A Duet for Piano

Edited by Rachael Spillane

Printed by in the United States of America
First Printing September 2018

ISBN-13: 9780692185926 (Bleak Kismet)
ISBN-10: 0692185925

First Edition

Preface

Mental illness should always be taken seriously. It is a crippling, debilitating sickness that affects millions of people in the world. If you or a loved one is undergoing a difficult period of time, please seek help. There is always another option.

This content is not suitable for people of all ages. Heavy themes of depression, drug abuse, domestic violence, death, and suicide coexist. As a forewarning, chapters marked with an asterisk are chapters that portray scenarios that may be disturbing and difficult to digest for readers. Feelings of negativity or emotional angst may occur, but please keep in mind that the ultimate purpose of this novel is to educate.

A Duet for Piano

Prologue

Values we learn in life, from when we are old enough to comprehend information to the day we die, belongs to a social construct. During our pre-adolescent years, we learn to do our business on the toilet than on the bed and feel unsettling guilt when stealing from the cookie jar. We learn to trust our parents and veer away from strangers. By the time we reach adulthood, we have a utilitarian set of social assets: the ability to communicate with our peers, share our secrets with friends, and even love one another. These rules are a set of guidelines humans follow. All this is how humans have come to interpret life as they know it.

Everything metaphysical we learn in life imposes regulation. Moral evil—murder of a bank teller during a robbery, raping as a product of untethered human lust, extorting finances from a company—are all punishable by stripping the miscreant of their free will, and reprehensible by the public. Benevolence—donating part of your earnings to a medicinal facility, tutoring instrumental lessons in an underprivileged part of a city, tipping a few dollars to a frayed beggar on the corner of the street—rewards you with high merit and esteem. But what if there are other intelligent beings on another planet where murder is encouraged, and conversely, good deeds are taboo or condemned? To us humans, their reality is completely skewed and fallacious. But to them, *our* reality is completely skewed and fallacious.

So who is right and who is wrong? The right side is the wrong side. Or maybe yet, the reality that humans live in now may neither be right nor wrong, and rather one in a bottomless pit of other realities. We humans shape our realities, blinded by content, with no shred of desire to discover whether our reality is bona fide. Reality is fabricated by the path humans follow.

People's differences pique my interest. A multitudinous amount of different beliefs and religions shape people spiritually. Occupational varieties allow people to form an expertise in their field. A flight attendant gets to travel the world and bask in the sights. A homeworker stays confined to the vicinity of their house. Both are polar opposites, yet quintessential for a stable economy. Some people see the world in black and white—a product of their sedateness. Others see the world full of color. Is the sky bluer to you or the person next to you? Is the grass fuller? Is the dirt brown colored, or sepia?

When I speak the word 'bird,' you get a mental picture in your head of a small creature coated with feathered wings, two black eyes and twiggy legs, and a sharpened beak. But we must keep in mind that the bird is only named that way because it is something we have been taught, a shred of general knowledge passed down for millennium. When the cycle reaches a point of time in the past where years were not measured, what was 'bird' called back then?

You always read about people of the past—of their low life spans, living conditions, and usable technology. Has it occurred to you that we are going to be those people one day? Two hundred years in the future, when the human species have conquered the impossible, people will be reading about the twenty-first century—about us—and how technologically obsolete we were. Future generations will hold the same mentality that we currently have toward citizens of the eighteenth century.

The book you're holding in your hands right now isn't actually real; you think it is due to the grainy texture of the pages and rough spine discharging information to the sensory neurons on your palms and fingertips, but it's not. Your five senses: sight, hearing, taste, touch, and smell are all fake because you're trapped in a dream. And when you die in said dream, you wake up. Your brain realizes nothing was real. But the goosebumps on your arms and sweat on your forehead speak otherwise. How do you know you're not in a dream at this moment? For the ones who die, regardless of age, do they wake up to the real reality? Or do they wake up to another realm of life? Reality could be tethered to an infinite chain. You wake up one after the other, each time thinking you're in the real world.

Why do people dream anyways? Maybe it's because we're getting glimpses into our previous lives. Someone very close to me once told me: the fears you harbor now are gateways to how you died in your past lives. Seems far-fetched? What do you believe, then? Dreams are the one mystery of the world we may never come to understand fully. Dreams are both a blessing and a curse.

People rant about new experiences and skim over parts of stories in which they are at fault, and by no means am I an exception. There have been many times in my life where I have been ashamed of my actions, but I am powerless to change events in the past. Fate—c'est la vie.

Welcome to my journey.

1

"Honey! It's time to get up!"

The distinct sound of my mother's voice floats from across the hall into my room, where I am currently laying in my warm bed. I kick my legs out from under the sheets, turning the plain white mass to a crumpled heap. My brain struggles to liven up my stiff limbs.

"One minute!" I bleat wearily. I turn my head to my alarm clock and notice there are still a few minutes to go before it is scheduled to go off. I close my eyes, futilely attempting to return to dreamland.

It isn't that easy. My ears involuntarily perk up as I hear the soft treading footsteps of my mother walk into my room, and then the rustling of my bed sheets as she yanks them off with a single flourish. My toes automatically coil at the lack of warmth and I snap open my eyes, catching her austere expression. I sigh dejectedly.

"Alright, I'm up," I sigh again, sitting forward and swinging my legs off to the side of the bed.

"Good, because today's the first day of your senior year, and God forbid I let you be late again," my mother says in a stern voice. I give her the stink eye while stretching my limbs, letting out a few butch grunts in the process. Mom is already making her way out of the room, but she stops at the door before turning around. Something unidentifiable flits across her face for a split second before she tears her eyes off of my untidy figure and checks her uniform for any wrinkles.

"Breakfast is on the kitchen table downstairs. I don't want to receive another call from school saying you were absent. Do you understand me, young lady?" She is satisfied by her routine check because she clicks her tongue and looks to me for agreement.

I suppress the urge to roll my eyes and keep the apathy out of my voice before simply replying, "Yes, ma'am."

Her face softens, and she walks back to the bed and kisses me on the cheek.

"I know it's hard for you, but your education is important. Have a good day at school honey, okay? Try to enjoy your first day back. I love you." She gets up and exits the room, her keys jingling in the process.

"Love you too, Mom," I mutter as I stand up and walk to the bathroom. I open the medicine cabinet and unscrew the cap off a bottle, swallowing a pill dry with a grimace. I wet my toothbrush and begin brushing my teeth, taking in my disgruntled visage in the mirror.

Dull brown eyes stare back at me, and I internally cringe at how hardened and lifeless they seem. My hair is no different. The russet locks have long since lost their voluminous shade and now hang down in unkempt, straggly strands that feel like straw. My cheekbones are sunken, and my figure is so slim that healthy is an antithesis. If I pinch myself, I can see the faintest trace of pink blossoming over my alabaster skin.

Spitting out the toothpaste, I notice a tint of red seeping through. I catch the sight of a pimple growing on my chin after I rinse my mouth and quickly pop it before hopping in the shower. After a few minutes of deep thought, I reluctantly turn off the shower head and dry myself.

A crowd of gray greets me after I drag my feet to my closet. I pick out a random, drab sweatshirt and sweatpants. They slip on easily. The sky is dark, and it's raining outside, so I dig out a simple raincoat before making my way downstairs. I'm not hungry, but I pick up a slice of prepared toast and squeeze it into a sphere in the palm of my hand before inserting it in my pocket. Grabbing my bag, I leave through the door, taking care not to scrape off any more of the peeling paint.

The ten-minute walk to school is made miserable by my wet socks. Unfortunately, we only have one car, and my mother uses it every day to get to her new job as a waitress at a local diner. And because I don't my own cell phone, I can't ask Haley for a ride on dingy days. This leaves me with my own two feet.

My thoughts consume my attention, because the next thing I know a semi roars past me, trying to warn me by honking its horn. But my reflexes are less than sub par, and the large puddle of water along the side of the road tinted with mud splatters all over me and gets on my face and clothes.

I stand still for a second, in shock at how fortune seemed to frown upon me, before slowly wiping my mouth and eyes with the sleeve of my raincoat. I contemplate missing first period to change clothes but resist the urge to at the thought of Mom's wrath.

After a few more minutes of walking on the two-lane road, I see the familiar sign of my high school looming around the corner. *Starmount High School— Home of the Titans*, it says. Consternation works its way through my body, and it dampens my listless spirits.

I drag my feet to the entrance of the parking lot and notice it is almost full with a medley of old and ostentatious cars. I know I am running late, but a few lustrous cars catch my attention, and I take a second to admire them.

Another honk behind me causes me to flail about suddenly, and I lose my balance, almost plummeting to the ground. A bull bar on a heavy-duty truck is within arm's reach, and I manage to latch myself to it before causing myself even more embarrassment. The car that honked at me slips by me, and I can make out the shape of a laughing passenger inside. My face sets on fire.

I search for a nearby bench and make my way over, taking off my raincoat and wiping my bag free of grime—to the best of my extent—before tucking the jacket inside. A hefty helping of mud is splattered on my sweatshirt too, but I can't take it off unless I have no qualms about baring my naked body to the student population.

A few straggling students who probably think it's cool to enter class late are chatting in the parking lot, and they shoot me looks as I pass them. I ignore the scrutiny and walk inside the office building, trying to find my homeroom instead.

My school is small. There are just over eight hundred students, which leaves about two hundred for each grade. And our modus operandi is unorthodox. Although school starts at eight-forty in the morning and ends at three in the afternoon, students are free to choose which classes they want to enroll in, as long as a minimum class quota is reached. The principal gives a speech in the auditorium every year to the newcomers about how this helps us to 'establish a firm foundation for college life.'

Most people usually allot one or two free periods in their schedule, and that was how inevitable solidary divisions were formed. The jocks eat extra meals in the cafeteria, the hippies sneak off school grounds to dabble with drugs, the nerds assemble in spare classrooms to play video games; you name it. Then you have the misanthropes, who seek solitary confinement and daydream. You'd have to be pretty obtuse if you can't discern how sundry our school is.

I manage to locate my classroom from the bulletin board near the entrance, and I make my way to Room 261 as a bundle of nerves.

Standing in front of the door, I gather my bearings before I enter. The first thing I notice is that I am the last to arrive, and my eyes rapidly search for a clock in an attempt to avoid eye contact with anyone. I locate one and observe my tardiness. The teacher quirks an eyebrow at me.

"May I help you?" he asks, trying to be polite. Hushed whispers arise around me, and I finally take a quick glance around the room. I blush, knowing the whispers are about me and my distraught appearance. I hear a few people unconcernedly commenting on my skinny figure and pasty skin.

"Sorry I'm late," I manage to blurt out before tucking my head down. I walk over to the front row and plop down at a black fire-retardant table with the only vacant seat next to a blonde girl who wasn't even attempting to hide her disdainful sneers. I pull my sleeves over my hands and pray that I can disappear.

"That's okay." The teacher nods his head and resumes his speech.

"As I was saying," he states, brandishing a stack of papers. "I will be handing out schedules for the new school year. You will report to this room after the semester is over for your spring schedules as well. You are free to leave after I call out your name. Any questions?" He pauses, waiting for anyone to speak up. But no one does, and he begins reciting the random list of names in his hand.

"Valerie Abbott," he begins. A dark-haired girl slips out of her chair and walks up to the front of the room, accepting her schedule before leaving the classroom.

"Altha LaBelle," he continues. The blonde girl sitting next to me stands up and makes her way to the teacher with a haughty stroll. She snatches her schedule and walks out of the room as well.

I slump in my chair and tune out the rest of the name-calling until I'm the only one left in the room.

"Ah, you must be Hope Valentine." He looks at the schedule and walks over to my desk before handing me the white piece of paper students will depend on for the first week of school. I glance into his smiling face.

"Go on," he says, and I take the piece of paper and murmur a short, "thanks" before rushing out of the room. I keep my head down the whole time until I realize I have no idea where I'm going.

Taking a look at my schedule, I remind myself that my first class of the day is in the education block. It's in the same building. Thank God.

I enter the classroom and take a seat in the back of the class. The class is split into two groups: the tutors and the tutored. Well, and the teacher too.

I signed up for the class as a tutor during spring semester last year at my mother's suggestion as a way to meet new faces, but no one I had attempted to talk to remained friends with me for long, except one. Now, I'm just here because it's an easy A.

Naturally, since it is the first day of school, no one looking to be tutored was here. By the time the rest of the handful of tutors file in, the teacher gives an announcement saying we have the class time to ourselves. Instantly, the quidnuncs around me begin to discuss new transfers and summer vacation. I lay my head down on the desk.

"Hope?" A voice beckons to me not long after I have closed my eyes, and I pull my head upwards halfheartedly, recognizing the voice from anywhere. I see Haley sitting two seats next to me with a gentle smile on her face.

"Hey, Haley." I try to add as much enthusiasm to my voice as I can, but I still end up sounding blasé. Sleep. I want to sleep.

"Hey, Hope!" She scoots her desk closer to me, and I resist the warm fuzzy feeling that glows inside me. "How was your summer?"

"It was fine," I mutter, not going into specifics. "Are you a tutor this year?"

Haley grins. "Uh, and to be on your intelligence level? Impossible."

I frown to myself. After all this time, I still don't understand why Haley continues to talk to me. She's a fashionista, has a quaint doll-face, and is equipped with creamy skin that turns heads wherever she goes. Not only is she one of the most popular kids in school and the cheerleading captain, but she was even crowned homecoming queen last year. And throughout junior year, she was—and to this day, still is—the only one who could have a conversation with me without remotely losing interest within a few seconds. Maybe she's just always happy in general. Or maybe the stereotype is true—that blonde girls are dumb. I mean, why else would she hang out with me?

Don't get me wrong; I do appreciate her friendliness. It's always nice to say I have a friend. Last year, she spent so much of her time keeping me company after Dad's death. I will forever be grateful to her for that.

I swallow. My throat is dry.

"Hope—" Haley speaks in what I think is a beginning to a comfort speech. Her hand twitches toward me. But before she says what she was going to say, I hear the annoying voice of Veronica, one of Haley's friends, interrupt us. A small flare of annoyance sparks inside me but I snuff it out.

Being the cattiest and most loquacious person I have ever met, it only makes sense that Veronica and I don't get along. All she had to offer when I first met her was a litany of complaints toward the teachers and students, establishing her titular throne as the queen. And ever since Veronica sensed my dissatisfaction, I was the brunt of her bullying—a subject of her supercilious glares. All because I'm ugly. Because I'm a goody-goody two shoes who makes better grades. Because she thinks I'm trying to steal Haley from her. But hey, maybe she's finally matured some this year.

"Haley!" Veronica calls out her name, and I almost vomit at how nasally her voice sounds. She ignores my presence, and I gladly return the favor. I can't believe how dense most of her friends are. Haley deserves better, genteel friends. *Like me.*

"The teacher said we could leave. We're going to the cafeteria." Veronica waves her hand at Haley and finally looks at me as if I was gum on the bottom of her shoe, and I feel myself shrink in intimidation at her social status. But she doesn't say anything. I'll take it as a sign of improvement.

Haley gives me a sympathetic look before standing up. But she does wrap her arms around my shoulders in a warm hug. Her breath tickles the hairs on the back of my neck. When she pulls away, I try not to look too crestfallen.

"I'll talk to you later, okay?" she suggests. I flash her a forced smile.

"See you," I say. She gives me another small smile before walking out with her group of friends. A few minutes later, the bell rings and everyone, including the teacher, leaves the room. Only I remain in the class, left in my thoughts.

While all the girls would gossip and go shopping for new dresses, I preferred to read and play my keyboard. They date, party, have sleepovers, whatever. Everything a girl is supposed to do, I do none of. They *live*. Something I haven't done since my father died a year ago. A year ago—

I shake the morbid self-pity from my head. Now isn't the time to dwell on it.

Pulling out my schedule, I see that I have a free period. That means lunch. But I wasn't hungry. Just tired.

I place my head on the cool surface of the desk, and the next thing I know—

Ringringringring!

I jump to my feet, momentarily forgetting where I am before seeing the cluttered desks and blackboard. I steady my spinning surroundings and pull out my schedule from under me, wiping as much drool off the paper as I can.

I rub my eyes, only to see that they are wet. *That* dream again. A quick glance at the clock…it's almost one o'clock?! No, no, no! I just slept for three hours! Mom's going to kill me!

"Crap, crap!" I scramble to my feet and bolt out the door. The math building is on the other side of campus, and I power walk instead of running, avoiding unwanted attention. If I'm late, I'll get a tardy slip. Although it probably won't matter anymore. I am fretting not at the three classes I missed, because most of the teachers skim over their syllabus on the first day, but at how livid Mom was going to be. Time to start digging my grave.

I burst through the side door of the building and carry myself to the second floor of the math building, whipping out my schedule again to remind myself which room I belong in. 204.

212…211…210…I turn a corner, already panting from exertion.

Apparently tripping over my own feet is not enough humiliation for one day, because when I round the corner, I crash into something very solid. A sudden flavor of citrus and cardamom infiltrate my nostrils. I fall on my rear far before my reflexes kick in.

"Oomph!" My face contorts into a painful grimace as I fervently rub my tailbone with my hand in an attempt to dispel my screaming nerves. My hand slows down when I blurrily realize someone is speaking to me.

"Are you okay?" My eyes wander up the figure, and my face is instantly set aflame as my eyes behold slim jeans and a V-neck on Adonis in the flesh.

My breath hitches in my throat, and I lose the ability to speak for a few seconds before I finally peep. "F—fine."

"Here," the unnamed stranger offers an outstretched hand. I look behind me for good measure, but I see no one there. I turn back to him and see that he's setting his sunglasses aside with one hand, tucking the accessory into the nook of his turquoise V-neck. The other is still hovering in the air, waiting to help me up.

"N—no, that's okay," I finally stammer out and begin to prop my hands under my bottom in an attempt to propel myself upwards. Before I can fully sit up, a calloused, yet warm hand grabs mine and pulls me up. I gasp at the contact.

The second our hands touch, a most peculiar tingle shoots into my hand and travels through my arm and jolts my body to my core, involuntarily forcing a shiver out of me. I let out another gasp; the feeling is euphoric and engulfs me in flames. My eyes dart to his face for any reaction, but if he feels the electricity, he didn't show it.

"There. That wasn't so bad, was it?" He cracks a smirk, and my brain instantly clicks as it determines which social group he falls in. The smirk says it all. A smirk that belongs to a condescending jackass who goes through two girls a week and bullies the weaker population only because he has the full support of the football team. Although, by the accent he's sporting, it's probably safe to replace football with rugby. But that's not how society should work. You can have your first impressions, but you can't judge the person for who they truly are until you get to know the real them. One's reputation isn't measured by who they are; it's measured by how other people perceive them.

Therefore, I somehow manage to build up the confidence and look into his eyes, noting how his green eyes resembled jade. Jade green is my favorite color.

My eyes travel downwards, and my heart hammers in my chest as I realize he's still holding my hand. I blush even harder when I realize how close we are. He's so close I can see the individual stitches in his clothing. He's so close I can feel his breath fanning over my face, clouding my senses like an aphrodisiac.

"I'm Videl," he says, jerking me out of my thoughts. My brain blanks out for a second before I finally realize I'm supposed to return the introduction.

"H—Hope," I manage to squeak out. He shakes the hand he's already holding and laughs before dropping it. My hand twitches.

"I'm sorry to have caused such an accident. I was rushing to find my class and didn't watch where I was going," he offers an explanation and scratches his head. The ruffle of his hair doesn't escape my view, and I let out a whimper so soft he doesn't hear.

After a deep breath, I respond with, "That's okay. What class are you looking for?" Inner Hope cheers at my accomplishment in keeping a conversation going.

"Um," he hesitates and looks at his schedule. "Calculus…level two, I believe." The word calculus triggers my brain to come back to the present, and I emit an exasperated groan, slapping a hand to my forehead.

"I have the same class."

Videl quirks an eyebrow at my flat voice. "Let's walk together, then."

We end up arriving five minutes late. A quick skim around the room and I recognize some of the students to be peers I shared classes with junior year. They all look at me with a mixture of emotions. No one is happy to see me, except for Haley, who is waving her hand in the air at me like some maniac. I meekly raise my hand and return her greeting with a half-hearted gesture.

"You two are late," the teacher scolds. "Mister and Miss—"

"Videl," Videl answers, and I grumble, "Hope," turning the color of a tomato at how connubial her statement sounded.

"Explain yourselves," the teacher commands. Oh, boy, this class sure is going to be exciting.

I open my mouth and attempt to answer but Videl beats me to the chase.

"I apologize, madam. I was helping Hope to her feet after accidentally colliding into her out in the hallway. I'll make sure to be careful next time." His voice slathers with honey, and I take a look at the teacher to find that she looks befuddled. The ability to sweet-talk his way out of trouble. Another sign of a sanctimonious personality.

"Ah, well, it is the first day of school," the teacher clears her throat. I get a closer look at her and see that she's sporting a mullet. I stifle a shudder.

The teacher finally reaches a conclusion and says, "I'll let you two off the hook today, Mister Videl and Miss—" she forgets my name, so she hesitates and ends up finally settling with "—but don't be late again." She hands us each a syllabus before continuing her introduction on the projection monitor.

"Of course, Miss—" Videl's eyes dart to the blackboard. "—Vance," he purrs, and before I can protest, he grabs my hand and leads me to the back of the room. The same shock shoots throughout my body, and I stumble at least three times during the endless journey to the desks. Eyes widen as my classmates notice our entwined fingers. I try my best to ignore the scrutiny. We finally make it to the back, and I sit down faster than my face can burn.

Ms. Vance begins rambling on about the syllabus, which I tune out after a few minutes of false attention. Giving a verbal dictation on a piece of paper that I can just read myself is like Mom telling me to eat food because it's healthy. I end up chancing a peek at Videl instead.

His clothes don't do him justice. The turquoise V-neck hugs his chest tightly, and for a second, I grow jealous of his sunglasses. A pair of dark-blue washed jeans fit snugly around his legs, but not overly so.

He's handsome. I've never really paid much attention to boys, but he's different. There's something rugged about him that easily tears apart my inattentiveness toward the male gender and establishes him at the top of a newly-formed list of bachelors. His cheekbones are prominent, but not too shallow, and his face is chiseled in a way that puts Michelangelo's statues to shame. His revealing top shows his carved muscles in all the right places, and they are a perfect shade of tan. His sun-kissed, sepia hair looks extremely soft, and for some reason, I find myself wanting to run my hands through it. And then—

He turns his head and catches me staring at him.

My brain whimpers at being caught, and I immediately avert my eyes away from him to the teacher, who is rambling about nothing in particular, and I blush again; what is wrong with me? I take a chance, looking back at him, and see that he doesn't seem to mind the obtrusive stares. I feel obligated to say something to him at this moment.

"T—thanks for getting me out of trouble," I blurt out in a whisper. Great. Come on, Hope. What a generic start.

He chuckles softly and looks my way. His eyes enthrall me. I can almost see his thoughts swimming underneath.

"It's not a problem," he replies. "It seemed like you were about to have a panic attack at the mere thought of a tardy slip."

My social skills form a conjecture that Videl's teasing me, and I find myself unable to come up with an adequate response.

We lapse into silence and I have no idea whether it's a comfortable one. The rest of the period passes by faster than I can stutter, and before I know it, the bell rings.

"This class is going to be torture." Videl stretches his limbs as the chairs scraped noisily against the floor. "I've never been very competent at math." I open my mouth to respond but am cut off by Haley, who has made her way to us without me noticing.

"Hey, Hope! What do you think about this class?"

I try to fight down the feeling of insignificance. "It's alright." Haley's a celestial being, a blonde sent from the gods themselves, and I'm just, well, me.

"Is this your friend?" Videl asks me with a raised eyebrow.

"Y—yeah," I stammer out. Remembering how introductions work, I say, "This is Haley." Haley sticks out her hand, and he shakes it.

"It's nice to meet you, Haley."

"Likewise," she returns the greeting, shuffling her feet and smiling coyly. Videl lets go of her hand and turns back to me.

"I have physics, so I should probably get going. Don't want to be rushed and accidentally crash into anybody again," he smirks at me and a rush of blood shoots in my face. "I'll leave you two ladies to your own." He smiles at us and gets up from his seat. My eyes stare at his receding figure until he vanishes from sight.

"Oh my God, I heard he's one of the new transfer students!" she asserts with a giggle, right after he leaves. This breaks me from my concentration.

A transfer student? Well, it does make sense, after all. Why else would he have an accent and tasteful fashion?

I shrug my shoulders and try to act nonchalant.

"Maybe he's a European model. He's really hot." She continues talking about Videl. A small flicker of annoyance blossoms within me.

"Yeah," I absentmindedly agree, and Haley's mouth falls open. I catch my blunder, but it is too late.

"Wow, Hope! Finally got your eye on a guy!" She slaps my shoulder playfully while I internally bash myself.

"I—it was—I didn't—whatever," I grumble, unsuccessfully trying to backtrack. She giggles.

"It's okay, after all, if anyone deserves him, it's you. You're never happy anymore." Her tone goes from ebullient to downcast, and she looks at me with sympathetic eyes.

"It's not like that," I grunt. "I don't like him that way. He probably has a girlfriend."

"I don't think so. If he's a transfer student, he must be from somewhere far away. I don't think he's the type to keep a long distance relationship. He gives off a bad boy vibe," she says, and I secretly agree with her.

"Wouldn't you want to date him yourself, anyways?" I ask, my eyes focusing on a mud stain on my sweatshirt.

"You wound me!" She clasps her right hand over her heart in a jesting manner. "You know very well I would never cheat on Chad."

"Look, Haley. I just met him today, and I *don't* like him," I emphasize. "Can we please drop it?" I plead desperately.

"Alright, alright. What class do you have next?"

I sigh and flip open my schedule.

"P.E.," I groan, clasping my hands to the side of my head. My headache is getting worse.

"Ah," Haley replies, and I know what she's thinking. If I can't walk without falling, then how do I compare when playing sports? I don't. "I have the same class!" she gazes at her schedule, her face breaking into a wide smile. "We can suffer together. Let's go!"

The rest of the day passes by in boredom and embarrassment. I trip over my feet twice during our laps around the gym, much to my chagrin and the class's humor. So it is with great solace that I finally finish the first day of class and begin walking back home after a hurried 'good-bye' to Haley.

The rainclouds have parted by now, and beacons of sun rays stream down through the sky, working its evaporating powers on the rain that has yet to disappear from the roads. Many people say the pavement smells like wet dog on a rainy day, but I love the odor. I hear birds chirping a chorale, and I let myself go and fall into their harmonious song.

How I yearn to be a bird; how I yearn to be free. I see the little creatures fly in the sky without a care in the world, spreading their wings whenever. Unconfined to society's conventional mindset. Not having to worry about materialistic, artificial things, or external opinions—I desire this life.

The shabby, two-story home comes into view, and I make my way onto the front porch and let myself inside. My headache has gotten worse, and I'm starting to feel lightheaded.

"I'm home, Mom!" I yell out. Silence. I walk to my room and change into a tank top, making sure to throw my dirty sweatshirt and jacket into the laundry basket. Heading back downstairs, I plop my school bag onto the sofa and walk over to the fridge. I pull out an apple, not bothering to wash it before I take tiny bites.

I walk back to the sofa and pick up my bag, spilling out my books on the kitchen table. I decide to work ahead on my assignments before they become too much of a burden. The soft scribbles of my pen and occasional crunching when I take a bite out of the enzymatic browning apple are the only breaks in the silence.

The next time I check the microwave clock, it's past six. I pack away my progress and scour the fridge for something I can cook for Mom and Roger. A frozen bag of broccoli and chicken breasts catch my eye.

The table has just been set with supple servings on plastic plates when the front door opens and Mom, and her new husband—my stepfather—stumble in. Mom instantly walks over to me and engulfs me in a hug, cutting off my supply of oxygen.

"Mom, get off!" I muffle as I half-heartedly try to pry her off. She laughs.

"I've missed you! How was school?" she asks, after finally letting me go.

"The same as last year," I reply dryly, brushing off a few dislocated stray hairs from my shirt. Mom's face falls, and she drops the subject immediately.

"Smells good in here," Roger compliments me as he makes his way up to the front. I recoil away from him. He cracks a smile at me, but it doesn't have the same effect on me as it does on Mom.

"Mom, is it okay if I go work on my homework?" I lie, but she can't tell; I've perfected my stoic face. Mom's one of the few people I can retain eye contact with for prolonged periods of time. I put it to good use when telling fibs.

"Are you sure you don't want to eat anything? The food you cooked looks amazing," Mom adulates. "And there's more than enough for the three of us. I don't remember the last time we all had dinner together. With Roger's company and your schoolwork…" she drifts off. I shake my head.

"I had a lot to eat during lunch. I'm not hungry." Even with my reticent expression, she must know it's a lie. My skin and bones isn't something a person can just overlook.

She stares at me with a tempestuous expression for a few seconds before her face softens.

"Sure, honey," she finally says. Ignoring Roger, who already has his face buried in his plate of food and slobbering away, I make my way up to my room with my backpack in hand, locking my door behind me.

I head straight over to my keyboard and plop down on the cushioned bench, adjusting the volume to a low degree and slipping on my headphones so I don't bother Mom. My emaciated fingers drift over the keys, and I lose myself in my melancholy improvisations for the next few hours, experimenting on different tunes while pondering life's meaning.

I moved to Roseden with my mom after she had started dating again, about a week before my junior year commencement.

'You'll make tons of new friends,' she had said. I still remember how cheerful she looked, and it wasn't until a few months later that I came to understand it was just a false front. And *tons* of friends? Well, I guess Haley considers me to be her friend, but I still don't understand *why*.

My headphones offers me no protection because raised voices ring throughout the house and shake me from my reverie. I pause my playing and look at my alarm clock. The glowing red nine o'clock peers out at me. It's laughing at me. It's scoffing at me. Somehow, I had lost track of time and failed to realize it was already dark outside.

Nine o'clock. Sounds about right.

Sure enough, the arguing between Mom and Roger downstairs escalates. I scuttle over the bench and walk over to my cheap music speakers, turning them on. A random pop song begins playing, but my focus is shattered. I crank the volume knob as high as it would go without hurting my ears, my hands shaking in the process. It doesn't work.

Loud crashing noises and high-pitched screaming filter under my door and through the walls, and the next thing I know, I'm in a fetal position at the foot of my bed with my hands held over my ears. Tears begin to trickle down my face and wet the carpet. I sniff, trying to get rid of the unappealing sensation of snot in my nose.

A feeling of hopelessness engulfs me as old memories of Dad's death assault my brain. I try my best to shut the visions out, but they are unrelenting and angry. My chest constricts. I can't breathe.

My lungs are unable to function. I stumble to my bathroom with a cloudy field of vision and scramble to open the medicine cabinet. The cap twists off. I twitchily pop three of the white pills in my mouth, filling up my glass with water and chugging it as fast as I can. I keep the sink running; combined with the speakers, it helps to mute the shouting below. Crawling inside the bathtub, I drape the shower curtains over my head. The medication is quick to work its magic.

I spend the night alone on the cold, acrylic surface of the bathtub.

2*

The first sight I'm greeted by is the plastic shower curtain. It takes me a while to get ahold of my surroundings.

"Ow, ow!" The familiar sensation of a stiff neck assaults my nerves and my eyes begin to water.

I choke back a sob and collapse back down in the tub as I try to rub away the unpleasantness.

I don't have the motivation to pull myself up and start the day. What's the point? Every day is a cyclic schedule. I wake up, go to school, do homework, and try to sleep. Oh yeah, and don't forget to rinse and repeat. And for what? A diploma that leads to a degree in college? Which then leads to a life of constant stress? Working for a living until you're old and can't move anymore? No thanks. I wish it doesn't have to be that way, but it is. That's just how society works. And I'm just a measly product of it, born into the wrong world. I'm the worker ant, and society is the queen.

The pain in my neck finally recedes to something more tolerable, and I reluctantly pull myself up and check on the time.

The alarm clock on my nightstand reads seven in the morning. I'm up an hour early. I return to the bathroom to start my daily routine by brushing my teeth and taking a shower, remembering to take a pill. To be honest, I don't even think these suckers work anymore.

After the shower, I dig through my closet and throw on another sweatshirt and sweatpants before jostling my backpack over my shoulder and cautiously slipping out of my room.

Mom's door across the hall is open, which signifies her absence. Early call.

Tiptoeing is a shrewd decision, for I see Roger splayed out on the sofa next to the kitchen after I reach the bottom of the stairs. Two beer bottles are stacked on top of each other like he was trying to play some ridiculous game, and many more are littered on the carpet at his feet. New carpet stains are evident, a result of the spilled bottle that slipped from his hand right as he passed out. The sofa arm is damp from his drool. His snoring injures my ears.

My face morphs into disgust, and I don't attempt to hide my repulsion at his obscene appearance. I hold in the temptation to vomit when the smell of alcohol invades my nostrils. Hopefully, he'll be gone by the time I get back.

I manage to make it to Starmount High without any humiliating incidents just in time to blend in with the rest of the horde of students that are streaming into class. My whole time in Education is spent finishing the rest of my homework that I didn't get to the night before. Luckily, I was born blessed in the smarts department, because it takes me less than ten minutes to knock out fifteen review calculus problems. It's the psychology homework that stumps me. There was a girl, Jackie, who offered to tutor me last year in this exact tutoring room, but her persona had scared me away. I'm not sure what happened to her.

The bell rings, and with a foreboding sigh, I make my way to the first class I missed yesterday: Chemistry.

I'm one of the first people in the class due to my earliness, and the teacher looks at me for a second before frowning.

"May I help you?" he asks, in the same manner as my homeroom teacher. He must think I'm here to deliver a note or something.

I shuffle around, digging out my schedule before showing it to him.

"I have your class," I tell him, trying to keep my answers as simple as possible. I hear the door open behind me and I know students are beginning to trickle in.

"What's your name?" he asks, but it feels more like an interrogation. "I don't recall your face."

"Hope," I respond feebly, and he strolls over to his desk before checking my name off on his attendance sheet.

"School started yesterday. Why weren't you here?"

"I, uh—I—I fell asleep in class and woke up late. Sorry. I'm sorry," I apologize lamely, a blush forming on my cheeks.

The teacher looks at me in disbelief.

"You fell asleep in class," he repeats. "On the first day of school." I nod and look anywhere but into his eyes. Unfortunately, that means I catch the sea of students who had filled the desks instead. I shift uncomfortably when I see the stares of several students, including the blonde girl who was scowling at me yesterday.

The teacher cocks an eyebrow and ends up shrugging, much to my incredulity.

"At least I know my class isn't the worst," he laughs, and I'm surprised at how fast his demeanor changed. A small feeling of relief washes over me at his smile. It's still a little too early to form impressions, but from past experiences, teachers all end up acting the same way toward me. They all realize I'm the smart one in class, and whenever no student volunteers to answer a simple question, the teacher will automatically call on me to respond. Sadly, this unwanted attention draws snickering and obloquies, and I usually end up answering the question with a red face.

"I think I'll have you sit beside Altha. She's new to the school and still needs a lab partner," he points to her, and I instantly freeze. *That* girl.

I trudge my feet over to the lab table with a heavy heart and meekly sit down in my chair, refusing to look at my partner. The teacher, Mr. Stern, goes on a dribbling tangent for half an hour, which I spend jotting notes furiously in an attempt to keep my mind distracted from the girl's boring stares.

"Okay, so today, we'll be diving headfirst in our first lab in polymer synthesis," the teacher says blithely after the lecture portion is over, and I can tell by the change in his tone that he's anticipating this.

"Take out your lab manual I handed out yesterday and spend the first ten minutes reading over the procedures to familiarize yourself with the experiment," he says, and I frown to myself, before mustering up the courage to raise my hand.

"Yes, Hope?" he asks. I feel some students watching me. Why do they always stare at someone when they have their hands up in the air instead of minding their own business?

"I don't—I don't have a lab manual," I stutter out.

The teacher rummages through a few of his drawers but then shakes his head at me.

"I seem to have run out. Just share with Altha for the next few labs. I'll send a request for more, and they should be here within the week." Dang. The hammer just hit the nail.

I wince but give a meek nod.

My fears are confirmed when I turn to the girl and see that she isn't even offering her manual to the halfway point on the table. Instead, she's looking at her manicured nails, giving no regard to what the teacher said.

"H—Hey," I try to say something. "Do you mind if we share?" My voice penetrates the atmosphere of veiled silence.

The girl finally looks at me, and my heart sinks as I recognize the same pejorative-filled expression on her face that I see on Veronica every time. Like I'm worthless scum.

Altha scoffs and shifts her notebook slightly, but it's still more on her side than it is mine, and I can hardly make anything out.

My self-esteem is hovering dangerously low in the negative zone, and I choose not to ask her to slide it over some more in fear of receiving uncongenial glowers. I spend the rest of the ten minutes craning my neck, desperately trying to comprehend the tiny font unsuccessfully.

"Okay! Time to start! The materials you need are over in the hood at the back. Don't forget the goggles!" The teacher claps his hand together resplendently, and the classroom comes to life as chairs screech across the tiled floor and the students scrabble for materials.

Altha gets up as well, but she takes her manual with her.

By the time she sits back down with the needed ingredients, all I have gotten are my goggles and gloves. She glares at my empty side of the table.

"You didn't get anything?" are the boorish first words I hear out of her mouth, and I notice she has an accent. I shake my head.

"Do you expect me to do all the work here?"

"No—no. That's not it."

"Can you not read or something? Are you dyslexic?" The words ring out callous and vitriolic, and I find myself wanting just to shrink and disappear.

"N—no, I just had trouble discerning the font."

"So what you are saying is that you are blind." Altha laughs, but it's not a chirpy, assuaging one. It's a dismissive laugh, and then she focuses her attention on the lab notebook.

"What's your problem?" I find myself losing rein of my emotions for a flash, and my voice comes out harsh. The fretful, worrying thought that I might have been too rude poofs away as Inner Hope cheers at how I stand up for myself.

"My problem?" she sneers, and her vindictive expression instantly snuffs my pride.

"You're just sitting there, lording about while I get all the materials. What is this, I do all the work, and you don't?" Her false accusation causes my jaw to slack. That's *not* what happened!

"I might have been able to, had you not kept the notebook under your crooked nose the whole time!" The words tumble out of my mouth before I can stop them, and a stunned silence fills the space between us. My hands clasp over my mouth. Altha's eyes widen, and they fill with a fire of hatred so incontrovertible that I can almost feel the flames lick me. And when she speaks, her voice is filled with heavy malicious vehemence scares me to my bones.

"Ugly? Me?" She laughs spitefully. "Have you looked at yourself in the mirror? Have you seen your abhorrent fashion style?" She eyes me from my toes to my hair. My limbs curl as a method of defense against her penetrating eyes. "I thought not…and here you sit, daring to talk with someone like me. Someone who is better than you." She finishes with a vainglorious smirk, and I realize she's trying to see how I will react.

The words sting me hard, and I break eye contact with her and whirl around. My vision immediately clouds up. I try to steel myself, but a traitor tear slips out.

"Is something the matter, ladies?" The teacher is standing in front of us. Instead of his cheery expression, Mr. Stern is sporting a frown at Altha. She doesn't respond, so for some reason, I do.

"No, sir, nothing happened," I say.

"Are you sure, Hope? You'll be spending the rest of the semester with the person sitting next to you, and the lab partnership will not work out if there are any hard feelings." He frowns again at Altha.

"Nothing happened, sir. I promise." He continues to frown but lets the matter drop without another word and walks back to his desk.

Inner Hope chastises me for letting Altha go unpunished, but I know I'm not a rat. That's not to say my feelings are immune to whatever is thrown at them, however.

The two of us fall quiet in an atmosphere of awkward animosity until she breaks the silence with a less-than-ladylike cantankerous sigh. I give a perfunctory nod to communicate my understanding.

Most girls tend just to avoid me or pretend like I don't exist. But it's different for Altha. I have *never* done anything to her, but she's already made it her life's mission to make mine as miserable as possible. I don't understand what Altha's problem is. I honestly don't. But if I had to guess, I'd say she's an opprobrious, narcissistic, snobbish bit—

The bell rings.

"Okay, class. Just leave your equipment by the windowsill and make sure to cover your beakers. We'll be resuming the experiment next class."

Altha stands up without doing anything he says and dashes off. She can probably tell by a single glance that I'm a perfectionist. Launching my own sigh, I begin cleaning.

Haley is already outside the hallway thanks to her free period, and greets me with a hug before the two of us walk to calculus together. She spends her time washing me with the most recent gossip to which I give minimal attention to.

"Who's that?" I point my finger at Videl from two doors down. He's leaning against the lockers with one foot propped up on the school property and his hands in his pockets.

"Uh, that's Videl. You met him yesterday."

I roll my eyes. "No, not him. The girl talking to him."

Haley turns around and rolls her eyes. "I was literally just talking about them. Were you paying attention to anything I was saying?!"

"Them?"

"Videl and Chastity. They're together."

"How do people get together after the first day of school?"

"It was *on* the first day of school," Haley corrects. "She shares physics with him, and asked him by the end of class. I don't know why, but I'm starting to think my earlier supposition is correct. That he is a bad boy. Look at them."

The nearer we get, the clearer I can see them. The girl is staring up at Videl with adoration in her shining eyes like he's a god and she's his loyal servant. There's a smirk on Videl's face. I ball my fists. He's *relishing* the control he has over her. He's using her. I've seen enough of these relationships to know they will crumble.

The warning bell rings, signaling for all the students still bustling about in the hallways to get inside the classroom before the teachers begin handing out tardy slips. Haley and I slip inside and sit in our designated seats. Videl walks in a few minutes later, slipping in right as the teacher kicks the door holder from under her foot. She scowls at him but doesn't proceed to dish out a tardy slip.

Videl walks down the rows of seats before he reaches mine. My eyes stay glued to him, but he ignores me and sits down at the desk next to mine.

Throughout the class, he catches me staring at him, but there's nothing on his face that would symbolize any flicker of recognition. Immediately, I know the popular kids got to him. They probably told him to stay away from weirdo Hope, brainiac Hope, and whatever else nonsense they spew. My stomach opens into a bottomless pit, and all my guts drop into it. Even as a senior, a judgement-free personality is too much to ask for.

Class ends with the ring of the overhead bell and he takes his time packing his bags and exchanging a short greeting with a girl on his other side before walking out of the room without a word. His departure is so abrupt that even Haley notices.

"What's up with him?" she asks after swerving through the mass hysteria of students trying to escape.

"Don't know. Don't care."

Haley rolls her eyes and mutters what sounds like 'denial' under her breath.

"What did you say?"

"Nothing, nothing!" she hastily says, as we walk through the horde of students to P.E. "So, uh, do you want to tutor your bestie in calculus?"

"Haley, it's the second day of school."

Haley stops in her tracks and instantly hits me with the adorable puppy look—eyes wide and begging, bottom lip jutting out, and eyebrows scrunching together.

"Please, please, please. I need better grades this year if I want to win a cheerleading scholarship into college, and I can totally snatch victory if I spend less time with Chad and more time with you."

Now it's my turn to roll my eyes. "Fine," I concede, mainly because I dislike Chad. "But in return, you'll let me take up some of your time this afternoon."

"Sure! What is it? Do you want to do something? Do you want dinner at my place? My mom loves your company."

I shake my head. "Thanks for the offer, but I was thinking about visiting Dad. It's been a week since I've seen him."

"Oh, of course! I'll take you after P.E. You should still come over for dinner tonight."

"I'll think about. Do you not have cheer practice today?"

"Yeah, but that's inconsequential. Today's tryouts day. Which means there will be a lot of new candidates. Every girl who's already on the team stays on. Guaranteed immunity, you know?"

"Like tenure."

~~~~~~

Haley drops me off in front of the cemetery once P.E. ends. She explains to me again her superstitious fears about the dead coming back to possess people; otherwise, she would come in with me. I tell her I'll be fine and I won't be joining her for dinner, so she begins the thirty minute drive back, probably eager to rush home and inhale her plate of food.

The burial site is on a lump of land too small to be called a hill, but too big to be called a mound. There's an oak tree—the oldest and largest in the cemetery—towering right above Dad's gravestone. And attached to the tree's largest branch is a wooden swing. Swinging back and forth settles me into a peaceful mood.

I learned in my intro to psychology class last year the term 'flow', and sitting in front of Dad's tombstone is a perfect example of it in action. I'm lost in the fond memories of Dad, and I don't even realize its dark until I feel a wet droplet on the back of my neck. I frown. Thunder crackles in the nearby distance.

Within seconds, the clouds spread apart, and a torrent of rain begins to coat my clothes.

I rise to my feet and groan; the soft, clay dirt I was resting my knees on is already mushy mud, and it's ruined my pants. I huff in annoyance, taking one last glance at the tombstone and whispering, "Love you," to the man buried below before retreating to the bus stop.

The bus would have roared by if it wasn't for me running and waving my hands frantically, trying to get the driver's attention. He sees, and I slip onto the bus soaking wet. I don't even stumble, let alone trip with my slippery shoes on. Impressive, I know.

I fumble around in my pockets and search for spare change. I pull out the remaining four quarters. Whew.

"Don't worry about it, lass," the man nods warmly. "Save your dollar and buy something good with it. This station is the last stop for tonight. Just tell me where you want to go, and I'll take you straight there." I look at the overhead time monitor and see that it says eleven.

I bite my tongue to avoid pointing out you can't buy much with a dollar anymore, and return his honest grin with a small smile instead.

"Thanks," I say, trying my best to sound appreciative.

"Not a problem. Where to?"

I notice the lack of any other passengers before giving him my street address in Roseden and finally taking a seat in the front. The bus hisses and its suspension elevates the vehicle.

My jeans are stuck to my legs, and it's a discomfiting feeling. I pinch the material and pull up, trying to get the fabric to relinquish its tacky grip. It falls back down with a silent smack and I sigh, focusing my attention on removing the rain from my face instead.

The bus eventually reaches a considerable speed, even in this crummy weather. I lapse into a jaded silence and my head against the cool windowpane.

Even in my uncomfortable, cold state, my eyes begin to droop. The next thing I know, I fall asleep.

Some time later, I'm drawn out of my nap by the squeal of the bus's tires, and I look around wildly. My clothes are damp now, and I seek the clock. It's past midnight.

"Your neighborhood's road is too narrow for me to turn into, so I'll have to drop you off here," he says. I wipe the fog away from the window and stand up, anxious to leave.

"Thanks for the free ride."

"No problem! A girl like you shouldn't be out this late. Be safe, and try to stay out of the rain! Have a good night!" The doors close with another hiss, and I'm left standing by myself. The rain has subsided and all that remains is the steady trickling of rain from the moist leaves overhead.

The buzzing streetlamps help to illuminate the road and guide me in the right direction to my neighborhood at the bottom of the small hill, and before long, I find myself safely approaching the vinyl siding of the house I live in.

The relief dies away and I frown. Roger's car is in the driveway, and Mom's isn't. She must be working a late night shift again.

For a moment, I seriously consider turning in the other direction to burn off a couple more hours before coming back, by then which he'll hopefully be passed out. But I shrug it off. I'm still half asleep from earlier, and even though I love the rain, I can hear the soft sheets of my bed beckoning, calling out to me.

I reach the front door and begin unlocking it. Big mistake.

The door swings open before I open it, and Roger is standing on the other side. I can tell he's drunk—his breathing is labored, eyes are glassy, and the horrendous smell of alcohol wafts to my nose.

"Engh? Hope? Hope? It's you!" He cackles and pulls me inside with almighty energy before I can regain my senses, take a step back, and run away.

"W—Where's Mom?" My voice fills with panic when he begins dragging me over to the living room with substantial strength. I gasp when I see the countless number of beer bottles littered around the table. This has to be a new record.

"Eh? Mom? Who's that? T—the only woman I n—need i—is you," he slurs. He throws me onto the sofa roughly, and I bounce a couple of times while staring at him with wide eyes.

His eyes lower to my chest, and his hand stretches over to me. My mind is telling me to run, escape, fight back; *anything*, but his malicious grin plastered on his demonic face binds me in place, embeds into my memory, and leaves me unable to act.

"Please," I plead. I can feel tears of fear trickling down my cheeks. "Please don't." My arms clasp against each other in a feeble attempt to protect myself.

"W—what are ya saying? You'll l—love this," he says. I can see a bulge growing in his pants and then I feel his hands make contact with my shirt, almost grazing my breasts. I snap away from him in desperation.

"Stop! Stop it!" I scream. My limbs finally come to life, and I push his hands away. I kick, hit, and pummel blindly whatever inch of him I can find, hoping, *praying* that he lets me go. I manage to keep him at bay for a few seconds, but all it does is rile him up.

"Playtime's over, girl," he snarls, and his spittle splats all over my face. I gag when some enters my mouth. He locks both of my wrists with one of his monstrous hands and begins lifting me up. My feet leave the ground, and I shriek and flail.

"Mother isn't comin' home for a few more hours," he smiles evilly, and oh God, it terrifies me. He leans in slowly, and I can smell the alcohol on his breath right before he smears his disgusting mouth on mine.

"MMNGH! NNNNGH!" I scream into his mouth, and my legs spaz so hard around my body that I feel like they are about to snap. His forced contact gives me renewed vigor, and I lash out deliriously. My left foot makes contact with something hard.

The next thing I know, his face isn't near mine anymore, and neither is his grip. My back collides with the coffee table, and all the alcohol bottles that are resting upright stab into my body. I howl as a searing pain reverberates through my soul.

Black spots dance in front of my eyes as pain explodes in my right arm. I whimper and try to raise myself up, but it takes me several attempts before I have a stable footing. I run up the stairs cradling my injured limb, fumbling on my feet, and gasping for breath. Only when I don't hear him following me do I turn around and see that Roger is red and moaning on the ground at the foot of the stairs, writhing in pain from my lucky kick to his manhood.

I enter my room and lock the door behind me before grabbing whatever I find and stacking them in a small pile against the door. Books, chairs, clothes, anything and everything, all while wet wails escape from my lips.

I let loose an uninhibited scream as the door vibrates.

"You can't hide forever!" he snarls. The erected defense vibrates at each and every one of his kicks. "You'll be mine, sooner or later!"

I choke back my fear and continue to assemble my blockade. The house is old, and the locks aren't sturdy.

I place the last portable object I can locate and step away from the door. I can hear him mumbling something unintelligible on the other end. My whole body is shaking, and my heart is still beating erratically. And my arm. I'm pretty sure my arm is broken.

I stumble to the bathroom and manage to lock the door before succumbing to nausea.

"Hugnh, ughn." I moan in suffering as I vomit my semi-digested lunch into the toilet, desperately trying to steady my stomach. I stay crouched at the foot of the toilet for a few more minutes until my breathing isn't so strained anymore.

The toilet lid has droplets of blood from my split lip, but I ignore the sight and limp to the mirror before looking into it. My eyes are swimming with fear, but other than that, they are blank and lifeless. A tuft of hair is missing. The drawstrings on my sweatshirt are pulled to one side, and the first signs of bruising are beginning to fester over my wrists.

I look at my hands. They're vibrating uncontrollably, and I clap them together in an attempt to stop the shivering, moaning as a dull ache undulates through my right arm in response. My teeth are chattering, even though the bathroom is at a warm temperature.

I collapse to the ground and crawl over to an open corner. My arm sears in pain, but I grit my teeth and bear through it and drag myself into an upright sitting position. I look at my feet and see I'm only sporting one shoe. Too bad I can't get rid of Roger as easily as my missing footwear.

Roger is still pounding furiously on the door outside. With nothing to do but wait now, the tears freely flow down my face, and I silently cry until only the dry hiccups remain.

I spend the next few hours trembling and traumatized. Crouching in the corner of my bathroom, I watch the door with haunted eyes. Please don't come in. Please.

3

Two weeks pass, and I find myself sinking back into the same routine. Exams are drawing near; I spend my time in tutoring class or the library pouring over my textbooks and notes, studying until my brain melts into a puddle of glop. Haley engages in conversation with me, and I grunt my way through it. Been there, done that. Altha retains her ice-queen composure, and Videl and I still share calculus—when he's in class. Call me a stalker, but he's missed four out of the last ten days of school. I can't help but wonder if he's skipping with his girlfriend—his *new* girlfriend. I've seen him with at least three already. He broke up with Chastity the day after I first saw them. The girl was a crying mess in the bathroom, and I felt terrible for not doing anything to comfort her. But, a surprising amount of giddiness had invaded my spirit. I attribute this to the ever-growing load of schoolwork.

Anyways, it's all the same. Well, except for two differences.

One, my arm won't stop throbbing, and it's swelled to a pretty appalling size. But I've been keeping it bandaged with athletic tape inside my sleeve, praying for the makeshift cast to work its magic.

And two, the jitters.

They say being in a drunken state of mind reveals the true side of someone that they keep hidden from society, and for good reason too.

The scarring night where Roger almost had his way with me is like a parasite; the memory never leaves my mind. If I spot his car in the driveway, I immediately backtrack and sit on the local park swings or visit Dad's grave, offering random school excuses when Mom questions why I return home so late. This doesn't turn out too well, because some nights he would plan on staying over, sleeping over on the downstairs sofa. I end up wasting many hours doing nothing, falling behind on my homework and worrying senselessly—several of my sweatshirts' sleeves have chew marks on them.

A week ago, I devised a little plan to leave my window unlocked and cracked just the slightest so I can climb into my room with help from the planted giant oak tree outside. The lens on my telescope that I received on my fifteenth birthday is currently sticking out the window so Mom doesn't think I left the window open by mistake. It's been working fairly well, and I hold a small pride at my accomplishment.

Currently, it's another one of those nights, and my outside air cravings end up with me in the local park sitting on the swing, alone without another person in sight. The screws squeak as I gently push myself, and I find them soothing, allowing me to collect my thoughts.

So why hasn't Mom, or someone, *anyone*, done anything yet?

Simple answer. Because I haven't told her.

Believe me, I've thought about it aplenty, but I know the outcome won't result in my favor. I can already envision the scenario in my head. I tell Mom what's going on, her face morphs into an all-too-often mask of concern; she confronts Roger about it, they yell, and then he unleashes his revenge on me the next time I'm alone.

I can't call social services or whatever it is either. If I manage to get ahold of them and tell them what's going on, I have no defense besides my own pusillanimous voice. They'll start an investigation, but it'll die away as they come up short with any evidence that can be used against Roger. He's careful not to leave everlasting marks. And then, back to square one. His revenge.

But the biggest reason I clamp my mouth is because he financially supports Mom. They bicker, and he drives her insane, but she, no *we*, rely on him to make our living conditions more comfortable. Mom is a high school dropout, and in today's society, there aren't many places that hire people with an incomplete education. Her position as a waitress is currently paying her two dollars an hour; the rest of her income is tips, which I doubt comes generously. When we moved here, I went with her, heart sinking as I observed how rickety and uncared for the building looked. There were only two other cars in the parking lot, and unless I'm mistaken, the restaurant hasn't become the booming business we had hoped for.

Mom had turned around, and I had seen the letdown swimming in her eyes. She had prayed for hours beforehand, hoping that this job would be better than her last. But it hadn't looked that way. It was pretty obvious the restaurant was about to go out of business, which means she'll be searching for another job soon enough.

She ended up snagging the job, but it's not enough. According to my calculations, Mom can't afford to raise me and take care of herself with her present salary. Gas is expensive. Clothes are expensive. Human wants are expensive. Her pride dismisses the mere thought of applying for welfare. And that's why Roger is here in our lives. Because with another source of income, we can indulge in just a little sumptuousness.

But even some costs are too outrageous.

The other day in my school library, I had searched how much it would take to pay to fix a broken arm without health insurance, and my jaw had dropped as I took in the exorbitant 15,000 dollar price tag.

I mean, seriously?! I remember scoffing. It's counterintuitive; if uninsured citizens provide reasonable evidence for their missing health insurance, then the hospital should cover the fees. It's not like we try to injure ourselves deliberately. We just don't have enough money to cover superfluous expenses.

But in the meantime, I'll just have to try my best and tough it out through the aches and discomfort. A broken bone will eventually heal on its own. Right?

As I hop off, the park swing creaks in protest. It's time to go home.

Exams draw closer, and then the dreadful week arrives. Those fortunate enough to have their tests spanned out over the course of one or two weeks are safe, but stress levels peak for those who have three or four exams in two days. Thankfully, I'm not a crammer.

I use the tutoring period to skim over my notes one last time before I proceed to ace my music theory, psychology, and astronomy exams. The last is calculus.

Ms. Vance distributes the thick stack of papers, threatening us with expulsion if we are caught turning the exam around before her clearance. I don't think she does a great job with the darkness of the font because I can read the questions through the back of the paper.

The classroom choruses with a large flipping noise at her signal, and then the scribbling of pencils. The test is straightforward; there is no critical thinking involved. I keep my head down, bent at an angle, so my hair washes over the sides of my face and prevents potential cheaters from copying.

We are allotted an hour for the exam, but I finish it within forty minutes. After double-checking my final answers, I turn my paper back over instead of handing it to the teacher at the front—all the surmising stares of being the first to submit makes me edgy.

Videl has his head down, much like mine was. He seems fraught—a new persona. His leg is jerking up and down and periodically while he fidgets in his seat. I may be imagining things, but I see a drop of sweat on his forehead. I can deduce that he is not going to score well, and it's his fault. He shouldn't have skipped half a dozen classes to indulge in his salaciousness.

Feeling smug, I focus on Haley across the room. She seems to be all right—her pencil strokes are plodding, but methodical.

The hour ticks by, and the teacher collects everybody's test. We have another fifteen minutes to cool down before class is dismissed. Haley immediately gets out of her seat and makes her way toward me.

"What'd you think of the test?"

"It was fine. Question 7b was difficult."

"Was that the one where we had to take like five derivatives in a row? I didn't know what to do afterward."

I smile. "Plot it on a graph with respect to y."

"Ah, looks like I got that wrong." She turns her attention to Videl. "Videl?"

"What do you want, Haley?" Videl's eyes are closed and he looks oddly at peace with himself.

"Sheesh, no need to sound so hostile. What about you?"

He runs his hand through his hair, and I bite my lip to stop the whimper. "Not well."

"Maybe if you weren't preoccupied sucking face all the time, you'd pass," she says. My mouth falls open.

Videl opens his eyes. I expect an annoyed retort, but he doesn't seem perturbed; rather, he launches his trademark smirk.

"Chad enjoys feisty women. Should I tell him? I'm sure he'd *love* your attitude," he purrs. Haley adopts a tint of red at the thought of what Chad would do to her.

"Hope, back me up here," she growls.

I raise my hands in surrender and mumble, "Leave me out of this."

Haley pouts. "I can't believe my best friend is ditching me. At least I get to revel in the satisfaction that we both scored higher than Videl."

"Excuse me? Who said I'm going to score the lowest?"

"You were basically sweating." Again, the words tumble out of my mouth before I can stop them. What the hell is wrong with me lately?

Videl finally pays attention to me for the first time since the first day of school—more than three weeks ago. Even though his face is unfathomable, I still find myself involuntarily sinking into those jade green orbs until time is no longer a measurement.

Haley hacks out a dying cough that pulls me back to reality. "Anyways, Videl, if you are so bent on skipping school constantly, Hope here can help you."

"Help me with what?"

"No, no, no, no!" I reject, blushing in the process as my brain catches up to the situation and understands what she's implying.

"Hope here—" Haley points both her arms toward me and wiggles her fingers—all while I'm shaking my head maniacally, "—is a tutor."

Videl faces me. "I pay you to teach me?"

"No," Haley answers. "It's free. There's a large classroom in the Education building where students go for tutoring. What's the room number, Hope?"

"I am not aware of this program's existence."

Haley narrows her eyes at me. "Hope," she warns.

"I'm not smart enough to be a tutor."

"Hope!"

"102," I mutter in defeat.

"This school offers peer tutoring?" Videl sounds surprised. "I might have to check it out." The bell rings and then he stands up like clockwork before Haley or I can respond. "Time to go to physics."

"Time to go to physics," Haley mocks, once his frame leaves our eyesight. "More like 'time to go fool around with Samantha,' am I right?"

I spin to Haley. "When did you and he get so peachy?" I hiss.

"Whoa, lioness, relax. He's like, best bros with Chad. We've gotten to know each other quite a bit."

I shake my head of any stray thoughts. "Fine. What is wrong with you?!"

"What? You and I both know he's skipping physics," she says innocently while we pack.

"No, not that! Why did you suggest he come to *me* out of anyone else for tutoring?"

"Well, who else would he go to? You seem to be the only girl on campus somewhat immune to his charms."

"S—Somewhat?"

"I see you ogling him every now and then." She coughs. "A few minutes ago."

"You—You're trying to get me to fraternize with the enemy!"

"Don't be so theatrical. He's not your enemy," she says. "You want to spend more time with him, don't you? This is a perfect opportunity. You help him; he helps you. It's an umm...what's the phrase?"

"Mutually assured destruction."

"Right," she agrees as we walk to P.E. "Wait, what? That doesn't sound right."

"Because it's not. It's quid pro quo." Haley scowls.

"I don't know why he's been ignoring you lately, but—"

I stop in my tracks, almost causing a boy behind to crash into me. He swears and swerves, shooting me a dirty look as he scurries by.

"You see it too? I thought I was crazy. He hardly even spares me a glance, and we sit right next to each other!"

"Seriously, though. I'd say he was deliberately ignoring you. Want me to bring you up and see how he reacts?"

I shake my head. "I'd rather not. He'll probably get the wrong idea and think I'm stalking him."

Haley gives me a skeptical look, her mouth curling up at one corner.

"Fine. I'll get Chad to talk to him. The two of them have no filter when it comes to each other. *And* you retain your anonymity."

Knowing Haley won't drop the subject, I relent and begin changing into my shorts.

In P.E., we preoccupy ourselves with volleyball. After an exhausting session, I can come up with one thing only: P.E. is an instated course solely for students to release all their pent-up anger and stress through physical beatings.

Two days later, to my great incredulity, Ms. Vance returns our exams which in itself fascinating. I don't recall any teachers ever in the history of teaching ever to return an exam before a week's time.

I hold my breath before flipping the paper over. I'm one point shy from a one hundred. My breath escapes out in a small whoosh at my careless mistake. I can't help but feel disappointed. When you get a B, you know there's room for improvement. But when you get a ninety-nine percent, just knowing you are one point away from a perfect score is enough to spur crestfallenness.

After P.E. ends, I head over to the Education building and enter the tutoring classroom. There are still some students here for some of the more demanding courses such as physics and statistics—I can tell by the foreign symbols scratched on notebook paper. School is out for the day, but students can stay on campus for however long they prefer until the doors automatically lock and security alarms activate at nighttime—eight o'clock. This is fortunate, for I'm overburdened on homework—an unwanted task best completed on a solid surface anywhere but my house.

I just manage to sit and pull out my experimental article reading for psychology when Haley bursts through the door.

"Hope!" Haley sees me tucked into the corner and begins bouncing toward me in her white cheer shoes and green and gold shell skirt.

"Hi," I respond, glancing around to see if anyone is listening in. "Don't you have cheerleading practice? What are you doing here?"

"I have a few minutes. But guess what?" She leans close to me and see how lit up her eyes. "They're introducing a new club this year, the music club. *Music club*," she emphasizes. "You're musically inclined."

"No," I flatly reject, turning my lackluster attention back to the article.

"But why? This is the perfect opportunity for you. Aren't you always complaining that your daily routine is always the same? Here's your chance! Stir things up a little, you know?"

"I don't think I'm *complaining*," I refute, blushing in the process. Haley looks at me suspiciously, but then the expression is washed away and is replaced by understanding.

"So you're just circumspect."

"What? No!" I spout adamantly. Haley gives me a stern look until I falter.

"Okay, maybe a little," I admit, shuffling my feet.

"Come on, please?" she pouts, giving me puppy eyes.

"I don't know…"

"You know what?" Haley grabs my backpack, yanks my uninjured arm, and begins tugging me out the door before I can firmly plant my foot on the ground.

"Wait! Wait! What are you doing?" Haley's grip is stronger than I'd have expected; it's locked around my arm like a strap on an electric chair.

"If my usual magical pleading eyes won't do the trick, I'll just have to resort to physical exertion instead. Quit sounding so panicked. You and I both know that you're desperate to see—no, to do—something new! Something that doesn't fall into your daily routine. So here. Get that butt of yours in here!" she grunts, pulling me through an entrance in an unfamiliar hallway before slapping my rear and shutting the door behind her.

"I'm going to kill you!" I yell uselessly, pounding my fist on the translucent door window.

I'm not even aware of the silence that ensued after my entrance until I hear someone clear their throat. I whip around and see a classroom with students sitting at each of the desks. They are all staring at me. Every last one of them.

"Are you here for the music club?" The teacher, whom I had missed during my first sweep, asks. My eyes widen as I take in the same facial hair and flannel shirt I had seen earlier that day—in Chemistry. I blush and nod, my voice scared away. He seems to recognize me a second later, though, and he smiles.

"Hope! So glad you could make it. We're just about to walk over to the new music room." He raises his hand up like a conductor and all the students stand at his behest, their chairs squeaking and tumultuously banging against the foot of the desks. I follow suit by inserting myself amongst the line, hunching my back to stay inconspicuous in the crowd of thirty or forty people.

The music room is newly established, a result of a multimillionaire alumni deciding to give back to his school. The teacher announces our arrival and shoos us inside the double doors, where my eyes pop out of their sockets as I scour the multitude of instruments in the room—drums, xylophones, guitars, keyboards, and saxophones—all enough to satisfy a philharmonic orchestra, band, and then some. But what catches my eye are two hunky behemoths tucked away, one in each corner, hiding under their covers so only their black polished legs are revealing.

Stern announces some general safety regulations about 'you break, you pay,' but I don't think anyone pays attention. The students disperse like a startled school of fish before he finishes his warning.

The three keyboards I locate all have beginners clunking down on the keys with exuberant expressions, like they had never seen a piano before.

I glance around. There's no other instrument available aside from the covered pianos.

I *really* want to play; not just because it's been over a year since I've touched a grand piano, but because I don't want to be the only person not doing anything.

The sound of my footsteps is drowned out in the mixture of dissonance by the musically inept. "Mr. Stern?" I ask.

He's busy jotting notes down on his attendance sheet or something, but at my voice, he looks up.

"What is it, Hope?"

"Are we allowed to play the grand pianos?" I ask him.

He takes a glance around the room. "I don't see why we can't. There are more students than instruments, so go ahead."

His approval is all I need; after I reach the grand pianos, I pull out the bench and adjust its height before running my uninjured hand over the piano, brushing my fingertips against the ivory keys. Immediately, I close my eyes and drift off to another realm; another world. Because my right arm has a reduced range of motion, only my left hand is playing. The tenor, rudimentary tune is still enough to lull me into a sense of paradise.

"That's wonderful playing." My eyes burst open to see Stern standing near the edge, right next to the C8 key.

"Thank you," I answer, without stopping.

Stern waves to someone beyond my field of vision. To my mortification, he drags over Videl.

"Videl here is a talented pianist as well. If it isn't too much to ask for, I'd appreciate if I heard the two of you playing something together."

Cryptic eyes. I stifle a shudder.

"Sure," he says, before plopping down on the other side of the bench. We're so close our elbows bump, and a shiver tingles down my spine—the same familiar tingle from the beginning of school.

Stern leaves us alone. The air of discomfort hovering around me probably scared him away.

"You heard the man," Videl says, placing his hands on the keys nonchalantly. He shuffles his side of the bench backward a little to give his feet some space.

"Do you play?" I ask.

"Not too well, but Haley tells me you do." That sly little fox.

"My piano skills are nowhere august."

"Scared?" My attention is brought from possible ways to punish Haley to Videl. Is he challenging me?

"No, no. I'm fine!" I say cheerfully, my voice an octave higher than normal. "Know any four-handed pieces?"

I shake my head.

"Something simple then. Bach's Prelude in C Major alright then?"

"Okay." I'm surprised Videl can't hear the hammering of my heart in its ribcage. I have never played with anyone, lest a stranger, and it renders me vulnerable. Like I'm sharing a big part of my life with him.

"Let's play with one hand each. You take the left hand, and I'll take the right."

Videl takes initiative and begins counting off the tempo. You know how you can tell a good pianist by their hand positioning and phrasing? His reminds me of a leaf lost in the wind, and I can't help but stare at his hand while we are playing.

Before long, even his presence can't surpass my slip outside of reality. I find myself in perfect sync with him—both our fingers enter and lift off each beat perfectly like we are one fused person.

We come to a close, and after holding the last note, I return to the real world. My ears immediately pick up the fact that there is no sound around us. And then my eyes grow wide as they see the huddled mass of students around me, staring at me wordlessly. Some of them have expressions of jealousy. Others are more inscrutable.

"Make way, make way!" Stern's voice sounds muffled, and a moment later he parts the crowd of students aside like Moses did to the Red Sea. "Let me get a word in with these two." The crowd doesn't budge.

"Alone," Stern clarifies. The mass grumbles before dispersing.

Stern claps. "Might I just say, that was beautiful. Bach? I have a daughter who is studying music in college."

"Thanks," I respond, my cheek color returning to normal. I know this isn't all that Stern had in mind; he could've complimented us around the group of students if that was the case. Beside me, Videl is already getting to his feet.

"Stay for a quick moment, Mr. LaBelle."

"What is it?" Videl asks; at the same time I say, "We're not in trouble, are we?"

"Not at all. How would the two of you like to play in front of an audience?"

"Like a band? Doesn't this school have those already?"

Stern shakes his head. "I'm not talking about band or orchestra. I'm talking about a talent show." He's already getting excited just by discussing his idea, much like when he's lecturing chemistry. "We have two talent shows, one per semester, and what better way to exhibit the gifts our student body holds than to have them participate in these events? This way, we can advertise our music club and keep it alive with fresh talent in the upcoming years."

"When is it?"

"The first is mid-January, right as winter break ends. Gives the students time to rehearse without sacrificing time to study for finals. With talent like yours, it would be a waste if the two of you didn't sign up."

"Who would we have to talk with to register?"

"Why, this year I am leading the contest. I can jot down both you and Miss Valentine's name right now."

"Sure," Videl answers before I ever have a chance to open my mouth to protest. But when I do, it's too late. Stern is nodding vigorously and scribbling our names on an official-looking sheet of paper.

"Great! I'm technically not allowed to pick favorites, but…" Stern winks at both of us before bumbling off.

I lose my shy demeanor and blow off the fact that he's been ignoring me for weeks.

"Why did you say yes?!"

Videl smirks at me for the first time, and I feel a bubbling sense of raw anger coating my timorous side. I've seen that smirk toward every girl he's been around and it makes me feel as if I am being compared.

"We make a compatible pair."

"You *think* we make a compatible pair," I refute.

"Don't think I didn't see the starry glint in your eyes," Videl says. "You love playing the piano." Immediately, the anger fades.

"I don't play in public anymore," I redirect, immediately blushing.

Videl eyes me closely like a hidden cat does to an exposed mouse. I suddenly realize just how close we are. So close I can smell his cologne: a whiff of cardamom and citrus, same as when I crashed into him on the first day of school. The bench creaks as I shuffle slightly away.

"It's still a few months down the road. We won't have to worry about it until a week or so prior."

"Just because you gave your answer with absolute certitude doesn't mean I agree."

"I'm not enthusiastic about this either; piano isn't my forte. I'm only doing this to get in Stern's good books. My sister has his class, and she doesn't think he favors her a great deal."

"He didn't say you had to play the piano."

"It was implied." Videl checks his watch. "I need to get going. Speaking of my sister, her car is at the mechanic's and I need to drive her home." Without another word, he leaves. How awkward. How stilted.

I roll my eyes and then start playing, this time alone. Thank god I don't have a sibling.

4

For the first time in a week, I return home before evening.

"Mom, I'm home!" I call out as I step foot into my house, wearing my daily dose of Hurt, by Altha.

"In the kitchen, honey!"

Mom is munching on a bowl of cereal and reading a thick, archaic novel.

"Hear anything about your tests yet? You seem a bit down."

"Just calculus. I made a ninety-nine." I pull out the exam crumpled in the bottom of my backpack and pass it over to her.

"This is great, Hope!" she praises. "All this looks like to me is a foreign language."

"Yeah, well, it's not a hundred." I open the fridge and grab a Granny Smith.

"Have you met any interesting people?"

I hesitate in my quest to bite the apple. The first person my brain jumped to was Videl, but he obviously wasn't a candidate.

"No," I settle.

"What about events? Is there anything new going on at school this year?"

I pause mid-bite, then set the apple down.

"Well, this year there is a music club we just had the first meeting. Evidently, the teacher who's in charge of the club signed me up to play in the January talent show."

"Really? If that's the case, I'll be there to root you on. I've always said you should do these kinds of things again. You have so much suppressed talent."

"It'll be difficult," I admit.

Mom shuffles to my side. "Not if you play your heart out."

"It won't just be me at the piano. I'll be playing with someone else."

"Girl or boy?"

"Boy."

Mom smiles. Is he your friend?"

I hesitate. "No. Mr. Stern—my chemistry teacher—paired us up because he heard the two of us play."

"Like a—what's it called again?"

"Duet."

"Have you picked your piece? Do you know which part you're playing? Where are you two going to practice?"

"Mom," I whine. "It's not until months later. I haven't given much thought to it."

"Well, I'm just excited for you. Maybe this is coincidence, but speaking of music—" Mom pushes over a folder on the table that I thought held her work schedule.

"What's this?" I query.

"I happened to spot this at a yard sale on my way back from work. I don't know if the pieces are at your skill level or whether you even enjoy—"

Mom's words are instantly silenced as I wrap my arms around her.

"Thank you."

"I guess it's safe to say you like them."

"I *love* them." There is probably over a dozen of musical works in the folder written by a variety of famous composers: Beethoven, Schubert, Bach, Mozart, Haydn, and plenty more. "There are even duets in here."

"If they're not too elementary, you can use them for the talent show with your partner. What did you say his name was?"

"It's too difficult to pronounce."

"Ah, well, I'm sure you'll learn sooner or later as the two of you become close. There's no better way to reach true love than through music."

"Mom!"

"I'm just yanking your chain, honey."

~~~~~~

It's the beginning of a new day, and as I walk down the hallway to get to my tutor class early for a quick nap, I think about how I couldn't sleep well at home from the rankle in my arm unless mitigated by painkillers.

As I turn the corner, my thoughts fly out the window as my eyes land on someone I never see here in this area of the school: Videl. He's furiously locking lips with someone. I instantly blush and accidentally squeak before Inner Hope can cap my mouth shut.

"Eek!"

The sound alerts him in the noiseless hallway, and he breaks away from the girl who has her hands around his neck and then his eyes settle on me. Some unfamiliar feeling twists my gut, and suddenly, I feel like passing out. Why is he outside my classroom door? And why is he looking at me like that? Why he walking over to me right now? Where are the teachers?

Now that he's standing a mere few feet away from me, he runs a hand through his seemingly soft-as -ever hair without saying anything at first. But he finally settles on a, "Hey, Hope," right as I slur a well-pronounced, "Um," together.

"You first," I offer.

"Right. I didn't know you would be here this early. Otherwise, I might have been more subtle," he cheerfully says, like I had disrupted a friendly greeting instead of two lovers kissing. He waves a hand in dismissal. The girl who's behind him gives me a look of death before stalking off. "Your turn."

Inner Hope questions why he would even care enough to tone down the degree of kissing in my presence instead of just stop entirely. I am not a voyeur.

"Um," I resume. "You just caught me by surprise. Hi." The word sounds more like a question than a greeting. "W—what are you doing here? I never see you here."

He shuffles a textbook tucked under his arm to his chest, and I see the integral sign plastered on the front cover.

"Here for the tutoring," he pops a smirk. "I think it's about time."

"Oh," I say. Given the amount of time I spend studying for my tests and worrying about Roger, it doesn't surprise me that I had completely forgotten about Haley's suggestion until now. "So you took Haley's advice and came."

"Well, it's not just because of Haley and my grades," Videl says, rubbing his chin for the first time that I've seen. "But her suggestion *is* a key part. I want you to be my tutor."

"Yeah, s—sure." Realizing it is rude to stand in clumsy silence, I open the door for him. "What's the other reason you're here?" I ask, curiosity getting the best of me.

"Well, that's for me to know and you to never find out," he smirks, gesturing for me to enter first instead. I comply with his cavalier behavior.

Videl's personality seems a bit singular, which in itself is peculiar. As I'm walking toward my usual seat, it takes me a few moments to pinpoint the reason behind his abrupt change, but when I figure it out, I'm no closer to the reason why. Videl and I are not on the best speaking terms. In fact, aside from the first day of class and the music club in which we were virtually forced into conversation by Mr. Stern, Videl hardly talked to me at all up until this moment. Now he has this air of familiarity around him as if we've known each other our whole lives and are on *very* friendly terms. But I brush this thought off to the side, positive that I'm conceiving things.

"I've never seen you at school this early," I state while navigating my way through the clutter of unorganized desks.

"I don't see myself here this early either. I'd much rather sleep. But my grade..." he cringes and runs a hand through his hair. "Well, I'm definitely not passing."

"I didn't know you cared about your grades," I say, and instantly regret at how hostile I sound. Videl laughs though.

"I wouldn't be here taking you up on your offer if I didn't care now, would I?"

I grimace as the other three female tutors gossiping amongst each other give me evident stares. "Just sit in any chair you like. Not that one, though. That one—" the seat releases a loud groaning noise similar to a victim's exorcism when he sits in it, "—shrieks."

"You said I could sit in *any* chair, and now you're eating your words? You'd make a great politician."

I ignore his sudden need to banter with me. "How badly are you failing? Your grades, I mean."

"Well…multiplying ten by five was my last test grade?" I cringe at his corny joke. "Trying to get in the mood for math. That sounded prosaic, even to my own ears."

"And your other classes?"

"They're fine. My brain just can't grasp numbers and strange squiggly lines."

Well, he can't be all looks and *all brains*, Inner Hope tells me. I hush her up.

"Fine. And do you need help reviewing your returned exam or would you rather we discuss what we're learning in class?"

"Where's option C, where we get to discuss *you*?"

My face immediately turns into the color of a tomato. It's the first time Videl's hit on me, and for the most part, I feel annoyance at his rhetoric. But a tiny repressed part of me deep down under is actually flattered. I stare at him and state firmly, "Returned exam or class material?"

"Class material," he relents with a huff. His book makes a thudding noise as he plops it down on the desk. Again, his shift in personality catches me by surprise, but I decide to deal with it. If he can spew snarky comments, then I sure as hell can return it with equal gusto. Challenge accepted.

"Okay, so L'Hôpital's rule and limits?"

"I thought it was pronounced hospital."

"Hôpital," I correct, letting the word roll off my tongue. "The guy was French. How do you not know how to pronounce a word from your own language?"

"I'm sure there are words in English you have trouble pronouncing."

"Well, at least you know how to say it now," I mutter under my breath. The closed textbook annoys me so I quickly yank it from his side of the table and flip it open to the correct chapter.

"I heard that. Can't we just go somewhere and have some fun?" he smirks suggestively. I can feel another blush rising out of me but I pin it down.

"We literally just got here, and you're already ready to bounce? No wonder you're failing."

"Well, you know what they say. You can't change someone who doesn't want to change." He props his legs up on the desk in front of him.

"Do you want my help or not?" I grit, annoyance levels steadily rising.

"*Fine*, tutor. Let's see what you got."

Trying to teach Videl is one of the most difficult moments of my life that I'll ever jot down in my non-existent diary. Every time I try to walk him through a practice problem, I catch his eyes looking anywhere but the paper—flitting across the room, observing the other felines and peering longingly through the window. But for the most part, they're usually on me, with his signature smirk in place. And even I, always able to retain a calm demeanor and steady focus on the topic at hand, lose track of the words coming out of my mouth when I catch Videl's jade green eyes. A couple of times he opens his mouth as if he's getting ready to say something, but he snaps his mouth shut before I can even blink once. Thirty minutes and a cranky Hope later, we only muddle through one problem. The situation is so miffing I almost laugh.

"This is impossible," Videl grunts as the bell rings, symbolizing the start of the first class. "I need a break."

I secretly agree with him. Another attempt at trying to get him to understand how to use this rule to evaluate indeterminate forms and I'm going to go crazy.

"Have you met my sister yet? Altha. I think she mentioned sharing chemistry class with you."

The irritable pulse disappears in a whim, and I have to turn my head to the side to hide the small gasp and widening of my eyes at his question. It all makes sense now. The same accents. The reason behind Videl's quick 'sure' to Stern's suggestion was so he could get shine his sister in a positive light. Stern's not stupid; I'm sure he knows of Altha's whisperings behind his back. Maybe that's why she's not in his good books. Because he knows about the bullying.

"I don't talk to her often. We don't sit near each other, and the only time I ever brush by her is when we're getting our beakers and flasks." Videl seems to buy my lie, or maybe he's just pretending to out of pity.

"Well, I'm sure the two of you will get to know each other soon. Fate has a jocular way of bringing people together."

I feel a need to add to my thoughts. "Some think it's coincidence."

"And you? Are you a fatalist or coincidentalist?"

"I'm somewhere in between. Some things you have no control over, no matter you do. On the other hand, with hard work, you can get almost wherever you want."

"Some people like the life of getting anywhere without ever having to do work."

"Well, that's not how I envision my life. I'd like to be a doctor one day. Maybe a neurosurgeon. The brain is fascinating."

"Any school would be lucky to have someone as smart as you."

I blush, then look down. "You seem to be the only one that thinks that."

"What, that you'd get into medical school? A girl with your brains definitely can; Haley told me you score perfect grades. Patience is just what you need to work on. Or maybe I'm just hopeless when it comes to calculus," he laughs.

"No, that being smart is a good thing."

Videl's nostrils flare. "I wouldn't worry about it. This is high school; turn a blind eye. Teenagers display their immaturity in the most unconventional of ways. What's wrong with being smart? Intelligence is what gets someone into college. It's what lands someone a well-paying job. It's a part of success. See those guys?" Videl points to a couple of guys who just stumbled in.

"See how they wobble around, like they own the place? How low their pants are sagging? No one wants to see their checkered underwear."

"Girls seem to like it."

"*Immature* girls. They ignoring you is a sign of immaturity as well. I'd bet copious amounts of money that half of the population is jealous, and the other half is just too stupid to realize how imperative an education is."

"You sure have a high opinion of school, seeing how you skip every other day."

Videl's threaded eyebrows skyrocket at my sass. I don't even know where it came from.

"Would you believe me if I told you I'm a superhero in disguise, and the reason I skip is—"

"To rescue cats from a tree? Yeah, I'd believe that." A soft snort escapes from my mouth, and a pink tint spreads across my cheeks from how unattractive the noise sounds. Videl doesn't seem to mind, and he presses on instead.

"Rescuing trapped baby turtles trapped under the sand makes for a better, less cliché chick magnet."

"Don't tell me any girl has ever fallen for that previous statement."

"Of course they have. No girl can resist an environmentalist. It's the new trend these days. All you have to do is tape a sign to your forehead with the word 'environmentalist' and before long, you'll have a *flock* of females swarming around you."

I chuckle. "That, or rallies for social advocacy."

"See? You already catch my drift. So," Videl continues.

"So?"

"So what medical school are you trying to get into?"

At his question, I freeze. I've given it some thought, but there's no way I'll be able to attend medical school, let alone college unless I win the lottery, financial aid, or a scholarship. Preferably all three. I won't even ask Roger for little things like an allowance or occasional change, let alone a fifty-thousand dollar loan for medical school.

"Any medical school, really. I don't have any preferences. I'll probably take a year off after high school or college. Go traveling," I lie. I don't know what my future holds. But if it comes down to the worst and I don't get any of the three lucky callings, then I'll just have to relegate myself to manual labor after graduating college.

"You're a terrible liar."

"W—what?"

"If you were really planning on traveling, you'd be more animated. Your eyes would light up at the prospect of visiting new places packed with different cultures. Instead, you ignored my eyes and clenched your teeth."

"It sounds like you already know." My face heats up. If he knows I lied then, did he know I lied about not knowing Altha?

"I don't mean to pry, but what about turning to your parents for help?"

"Dad's deceased. Mom's remarried…to Roger."

Videl's eyebrows almost disappear into his hairline.

"You don't like him," he asserts.

"He—he's not the nicest of people. He and Mom fuss over a lot of things. They spend more time bickering than getting along with one another."

"It's not easy, having to listen to your caretakers argue."

"Roger isn't much of a caretaker. He spends more of his time passed out drunk than sober."

For the first time since I've known Videl, he scowls. "What a first-rate role model."

"It's better for me when he's unconscious."

"What a pig. So that's why the piano is an avocation of yours. It offers you escape from reality."

"Yeah."

"I could tell by the way you were playing in music club how much you love music. Have you thought about what Stern asked of us?"

"The talent show? I don't know." I bite my lip.

"There's still almost three months before it's held. We should have more than enough to practice."

"Okay," I draw out, spurred on by the urge to not let him down. "If you do well on the next exam, I'll consider it."

My answer seems to satisfy Videl. He grabs his textbook and noses into it. "What are we waiting for? Tutor me."

5

This morning, instead of heading straight to the Education building, I make a detour to Chemistry.

I'm fed up with Altha.

The girl has done nothing but add to the ever-growing list of things that stress me out. Any more of her comments and I'll have a nervous breakdown in class, but it's not as if a lurid display of me crying will ruin my non-existent reputation anyways.

Stern is in the room. He's drawing up equations on the blackboard. The chalk scrapes against the board, and my ears threaten to bleed at the dissonant scratching.

"Hi, Mr. Stern." He stops writing and dusts his hands before walking around the desk to me.

"Hello there, Hope."

Inner Hope tells me that the twinkle in his eyes aren't just for show; they hold a shred of insight.

It's stupid just to retreat after coming all this way, so I blurt, "Is it okay if I switch partners?"

As if expected, Stern flips open a handheld calendar.

"I'm sorry, Hope, but it's already been a month of school. All the students have settled with their partners, and asking someone to switch with you or moving to a new group would just cause problematic tensions that would take more time to resolve."

Just like that, my heart sinks into the bottomless pit that was once my stomach.

"Is there a reason behind your request? If it's serious, I could probably rearrange something."

He already knows, but what am I going to say? That I'm a victim of bullying? A senior in high school, being bullied. How ironic. If I tell Stern about my issues with Altha, he'll become impudent. And I don't want that. Stern is my favorite teacher.

"No. She and I just don't get along."

"I see." A sharp glint passes over his eyes, and they're so calculating my eyes suddenly become interested in the laces of my shoes.

"That's all I wanted to talk to you about."

"Wait." For a split second, I think he will take me out of my misery. But I am wrong.

"You only use your left arm in experiments. Not a very efficient way to handle volatile chemicals. Also, in the first meeting of our music club, you were only playing with your left hand. Is there anything wrong with the other?"

"Um," I give a half-assed shrug that can resemble nothing but positive verification toward his question.

"Here, let me see."

"N—No, that's okay. It's nothing."

"Teachers spend all their time around students. We know when one is lying," Stern chuckles. He gestures firmly with his hand, and I know the argument is over. I drag my arm out of the sweatshirt's pocket as fluidly as possible.

"You're in pain," Stern declares, noticing my grimace. He takes his hands and gingerly lifts my sleeve back.

"Ouch," he says. Ouch is right. The only times I have glanced at my arm is when I'm in the shower. Bruised would be the most relatable word to summarize the appearance. Blotches of red, purple, and mostly yellow splay out in unsystematic locations. It's like my arm's the xylophone and someone banged their mallets on it.

"Do—do you think I need to go see a doctor?" I ask, my shame washed away.

Stern makes a tsking noise. "You're lucky. It's a sprain. No broken bones or anything."

"Are you sure?"

"Positive. Trust me. I was an RN many years ago."

"You were a nurse?"

"Is that so hard to believe?" he chuckles.

"I mean, the majority of nurses are just…you know, women. Why are you teaching chemistry now?"

"I'm not the type of person who stays in one profession. A few years here and a few years there, but I have to switch occupations to preserve my sanity. I couldn't begin to imagine working as a nurse for the rest of my life. But luckily I was one, eh? It looks like fate brought you to me so I can fix your sprain."

At this, I chuckle.

"What's so funny?" he asked, eyes glued onto mine.

"You mentioning fate," is my reply. "I've had enough shares of that over my lifetime."

Stern makes a humming noise. "Believe me, when you get to the age I am, you'll have racked up plenty more. It's not something we can escape, so we may as well stay for the ride."

The conversation stills while he takes another thorough evaluation of my arm.

"You should recover naturally. You can tell by the coloring that your arm is almost healed, but we shouldn't take risks. Medicine is never a guarantee, especially when it comes to the human body. There's always a chance for something to go wrong. A very slim chance, but a chance nonetheless."

Well, that's certainly mollifying.

Stern pulls open drawers at his desk and digs through them messily before he finds what he needs.

"There we go," he says, pulling out some tan gauze and a pair of scissors. "You have a Grade 2 sprain. How long have you been this way?"

"A month, I think."

"Grade 2 sprains take a while to heal. But don't worry. You'll return to normal in no time," he says, busying himself with my arm.

"Better than having a broken bone, I guess," I respond.

"True. You're all set. Come to me every other day, early in the morning, so we don't run into any students, and I'll redo your arm with fresh gauze. It should be restored in a couple of weeks. Sound good?"

I test my arm. It still hurts, but less than usual. The gauze restricts even more movement than before, but this is a good thing. The more I move, the greater the pain.

"Thank you, Mr. Stern." I'm grateful he didn't ask me why I didn't see a doctor at first glance, or how I got injured to start. He'd detect my lies in an instant with his 'teacher power.'

"Call me Greg," he says. "See you in class later."

I smile and wave him goodbye with my free hand.

It feels like I was in Stern's room for half an hour, but I still have ten minutes to spare before tutoring starts, so I wait outside the door for the puerile boy, who—I hate to admit—is making *some* progress in understanding the course material, even though he spends most of the time flirting instead. Finally, after the bell rings, he shows up.

"You're late," I opine. Videl cocks his eyebrow at my boldness before firing back a swift response.

"It's not like you're going to punish me for it."

I immediately blush at how provocative he made 'punish' sound. A second later, I clench my teeth and begin walking away from the room.

Videl catches up to me in no time. "Wait. Are you ditching?" There's no panic, only a hint of curiosity.

"Your tutoring will be held in the library from now on."

"What's wrong with the classroom?"

"I don't like how crowded it gets. The library is much more open, and not many people are there at this time of day." I don't tell him the real reason: the increase of females "needing" to be tutored in the early morning. What a bunch of thirsty degenerates.

Videl shrugs, thankfully. "Sure, why not. That means less interrupted time between the two of us." He smirks.

"Okay, that's fine, but a new rule: you're not allowed to talk to me unless it's about homework."

The library is vast, a haven for bookworms. Shelves and shelves of books, colors of the spine varying from black to white and everything in between are standing sentinel as if they are protecting a hidden secret. The ceiling is adorned with golden stripes that reflect cozily off the darkened tan shade of coating spread over the wall's foundations. The thirty foot dome-shaped Palladian ceiling threatens to hypnotize you the longer you stare, and if you wanted the allure of crackling noises, the central fireplace would be active during the colder days. The library is our school's diamond.

The table we sit at is ushered off to the side, surrounded by a few lounge chairs leaning against a rare windowpane. I can still see the librarian. She's slim with reading glasses and a fat hair bun. Videl better not draw any unwanted attention. I teach him through the section we learned—trigonometric derivative tests. Easy enough to understand, but a foreign language to those who, ahem, well, never mind.

"Do the problems first," I point on his blank sheet of paper after we finish. "Then we'll talk."

"I don't like this rule. If you can give, you have to be able to receive. My rule is—"

"I'm *giving* you my rule so that you can *receive* a passing score on the next exam."

"You're such a pain."

I roll my eyes. "Your attempts to rile me up are failing. Miserably, I might add."

His smirk disappears, and he growls before tipping his head down and scratching on the paper. I bury my nose back in my book and absorb the juicy details between the transformative protagonist and his demented counterpart.

Not more than thirty minutes later, Videl says, "Done." He whips the paper up in a flourish and sticks it in my face, so close that my nose touches the paper. Even though it takes a conscious effort on my part to discern his illegible handwriting, everything looks solid. I grumble to myself. There goes my undisturbed peace.

"This means we get to talk now, right?'

"Fine," I sigh. "What do you want to discuss?"

"You."

"I see your disposition is still in place. What is it with your fascination toward me?"

He takes a few seconds to think to himself. "I like you."

I choke on my spit. Seconds pass in verbal silence until I manage to confine my coughing.

"You're kidding me," I croak, my eyes watering.

Videl's eyes remain enigmatic. "And if I wasn't, what would your response be?"

"I don't date players." *You don't date at all*, Inner Hope inserts.

"Who said I'm a player?" he asks, an aura of innocence immediately surrounding him.

"Your reputation." Inner Hope is working hard at fanning my face to a normal shade of pink.

"Labels are just labels. Someone's reputation doesn't determine who they truly are, just how—"

"—other people perceive them as," I finish.

"Oh, so you understand the adage," Videl claps his hands once before leaning back.

"Oh, I understand all right. Don't think I don't spot the runny makeup and tears in the bathroom sinks from all the hearts you've broken."

He shrugs. "Those girls are shallow. Equipped with curves, but lacking intelligence. Meretricious."

"You're dating Ashlyn though. The dumbest girl on the cheerleading squad."

He shrugs again, ignoring my insult. "Speaking of Ashlyn, are you going to Veronica's party?"

"The one on Halloween? I don't know. It's supposed to be some costume-themed party, no?"

"Yes, but costumes aren't pertinent to her parties. The point of all the girls going is to try to show off as much skin as possible."

I shake my head. "I don't do parties."

"And why's that?"

"I just don't," I grunt. I have too much dignity to preserve to tell him I've never been invited to one. "Plus, Veronica is the host. She's oil, and I'm water. Immiscibility at its finest."

"How about we go together, then? You can be my guest," he offers.

"That doesn't give me any more incentive to attend."

"How about this, then?" I look up from my book to see that Videl has leaned in *way* past my comfort bubble; I can feel myself going cross-eyed trying to hold his gaze. He's so close the citrus and cardamom almost cloud my judgment. He's so close I want to touch him all over.

Coming to my senses, I immediately push my chair backward until my back hits the bookshelf, all while becoming mindful of the pounding heartbeats thudding painfully in my chest.

"Does t—this look like a game to you?"

"No." But his insufferable smirk says otherwise.

"It does to me. Were you about to *kiss* me?!"

He takes his eyes off me and looks out the window. "Perhaps," he drawls.

"In case if you haven't realized, you're in a relationship right now. You have a *girlfriend*."

"Loose term, in my opinion." Videl turns his attention back toward me.

"It doesn't matter! She's your girlfriend, for God's sake!"

"Are you saying if I didn't have one, you'd let me in your pants?"

I stand up, the textbooks spilling onto the floor in the process.

"I think it's time for you to leave." I try my best to contain my anger, but my hand still shakes as I point him to the exit. Some of my vexation threatens to spill over the edge, like an over-filling bucket of paint.

"You're supposed to be looking over my homework and tutoring me."

I take his homework and throw it back in his face. The piece of paper soars through the air and plops down on the ground like a wilting flower exposed to too much water.

"Leave."

"Why don't you make me?" he feverishly grins.

Unable to quell the surge of anger, I smack him right across his conceited face with my left hand. Hard. His grin seems to slip down just a notch but remains on his defined face nonetheless.

"You know, you're cute when you're all flushed."

"Get out! Get the hell out!"

"This is a public area. Speaking of which, you're drawing attention."

Sure enough, through my clouded-red vision, I see students eyeing us suspiciously and the librarian on the verge of coming over and whispering a few obscenities at my racket.

"Fine. *Fine*," I grit my teeth, unable to bear him any longer. I stoop down and collect my textbooks and stomp out of the library, but not before flicking Videl off and giving him a mocking wink that seems to unsettle him into a stupefied state, if only for a split second.

~~~~~~

"You're really red."

"Thanks. Seems to happen a lot. Genetics, hear, hear."

"Yeah, but I don't see any hunky guys or hear any erotic whispering. Unless you're listening to some raunchy music right now?"

I take out my earbuds before I gape at Haley, dumbfounded. She gives me a concerned look before snatching one of my buds and plugging it in her ear.

"Music checks out."

"Haley!"

"I'm just joking with you. So why are you red? Apart from your previous genetics hypothesis."

"Take a guess." I grind my teeth together in impatience.

"Videl." It isn't even a question. "What did he do this time?" she sighs, before plopping down in the seat next to me and pulling out her books.

"I hate that I always become flappable in his presence," I grumble, toeing the empty seat in front of me. "Sometimes he can be tolerable, but he always has that condescending smirk on his face, and it's getting on my last nerves. It's like an itch that won't go away, no matter how hard you scratch"

"Okay…" she draws out slowly. "But isn't that what usually draws you to him?"

"No! I hate how he always has some snappy retort ready for any attempts I make at a serious conversation. He never stops hitting on me, which is strange in itself, because not even two weeks ago he spent all his time ignoring me!"

"Hmm. Remember when I told you I'd ask Chad to ask Videl why he was so unresponsive toward you?"

"Yeah. What did he say?"

"Nothing. Chad came back the next day with a furtive look on his face and wouldn't say anything."

I release an exasperating groan. "How is that supposed to help me in any shape or form?!"

"Okay, okay! So judging by your tone, you want to have serious conversations with Videl? And date him, yeah?"

"Can you stop twisting everything I say?!" I throw my hands up in the air.

"Okay, Miss Dramatic! Want to hear my professional diagnosis? It'll come free of charge."

I say, "Fine," just to try to get her to shut up.

She slides her seat closer to me. "You're sexually frustrated," she states matter-of-factly. My irritation disappears as my eyes bulge to the size of saucers.

"WHAT?! I am not! No way! No way, no way, no way!" I clamp my hands down on my ears and shake my head back and forth distressfully.

"You're getting flustered again."

"S—so? I'm just sensitive about these kinds of subjects. It's not true!"

"Oh, come on, Hope. Remember the first day of school? When you two sat next to each other in calculus? When you introduced me after class?"

"So? What of it?"

"You were ogling him."

"No, I wasn't."

"Whatever. I'm your best friend. You can't deny that you at least *are* attracted to him."

All my movements cease. My mind, a couple of times if I recall, has strayed over to the dream world of Videl and me dating, but the thought was always veered away from me like two electrons trying to mesh onto one another before I could critically ponder on it.

Is Haley right? He is obnoxious, but I always find myself forgiving him. I always find myself *wanting* to be around him, even if he's at the bottom of my cordial list. And lately, this feeling has amplified due to his sudden change in the way he treats me: from ignoring me to full-blown annoying me.

"Okay, okay! I'll stop!" Haley puts her hand up in surrender. "It's not like I'm *entirely* supporting the two of you together."

"What do you mean?" My breath hitches and I try hard to ignore the remote feeling of disappointment that worms its way into my heart at her disapproval.

"Forgive me for saying this, but the two of you aren't really compatible. From the year I've come to know you, I've learned that you're reserved and shy. Taciturn. And Videl, he—"

"—will never obtain my deference. He's a good-for-nothing libertine," I finish.

"And that is—?"

"He lacks a moral compass."

"Well, if a hottie like him has no morals, sign me up for the next one," she wags her eyebrows. I roll my eyes at the display of her infantile behavior.

"What you said didn't even make sense. A couple of weeks ago—"

"He asked you out?"

"No. He finally decided his grades needed amelioration and came to me for tutoring. But I wasn't in the room, so he decided to wait outside the door, eating some girl's face."

A wide smile spreads across Haley's face. "Wait. What did she look like?"

"I don't know. I was trying to avoid them and their throes of passion in general."

"Come on. You don't remember anything about her?"

"I guess she had dirty blonde hair. Uh, she was carrying a glittering purple purse." My eyes narrow. "Why?"

"Hello? Cheerleader here," Haley points to herself. "It's in our genes to be voluble. But you're referring to Francine."

"Great. Now that I know of this girl's ability to open doors of satyriasis in Videl, I'll be sure to remember her name for the rest of my existence when I jot it down five hundred times in my diary every day."

"Do you ever breathe when you speak a ten-second long sentence?"

"No."

"Well, *anyways*, what I was trying to get at is that she's single now. Videl dumped her a few days ago."

"Great. More news I don't care about," I retort, snuffling the same remote inkling of uncertainty.

"He's dating Ashlyn now."

I completely forgot about her. "Oh, yeah, her. Videl told me. And then proceeded to ask me to Veronica's party."

Haley clasps her hands together. "Please tell me you accepted."

"No, why would I? Parties aren't my thing."

"It doesn't matter if parties aren't your thing. He invited you. *Invited* you. He wants you to go, and you better not let him down."

"I'd rather be home. And I will be."

"No, you're not. Seeing how you're planning to be in your home all night, I'll be there Halloween night, nine o'clock. We, Hope and Haley, are going together. End of discussion." Haley clamps her hands down on her ears and sings random nonsense as she walks to her seat.

"You're so immature!"

She turns around and sticks out her tongue, further demonstrating my point, before putting a finger to her lips and pointing to the door. On cue, Videl walks in, clad in his perfectly fitting brown chinos and buttoned shirt with the rolled-up sleeves. The most unnerving thing is that his eyes lock on mine the whole time he is walking. Even when he sits down, he doesn't break eye contact. He doesn't say anything, so I do.

"What do you want?" I mutter, still slightly irked from this morning.

"I'd like to apologize for my behavior this morning."

I sit still for about ten seconds in a state of semi-shock. "*You*? Apologize? Didn't realize that was a part of your vocabulary."

He growls, and it sends tingles racing through my fingertips.

"It's not, but I admit…I took things too far." His right hand comes out from behind his back, and he presents me with a gift.

A rose. It's a rose. And not just any rose, but a yellow one. I stare at it, dumbfounded. My brain hurriedly flips through years of mundane sitcom romance television shows and movies to try to interpret what his gesture represents.

"What does this mean?" My breath hitches and I feel my cheeks flaming. There's still ten minutes before class starts, but a third of the seats are already filled. I can sense stares boring holes in the back of my head. The endowment, to an outsider, makes it seem as if he's trying to court me.

"The rose, or us?"

Both, I guess, but I say, "The rose."

"You're a girl, and you don't know the significance of yellow roses?"

"Do you ever let up with the insults?"

"I tend to think of it more as convivial banter. But that's not all."

Out comes a stuffed animal—a teddy bear. As if the rose wasn't already enough, my brain decides to short-circuit and I stare at him, mouth open like a fish out of the water.

"Are you going to accept the gift or am I going to have to kneel?"

Any more of him and my face will combust to ashes. "No, please don't." I take the teddy bear in one hand and pluck the rose from his outstretched hand with the other. My nose captures a waft of its scent and my eyes close.

"Don't think you'll be able to take advantage of me this easily in the future," I say, taking another deep draught, my lips curling into an involuntary smile.

"Agreed." I don't even have to crack my eyelids to know he's smirking.

"I'm your tutor. I'm not a toy. I'm not something you can use at your own pleasure before disposing of me whenever you're bored. I mean it."

"There's no guarantee that I won't subject you to my incessant and well-timed quips. As long as you continue tutoring me."

I tuck the rose into my backpack's side pocket and leave the teddy bear on the desk for display. For the first time this year, it is me who does not focus on calculus.

6

"Honey! Can you come downstairs for a minute?"

"Just a sec, Mom!" The piano makes a dull thud as I draw the lid over the keys after playing the final notes to a piece from the folder Mom bought. I rotate my right arm, pleased at how I can twirl it around without any hindrance.

I take another glimpse at the now-dead rose still sitting in a glass of fresh water before I hurry down the stairs. Mom is sitting at the table, her nose buried in another unrecognizable novel.

"You need me?" Mom takes off her reading glasses and shuts the book.

"I hope you don't mind it being wrapped. A mother's old tendency is hard to break." She gestures toward the other end of the table. There sits a small box adorned with yellow wrapping paper covered in ladybug designs and a small green bow.

"What's this?" I take the box, afraid that the slightest touch will ruin whatever is inside of it. I find the sticker on the bottom of the bow and ease the ribbon off before turning the box on its side and ripping open the wrapping paper.

A phone. It's a phone. Not just any ordinary phone either, but a fancy one. One that I see predominantly used by the school population. Flat, not a flip phone, with a large touchscreen and sleek black design that my fingerprints vanish off of after a brief touch.

"Wow."

"Consider it an early Christmas gift." My head spins back to Mom.

I immediately get out of my chair and throw myself on her, hugging her ferociously.

"Thank you! Thank you! I love it! Thank you!"

"Don't thank me," she chuckles. "Thank Roger. He got it for you."

My happy demeanor bubbles away into a pit of lava until all that's left is a bewildered frown.

"Roger? He got this for me?" Mom gives me an affirming nod. "Are you sure?"

"Yes. He bought it for you last night and told me to give it to you this morning. Why? Is something the matter?"

I set the phone back down on the table. Maybe he got it because he felt bad about what happened that one night, but I doubt it. Roger is incapable of feeling remorse. He can't possibly think I'll forgive him just because he got me a cell phone.

Maybe he got it because he wants to turn over a new leaf. I shake my head. There's an even lesser possibility of that option coming to fruition.

"Honey, are you sure you're okay? You seem out of it."

"I'm fine," I dismiss, returning my attention back to my mom, who's staring at me with evident worry. "But since we're on the topic of Roger, how are…you two? I hear some things…downstairs sometimes," I finish lamely, blushing. It feels anomalous, discussing Mom's relationship with the lady herself.

"Where's this coming from, Hope?"

"I haven't asked about your relationship with him since you two began dating, so I thought I'd ask now," I shrug half-heartedly. Mom blinks at me a couple of times. Right when I think she's not going to respond, she tells me.

"You said you hear us downstairs?"

"Yeah. You two are…quite truculent." I try not to sound like I'm blaming her but that's just what it sounds like, for she sighs.

"Honey, Roger and I do argue a lot, but in the end, I love him. And he loves me. I see the distrusting looks you give him, but he hasn't given you—no, us—a reason to dislike him."

"I don't know what you see in him. He is nothing like Dad."

"Honey, I miss your father too, but we all have to move on sooner or later. You know me," Mom surprises me with a wink. "I'm not too picky when it comes to dating."

"Right," I mumble, unconvinced. My fingers absentmindedly toy with the phone.

"Is there something you know about him? I know you said you were curious, but I can't help but feel like there's an unprecedented reason as to why you're asking."

I bite my tongue. "No, no. I was genuinely inquisitive."

"Hope, you know that I will choose you over *anybody*, right? I just want you to realize that noone is more important than my own daughter."

"Thanks, Mom." I hug her again. "Everything is fine. I promise." They may fight, but she loves him to death. And, as much as I hate to admit it, he does support us. There's a roof over our heads, and he just bought me a cell phone. A new start-of-the-art phone I see Haley and other students using to text their friends during class. A habit I pray I won't pick up. For the sake of my phone and the sake of my teachers' sanity.

"Honey, you're drifting off again."

"Hmm? Sorry," I sheepishly grin. Mom gives me a nod and then glances at the oven clock.

"Didn't you say you were going to spend some time with Haley at nine? It's that time already."

As if Haley herself was standing outside my door waiting for Mom to dismiss me, the doorbell suddenly rings.

"That's her," I say, marching to the front door and yanking it open. Sure enough, Haley is standing on the other side looking like a prim little doll. Her eyeshadow is smoky and her eyeliner curls off the corner of her eyes into wing tips; when she narrows her eyes, I imagine a fiery snake about to strike. Her hair is straightened so its voluminous strands dangle down to her stomach, and her body is covered by a taupe pinafore dress and dark forest green heels that makes her legs to die for.

"Hi, Haley," I greet, my eyes lingering on her figure.

"Hey yourself!" Haley greets, wrapping me in a hug and kissing my cheek. "Are you ready?"

My cheek tingles and reddens at where her pink lips made contact. "Yeah, hold on. Let me put my shoes on." My usual sneakers are missing next to the shoe rack. "I must have left them in my room. Why don't you come in for a minute?"

"Yeah, sure!" She virtually glides in and then slips off her jacket. "I like the house."

I blush, because it's not a nice house. "Mom! Haley's here!"

"Oh, you're Haley?" Mom rounds the corner and gives Haley an earnest hug, to which she returns with just as much fervor. "Hope talks about you all the time."

"Really now? What's she say?" Haley asks, waggling her eyebrows at me. I stick my tongue out at her, and she pretends to bite it.

"Just how grateful she is to have such an amazing friend like you."

"Mom," I whine. "Can you stop sucking up to her?"

Mom chuckles. "Sorry honey, but Haley does seem to soak up the attention." I turn my attention to Haley, who's puffing her chest proudly and pounding on it with her fist, like King Kong. I roll my eyes.

"Hey, sophomoric child, quit acting so silly." Haley immediately drops the act and begins pouting.

"So where are you two planning on going?" Mom intervenes. Uh-oh. Luckily, I'm out of her field of vision, so I urgently lift my hand up and make slicing motions across my neck while frantically shaking my head back and forth.

"We're just going to go back to my house and watch a movie. Is it okay if Hope spends the night?"

"I don't see a problem with that idea," Mom says. "But why are you wearing a dress for a sleepover?" Uh-oh again.

"Er—" Haley stutters as she fumbles for an answer. "I just came straight from a club event at school. I haven't had time to change."

"Alright, then. Just make sure to text me if you need anything, Hope."

"I'll have her back bright and early tomorrow morning, Ms. Valentine."

"Call me Chloe." Mom laughs, which is her sign of approval.

I head upstairs and slip on my sneakers. When I come down, Haley regards me with a strange look, but we end up leaving the house successfully without any more interrogating questions. Parents will be parents.

As soon as we're outside and out of the vicinity of Mom's ears, Haley spins around so suddenly I bump into her and almost step on her expensive shoes.

"Why are you dressed in school clothes?" she asks innocently. "Did you actually think I would let you opt out of your first party?"

"What?"

"Your *clothes*, Hope. Where is your dress?"

Her words suddenly dawn on me, and I blush.

"I don't have a dress." I stare at my feet, ashamed, wondering if Haley will scoff at me. But a warm hand caresses my cheek, bringing my head up.

"You don't have a dress?" Haley repeats.

"No."

She takes a calculating look at me before sighing.

"I doubt we wear the same size, and I don't have dresses or anything that counts as party appropriate for you. I guess what you're wearing will have to do." I shuffle my feet, trying to throw off the repeating sound of 'poor' resonating in my head.

"How about I take you shopping next week?"

I give a half-assed grunt that makes even me question whether it was an agreement or not. But all it does is make Haley giggle and drag me to her car.

I'm shivering after spending only a few minutes in her sedan. Haley seems to have some tolerance to cold weather because her air conditioning is cranked to the coldest setting. And the music she blares out of her speakers is so loud it reminds me of the cheerleading coach and his megaphone. Poor speakers. They could implode any moment.

The sinking feeling in my gut worsens when we turn the corner. Haley turned off the music a few minutes ago, complaining about how radios only play mainstream songs over and over again without any throwbacks. This allows me to hear the slight murmur of music creeping up from the end of the street.

"You'll be fine." Haley flashes me her promising grin. "Everyone here has been in your shoes before; you'll fit in quickly. Don't worry."

"If only your words compelled me," I bite my lip. Haley parallel parks the car on the side of the street a few hundred feet from the house and cuts the engine.

"Listen Hope. I won't leave your side for a second. Well, unless you want me to. Or if you see some Videl. Or if—"

"Haley."

"Right. Sorry. Let's go?"

"Do you promise?" *It's only a party*, Inner Hope explains. Something that all high school teenagers experience.

"Yes," she sincerely answers, before we step out of her car.

"How is Veronica throwing this party anyways? I mean, do her parents not care?" I ask, trying to distract myself from my impending doom.

"You really are clueless about how social life works, aren't you?" I feel a little hurt at her remark, and it must have shown on my face because she grimaces. "I didn't mean it that way. Sorry."

"No worries," I shake my head. "Honesty's important."

"Here. Let me fill you in on what goes inside Veronica's tiny, tiny brain. She acts all, let's say dolly, and that serves as a guy magnet. They come flocking to her, and she sleeps with them. She's picky with her guys, so they're usually popular, handsome, or preferably both. Do you follow me so far?"

"Uh, sure? Where exactly is this going?"

"You'll see. So she gets all of their numbers, and then whenever her parents are gone for the night or out of town, she throws a party and invites her 'friends' and the tools she sleeps with. The boys flock over like lost puppies for another attempt to get into her pants, and well, partly because they like booze. And they bring their friends too. So Veronica ends up with fresh meat and a boost in her popularity." Haley presses her palms together then moves one hand up accordingly.

"It sounds like it would be convivial at first, but in the end, wouldn't it be better to have a small group of closely knit friends than a large group of faint acquaintances? Surely she doesn't have time for everyone," I say.

"Exactly. You catch on fast." Haley sounds impressed. "She's living in the present, when she should be looking ahead over the horizon into her future. I've tried to help her, but people don't change if they don't want to change. For the record, I like you a lot, Hope. You're a great friend," she points at me.

I blush. "So how are Videl and Ashlyn?" I ask, trying to arrive at a different subject of conversation.

"I think they're over, but I'm not too sure. I haven't been paying much attention. Rumors are he's dating Veronica now."

"You mentioned the only reason she hosts these parties is to hook up with guys. If they're dating, doesn't that mean Veronica's cheating on him?"

Haley gives me an 'are you dense?' look.

"Please, Hope. Since when have Veronica and Videl demonstrated any fidelity in the slightest?" she emphasizes. "I don't know how some people can have such misguided morals. I mean, checking someone out while you're in a relationship is one thing, but cheating on them while the other person knows? And they're okay with it? That's messed up. They probably have orgies or something all the time."

"I guess they have a very open relationship," I say, trying to defend Videl. But the thought of him sleeping with more than one girl at a time churns my stomach.

"You're still hardcore crushing on him, aren't you?" Haley nudges my shoulder, taking notice of my queasy face. "You accepting him as his tutor sure has brought the two of you closer together, from what you've told me."

"Yeah," I admit. "A lot, to be honest."

"Look, Hope. I'm saying this as your friend." Haley juts out her neck and turns me sideways to face her. "It's obvious you have a crush on him, even if you're in denial about it." She holds up her hand at when I try to interrupt. "And if the two of you end up dating, *please* be careful. That boy will bring nothing but heartbreak to you. Believe me. Chad hangs out with him all the time. I know you already know this, but Videl's a womanizer."

"He still comes over to be tutored," I point out. Haley narrows her eyes.

"Well, just keep the relationship as friendly as possible, okay? The last thing I want to see is you get hurt. Then I might have to beat Videl up for you." She giggles, but then it dies away. "You don't want to be used like all those other girls he has wrapped around his pinky, do you?"

"Not at all," I guiltily say. Haley's right. It's ironic how she was half-heartedly urging me to get closer to him but is now telling me to back off. Maybe she didn't believe the two of us would actually grow to be semi-close. I mean, the rose was *way* more than just a friendly gesture. I don't know. Blonde girls are confusing.

"Exactly. Take my advice to heart, will you? Let's not discuss him anymore. We're here to have fun and loosen up after a long week of school." She winks and then leaves the topic at hand alone, for we finally arrive. The front gate of Veronica's home is unlocked, and we slip through.

The party's on full blast when we navigate our way to the front door; there are already people passed out and drunk in the yard. I crinkle my nose. The smell of alcohol is so malodorous that my head spins.

"You sure this is where students go to have fun?" I whisper loudly to Haley, wishing I was tinkering with my telescope or keyboard instead. We pass through the front entry hall, where I almost trip on a rug sitting by the door.

"Of course. Smell the alcohol? It's like an aphrodisiac to me." She shudders and drags me inside to the kitchen counter. There's some weird upbeat music pounding through the house, but it's almost drowned out by the shouting conversations people are having with each other. Amongst a large pile, Haley snatches a beer bottle. My body tenses when I recognize the all-too-familiar label.

"Want one?" she asks. I shake my head no.

"How are there already people passed out on the front lawn?"

"Party actually started at eight. I thought it'd be easier if you slipped in when Veronica isn't anywhere outside her bedroom. You sure you don't want one?" Again, I shake my head no.

"Don't be such a worrywart, Hope! No one will know there's underage drinking here. Private property," she grins, before popping the cap off like a pro. Smoke gently fumes out of the opening, the water vapor dispersing throughout the room.

"No thanks, Haley."

"Suit yourself. Maybe next time. Here," She and pulls me forward through another door. "Let me introduce you to some people." Before I can protest, we wind through the kitchen into the living room. The multi-piece sofa set and futon off to the side are occupied by strangers, although I do recognize some faces I see now and then in passing in the school hallways. Girls are in their finest dresses, perfectly cut and with even smoother fabric, sitting way too close to guys to suggest anything abstinent in the least. Roaming hands and glassy, lust-filled gazes entwines all the inhabitants together like they're one long animal skin splayed out on the sofa.

"Hey, guys!" At the sound of Haley's voice, the laughter and conversation dampen. They fire back a chorus of greetings. The alcoholic stench is almost unbearable. I feel like I'm breathing in toxic fumes from a waste dump.

"Everybody, meet my friend, Hope." Haley puts a hand on my shoulder and begins pointing at the people drinking on the sofas, ticking off their names one by one. I don't understand how she expects me to remember everyone. There are at least three Emily's.

A couple of guys seem interested or conscious enough to wave a hand, nod, or say 'hey' toward my general direction, but I'm positive it's the alcohol talking. And for the most part, the girls ignore me after a quick eye over and scoff at my attire.

"You attend Starmount?" A guy sitting in the corner of the futon asks.

"Y–yeah," I stammer. He nods and then pats the tiny opening right next to him, inviting me over.

"Cool," he says. I hesitate but then decide to try to situate myself. So I take his invitation and sit next to him. I manage to squeeze in between him and the futon arm, but now our shoulders are scraping each other's.

Thank god Haley sees the distressed whimper on my face because she follows suit and sits next to me on the futon arm itself. She lets me draw circles with my fingertips on her exposed thigh, and the touch gradually evens the acceleration of my heartbeat.

"So what year are you?" My attention is drawn back toward the guy, and my neck cries out in pain when I have to twist it a hundred degrees just to see him.

"I'm a senior. You?" Can I be any more simple and straightforward?

"Sophomore." A tinge of envy hits me. "You new? I'm pretty good with faces, but I haven't seen yours around here."

"Here—" I crane my head to emphasize my point. "As in Veronica's party?"

"Well, yeah. And school."

We continue speaking in telegram language. The more we speak, the closer his hands draw to my leg. After a few minutes, he touches it. I immediately pull it off and set his arm back on his chest. Not even a minute later, it's back on me.

I bolt from my seat, pushing myself out of the squished area with superhuman strength, sputtering nonsensible excuses.

"Hope!" I hear Haley's name behind me. "Hope! What happened?"

Empty beer bottles sift around in the sink when I wash my hands deliriously.

"Parties just aren't for me, Haley," I grit, squirting another load of liquid soap onto my palms.

"I thought you were enjoying Emily's story?"

"Who? Well, you thought wrong. Look at this!" I exclaim, rotating around on my heels, splattering water and foam everywhere. "You know I'm one to sit in my room and read on a night like this. Look at all these intoxicated primates improvidently frolicking around! Even now, my outdoor voice is in full effect because of how blaringly loud this inbred music is!"

"Okay, okay, can you tone down on the vernacular? I get it!" Haley puts her hands up defensively after wiping some bubbles smeared on her eyebrow.

"I wasn't *enjoying* myself. I was trying to settle in. But that doesn't matter. He, a human species of the male gender whose name I do not even know, tried to grab my boobs! And then proceed to whisper under his breath about things he'd love to do to me!"

Haley takes a calculating glance at my fingers pointing to the small mounds on my chest before launching herself at me and playing with them, one hand fondling each.

"Haley!" I jerk backward.

"What? You're letting me grab them now." She continues massaging them.

"You're different," I yank her hands away, a warm blush blooming in my cheeks

"I know. Just trying to lighten up the mood. But on a serious note," Haley begins. "You don't have to take everything so seriously."

A vein in my temple throbs.

"Seriously?"

"Yeah, like try to loosen up. In no way am I suggesting you take Bates up on his offer, but at least try to have some fun, you know? Have a couple of beers. It'll make you feel good."

"No," I reject.

"Suit yourself. Oh, hey babe!" Babe? I take my attention off the menacing beer bottles and turn over toward Haley, who is staring at the sudden appearance of her boyfriend.

"Hey, baby," he smiles. But then it disappears as he notices me. He whispers something to Haley, and her face changes from happy to sad to upset.

"Hope, you don't mind if I go with Chad? I need to talk to him about something important," she asks. My chest constricts. I don't want to be left alone by myself in my archenemy's lair.

But for some reason, "No problem," is what slips out of my mouth. She gives me a faint, dim smile before mouthing 'I'm sorry,' and then she's gone. Well played.

I spend the next half hour or so with my eyes glued to the oven clock. Never have I felt so out of place. Now and then, more familiar faces I'd see strolling the school hallways show up and grab a couple more drinks. Some ignore me, some shoot me skeptical looks, and twice, guys come up and actually have the audacity to try to dirty talk me into one of the beds upstairs. Inner Hope glowers at them, and I quote from her voice to mine, 'beat it.'

I want Haley to come back so I can pounce on her and ask her to take me home. I feel slightly betrayed at her failed attempt to keep her promise, but it seemed like she had a good reason to leave. With nothing but shelves of beer to keep me company, I heave a heavy sigh.

"I thought you weren't going to show. Penny for your thoughts?"

"I didn't know that phrase was a thing anymore," I reply dryly without thinking, continuing to run my hands over the smooth, granite countertop. "Don't you have a better conversation starter?"

"It's not. You're clearly uncomfortable. Here."

The distinct cologne hits me first right before the familiar sound of his voice, and then my brain clicks right as I see his hand offering me a beer.

"O—Oh. Oh! I mean, oh. Hi?" I'm already at a loss for words, so I take the bottle from him, averting his gaze and concealing my flushing cheeks. "I didn't know it was you."

"I figured. I've never heard you use such a defensive tone before. My guess is that you've had your fair share of guys hitting on you tonight." Videl's breath smells of alcohol, but it isn't as prominent as that of the rest of the partygoers. I take a few seconds to analyze him. He's wearing a patchy, brown V-neck and my eyes focus on the tight fit around his shoulders to the point where it can be considered creepy. He's also wearing a pair of honey-colored chinos, which brings out the waviness of his hair. Honestly, he'll look good in anything.

"Drunk. Drunk guys," I correct, finishing my analysis. "And if you're referring to their incoherent, slurred, 'Hey baby, let me show you a good time upstairs' as 'hitting on me,' then yes, you are indeed accurate in your claim."

"They what?!"

"Don't worry, I'm still here in the kitchen, aren't I?"

"Huh. First party, isn't it?" Videl cocks his eyebrow. I remain silent until he starts chuckling.

"Hey! Stop laughing at me!" I whack his arm while Inner Hope slumps further in her confidence chair.

"Don't worry Hope. Everyone has a first."

"You and Haley should recite proverbs to one another."

Videl smirks. "Tell me about it."

"I hate this place. It's so crowded, and people are just acting like feral animals, groping and making out and getting wasted like it's the last day before the apocalypse." I look at my beer bottle distastefully. It's hard to believe this drink has the innate ability to bring out a whole different side to people.

"I completely understand. Most people here are pressured by their friends to come. In the end, we all just want to fit into the social construct."

"Amen to that. Haley was the one who dragged me here. I need to put my foot down next time a preposterous idea comes to her mind. She suggested I loosen up and basically told me I should let Bates, or whatever the hell his name is, grope me."

Videl growls. "Bates did that? That's not like him."

"Like I said, humans plus alcohol equals cave people."

"Well, I hate that loser anyways. He's had a confrontation coming for quite a while now." Videl starts to walk toward the living room, but I quickly pull him back after my brain realizes what he's about to do.

"Don't," I say. "He's not worth it."

"Who cares? I haven't gotten into a brawl in ages. And calculus homework been such a pain lately, it'd be nice to vent." His signature smirk is missing, and in its place is a deadpan expression.

"We're at a *party*, Videl," I remind him. "Not a fight club. Come on." I tug him toward the opposite direction of the living room. This area is a darker corner of the house, and there aren't many people in this hallway.

"You have no idea where you're going, do you?"

I shake my head, defeated.

"Well if that's the case, want to get away?" Videl offers. "Not in the sense of the guys trying to court you to bed." Never mind, the smirk's back.

I chuckle before saying, "Yes. Please."

"Follow me." Videl pulls me to the end of the hallway and up the stairs. I follow him, taking note that the music grows softer with each step as if an invisible curtain at the foot of the steps divided the realm of chaos and utopia.

We wind our way past a couple of rooms, one of which I can hear some more-than-obvious, uh, copulating noises. Videl opens the door at the end of the hallway, and when I follow suit, I see him lifting open the window.

"You're not scared, are you?"

"No." My voice trembles, but this sounds a lot better than spending time downstairs alone. He disappears out the window for a few seconds, but then I see his hand. I take it and push myself up with one leg until my whole body is outside on the roof.

"Sit." Videl is already splayed out near the edge, one arm propping himself up, the other resting on his knee. I join him warily, but my thoughts of concern fly out the window as I look to the sky.

"This window faces the backyard. It's the best place to stargaze."

"The stars seem to be glowing with such intensity," I point. "They're—"

"Mesmerizing." My head spins toward Videl to see him raptly looking at my face.

"Yeah," I breathe. I turn my attention back to the angelic beauty of the stars.

"Look. Big Dipper." Videl asks after a few minutes of quiet. I follow his finger up to the sky.

"And there's the little one," I say with a smile. He grunts after a few seconds.

"I can't find it tonight."

"Look above the big one."

"Yeah, I know. I still don't see it."

"Look a little to the right then above the big one. Try not to focus your eyes too hard, otherwise, you'll miss it. Do you see it?"

"I think I do. I see it! Wait, now it's gone. It's here again! And it's gone." He lets out a dramatic sigh, and I giggle.

"Some faint stars you can't see if you're actually trying to see them, if that makes sense. What I do is just let my eyes lose focus and let the peripherals do the work. You have more rods there." I take another look at the pair of Dippers. "There's Hercules. And right above it is Draco."

"I know you're trying to point them out, but unless your finger shoots a high-power laser beam to that constellation, there's no way my eyes can see them. That being said, you sure know your constellations."

"Not really. I'm just a really big space geek," I blush. "There's nothing quite like it."

"No, I completely understand. I'm a space junkie myself."

"Really? Test me," I challenge.

"Do you ever get an inexplicable feeling when you look up to the sky and realize just how big the universe truly is? It's difficult to explain."

"Yes! The infinite mystery of space. The size is indescribable, and it magnifies just how small we are." The few people that I've gotten close enough to talk about space to were all too down-to-earth; they either didn't really think about what was out there for us to dream about, or were too wrapped up in the social structure of life—finishing education, finding a well-paying job, and starting a family. But Videl...

"Yeah, can you believe there are people who don't believe we landed on the moon? What a load of garbage."

"Yeah, I know, right?" I agree. "Also the fact that there are people that think the earth is flat." I chuckle. "I mean, if you were in New Zealand staring up into the sky, the landmarks on the moon would be flipped upside-down than if you were somewhere else halfway around the world."

"Maybe they're secretly from the golden ages, before Pythagoras's time."

"There is physical evidence that we have been to the moon. A shuttle goes a little under eighteen thousand miles per hour, and the moon is how far away? Two—"

"—hundred and forty-thousand miles," Videl finishes. "About a fourteen-hour ride, theoretically. Three days, realistically."

"To some people, that seems like a great feat."

"You don't think that?"

"It *is* a great feat, but there's always the possibility of 'what else.' Human technology is so rudimentary. I wish I could be alive two hundred years from now, just to see how far human space exploration has progressed. I bet we'll have domesticated interstellar space travel."

"Imagine what the future humans would have to say about our paved highways and fashion."

"If I had one ability, it'd probably be to live forever. The only hard thing would be to say goodbye to my loved ones. To Haley and my mom. Oh, and probably you too," I roll my eyes after Videl quirks his eyebrow.

"I'd like to see how history evolves through my own eyes, not just read about it from school textbooks. It would be nice to know that there is a Fountain of Youth waiting for us somewhere."

"But without the addition of preternatural human abilities, like vampirism, werewolves, undead zombies, and whatever else I can't think of right now."

"Gods, deities, or the protagonist of an upcoming feature film."

"Yeah. Maybe in our lifetime, astrophysicists will create some cryogenic spaceship that will be shot off somewhere far away, where Einstein's time relativity comes into play. Then when we land back on earth, hundreds of years will have passed, but we've stayed young and pristine."

"Could you do it, though?" Videl asks, taking a gulp of his beer. "Leave everything behind? Imagine if we humans had the capability of interstellar travel, and you were to leave right now. Once you're in the abyss, nothing we have on this earth means anything outside of it. Our cell phones, laptops, clothes, whatever. To the vast space, there is no existence of this useless junk. In a sense, we're reverting to the most fundamental part of human life."

"Right," I nod, veiling my zest. "War impacts us all on earth, but regarding the universe, the problem is lesser than a grain of sand." Videl cocks his eyebrows. "Carl Sagan," I blush. "My favorite astronomer. And cosmologist. And astrophysicist. Probably author too." Shut up, Hope!

Videl laughs, and it sounds like running water.

"That blush becomes you," he states. I immediately turn even redder.

"T—thanks." I try my best not to come off as awkward. To get my mind off of his comment, I take a sip from the bottle he handed me earlier.

"Gah!" I instantly spit out the revolting drink. "How can people drink this?" I offer the bottle back to Videl, keeping my face as far away from it as possible. He takes it away from me.

"I dunno. Peer pressure, acquired taste, or maybe they're just crazy enough to like it." Videl takes a drink himself and winks. "I must say, though, it is attractive seeing a girl hold her alcohol."

"You don't seem like the kind of guy who succumbs to peer pressure. You definitely seem crazy enough."

"This might be news to you, but France's drinking age is sixteen. So the answer you're so desperately seeking is B: acquired taste. You Americans have funny-tasting beer," he mutters the last sentence.

"Really? That young?"

"Most of Europe's drinking age is sixteen. You should've seen the expressions on people's faces after I told them. As soon as I mentioned sixteen, they all begged me to take them to France."

I scoff, rolling my eyes. "In your private jet?"

"How'd you know?"

If I had anything in my mouth, I'm sure I would have spat it out. "Come on," I clap slowly. "You really think I'll fall for that?"

"It's not a joke. I have a private jet. Or, rather, it's my father's."

"You can't be serious."

Videl's face remains stoic.

"Your family owns a jet?!"

"Yeah."

"That's so cool. What's it like? Can I see it?" Suddenly, I stop. I don't want to sound like I'm on of Videl's 'friends' so that I can use him as a sycophant. His comment about his usual company brings up the earlier conversation Haley and I had about him and Veronica, so I ask him a question about her, trying to play it like a discrete topic shift.

"So…how are you and Veronica?"

"Veronica," Videl repeats blankly.

"You know, the cheerleader, the complete bit—"

"Oh, her," he interjects. "We're fine," he says, but I detect a hint of hesitation.

"The two of you have managed to stay in a relationship longer than usual," I twiddle.

"Keeping tabs, are you? We're okay. It's a pretty open relationship between us two." He thinks to himself. "Actually, I mean really open. She's probably with a guy in her bedroom right now." My stomach rumbles with unease at his words.

"That doesn't bother you?" I ask incredulously. He shakes his head.

"Not at all. We're not ones to remain monogamous," he explains.

"D—do you, um, love her?"

"Veronica? Love is hardly the word I'd use for her. Holding slight, if not invisible attraction toward the blabbering bimbo is more along the lines." He laughs, and I even let out a small chuckle. "All she's got going for her are her looks and popularity."

I don't bother hiding my grimace, and he spots it.

"What's the matter? Can't believe that a guy like me could ever fall in love?"

I look into his eyes. "Do you think it's better to be loved once and then hurt or never to have been loved at all?"

Videl takes another sip of his beer and then sits in silence for so long that I think he didn't hear me. Right as I'm about to repeat myself, he speaks. And when he does, his voice is hushed.

"We all get hurt every now and then, but love is interminable. If you haven't loved, then you're not living."

"So does that mean you're not living?" I jab.

"I never said I wasn't ever in love. Even now…" He takes a long draught from his bottle.

I shake my back and forth, trying to clear my head. "Do you believe in true love?"

"Yeah. When you make eye contact with someone or touch them for the first time and get shivers through your spine and tingles racing through your fingertips when you brush them—that right there is true love."

My mouth starts to falls open at his explanation, but I manage to shut it in time before he sees. Maybe he just touches a lot of that Velcro stuff, but the tingles and shocks he described sound exactly like the ones that I feel every time we make contact.

"Your eyes just widened. Do you agree?"

I choose my words wisely, painfully aware of the thudding heartbeats against my ribcage.

"Yeah, I espouse that statement. Have you—have you ever felt it?"

"Of course I have," Videl says. "Otherwise, how could I answer your question with such certitude?"

"And is it always mutual?" I ask, curiosity having gotten the best of me.

"If it was, then I wouldn't be where I am now, dating Veronica, would I?" Videl turns to me and gives me a small smile. One innocent and shy. One that holds something deeper than the open expressions he wears on his face. One I've never seen strewn across his face before.

Realizing that I brushed too sensitively on the topic, I backtrack.

"So you're a love at first sight kind of guy. Why date all these girls then? I mean, they're obviously not 'the one.'"

"There's nothing wrong with having fun, is there?" Videl says, his voice confident again. "And besides, they're just there to pass the time."

"And what happens after all the time has passed?"

"Humans can't predict the future. I'll worry about it when I get there." Videl gets to his feet. "Wait here. I'll be back in a few." He enters the house through the window.

The weather starts to get chillier as the night surges on, so I draw my knees up to my chest and wrap my arms around them. I should honestly be terrified at the thought of how accurately I fit in Videl's description of true love, but our lengthy conversation has set my brain in a state of ease to the point where I can't be concerned about anything. So for another few minutes, I stare into the black abyss hovering above my head until Videl comes with two red solo cups, their contents sloshing around and threatening to spill over the sides.

"Here," he offers.

"What's this?" I look into the cup to see some reddish-purplish liquid. It smells fruity. "You're not trying to drug me or anything, are you?" I ask in all sincerity.

"You're silly. It's party punch. I reckon if you dislike the taste of beer, you'll love this instead. Trust me." He holds his cup to me, and it takes me a few seconds to realize he's offering a toast. I tap my cup to his, and the boing spills out some punch.

Hmm. Not bad. The punch tastes like a sugary drink—not saccharine—with a slight molasses flavor and a zesty zing that leaves my tongue humming. Actually—

"This is really good." I look into my cup to see it's already half empty. I put the cup back to my lips and chug the rest of the drink down, wincing at a strange burning sensation that spreads in my chest.

"So. Space," Videl begins again, chuckling at my reaction. "Did you know there's an ongoing program planning on sending humans on a one-way flight to Mars?"

"What? As in, never coming back to Earth?"

"Mind-boggling, right? To start a new life on another planet millions of kilometers away. The first civilization."

We talk longer than I can keep track of, but before long, there are several empty cups turned upside down arranged in a neat little pyramid formation. I realize after the fifth cup there's actual alcohol in it, but for some reason, I can't stop drinking. My chest and stomach is really warm. I have to pee. Badly.

Where am I again? I quit admiring my project and hold up my sixth or seventh, or even eighth. I don't remember anymore. I bring the cup to my lips, only to have it snatched away by Videl. Party-pooper.

I stumble to him but end up slipping on my feet and crashing into something firm.

"Gimme it back," I slur. He looks torn between taking responsibility and laughing at my drunkenness.

"You've had too much. Go use the bathroom and sober up a bit." I stick my tongue out at him before I snuggle up to his arm and attempt to focus in on his face.

"You're so controlling," I purr mischievously, and with the alcohol fueling my boldness, I adjust myself in his grip so that my arms are around his nape of his neck.

"Okay, Hope. You've definitely had too much to drink." Videl resists my advances and easily pries me off of him.

"What's—what's the matter?" I hiccup. "Do you not like me or something?" I pout at the lack of his touch.

He mutters something under his breath that I don't catch.

"Speak up," I giggle, before caressing his chest.

"Okay, you need to head home. Here. Let's find Haley."

"But I like you Videl. Really, *really* like you." Stupid alcohol myopia. I hiccup again. My vision is blurring, and the world is starting to spin around me. "Why do you have to keep dating Veronica? Wh—why can't you date me instead?"

"Enough, Hope," Videl pleads, but I'm not done. Now that I've started, I can't stop myself. Inner Hope is passed out drunk on her couch and in her place is an alcohol bottle garbed in her clothes waving pompoms in the air and spewing non-filtered, repressed secrets.

"You know—I hated you. I hated how you were so good-looking and could get any girl under your belt. I hated how you always had that st—stupid smirk on your face. Yeah, and I hated your snide remarks and facetious humor. But lately your dumb banters are beginning to grow on me. The first time we met—" I hiccup again. "In the hallway, when you pulled me up, those tingles you described—I felt them. That makes a lot of sense to your theory. The love at first sig—"

"Hope," someone warns. I think Haley just joined us on the ledge.

"L—let me finish, Haley. Those tingles and stuff, you feel them too, right?" I lean forward with my hand and touch Videl's hand, bubbling exuberantly when the fireworks shoot through my arm again. "See! There it is again! What do you have to say about that, V—Videl?"

"Hope." Videl's voice is weak. His eyes shut, and his jaw clenches almost reflexively. Through my blurry vision, I can see a strangely vibrant colored bond linking us.

"Hope, you need to stay awake."

"No, Haley," I giggle. "Leave me alone. I don't want to forget about him. I've been trying to tell him that I like him but he's just going to laugh at me. Me, Hope, stand a chance? Ha!" I start laughing to myself deliriously until I run out of air. The stars in the sky begin to rain down upon me like meteors, and the next thing I know, the world goes black.

~~~~~~

At first, I think someone's shining a flashlight in my eyes, but then my eyes crack open and spy the torrent of sunlight peeking through the ornate, cream curtains.

My head whips around and I cringe as my brain rattles in my skull. I'm in an unfamiliar room. What I originally thought were curtains is a large mosquito net draped around the posts of the bed I'm in. My legs kick around in the sheets, and I almost moan from how soft and silky they are around my legs. Which is funny, because the last time I remember, I had pants on. And now, I'm in my underwear and an overlarge t-shirt.

The lock suddenly clicks. I try to pull the covers over me, but the door swings open too quickly, revealing…Videl in a tight gray V-neck?!

"Rise and shine, sleeping beauty," Videl exclaims, opening his arms. He walks over to me and offers me some pills that are in his hands.

"Aspirin. You must feel like there's a jackhammer drilling into your skull."

"One? More like a dozen." I take the pills gratefully and chug them down with some water he procured, my face burning from the earlier endearment.

"I'm not too surprised. You chugged six cups of party punch like it was the richest water you had ever laid your hands on. By the time I returned to the roof with some actual water, you were already passed out."

So that's where I was. Veronica's party. Racking my brain, I recall the testosterone-riddled males and pulsing electronica music. But after that, it's a black abyss.

"I can't—can't seem to remember anything." Oh god. I've definitely seen enough television shows to realize that I probably said or got myself tangled in an imbroglio. "Please tell me I didn't do anything ignominious."

"Nope," he winks. "We were talking about space, and then you just passed out. I called Haley and let her know I was   taking you back to my house. I figured you'd prefer to wake up in a bed that wasn't Veronica's."

Now that Videl mentioned space, my memories unfurrow themselves out of the haystack. Yesterday's conversation was the first I've had with Videl where his signature foibles were missing—no signs of his irksome smirk, no signs of his crude remarks, and no signs of his sarcastic banter—for once, Videl and I had a serious, pensive conversation that consisted of more than a few nugatory, superficial questions.

"Thank you," I reply gratefully. But then the scenario finally hits me. I'm with a friend, no someone, *whatever* Videl is to me, intruding on his privacy with his clothes on. And to exacerbate things, he's dating Veronica. I'm in his bed. Inner Hope chastises me.

"I need to leave," I firmly state. I kick my legs out from under the sheets over to the side of the bed, only to lose my balance and fall to the ground in what would be a painful thud if it were not for Videl's waiting hand.

"Thanks," I blush after steeling my wobbly legs.

"Let me make you some lunch first."

"I really can't. I have to get back home. My mom is going to kill me. She's probably called my phone a million times. Where's my phone?" I look around.

The medicine has already begun to kick in, so my headache is tolerable in my sweep this time. Videl slides open the nightstand drawer and pulls out my phone. I breathe a sigh a relief after a brief examination reveals no scratches or cracks on the surface.

"Thanks," I say again, taking the phone from him. "And, uh, where are my clothes?" I try to brush by him, but I bump into his unmoving figure instead.

"After you eat lunch. It's not a good idea to skip a meal, especially after a hangover."

I'm all too aware of how close we are to each other. His scent washes over me and leaves my brain suddenly unable to function.

"O—okay. Sure."

I follow Videl out into the hallway and down the steps, passing through the living room. A large—at least eighty inch—plasma television is mounted on the way. The sofas are plump; the pillows and cushions are a light brown color, with patterns suitable for a nineteenth-century ball. I shake my head, addled.

I make sure to send my mom a short yet reassuring text telling her I woke up late at Haley's and will be coming home soon.

The kitchen's countertop is made entirely of white marble, and not a speck of dust is in sight. A large chandelier—I wouldn't even be surprised if it was made of diamond—dangles over the dining table, which is burgundy in color. In the corner stands a man sharply garnished in a coattail, and when he sees us, he begins moving.

"Videl," the man nods before shifting his attention to me, his eyebrows quirking in the process.

"And who might you be?" He switches from French to English without a hitch.

"This is Hope, a close friend. She's pretty hungry, so I'm—"

Whatever Videl says next gets lost in my thoughts after I heard his label. A *close* friend. Being decent friends would be stretching the truth quite a bit, but a close friend. My chest swells.

"It's fine. I'm making her oatmeal, not a goddamn bowl of bouillabaisse." My attention reverts to the conversation at hand. Videl looks rather irked.

"What's bouilla-something?" I query.

"French dish. You like seafood?" Videl lifts his head from the pantry cupboard, hands full of food packets, annoyed expression gone.

"Yeah. I've eaten fish before."

"Good. Bastien here makes a fucking fantastic bowl of bouillabaisse. You'll have to try it sometime."

Bastien strings some French words in what sounds like a complaint, but Videl waves him off.

"Not now, Bastien." Videl busies himself with the food and I use the time to peer around while Videl locates all that he needs. After almost tumbling out of the bar seat, I finally situate myself at the countertop.

"Would you like anything to drink, Miss Valentine?" Bastien asks, standing off to my side.

"Um, sure." I'm not very thirsty after drinking the glass of water in Videl's bed, but Bastien seems like the kind of person you don't want to deny. "What do you have?"

"We have water, milk, juice, and a selection of wines."

"No," Videl interrupts, clapping his hands together to get rid of the residues on his hands. "No wine. Absolutely not. Anything alcoholic is strictly off-limits to her."

"Hey! It was only a few drinks!"

"Don't listen to her, Bastien. It was six cups of twelve-ounce party punch, full of that vodka shit Veronica loves."

"Okay, first off," I state, scooting myself off the seat and planting myself firmly in front of Videl with my arms at my hips. "You're not my parent. Second off," I continue, getting closer and closer to his face. "I wasn't going to drink wine at noon anyways. May I have some water please, Bastien?"

"Certainly, Miss Valentine."

"Call me Hope."

"You," Videl says, spinning me back around to face him. "When'd you get so sassy? I like it." His lips curl into his traditional smirk.

I find the corners of my lips rising into a smirk of my own. "Maybe because I have the power to. Shouldn't you get back to making my meal, *servant*?"

Videl cocks an eyebrow but remains silent.

My cheeks suddenly flame when I realize how smutty I sound, a product of lingering alcohol still floating around in my bloodstream. To try to cool off and fill the awkward silence, I grab the goblet glass in front of me and hastily gulp its contents down in its entirety. Bastien, who is watching me in the corner like a dog to a tennis ball, teleports beside me and immediately refills the glass with more water from his decanter.

"I find the fact that your family owns a private jet more believable," I say, scrolling back and forth between Videl and Bastien. "Are you like a multi-job aficionado? A jack of all trades? Do you double as a butler and pilot?"

Bastien glances at Videl.

"She wouldn't stop fucking pestering me at the party, okay?"

"Young master, I know it will be difficult for someone as incompetent as yourself, but do put forth a modicum of effort and refrain from using such obscenities in front of a lady."

I snort into my glass. "Yeah, Videl. Listen to the man."

Videl shoots me a dirty look, while Bastien looks upon me with praise at my agreement. I don't think he understands sarcasm. Or any sort of teasing, for that matter.

Ten minutes later, a steaming hot bowl and another glass slide from one end of the counter to the other.

"Oatmeal and Gatorade?" I ask, a bit skeptical.

"Maple oats and Glacier Freeze. Two best things I find that help after an excessive night of drinking. And you, madam, have quite the hangover." Videl pushes the bowl over to me. "A scoop of brown sugar and some dried cranberries for extra flavor." He grabs a sugar shaker and a pint-sized bowl of cranberries. "Here are some extra condiments in case if the taste is still too bland for you."

I take a tentative bite, and sure enough, it's what he says it is. And my god, it's delicious. The oatmeal melts in my mouth like cotton candy.

"This is so good," I admit, before taking another bite, this one hasty. "I could eat this every morning. Make it for me."

"What's in it for me?" he smirks.

"Young master dreams to be a chef," Bastien interjects from the side, eyeing my untouched second glass of water.

"Really?" I look to Videl for verification. I blush after I realize there's still food in my mouth, so I quickly swallow it, scorching my throat.

"Yeah."

"I mean," I fan my throat. "That's wonderful! Is that why you came to America? To attend an American culinary school after graduating Starmount?"

"This may come as breaking news, but the French are more refined in culinary expertise than your country is and ever will be. Ever wonder why the French are all excruciatingly good-looking? Because we aren't pumped full of artificial, fat-infested foods and GMOS. 'Grease, grease, and more grease' is America's slogan."

"Better watch that mouth of yours around in public."

Videl waves his arm around. "Whatever. Anyways, when I was in lycée—"

"What's that?"

"French secondary school. You and Bastien need to have a competition for the most interruptions in one minute. Need I remind you of how drunk you became yesterday?"

I flush. "No, that's alright."

"I had to cook my own breakfast. It started off small, with a scrambled egg, but progressed into something greater, like omelets."

"You just about burned the house down twice."

"How astute of you, Bastien. If I recall, you were lounging about in the living quarters, reading a newspaper on pronatalist policies. You were supposed to prepare my breakfasts."

"Ah, well. Your mother's orders; she, at least, wished for you to grow up with a smidgeon of independence."

"You're worse than Altha."

"Someone called?" My giggles cease when I hear the familiar voice of Altha cutting through the air from somewhere in another room, but there's something different. There's no hostility to it.

"Oh boy," Videl breaths. My eyes follow his newly directed gaze to the living room. I strain my ears. The footsteps are drawing closer. Heels maybe.

The she-devil rounds the corner and hits us with her presence. She's digging in a designer purse but stops when she sees me, her eyes widening.

"What's she—"

"Don't worry about it," he says. My ears perk up. Videl sounds...protective?

"Well, I'm about to get a bite to eat before I head out and I really would prefer my appetite to remain unspoiled. So—" Altha waves her hand with a sour face. "I hope you have an answer. Otherwise, the front door is in that direction."

"Altha." Videl's tone grows dark. "Leave her alone."

"Defensive much," she says, holding her hands up in the air. "Why should I? Are you trying to make her one of your conquests?" At Videl's silence, she continues, staring me right in the eye.

"I suppose it wouldn't make sense for you to be interested in her. She doesn't look your type. Ugly. Lacking love handles. Oh boy, you can use some weight, don't you think?" she smirks heinously. The insults flow out of her mouth easily, and although I've heard them time and time again, they still hurt. Like always. My cheerful mood is slapped away, with tears forming in my eyes. The overweening personality I displayed earlier is now infinitesimal.

I'm about to duck my head to shirk away from Altha when I feel tingles— Videl's caressing hand on my shoulder. My head turns and I see him with his jaw clenched. He starts stringing along a batch of French, probably for my ears' sake. Altha starts arguing with him, and it doesn't take long before they're full-on shouting at each other. I take a furtive peek at Bastien, and even he looks troubled, but he catches my gaze and gives me a reassuring smile, sending some encouragement my way, nonverbally telling me I should stand up for myself. He's right.

I turn my attention to Altha and see her seething, murderous expression. Never mind. Maybe later. Let me just tilt my head down and preoccupy myself— by stuffing my face.

"Fyeuh," is the sound that comes out when a napkin starts running over my mouth.

"You have some food on your lips," Videl says. My heart flutters at his touch but fades away when I see Altha glaring at me. Bastien is standing in front of her with his hands on his hips, seemingly lecturing her, but her attention is on me. The next thing I know, she huffs and sits down at the other end of the counter, pulling an apple from the basket of fruit.

"Just ignore her. Are you done eating, or do you want a second helping?" Videl inquires.

"I'm done." My voice is timid. Videl takes the empty bowl and hands it to Bastien, who is already busying himself with my water glass.

"Come on," he says. I follow him out of the kitchen and back up the stairs to his room. He pulls the door open to a wardrobe, similar to mine back at home, and retrieves my missing clothes.

"The bathroom's right there." He points to a door hidden by the shadow of the wardrobe. I take my clothes graciously and head over to the bathroom.

Videl is still standing outside the door after I change and relieve myself.

"Are you okay?" His usual, goofy demeanor is missing, and it bothers me. I'm not used to seeing him expressing concern.

"Yeah."

We make our way out into the hallway and down the stairs again, but stop at the front door.

"You don't play off the poker face well."

"What do you mean?" I continue to play dumb.

"Before Altha's entrance, you were bantering so well I almost couldn't keep up with you. But now, you're hushed. Reserved. Your eyes find the floor too interesting, and your shoulders sag."

"Does nothing slip by you?" He doesn't answer, so I fill in the void.

"It's nothing. Altha just says some hurtful things sometimes." Just saying it aloud brings tears to my eyes and I turn around and wipe them away.

"You know," Videl's hands rest on my shoulders. "You don't have to hide your tears from me."

And then it just bursts out of me.

"Your sister is such a bitch!" I hiss, a mix of plaintive and angry tears slipping down my cheeks. "I hate her! I never gave her any reason to despise me. Yet every day she just has to meet some quota of abject aspersions."

"Look," Videl begins, after I cool down. "My sister can sometimes be a condescending freak. I know you're struggling, but let me talk to her. She'll listen to me."

I nod pathetically. "Why are you so kind to me? Veronica, your sister, they all share the same opinion of me. So why don't you?"

"There's more than just one reason."

"I've got time."

"Judging by the way you were acting in my bedroom, you're actually in a hurry to get home." I ignore his jab and remain silent until he relents.

"Well, for one, Bastien likes you," he mutters.

"Why?"

"The man may not look it, but he's a great judge of character. He's fond of you already."

"So that's what you two were muttering about in French."

"No, we were plotting conspiracies and political assassinations." I give him a lighthearted shove.

"I'm serious here."

"So am I."

"You're incorrigible."

"I think you mean irresistible."

"What's the other reason?"

"Another story for another day," he chuckles

"Goodbye, Videl." I stand there smiling like an idiot before he pulls me into an embrace. The hug lasts longer than I'm accustomed to but the scent of his cologne still sends Inner Hope spiraling into her happy place until someone clears their throat.

"Hope. Hope?" My thoughts spiral back down to earth.

"Yeah, sorry. Wow, I really blanked out. What's going on?" I ask, after interpreting his slightly edgy tone.

"Veronica's at the door."

"Oh, okay. Wait, what?!"

"Yeah," he sighs. "I suppose you wouldn't be averse toward hiding somewhere?" I nod my head. "Behind me," he says. I oblige.

The door clicks open and my ears retract into my head at the nasally voice.

"Sugar booger! I couldn't find you last night, where were you?"

"I left early. Didn't feel too well." I strain my ears to hear more.

"Well." Something thuds into something else. "I missed you. Why don't I come in and make things better?"

Push it down, Hope, Inner Hope advises.

"Actually, I'm about to leave. Altha and I have shopping duties for the week."

"Come on, yummy-buns," Veronica purrs. And I try to stop myself from giggling, I really do, but a squeal just slips out before I can my cover mouth with my hand.

"What was that?" Veronica asks. Videl mutters something, but then the door flies open, revealing Veronica dressed in a scanty, licentious dress. Videl's standing there with a prospecting grin on his face.

"What's she doing here?!" Veronica screeches, twisting her head back and forth between Videl and me. "And why are you hiding her?" A few seconds pass and then her eyes widen. "Don't tell me?! You slept with her? This *loser*?" Her outrage is a mirror reflection of Altha's early one, and electricity burns into my veins. One person, I can stand, but two?

My vision clouds and my anger spikes to a degree that even scares me. Videl notices my sudden change and begins to step forward, but it's too late. I curl my hand into a fist.

"Screw you," I spit and punch her right in the face. Veronica's nose instantly begins spurting blood and she staggers back. She wipes her nose, disbelief etched on her face.

"Y—you bitch!" she roars and then pounces on me. Her landing knocks the wind out of me, and I teeter back, hitting my head on the floor, but the raging fire in my body deflects all the pain I would normally feel, and I instantly retaliate by pulling on her hair and head-butting her so that I end up on top of her. Her hands begin flailing wildly and ripping at my chest, ripping at my clothes, but I don't care. I land punch after punch on her face, neck, stomach, anything I can land my fists into, while she's screaming at the top of her lungs. I attempt to land one more punch for good measure, but before I could do so, stronger, larger hands wrap themselves around my waist and yank me up. I comply without resistance.

"Enough." Videl's voice is detached and betraying nothing, another first for me. He pulls me up into a standing position and Veronica instantly scrambles to her feet. My eyes widen as I take in her disheveled appearance—her expensive dress has a long gash running from her left shoulder blade down, and her hair is in a tangled heap of mess. Her makeup looks like it had just run a marathon. Her right eye's swollen shut but the other eye is glaring daggers at me like she's trying her hardest to condemn me to hell. And then a wave of contriteness so strong hits me it almost knocks me to the ground.

"Oh God, I—I'm so sorry, I don't—I don't know what came over me."

Veronica doesn't say a word. We're both breathing heavily and confused about to what to do next. Then something flits across her face. She grabs her purse from the ground and exits the front door silently.

"Oh, my. Oh my, oh my." Bastien appears in the living room from out of nowhere with a surface spray in one hand and hand towel and crouches down, getting to work on the droplets of blood staining the floor. "That poor, poor girl."

"She got what she deserved." My head whips up to the hallway balcony to see Altha regally leaning against the railing in her short high-necked golden dress. She has a smirk that rivals even her brother's and a slight shadow on her face, but even from here I can tell she looks vaguely impressed.

"Isn't that hypocritical? You say similar things about me that Veronica does, if not worse."

She shrugs. "And yet, you haven't done anything to me. I must be doing something right."

Inner Hope's craving for blood flares back up but I have enough control to push her back down. "I wouldn't push your luck."

Altha's smirk widens at my empty threat. "I'll be waiting."

Videl's voice pipes up behind me. "I think I'm going to have to get you riled up more often."

"Excuse me?" I spin around on my feet and face him. Like brother, like sister, he has his lips curled up in that trademark smirk. "You just watched me beat up your *girlfriend*. The person who just left in shambles without your aid. And yet you stand here, grinning like an idiot."

My words have the effect of gasoline, for the fire in his eyes blazes even higher.

He gives a nonchalant shrug, and this sets me off.

I whip my hand back, enraged at his unruffled behavior, and smack him hard across the face. His head flies to the side. I slap him again and then shove him with all my might so that he ends up toppling to the ground.

"You think this is sexy?" I slap him again. "Do you always feel schadenfreude?"

"Um, Hope?"

"I'm not done! Just when I thought I finally spent some *normal* time with someone I care about, you pull this imprudence out of your ass!"

"Hope!"

"Shut up! I can't—"

"Hope!" he roars.

"What?! Finally going to apologize?"

"Not quite." Videl's eyes move away from my face. I follow his gaze and discover my hands are propped up on his chest, arms perpendicular to his body. My legs are spread out, one on either side of his hips in a pose that can stand for nothing but suggestive.

I scramble to my feet at a speed as if my life depended on it, fully aware that I am beet-red. "Quit pushing all of my freaking buttons!"

"You have cute buttons though!" he protests, following my lead and climbing to his feet.

"Brother, any more from you and she'll combust," Altha adds from above.

My face turns to a whole new level of red when I realize Altha is still posed next to the handrail. "Altha! Why are you still here?!"

"The fight was entertaining. Never really liked Veronica."

"You don't like anyone but yourself," I mutter, outside of her hearing range.

A text from Haley tells me she's outside waiting and that Mom's getting suspicious of where I am. My brain switches settings, and I hurriedly tell her I will be out the front door as soon as possible. Videl instantly understands and leads me to the exit.

"So what does Bastien say about Veronica?" I ask him, wanting to get one last question in before I have to leave. I check my clothes for any rips.

Videl shakes his head. "You're the first person outside the family that's been here."

"You haven't invited her over." He nods, and I suddenly feel very exposed. Like I'm caught up in a plot unbeknown to me. Because I was the first girl privileged enough to see his home.

"Judging by the situation that went down, I don't think his impression of her is too revering."

"I don't think anyone could admire Veronica, given the nicknames she insists on using."

Videl cringes. "I'm about to break up with her anyways."

"Over nicknames?"

"No. She's too bitchy. I have a threshold when it comes to snobbery."

"Oh."

"And Hope?"

"Yeah?"

"I care about you too."

7

Ms. Vance knocks the pages of our recent exam against her teacher's desk until the edges line up.

"Let me see." I stretch my hand out to Videl, tapping on his desk after he receives his exam. "Give it here."

"Sheesh, woman. Simmer down and let me bathe in the glory of my intelligence for at least a minute." He hands me his exam, and I'm pleased to see a big fat B circled in red with the words 'Well done!' underneath. Of course he gets a compliment.

I glare at him. "*Your* intelligence?"

"Augmented by your unprecedented tutoring skills?"

"Still. Great job. Looks like some of the stuff I'm teaching you is actually getting through that thick skull of yours."

"What's so thick about it?"

"How am I supposed to know? It's your brain." The teacher breezes by my desk and places my test facedown without saying a word. I relish in the tiny bit of adrenaline that courses through my body as I lift the corner of the paper up.

"An A, as usual." Videl sighs in defeat.

"All I can do is teach you the material. What you do in your spare time is entirely up to you."

"Has it ever occurred to you that you're simply more intelligent than most people?" Videl stretches his arms. "Looks like I'll have to wait until the next exam to beat you. Although that hope is growing dimmer and dimmer by the second."

"Maybe you'd be smarter if you stopped fooling around all the time and actually focus on studying."

"How about we study together then? You get to knock out two birds with one stone. Study for your lovely little exams *and* bask in my almighty glory."

"We already spend enough time together."

"So? What's wrong with spending more?"

"Spending more time with you comes a greater desire to repeatedly bang my head on a table," I retort.

Videl mouth opens. "Regardless, we have to celebrate. Have you eaten anything for lunch?"

"Sure. I don't mind eating at the cafeteria. Are you sure your popularity won't take a hit?"

Videl laughs. "Cafeteria food tastes like muck. We're going out."

I narrow my eyes. "Skip? Are you crazy?"

"Why, thank you! Let's go after—"

My stomach grumbles. Not just a soft, tiny one that is easily stifled by a quick squeeze of my abs, but one so loud and lingering that it sounds like someone flatulating after drinking five cans of carbonated beverages.

"Say what you want, but your body knows what it wants," Videl smirks.

I blush. "We can just eat in the cafeteria. I don't mind."

"No. Hell no. I'm taking you to a restaurant that serves *real* food. Besides, I'm sure you don't want to be surrounded by hungry, sweaty, prepubescent kids."

I roll my eyes at his inexact description. "Fine."

Calculus class ends and we sneak out to the parking grounds. I send Haley a text to which she responded with a winking face. What a child.

Videl unlocks the passenger door to a yellow beetle, beckoning me to sit down in the seat.

"It's Altha's car," he quickly responds. "Mine's at the mechanic getting its clutch replaced."

"Where are we going?" I ask, buckling up. The car makes a strange cranky noise when Videl starts the ignition as if it is rudely disturbed from its deep slumber.

"There's no French restaurants here anyways. Apart from my home," he winks. "Do you like Italian?" I shake my head.

"I've never had it, but I wouldn't be opposed to trying it."

"Italian it is then."

We drive for fifteen minutes in silence before he turns into a large shopping center and parks in front of a restaurant called 'Carmine's.' The windows are tinted black, but I can still discern the little carved pumpkins placed on the window ledges even though Halloween is over. Scarecrows plop on a rectangular bundle of hay next to the front entrance, demonstrating the restaurant's holiday spirit.

My heart grows heavy as I take in the excessive ornamentation and cleanliness of the place. The tables each are decorated with real candles and tablecloths that have little extensions of crystal beads dangling off at the edges. The lighting is dim enough to emit a romantic ambiance, and this thought of mine is proven when I see a dozen, perhaps more, people dining in at the restaurant, with the majority of them looking like they're couples out on a date. The men dress in V-neck sweaters with the tips of their dress shirts poking through below their chin, while the women are all clad in colorful silk dresses like they were in a fashion contest to outdo the person sitting at the table next to them. Suddenly I feel like a sore thumb in my sweatpants and excessively large sweatshirt.

The waitress greets and seats us in a small two-person booth. Although it's in the back, it gives me full access to the entire room, allowing me to people-watch at my leisure.

"Hey. Are you alright?" Videl cups my hands and my attention suddenly zeroes in on how warm and electric they are. "Is this place fine?"

I bite my lip to stop my protests.

"Yeah, it's fine." Videl stares at me for a moment before chuckling.

"You're a terrible liar," he says.

"You're too good with that. Mom doesn't even know when I lie."

"One of my many undisputed talents."

"Are you always this observant?" I'm not sure whether to feel invaded or innocuous.

"Only around a girl like you," he says ambivalently, which causes me to blush. Order whatever you'd like; the check is on me." I open my mouth and try to begin arguing, but my stomach growls and forces my eyes to scan the menu instead.

I end up ordering gnocchi, and it is delicious! Videl orders some kind of spaghetti, and we start talking about trivial things. Near the end of our meal, though, we start playing a game.

"Okay, that table over there." Videl points behind me. I turn around and see a man and a woman, both in their sixties, slowly delving into their dishes.

"Well, the woman's wearing a fancy brooch. Maybe a forty-year anniversary gift outside the Louvre? Two boys. Twins."

"I think she only has boys, but I don't think they're twins. I bet one's in engineering and the other is in the military. The old man looks like a vet."

We run through six or seven tables, playing this same game. Some stories are absurd. For table four, Videl suggests that the lesbian couple met through a local cocaine convention. I lost it there.

"Table one. Right next to the entrance," Videl says when it's his turn again.

I turn to the front table, but the young couple there disappears altogether when a man makes his way into the restaurant. He walks to a different corner of the restaurant so I can only his side is visible to me, but his hair and just-trimmed stubbly beard are exactly the same as it was when I last saw it a year ago.

"Dad." My voice comes out in a whisper, but it's enough to draw Videl's attention.

"You'll need a better description than that," he chuckles.

I ignore him. Dad is walking away from me. He's walking to the other side of the restaurant. The other side of the hallway. He's walking away from the land of the living.

"No. No!" I scream. "No! Don't leave me! Don't!" The plates of food flip over the edge of the table and shatter into a million pieces on the floor when I catch the tablecloth with my feet. "Stop! Come back!"

"Hope! What's the matter?!" In the back of my mind, I hear Videl's voice, and I have just enough logic to pinpoint the underlying emotion. He's scared.

My eyes scour across the room.

"Hope! You look like you've just seen a ghost!" I look up to see Videl with an alarmed expression on his face, shaking my shoulder furiously.

My voice trembles. "Dad. Come back. Dad." I try to run toward the direction he went, but I slip on something slippery. My food.

Videl has a bewildered look on his face, but in less than a few seconds, he bolts over to my side and scoops me up, slapping a few bills on the table. My eyes freeze to the man who is still walking toward the end of the restaurant. I want him to turn around so I can get a clear view on his face. I want him to turn around so badly I bite my lip and draw blood. Let me see what's on the other side of the brown overcoat. Something is sticking to my skin. There are voices ringing in the background. Flashes of black sweep around me. The waiters.

My senses don't even interpret where we are until Videl cranks the temperature knob in his car all the way to the hottest. For a second, I think he's trying to take advantage of me, but then I realize he just wants to help take off my sweatshirt so the damp shirt underneath would dry faster to the heat.

"Will you tell me what's going on?" Videl asks after we're back on the highway. I shake my head, causing him to curse in French.

"I can't help you if you don't tell me, Hope!"

"It's not something I have control over!" I snap. "The world doesn't revolve around you Videl! Just—just leave me alone." My eyes are wet from the melancholy in my chest, and I wipe them with my fingers, sniffing in the process.

"I just want to help."

"Why do you care so much anyways?" My anger begins to fizzle out, and I realize my hurtful words a little too late.

"Try me," he argues.

"I said no!"

"Hope, don't pretend like I can't see the hurt in your eyes! Something happened to you, and I swear I won't abuse your trust!"

"Fine! Fine! You want to know?! I thought I saw my *dad*. Are you happy now? He's been gone for a year, I thought I saw him and freaked out! Go ahead, make fun of me!"

Instead of his expected scolding, my left hand envelops in his much larger, much warmer one.

"When you mean gone, do you mean—."

I give him a meek nod, and this seems to spur him on.

"It's etched in your soul. You blame yourself, and that's why you can't get over it. Have you confided in anyone?" I shake my head.

"I'm sorry."

Usually bromide remarks irk me, but the sincerity in Videl's voice calms me down instead.

"Will you tell me?" he asked.

I'm not ready to tell him. I'm not ready to relive the past.

I shake my head. Videl understands, for he gives me a soft smile and continues holding my hand, squeezing it.

The pressure on my hand drags me out of my reverie and I suddenly realize we've already stopped. I quickly glimpse out of the window and see my house on the side.

The two of us silently get out of the car. Videl comes over to me without a word, and I melt into the much-needed hug he offers.

"It's all my fault." My voice comes out muffled and nasally.

"I know you're hurting." He brushes my hair gently. "But this just means you're alive. Things like this can eat you up on the inside. I will always be here, for when you need someone to talk to." He doesn't relinquish his hold on me, and I make no attempt to escape.

We remain still for another minute, basking in other's body heat.

"You know, Mom always says that time heals everything. So why do I still feel the same as I did a year ago?" I tighten my grip around his waist, trying to savor his presence before I go inside.

"Time doesn't heal the wound," Videl answers shrewdly. "It's always there, but gradually you learn how to walk around the hole, rather than falling into it."

"The way you said that—you've lost someone close to you too, haven't you?"

I hear the disturbance of air as Videl inhales sharply.

"I had a cousin a couple of years ago who was murdered back home. He was just at the wrong place at the wrong time. He left the world too young."

"I'm sorry. I didn't mean to—"

"Don't apologize. It looks like we've both experienced losses, so I can say with utmost certainty that I completely understand what it's like to lose someone close to you."

Ten seconds later, I feel Videl pulling away. I allow the separation, feeling as if I've intruded in his personal space—figuratively and literally—for too long.

"Will you be okay?" Videl asks. I give him a hesitant nod.

"Call me if you need anything, and I'll come." His words make me feel slightly better, and a thin smile works its way on my face. He kisses my forehead before leaving.

I open the front door and walk inside, mindlessly touching the spot he kissed me. The house is empty, or so I thought, until the sight of new empty beer bottles littered around the living room point my eyes to a hulk of a man sitting upright on the sofa.

"What you been doin' out so late?" Roger asks. The sofa creaks at his shifting weight as he stands up and begins to wobble unsteadily toward me like a grotesque figure from a horror movie.

"Where's Mom?" I keep my voice steady, a false mirror of the fear brewing in me. However, my legs betray me by slowly pacing backward, and he catches the motions. Roger smirks.

"Work."

Inner Hope yells at how stupid I am for not checking the driveway, right before he grunts and launches himself at me, wrapping his heavy hands around my wrists.

"St—stop!" My body refuses to clam up this time, and I begin kicking him as soon as he makes contact with me. He must have been expecting the opposition, because his hold tightens tenfold, cutting off my blood circulation to my wrists. I yell out in ear-splitting pain as he squeezes even harder. This is nothing like last time. Roger is out to do real, lasting damage, but I come to realize there's a seed of courage planted in me. Memories of my father are fresh in my mind. I have renewed fire in my veins. Roger's not my dad. He will *never* be Dad.

I plant my feet on his thighs while he tries to pull me closer to him, increasing the force between us, before I yank my head back and then release my foothold; at the same time, my head snaps forward, hitting him in his mouth with a loud clash. He falters and staggers back, more dazed than I am and dropping me on my feet, but then charges at me. He spits on my face, and I detect the metallic tint of blood and alcohol right before his flying fist ends up directly in my gut. The air escapes from my lungs like a deflated balloon, and I collapse to the floor, wheezing and twitching uncontrollably, trying to get the oxygen I need. I vaguely hear Roger muttering incoherently right before I sense his hands move to my neck and begin squeezing. My throat instantly stoppers up, and I begin gagging at the lack of air my already-flat lungs need. I feebly call out for help, for Roger to stop, but it's of no use. Black spots begin dancing in my vision, and my surroundings begin to grow dark. My legs slow their kicking—

Whack! A tremendous noise rings throughout the room. My body vibrates leadenly before my hands shoot to my throat and begin massaging it reflexively, and I graciously gasp as wonderful air flows into my mouth and fills my lungs. The blurry vision melts away little-by-little until all that's in front of me is an unconscious Roger and Videl holding a frying pan in one hand and my sweatshirt in the other with a horrified look on his face.

He turns his attention to Roger, prodding him with his toe before nodding once and then offering his hand to me without a word. I accept his help, and he carries me in his arms as we walk to the front door. Only until he's speeding down the neighborhood do I crack and speak in the suspenseful atmosphere.

"Hi again," I let out a nervous chuckle, trying to dissipate the tenseness.

Videl swerves the car. The movement almost throws me out of the seat.

"This isn't funny, Hope!" he yells. "Is this what you mean by disliking your stepfather?! Because he rapes you when you come home?!"

"Videl, please," I say, cringing at the word and the loudness of his voice.

Videl takes a deep breath and steadies the car.

"I just can't believe how sickening your stepfather is!" he snarls. "I can't *believe* that—that monster would do something to his own daughter."

"Try is the key word. He hasn't managed to get his way yet." I realize my mistake the moment it slips from my mouth.

"Yet?! You mean this happens on a regular basis?" The indignation that he reined in not even one minute ago manages to break out of its cage. "How. How many times, Hope?" he asks, voice cracking in the process.

"Videl, please calm down." I put my hand into his and squeeze it gently. It seems to work because his jaw unclenches and he relinquishes his deathly-white grip on the steering wheel. We spend the ride in silence until he slides Altha's car into the garage and shuts off the engine. The two of us sit in the dark car.

"I never knew," he croaks. "I'm so sorry."

"You have nothing to apologize for," I genuinely answer. He gives me a strained smile and helps me out of the car and into the living room, where I see Bastien hunched over watching a French drama on the television. He greets us with a hello, unaware of what went down. Altha is nowhere to be seen. The evening has made me tired, and I release a pent-up yawn.

"You can take my bed tonight," Videl intuitively says. I pull him back and shake my head.

"Spend the night with me," I ask. There's no shame, no embarrassment, and no blushes. He looks at me for a few seconds, probably taking in my clammy skin, before nodding his head.

"Alright," Videl says. He scoops me up in his arms again, and we head to his room. Once we're in his bedroom, he locks the door before getting into bed. I follow suit, positioning myself so that my head rests on his chest. The false front I had erected begins to crumble from the earthquake my sobbing chest elicits; tears that I had held in for so long finally break through the dam and I spill my eyes onto Videl's shirt, while he runs his hand through my hair and whispers soft reassurances in my ear.

At this moment, I don't even care if he is my saving angel. I don't care that he is a philanderer. I don't care that he knows my deepest and darkest secret. I don't care that I might be crossing the friendship border between us and starting something more intimate. I don't care. I need companionship. I need someone to comfort me from Roger's abuse. To protect me.

In Videl's arms, I fall asleep in no time, sleeping away the night until the next thing I sense is the stirring of our bodies and the soft warmth of sunlight streaming down on my face.

Immediately, I jerk wide awake and look down to see his muscular arms clasped gently around my thin waist. My face lights on fire, and I start panicking. This is too far.

I tell myself that last night was a moment of weakness. So with quick, yet methodical movements, I peel his arms off of me. I'm successful because his eyelids remain closed after I roll off the bed. Grabbing my shoes, I tiptoe to the end of the room where I spend the next minute trying to open the door without the hinges gently squeaking.

I'm in the middle of the hallway when I hear rushing footsteps behind me, and then Videl's hands clasp on my shoulders. The usual shivers shoot through my spine.

"Where are you going?" His voice sounds almost accusatory, and I have to consciously refrain from squinting my eyes at how controlling he sounds.

"I didn't want to wake you."

Videl takes a step closer to me, and his scent immediately clouds over my common sense.

"Listen, Hope. I know what you're thinking right now, but rest assured, us sleeping together means nothing more than the denotation it presents. I won't tell anyone about this. I know how much you treasure your reputation and dignity."

I blush, fears allayed at his sincerity. But with the relief also comes a wave of disappointment deep inside. The anti-Hope, the girl residing deep inside me that is opposite in personality and demeanor, wants to flaunt this knowledge to the outside world.

"Hope, you have to do something," Videl urges. It takes me a few seconds to realize he's referring to the fiasco he witnessed yesterday. And when I do, the atmosphere completely changes. The trauma was already repressed to the back corner of my brain, a result of conditioning over time. So although I remember what went down last night, it is a part of my past, and not my present. And now Videl just has to bring the memories back to the surface.

"I will," comes out of my mouth. What else am I supposed to say? He walked in the house with Roger on top of me. Even with my clipped answers, there is no way I can reduce this situation's severity.

"Hope, I can tell when you're lying, okay? What goes on in the house between you and Roger makes me sick to the stomach. I don't see any practical reason why you want to protect him. Unless you—"

"Don't," I hold up my hand. This time, I read his mind. "Are you seriously going as far as to question whether I *enjoy* his hands on me? News flash: he was choking me, remember?"

Videl cringes.

"It was impetuous of me. Why don't you want to see Roger arrested? He'll get what's coming to him."

"It's not that simple. As much as I despise him, Mom loves him. Also, we only live in a house and not a trailer because of him."

"You call that support? I'll supply you and your Mom's needs if it means you stop living with that sick freak."

"Stop acting like this, Videl! Do you see the clothes I wear? These old hand-me-down sweatshirts and saggy pants?" I self-consciously point to my secondhand clothes. Videl follows my attention but his eyes only hover around my body briefly before coming back to rest on my face. "I know these aren't the best, but this is still better than nothing if it had not been for him."

Videl's body shuffles even closer to me, and he takes the fabric and rubs it back and forth between his fingers as if analyzing the composition. After he's done, he drops his arms to his sides but doesn't move away. Suddenly, I'm aware of the narrow distance between the two of us. But there's no intrusive feeling of him violating my personal space. His presence calms me and sends my mind spiraling into a haze.

"I can't believe he'd do such a thing."

"Listen, Videl. You help me in more ways than one, and I will forever be grateful." I reach with both my hands and rest them on his chin, saying, "But your concern is appreciated, not necessary."

Videl's outburst dwindles away as stares at me before bringing his hands up to mine and rubbing them with his thumbs while he hypnotizes me with his eyes. All of a sudden, our tense conversation stills and a more amatory spirit fills the space between us. With the electric tension growing faster than ever, I subconsciously chance a peek down at his lips before back into his eyes, only to see that his orbs are fixed on my lips. The scent of cardamom and citrus swirls together in the forefront of my mind, mingling and distorting all of my senses until my ability to think straight is completely obliterated. He slowly leans forward, and with a hungry craving gnawing at my insides, I return the favor, closing the gap—

"Ahem." The clearing of someone's throat causes Videl to pull away.

"What do you want Altha?" Videl grits. Sure enough, his sister is leaning against the railing with a patronizing smirk on her face.

"Nothing. Just needed to go to my room, and the only way to do that is to pass through this hallway. But please, don't let my interference stop you two lovebirds," she laughs derisively before brushing past us.

"I—I need to go," I gasp, coming to a realization of what I had almost done. He's still so close that I'm about to combust. Six inches forward is all it will take to touch him, to lose myself to my desires. "I need to go," I repeat, before stumbling down the stairs and out the front door. Outside, I steady the shakiness of my legs before walking home in a drowning pit of swirling emotions. But through the fiesta of feelings, one is easily identifiable. It's the worst feeling: regret, knowing that he let me go.

~~~~~~

Life resumes in its same repetitive pattern; only one thing is different. Something between Videl and me has changed after I revealed my darkest secret. I mean, he still teases me and constantly smirks that stupid cocky grin, but there's something else. Something he wants to protect. And I think that something is someone. Me.

Every day, he's always standing in the hallway in front of the library growling at anyone brushing too close to me, leaving the scent of his cologne in my nostrils for the next hour afterward. One day, he even brought me a cup of coffee in an attempt to be sweet. I told him I didn't drink coffee, but I loved the gesture nonetheless. Even with my poor empathetic skills, I can tell that whenever he is near me, some unknown weight on his shoulders seem to vanish and he would visibly relax. And since he attends calculus every day now instead of twice a week, I would catch him staring at me multiple times throughout the class period. Sometimes I pretend I don't see him, but that doesn't work because I would always blush, a telltale sign that he knows I know. But other times, when Inner Hope is feeling flirty and bold, I would meet his gaze and wink at him, allowing a coquettish, sly smile or two.

"You're totally high on love." My head whips around to see Haley smirking impishly at me before she takes her seat.

"Am I really?" I ask her while watching the teacher trip through the crack in the floor. He manages to regain his balance and preserve the orderliness of his papers. Good save.

"If you hand me a mirror, I can show that your pupils have become little V's with tiny hearts."

"Haley, stop talking so loudly!" I urgently whisper, blushing for the fourth time that day while scanning my surroundings. "People can be listening!"

"Hope, if you haven't realized, I'm sure at least half of our grade know about some sexual tension between you and Videl. You see that girl in the back corner?" She stabs her thumb behind her back, and we both turn around. I see a girl with scraggly blonde hair resting her chin on her desk, not even bothering to talk with her circle of friends.

"Julia. She was dumped by Videl almost a week ago. He's also no longer dating anyone and claims the need to 'take a break' from girls. Of course, this spurred on questions regarding his sexuality, but I don't think the gossip affected him that much. *Real* rumor has it—" Haley scoots closer to me. "—that he dumped her because he can't stop thinking about someone else." She nudges my ribs. "And in case you're too dense to understand, that someone else is you. Y—O—U."

"Veronica," I sigh, ignoring the facetious jab. "She's the one spreading the rumors."

"But are they rumors? I mean, even I can tell—I knew on the first day—that there's something special going on between you two. That whole him handing you coffee thing was seen by at least two girls on the cheerleading team. And what's with his attention span in calc? Literally, like every time I turn my head to get a glimpse of him, all I get is the back of his head because his eyes are locked on your face."

"I probably have a zit growing."

"Don't be so droll."

"I'm being serious."

"Hope, you honestly can't lie to your best friend and say that you don't have feelings for him. How long has it been going on? Like over two months, right? Don't be such a baby and go ask him out."

"Weren't you just telling me at Veronica's party that I should be careful?"

"That was before I realized you two were destined for each other. Now go ask him out!"

"I thought it's the male's job to do the asking in this society?"

"Since when have you ever been a conformist?"

I roll my eyes before my mouth betrays me. "I went to his house again."

"You *what*?!" Haley starts coughing so hard I have to beat my palm against her back until all that remains are the watery eyes and red face.

"Yeah. He took me out to this Italian restaurant in the mall area we went to. Then—" I recall what happened and opt to skip that part of the story. "Well, I just ended up spending the night. Like a sleepover."

"Carmine's?" Haley asks incredulously. I give her a candid nod. "You spent the night?" Haley's face morphs to a fish-out-of-the-water look.

"And *why* didn't you tell me?" She frowns and I realize part of her cheerleader side is starting to come out. You know, the one that likes juicy details.

"It just slipped my mind," I answer truthfully. "There was a lot going on that night. But if your heart truly desires my Videl story-telling, then I will definitely tell you anything that happens in the future."

"Of course I do. But don't you see what this means, though? Guys don't do sleepovers. So the fact that you spent the night at Videl's house means you two are basically together."

"I spent the night after getting wasted at Veronica's party that one time."

"That was different. You were inebriated and incapacitated."

I open my mouth to respond, but the teacher's voice cuts through our conversation like a hot knife through butter.

"Ladies, is there something you want to discuss to the class? If not, I suggest paying attention to the board!"

The next two days pass in a flurry of homework and essays. I begin to pack my own lunch, making a small sandwich consisting of a slice of lettuce, tomato, and ham. For some reason, I'm getting hungry again. Before Dad passed, I had three meals a day, with intervallic snacks. But for the last year, it's been one meal, if any, each day. Mom seems happy about this change, though. She walked in on me grabbing a hot dog and scarfing it down, then proceeded to hug me and whisper some 'your appetite is back' nonsense.

Haley and I get to calculus with ten minutes to spare. We discuss her upcoming state cheerleading tournament for a few minutes before Videl strolls in. He's dressed in a leather jacket with cuffed jeans, and he walks with a purpose. You know when you can tell when someone is going to begin talking to you? This is him right now, and Haley breaks out into a knowing smirk before shooing aside.

"So," he begins, after he situates himself in the tiny desk, handing me a cup of water. I graciously accept his gesture while avoiding the stares from jealous females. Sometimes I don't even realize I'm thirsty until my eyes land on the water.

"So?" I repeat.

His eyes flit to the front. The teacher is beginning to drone on about Taylor series.
"I've been thinking about this for quite a while. I want to show you something next
Wednesday. Something that I think you'd like, but it's going to be a whole afternoon and maybe even night thing."

"Whole day…with you?" I ask indecisively. Then it hits me like a truck.

"Wait. You're asking me on a date?" My eyes widen and my heartbeat skyrockets until I can hear rapid *thudthuds* in my chest. My rushed tone draws some nearby students' attention, and they seem more dumbfounded than me. I blush until they return to the teacher's lecture.

"No, Hope. I'm asking you on a tryst," he answers sarcastically.

I hastily take a sip of my water and lick my lips. "Uhh…"

Videl's eyes hone in on the tip of my tongue. "Yes, a *date*." He emphasizes the word like hot chocolate is sliding down his throat and it makes my insides boil.

"I—I don't know." My voice suddenly becomes squeakier than a mouse's. My brain is praising me at my answer, but my heart is admonishing me, asking me why the hell I wasn't agreeing.

"You don't know?" Videl repeats, cocking his eyebrow. Am I that blatant? I mean, there was that time where we almost kissed in front of his bedroom door, but—

"Mom doesn't like it when I skip class."

Videl looks at me like I'm stupid but then snorts in silent laughter.

"You know, if I didn't know you the way I do, I would've wholeheartedly thought you were serious. Wednesday it is then."

"Wait! Really, I can't do Wednesday. Mom's birthday is then."

"I'll be out of town Tuesday. So Monday it is then."

"Y—No. Yeah. What? Fine," I turn red and stoop in my chair, covering my face with my hands. I get asked out for the first time in my life, and this embarrassing tongue twisting ensues.

"You really are cute when you blush," Videl throws out of nowhere. Just like that, my next week's worth of focus flies out the window.

Damn it, Haley was right.

8

Haley and I set up a time and place to meet on Sunday, and I almost call it quits after she gurgles out about fifty store locations scattered throughout this state and the next one over.

I try to predict how much money Mom will hand me. My insides squirm as I dig through my memories of girls at school talking about the prices they pay for their clothes. I really shouldn't be asking Mom for her hard-earned money. And I'd rather not go on the date at all than ask Roger for his dirty cash.

"Hey, Mom?" I ask as I round the corner to the kitchen. She's still in her plaid pajamas, working away on a bowl of cereal and reading a thick book. At the sound of my voice, she looks up.

"Hope! What brings you out of bed so early? It's Sunday."

"I'm planning on going shopping with Haley, but I don't have any money. Do you—" I take a deep breath. "Can I have some?" Good job, Hope. Of course she knows you don't have money. Way to remind her of the reason why you don't have an allowance in the first place.

I swear Mom makes a crestfallen face, but in the next second after I blink, all I see is a smile instead.

"Sure," she says. "What do you need it for?"

"I just feel like I need some new clothes, you know?" It's a half-truth, but a truth nonetheless. I'm not too sure what her policy is on dating, so I avoid telling her the whole truth.

"Honey, of course, and that is a wonderful idea!" Mom says with genuine zeal. "Your old clothes are—" Her face scrunches up, and she stops talking. We've never really discussed my insipid fashion sense, and I think she's figuring out the best way to tell me it's time for a wardrobe change without actually commenting on the current state my pieces of clothing are in.

I take her out of her misery by leaning in and giving her a hug, saying, "Thanks, Mom," to which she chuckles to before rummaging in her purse and pulling a modicum of bills and handing them to me. I take the money, holding it in my palm gingerly as if the slightest graze would tear the paper apart.

"I wish you'd let me get a job," I state suddenly. Mom's smile remains in place, but it loses some of its gaiety. Inner Hope slaps her hand on her forehead blenchingly.

"You know I can't let you do that. I can't let distractions influence your education and have you end up on the same path I did. I don't want you to turn into me," Mom wistfully proclaims.

"What's so bad about taking after the greatest Mom in the whole world?"

Mom laughs, but her hardened eyes remain. I know the subject at hand is closed. So instead, I give her another hug and a kiss on the cheek before heading out.

Haley is wearing aviators and leaning against the door of her car, much like I see Videl doing in the mornings when he's not skipping school. She drags me inside the vehicle.

"Do you have any idea how long I've waited to go shopping with you! It's going to be so much fun!" she exclaims, after we're on the road.

"Where are we going, anyways?"

"To the mall? Where else?" She looks at me skeptically.

"Oh. I didn't realize we had a mall."

"What? If we didn't, I'd have moved already. Have you ever been?"

I shake my head.

"Ah, well don't worry about it. There's a cute little store that holds the most *perfect* outfits. You'll see once we get there. I'm going to turn you into the most desirable girl on campus."

Before long, a massive building looms out in front of us. I recognize the mall to be in the same shopping center vicinity where Videl took me to eat.

We make our way into the mall and wind through several confusing hallways which remind me of the Minotaur's labyrinth. I tail Haley like an insecure puppy following its owner. If it weren't for her guiding me, I would've gotten hopelessly lost a long time ago. My naiveté makes me pay close attention to the little shops—confectionaries, bath works, cell phone providers, video game retailers, haberdasheries—you name it, it's all here. It feels like a contemporary, posh flea market.

"We're here!" Haley exclaims, and I accidentally bump into her from lack of attentiveness. My focus was on a display of digital pianos lined up harmoniously on wide shelves instead. White, brown, burgundy, black—every color imaginable was there, wrapped around those sleek pianos. But the innumerable price tag...

"Hope? Earth to Hope? Do you read me, do you read me? We have arrived."

"Uhug—what?" I whip my head around, my thoughts jerking back to reality.

"You have some drool leaking out the corner of your mouth," she points out, giggling like a madman.

I blush and quickly bring my sleeve to my mouth and wipe it off.

"Yeah, sorry. Are we here?" I revolve my head to try to find the store, resisting the urge to look back at the pianos. I can't stop myself, though, and glimpse one last time at them.

"Hold on, Haley," I say.

"Hope, the clothes store closes in seven hours!"

"Just—just let me take a quick look," I tell her. I stroll into the same store with the digital pianos and walk up to the first display table before scooping up the object of attention. I wind the key constructed into the side of the piano until the pressure is too great, and then I release my grip. A warm, melodious tune comes out of the hidden speaker while a ballerina figurine spins around in a circle, hands held high in grandeur.

"Aww, it's adorable!" Haley coos, popping up next to me without warning. "And it's cute how you're already buying Videl a gift. Although a guy like him probably wouldn't like a music box," she trails off.

"It's not for him. Mom's birthday is in three days." I flip the music box upside down and label the price sticker. I have just the right amount of cash—ten dollars for an emergency—left over from selling my textbooks the year before, so I take it to the counter. The guy asks if it's a gift, and when I say yes, he pulls out gift wrap and bundles it with his agile hands. Free of charge.

"Do you think Mom will like this?"

"She'll love it. I promise," Haley says. "But enough of that, and back to the main topic at hand. This." Haley points to the store we're standing across. I take a quick glimpse inside and see a vast assortment of clothing. "Let's go!" She tugs me into the store before I can protest and instantly begins digging through the first rack of…

"Uh…so what are these?" I dumbly ask while scanning my surroundings. Installed speakers rest throughout the store ceiling blasting some pop song I vaguely recognize. Because it is Sunday morning, not many people are out shopping; they'd be in church right now, like Mom currently is.

"These?" Haley pulls out a green one. "Cardigans. I think you'll look cute in them. Whaddya think?" She presses the cardigan against my chest then frowns.

"Hmm, this size is a little too big. Let me find a smaller one, okay?" She turns her attention back to the rack.

"Haley."

"Hmm? Wait, wait. What about this one? It's a size smaller."

"Haley."

"Yeah, what's up?"

"I don't like it."

Her face falls, and she juts her bottom lip.

"Why? Isn't green your favorite color? I thought you liked it." She puts the cardigan to my chest again.

"It's not the color. I'd just prefer not to match something a mother would wear." I wrinkle my nose. Haley takes one last look at the cardigan before sighing and putting it back.

"Well, that's okay. There's more of the store you haven't seen yet." She goes deeper into the depths of the store, and I follow.

"How many girls from school shop here?" I ask as she peruses an accessory booth.

"In our class? Veronica shops here," Haley starts and my heart sinks. "But she only comes here a day or two before her parties, and I haven't heard of any new ones planned, so if you were worried about running into her here, don't. Even by the off chance that she was here, I'll take care of you," she shoots me a wink. "Since Videl isn't here to."

I swat her arm and then turn my attention to the apparel.

An hour later, we're still up short. Either I'm picky and turn down the article of clothing—I said hell no to dresses—or they just don't look good on me, like the store's skirts, blouses, tunics, tube tops, and a bunch of other stuff. I'm already getting impatient, and the more racks we go through, the more irritated I get.

"Listen, Haley. Can we take a break? Or go to another store?" I exasperatedly clench out after going through another shelf. I would have long called this shopping trip off if it were not for my desire to impress Videl tomorrow.

"We're almost done, Hope," Haley gestures behind me. "There's just a few more rows of clothes left to go through. Then if we haven't found anything, we can try somewhere else, okay?"

"Ugh! Fine."

We continue searching for something that catches my eye. I really don't see how Haley can tolerate flipping through one article of clothing at a time at a rack in dozens without going insane. We go through athletic gear, vibrant socks, and even scandalous underwear to which I blush furiously upon seeing. Who would even wear such a lecherous item? One thing's for sure: there is no way in hell thongs are comfortable.

Haley and I continue to browse. The front window and several first racks are already stripped clean of prospective items, and the middle one is no different. But when we finally reach the clothes near the back, my eye zeroes in on a clear winner.

"Whoa. Is this a leather jacket?"

"Hmm? Oh yeah, it is!" Haley slides it off the hanger with ease. "Now that you mention it, I think this is more your style." She throws it at me but then yanks it back before I can slip it on. "Wait. This one has too many pockets. Simple is better. Here, try this one."

"I don't think it'll look good on me at all."

"Nonsense. You're blessed in the beauty department. I haven't seen anyone look as good as you without makeup on. The only problem is that you have no confidence."

"Gee, thanks," I mutter dryly.

"Oh, come on. This is going to be perfect on you. Just make sure to walk straight with poise, and don't slouch. People tend to associate leather with confidence, so make sure you adopt an air of it. Just make sure you don't turn into an egotistical hellion, like Altha." She shudders before throwing on the jacket and walking down half the hallway to demonstrate. I chuckle at her strut. Fashion models.

Haley returns to me and hands me the jacket.

"You have a penchant for slouching your back and looking at the ground a lot too so make sure you work on that. And try not to trip on anything. Oh, and before I forget, don't blush at every—"

"Okay, okay!" I hurriedly throw on the jacket in an attempt to shut Haley up.

Haley adjusts the sleeves and then spins me around so that I'm facing a mirror. "Ta-da!" she beams.

Wow. I do look good. The jacket hugs my shoulders snugly, but not overly tight, and I look kind of badass. Scratch that out; I look *really* badass. I've always admired movies where the female protagonist donned some leather jacket and studded boots look to give themselves a punk-rocker, phlegmatic, biker chick kind of vibe.

"You like?" Haley grins.

I give her a forthright nod.

"You're right; this does fit me well." I look into the mirror and Inner Hope beams at me. My confidence boosts up some.

"You'll be the desire of every boy on campus," she agrees.

"Haley, I'm not trying to be fantasy material for any male at our school," I reject. "That's gross."

"Gross?" Her eyes widen. "You don't mean to tell me that you're–you're a lesbian?" She puts her hand over her heart mockingly.

"Haley, shut up!" I laugh gaily.

"It's okay to be gay, Hope," she comforts teasingly. "If you are gay, you'd be my *best best* friend, if you know what I mean," she nudges.

"Okay Haley, if it'll get you to shut up, I'll buy the jacket."

"Yes!" she pumps her fist.

I take the jacket off, and my grin fades away almost instantly as I manage to locate the little square price tag. *$70*, it said. My heart sinks as I reflect on how Mom's money in my wallet doesn't come to meet the price of the leather jacket. My shoulders slump.

"I can't afford this," I admit to Haley, my cheeks flaming. Just like that, my confidence shatters. From one little two-digit number, my excitement vanishes. Why couldn't I have located the price tag beforehand and saved myself all this shame?

"How much is—" Haley spots the price tag. "Oh. Seventy dollars."

"Yeah, I can't. I only have fifty with me." I dig through my wallet and brush the three bills. It feels like chump change in comparison to the article of clothing in my hand, and I immediately feel guilty because I know Mom worked hard for this money.

"Hand it over." Haley's sentence jerks me out of my thoughts.

"Why?"

"Hand it over, I said. I'm paying for it." She looks at me steadily.

"I don't need your commiserations, Haley," I mutter. All of a sudden I just feel like going home and calling this whole plan off.

"Hope, you must not know me the way you think you do if you think I'm going to walk away from this. I *am* your friend," she angrily exclaims. "And friends care for each other." She snatches the jacket out of my hand before I can protest and shoves me away with her free hand.

"Go look for something else," she waves. "The jacket's on me."

"B—but."

"No buts. Look for something else you like, or would you rather I tie you down and purchase everything for you?" she threatens. A huge swell in my heart raises my spirits at her commitment.

"Haley…thank you."

She turns her face away from me. "Don't pay me back for it either. This is your present. For the best day you'll ever have tomorrow. Shoo."

I don't need any more encouragement, so I turn around and walk off further into the back of the store. I flip through racks of pants, taking heed of their price, making sure that I can at least buy something. If you ask me, the store holds some pretty elicit, promiscuous lower wear. Their daisy dukes, short shorts, jean shorts, hot pants, and a bunch of other shorts that I have no idea what to call are on all sale from the frenetic transition from summer to fall. I move past this rack into the jeans after a quick sweep. They are all too expensive; the store only holds designer and each pair is either the same price as the jacket or so expensive that I have to rub my eyes twice to make sure what I am seeing is real. It isn't until I reach a secluded corner of the shop that my eyes land on a small selection of yoga pants and leggings. The yoga pants only come in one color—black—but the leggings come in black and gray as well an assortment of colors to match the rainbow.

I draw out a pair of black and simple leggings and check the price tag, sighing in relief at the fifteen dollar price tag. I don't know if this is considered cheap, but I think it'll match the jacket just fine. So I pick out a small pair and walk into the fitting rooms. Luckily, they fit well, but I've never worn anything that clings to my skin so tightly, lest it is too revealing. But it gives me a sense of fashion de novo, so I decide to keep it. It's time for a makeover.

I stumble out of the closet and am just about to walk out of the fitting rooms until my eyes hone toward a protruding bulge in the returned items cart full of clothes. I approach the cart and sift through the distasteful shirts until I identify the object of attention—a pair of combat boots. I yank them out of the cart and hold them at an eye-level, arms-width distance, directly below the ceiling lights so that it looks like a shiny object of importance. I begin to hear the chorus singing hallelujah in my head.

There is a red clearance sticker on it, labeling the boots for thirty dollars. I make up my mind in a split second; the deal is too much to ignore, especially for shoes this chic. I'm not a fashion pundit, but this will definitely match everything else. The boots run a bit past my ankles and are laced all the way down toward the front. I wonder why it's so cheap, but after some scrutiny, I realize the left shoe has a blemish on the side. A straight line runs two inches long, providing some lighter discoloration in contrast to the black surface, but it's not enough to deter me.

I do quick math in my head, and a grin breaks over my face as I realize that even with tax added, the total wouldn't surmount my budget. Thirty for the shoes and fifteen for the leggings is forty-five…and tax is eight percent? So that's like a buck shy from fifty.

I scan the store and see Haley waving her arm in the air, beckoning me toward her. Several lengthy strides later, I'm in front of her, holding out my picks.

"What do you think?" I ask. She runs her eyes over them and beams at me.

"They're perfect for you." Relief washes over me at her compliment. "Here," she says, holding out the plastic bag in her hand. "I got you some tees."

"Oh Haley, you didn't have to."

"Don't worry about it. Being a regular member here does have its benefits. Discounts and all." She pulls out two, three, no, *five* T-shirts. Graphic ones. I can't even tell what they depict. Haley's fashion bud is like a five-star restaurant, only without the cost.

"I love them all. Thank you." I wrap my arm around Haley, enveloping her in a hug. She disappears under my taller frame, and her hair tickles my nose.

"No problem." Haley pinches her index finger and thumb together. "You should probably check out now, though. Veronica just texted me saying she was coming here, probably to buy the whole store out. That girl's wardrobe is fatter than her dad. Bleh."

I chuckle before heading to the cashier.

9*

My eyes open and within a few seconds, I'm instantly awake and alert. But instead of a gloomy feeling perpetuating in my toes and rising through my stomach, an alien sensation engulfs me until I place my finger on it. For the first time in years, I'm *wholly* exuberant. I'm going on a date, something that I've spent the last year hearing everyone around me gossiping, crying, and gushing about.

I swing my legs off the bed and instantly hop over to my shower with a vigorous spring in my step. I brush my teeth and then take a hot shower, in which I spend my time humming my recent composition.

I get out of the shower. For a countless number of days I had gone without my pills and today is no different. I go for a new look and straighten my straggly hair, which has some luminosity restored and is now a shade brighter than which it used to be.

After I'm satisfied with the results, I make my way to my piano bench, which has my newly bought and fresh pieces of clothing I purchased from the mall yesterday. I bite my lip in averseness; the outfit itself isn't considered to be anything new or trendy to the female school population, but it's more than the usual colorless tatters I usually don. I'm worried it'll draw attention from people I'm hoping to avoid. Like Veronica and her simpleton friends.

But then Inner Hope grabs my dubiousness and crushes it in the palm of her hand, telling me to stop being such a wuss and throw it on. So I worm into the multi-piece outfit, making sure none of the tags are poking out. I take a lingering glimpse of myself in the mirror, and I'm not going to lie, Haley did a great job picking out the outfit. I lick my lips. I look *hot*.

Next, the makeup. Probably the most noticeable change I'm partaking in. I sit down at my dresser and open up the bag of assorted accessories, staring blankly at the clustered tools. Yesterday, when Haley was over my shoulder doing my makeup for me, I felt confident, and when she had me do it, I could replicate it perfectly under her reassuring words. But now that I'm left to attend to the task alone, I completely forget the step-by-step instructions. I should have written it down on paper. Is it a light flick of my wrist originating from my tear duct or the opposite side?

In the end, I avoid the eyeliner and decide to work on putting on my mascara instead. But after several futile attempts, my inferior application looks like the equivalent of a five-year-old given free reign over his brand-new coloring book.

I head over to the bathroom and wash the sloppy mess away, taking care to avoid wetting my clothes. Haley's number pulls up on my phone.

"Hey, Hope! Ready to show the whole school the hot new you?"

I blush. "Almost, but I need a little help applying the makeup." How does she manage to sound peppy this early in the morning? "Can you come over? I know school starts soon, but…"

"Oh, Hope, I would love to, but I'm already at school. What's the issue?"

"I don't know, yesterday I was fine, but today my fine motor skills are faulty or something. Every time I've tried to apply makeup, the end result looks like a kid scribbling profusely over my face."

"Okay, how about this," she giggles. "Text me when you get to school. I'll meet you in the bathroom in the Education building and then do your makeup for you. Sound good?" she chirps.

I nod and then slap my palm to my forehead when I realize she can't see the pantomime.

"I'll meet you there in ten minutes."

"Okay! See you!"

"Bye," I mutter, ending the call.

Letting out a sigh, I send a quick prayer, the first in a while, hoping that I won't mess things up today before heading downstairs. First date ever, and I'm so nervous my legs won't quit bouncing up and down. I'm more jittery than the time I went to Veronica's party.

"Hi, Mom!" I shyly greet as I walk into the kitchen casually, opening the fridge door and double-checking to see whether her favorite flavor red-velvet cupcake I bought for her yesterday is still securely tucked in the back corner of the fridge. It is.

Mom is hovering over the bowl of cereal with her mouth open, just in time for me to catch her mouthing a silent wow.

"Honey…you look amazing!" she finally says. "What's the occasion?"

Crap. I completely forgot.

My smile reduces in concavity as I furrow my brows for any excuse, in fear of her opposition. But I realize the longer I keep her waiting, the more suspicious she'll get, so I decide to settle on another half-truth.

"I'm going to hang out with a friend after school today. Is that alright?" I make sure to keep my voice steady and intoned.

"Of course honey. And is this friend a boy or girl?" she interrogates, a devilish glint worming into her eyes.

Hook, line, and sinker.

"Mommmm," I whine, but she doesn't give up. "It's a guy," I finally mumble, waiting for the axe to fall.

A few moments pass in silence, and I use the time to admire the reflective qualities of my jacket. Then…

"I knew there was another reason behind getting new clothes. And speaking of which," she says, giving me an eye-over. "I certainly hope you enjoy yourself."

My head snaps up. "You approve?" I ask in disbelief.

Mom gets up from her seat and walks over to me, placing her hands on my shoulders.

"Oh, Hope. Of course, I approve. I completely trust you and know you're old enough to make the right decision. Besides, I haven't seen you this happy in a year—you practically pranced down the stairs this morning. If there's a smile on your face, then he must be worth the trouble that comes with the common male gender. What's his name?"

"Mom!" I scold playfully. "His name's Videl."

"Ooh, that sounds foreign. Is he foreign?"

"Yeah, Videl's from France. He and his sister are visiting the states."

"Wow, imagine if they're here to find shelter because their father is a drug lord who's neck-deep in trouble right now. Does he have an accent?"

"Mom, your imagination is a little too quixotic, and yes, he does."

"Sorry, sorry! I mean, wow. Even I'm feeling a little excited now." She fans her face with a hand in a melodramatic manner. "Is he the one who's your duet partner? Is he attractive?"

"Okay, okay, what is this, twenty questions?" I laugh. "Yes and yes, he's attractive and everything about him is just so refined and—and perfect. He can get any girl in the school, but he settles for me instead. I don't understand it."

"Honey, don't look into it too hard," Mom reassures. "You've already grown into a beautiful lady. And I'm not saying that because I'm your mother and obligated to. It's the truth. You may think you don't deserve him, but the truth of the matter is, he deserves *you*."

The next thing I know, I'm swallowed in an enormous motherly hug—which is kind of difficult for her with my backpack on, but years of practice has led to perfection.

"It's a little cliché, but just be yourself," Mom whispers in my ear. "And I hope he comes over for dinner sometime soon."

"Thanks," I say, my voice slightly muffled. We break apart from the hug and Mom observes the oven clock.

"Oh, it's time for you to get yourself to school. Otherwise, you'll be late." Sure enough, it's twenty after eight.

"Can you give me a ride?" I ask, my nerves returning.

"Sure!" Then she sighs. "Wait, I can't. Roger is out front fixing the car. Something about a brake issue, he said."

Damn. There goes my ride to school.

"Does that mean you don't have work today?"

"No, I'm covering a girl's shift a few extra hours tonight instead of heading in this morning. I'll be leaving around midnight. The extra cash will help." Mom turns her head away.

"Oh, Mom," I console.

"Don't worry dear. Customer turnout is actually on the rise. We got a new cook and to say she is talented would be the understatement of the year."

"Wow. That's great, Mom!"

"Thanks, honey. Anyways, just remember to make sure you're home before I head out, and no matter how attractive he is, I don't condone sex until—"

"OKAY, MOM! No need to go into the birds and the bees!"

"Love you honey!" she calls when I'm at the door.

"Love you too!" I yell back.

Right as I'm in the process of shutting the door, I hear a, "Remember to be home before midnight! You're going to tell me about your afternoon before I leave!" which causes me to chuckle.

The smile drops from my face as I spot the dirty jeans and holed shoes sticking out from under Mom's car, and I try my best to sneak past him without detection, I really do. But his sixth sense is like a honing magnet to my presence because he slides out from under the car on a mechanic's creeper and grins at me maliciously with a predatorial glint in his eyes.

"What are you doing?" Voice steady, Hope. Don't quiver.

"Oh, nothin' much. Just fixin' the brakes on ya mom's car," he sneers menacingly. "Ya still wastin' my money attendin' school? Rather ya stay home, with me."

I ignore the jab.

"What's wrong with the brakes? And what would you know about fixing things?" My fist clenches tightly. He's eyeing me like I'm fresh meat, and it pisses me the hell off.

"She complained about 'em being too wiggly or squeaky or somethin'."

"I think you should let me take a look at it." My offer is a bold one, but I'm sure he'll accept it for any chance of getting to grope me, especially after his last attempt ended disastrously for him. Something seems suspicious about the whole situation here. Not just because Roger is a shady mongrel, but I've never seen him up and sober this early before.

But to my immense surprise, he shakes his head.

"Nah, I got it," he sincerely answers, and my eyebrows shoot through my forehead.

I recognize his dismissal when Roger slides himself back under the car and resumes tinkering. I stand for another few seconds in stunned silence before shaking my head and beginning the trek to school.

I spend the entire walk to school not worrying about my new outwards presentation toward the student population, but rather trying to unveil Roger's aberrant behavior. Unfortunately, I can't think of any low, dirty deeds even he would succumb to. Mom said she loves him, and he loves her. And if I can't trust her words, then I can't trust her.

The parking lot is filled with the usual cars in the same spot. My eyes automatically hone toward Videl's, which I know is always parked in the corner of the lot to ensure his privacy when he's acting debaucherously with his flings. I shake my head, ignoring the insecurities over whether Videl is actually attracted to me. And then my heart races when I see him purposely walking toward me.

"You look absolutely *ravishing*. Did you do this for our date?" he winks at me when there's only a foot or two of concrete between us.

"Um, sure. I thought you were meeting me after school?" I avoid his eyes, flushing. My phone begins to vibrate, and I quickly switch it to silent.

"Change of plans. We're skipping class for today. The earlier we get there, the better." His slightly darkened eyes appraise my outfit and for once, I don't feel scrutinized by another pair of commiserating eyes casting themselves on my clothing style. In fact, quite the opposite. His compliment makes me feel special.

"But—"

"Please, Hope." Videl leaves me with no chance to argue because he pouts and hits me with full-on puppy eyes, turning me to mush.

"O—okay," I weakly agree. He grabs my hand and pulls me forward, and my breathing immediately labors from the electric shocks at his touch.

"So what is it you want to show me?" I ask him, after catching my breath.

"You'll see," he says, as we approach his car. "Trust me; you'll love it." He opens the passenger door and invites me to get in.

Trust him? Do I? Yeah, I do. My wariness is all that's preventing me from hopping into the car without a second thought. For all I know, he might be harboring an arrière-pensée. Call me silly, but that's just how my brain functions. Always fearing the worst. Pfft. And maybe Roger *was* trying to be a nice guy for once.

"Is it somewhere close by?"

"Not especially. It's ninety minutes, tops. You'll love it, though, I promise." His voice is filled with genuine probity, and I make up my mind and say, "Okay" before getting into the vehicle. He shuts the door and strolls around to the driver's side, plops down on the leather, and cranks the engine on. A feverish shudder runs down my spine when I hear the start-up, and the soft, menacing purr of the vehicle as it sits in park.

He sets the gear stick in forward and floors the gas pedal. The car zooms forward with an obnoxious rumble and the engine *screams*. All I can do for the first few minutes is sit in a hazy mixture of excitement and nervousness as the trees and houses whiz by in a blur, and admire the lush, burgundy leather interior and smooth suspension system.

Altha's car definitely doesn't meet his expectations. I bet when he said an hour and a half, he meant it at his pace. I let loose a small chuckle of unbridled giddiness at the thought, and because the car does such a marvelous job at quelling exterior sounds, Videl hears me.

"What are you giggling about?" He turns to me, taking his eyes off the road in the process while keeping his manic speed. His right hand—the free one—drums on the gearbox and I find the tapping oddly comforting.

"Conspiracies and political assassinations," I murmur after an apt pause, twirling a hand through the strands of my hair and striving to come off in a mysterious yet teasing demeanor. Inner Hope proudly pats me on the back.

It works because Videl growls at me. A shiver of avidity crawls down my spine, and the hairs on my arms stiffen. Good lord, it sounded sinful.

"What have I started?" he moans and turns his attention back to the road. "You're an infuriating woman."

"Everything I feel toward you, I'm projecting at you," I shoot back, a grin teasing my face. My confidence is at an all-time high and conversation flows through my lips with a second-nature ease I have never experienced before.

"So…" I begin, kicking off my boots so I can sit comfortably with my legs crossed.

"So?"

"Are you going to tell me where you're taking me?

"No. I want it to be a surprise. You can ask about anything else," he offers. He shoots a wink at me, and my heart skips a beat.

"Uh…what do your parents do for a living?" It is a banal question, but I am actually curious to know. In the meantime, my brain chides my heart for its sentiency.

"Well, my mother is a novelist in the criminology genre. She has a private study in our home back in France, which allows for a lot of leisure time to keep the house up and running. She doesn't have any quotas to fulfill other than the writing workshops she's charge of once a week; it's a relaxing occupation, from what she's told me."

"And your father?" I ask after he falls silent. He doesn't respond at first, and I'm not sure if it's because he didn't hear me.

"My father is a businessman…of sorts. He's the boss of his own company." His voice tapers off to a mutter, and I easily detect the reticence behind it. I don't want to come off as pushy, so I drop the subject.

"But hey, you want to know what Altha does?" His face suddenly lights up in a mischievous grin, and I have a feeling Altha has secrets she doesn't want him spilling. But hey, what she doesn't know won't hurt her, right?

My face breaks out in its own form of mischievousness and I nod. "Tell me."

"She sells dolls." At my snort, he grins.

"You don't believe me?"

"No, I believe you. I just find it hard that Altha, an ice queen and a word that I won't say in my calm and collected state—but rhymes with ditch—could ever partake in doll collecting."

"That's why you can't tell her. She still sleeps with her favorite one. Lacey-Macy is her name."

I burst out laughing then stop, feeling bad for taking advantage of Altha's privacy.

"Why are you even telling me this?" I query.

"I needed a smooth transition to talk to you about her."

"No, really. Why? I'm pretty sure you just told me her biggest secret."

"No, really, exactly what I said," he mocks.

I squint my eyes.

"Okay, forgive me for saying this, but you know how she treats you like a sack of caca?"

"What's caca?" I try my best to imitate the word.

"French for shit."

"Um…yeah." My voice subdues, and Videl sighs before looking over at me apologetically.

"Sorry. That came out wrong." Videl runs his hand through his hair. "Let me try again. She treats you like a sack of shit. No, that's literally what I just said." He sighs again, and it takes a lot of effort for me to hold in my smile. "What I'm trying to get at is that Altha is jealous of you."

"Excuse me?" My eyebrows shoot through the roof. "Did you say *jealous*?"

"Sure enough," he says. I pace my next words very carefully and deliberately.

"And regarding *me*, what is *Altha* exactly jealous of?" I ask.

"She's jealous of your simplicity. She wants a quiet, unhurried life. To have your brains, and your time management. She endlessly whines at home about not scoring higher than you on her chemistry exams. That's why she bullies you. Because she wants to break you with her words, so you feel what she's feeling. Pressured to make friends. Pressured to please people. Having little-to-no say in matters. She wants to be free. That's why she's so—"

"Bitchy," I finish. "Let her know I'm more than happy to switch anytime."

"I'll tell her," Videl nods. "The bitchy part, that is."

"Videl!"

"Relax, I know." He shifts his arm and then grabs my hand, resting them on the center console of his car. Tingles. Tingles. Tingles.

"Why can't she just treat me better? I mean, I'd be happy to give her pointers. It doesn't help that she's covering her true feelings by harassing me instead."

"Pride, Hope. Pride is her maxim. She's a snooty sister, but my sister nonetheless. She'd rather give up an arm than to admit her jealousy."

"People are so irrational."

"I know," he chuckles. "Human beings are strange."

Not even five minutes into the car ride and my eyebrows shoot through the roof for a third time. "No one talks like that, you know."

"Talks like what?" He looks over at me, taking his eyes off the road.

"Speaking as if you're not human yourself sometimes."

He chuckles. "So what, you think I'm supernatural being with an affinity for multitasking or whatever unrealistic stuff floating around in the world of teenage novels?" I stay silent.

"Sorry to pop your bubble, but Videl is human."

I smack his arm. "Whatever. But Altha, everything she's said—it's all out of jealousy?"

"Well, no, not *all*. It's true she doesn't like your figure or fashion sense, but I think her opinion would change if she saw your outfit today." He gives another wry smirk.

"Oh."

"Plus, I don't think the root of her jealousy stems from your lifestyle."

"What do you mean?"

"I think she secretly likes you."

"You don't say?"

"No, I mean like, as in *like, like*. She has a crush on you."

A thick silence engulfs the moving box.

"Hope?" Videl asks.

"Excuse me? You're telling me my arch nemesis *likes* me. Let me get this straight. Likes as in 'I am attracted to her' *like* or 'I want to be friends with her' *like*?"

"The former."

I laugh rowdily. "You're kidding. You should sit in Chemistry class and listen to her denigrating attacks and venomous eyes."

"She's in denial. Just the other day she came home, yelled at Bastien to make her a kale smoothie, then proceeded to grumble about you under her breath. Which was impressive, seeing how her mouth was full of that green stuff." Videl fans his mouth and makes a small gagging noise. "Can't believe she drinks kale."

"What did she say?"

"I caught only a few words. Infuriating, detestable, unbearable were a few of her vernacular."

"I say that stuff about you all the time."

"Yeah, so it makes sense. You like me. She likes you." I blush.

"Stop twisting my words!"

"Yeah, Altha was the same shade as you are now too."

We spend the rest of the time riding in silence. I have a lot of information to digest. What sticks to me the most is that Videl's Mom is an author. I've always thought it would be cool to write for a living. From what I've been told, I have a vivid imagination. But when I try to transcribe my ideas onto paper, it always comes out in a wordy jumble of nonsense.

Videl turns onto a one-lane road shy from the busy intersection, and the first thing I notice is all the underlying brush surrounding us. The weeds are at a disproportional size, a result of the road's obvious lack of use. Long, jagged cracks shaped like thunderbolts run from one side of the road to the other. I fasten my hand to the passenger assist grip when Videl begins swerving around the conspicuous potholes to preserve the welfare of his car's suspension system. I'm beginning to feel a little antsy.

We arrive in a spacious clearing, and it takes me a minute before I realize we're sitting in a parking lot. The white parking stripes have already long faded, and I continue to detect a countless number of cracks and potholes scattered all around us.

Videl shuts off the ignition, and after a drawn-out complaint, the car's engine dies. I remain still.

"We're here," he says to me, and his unsuspecting grin sets me slightly at ease.

I clear my throat. "Where exactly is here?"

"I'll show you right now," he says and steps out of the car. Much to my diffidence, my face heats up when he grabs my hand and pulls me toward a dirt road ahead of us. I really need to learn how to control my blushing. Or better yet, get rid of them.

We walk down the dusty path for a couple of minutes, and when we round the corner, my jaw drops as my brain processes the spectacle in front of me.

Amusement park. We're at an amusement park. And then it clicks. It's an *abandoned* amusement park. The desolate atmosphere, ruins of a once-popular tourist attraction—this is what Videl wants to show me.

And I'm not going to lie; I find it fascinating. There's something in the air about a deserted piece of artwork that hypnotizes me. Maybe it's the sense of solemnity or the feeling of lost potential. Perhaps even a representation of a connection to the lives long gone from the buildings; the remains of an empty shell being all that's left. Abandoned places make me think, 'Hey, once upon a time, someone was standing right where I am,' and then flashes of a fully functioning theme park with optimistic families as tableaus waiting in lines clairvoyantly perpetuate my vision. In black and white too, for theatricality.

I'm sure it also has to do with my proclivity. Haley always rants on about how perfect her dates turn out to be, and I never understand why. I mean, what's the point of a dinner date? We have to eat anyways, right? Dressing up and forking over a gratuitous chunk of money offers no shred of appeal for me. And as for the movies, I'd rather spend my time getting to know the person verbally rather than glue my eyes at a humongous monitor. This place that Videl has brought me to is definitely through the roof on the creative scale. I love it.

By the time my thoughts finish reeling, we're standing next to a standard silver fence with barbed wires at the top.

"There's a hole here we can crawl through," he points to the ground. There's a gap wide enough for a large dog. I could easily slide through prone, but Videl would need to squeeze.

"Uh, Videl, the sign here says no trespassing," I point out. Sure enough, there's a menacing black warning notice with a skull tacked on the rickety, rusty fence.

"Yeah, but it's just for show. No one comes around here anymore aside from hippies and parkour junkies." He mock bows and gestures toward the opening. "Ladies first."

I'm still a little hesitant, but when he looks at me and flashes a reassuring smile, I immediately lose all former pretense of arguing and begin crawling to the other side. Once I'm through, I breathe a sigh of relief after I do a full-body check and see my clothes still intact.

The air smells crisper. I can also feel the park's ghost beckoning toward me, inviting me into its lair.

"Help me through, I'm too fat," Videl grunts. His squashed figure is struggling to squeeze through the tight opening. I hold back my laughter at how absurd he looks, and instead, crouch down low and tug on his outstretched hand, until—after strenuous effort on my part—he pops through.

"—never been this hard to squeeze through before," Videl mutters while rubbing his shoulders.

"Maybe if you didn't work out so much it'd be easier," I suggest playfully.

"Definitely true, but I need these guns to impress all the girls," he retorts, flexing his bicep.

"I'm not impressed," I lie. "Does that mean I'm not a girl?"

The next thing I know, his face is only a few inches away from mine, and I have to remind myself twice to keep breathing.

"No, you're just a classy lady," he smirks. He offers his hand and I wobble to it.

We progress until we reach the entrance. The welcome sign has long faded—not a single letter is intact on light-blue paint that once captivated tourists' pointed fingers and anticipation. The two poles, attached to either side of the sign, have their bury points obscured by the thick shin-level weeds.

I close my eyes, letting the image burn into my corneas. "How did you even find this place?"

"A friend of a friend."

"So an acquaintance?"

"Remember, infuriating," he points to me. "But they come here to get high. Do you like it?"

I detect a need for approval in his voice, so I say, "It's beautiful." And it is. Thick vines are strapped tightly around the infrastructure of the welcome center, binding it to the ground and giving it a desolated, haunted appeal. That's the power of nature, taking back what's rightfully theirs.

Videl mouth breaks into a goofy smile, and he tugs me forward.

We spend the next ten minutes in silence, passing several desecrate attractions. For once, his touch doesn't drive me as crazy. The attractions make sure of this.

Unicorns with peeling paint on a merry-go-round blankly stare at me, never to be ridden again. Empty, square stands that once held mini-games—I imagine ring tosses and squirt gun races—stand silent. Bumper cars, whose circuits will never be reanimated ever again, sit rusting. Only the shuffling of debris and the brushing of leaves into the air from the gentle wind whispering in my ear reveals to me any sign of life. And then, when we round a corner—

"Oh my god," a whisper leaves me, and my voice becomes lost, almost muted, at the sight of the monstrous roller coaster looming a hundred feet before me.

"Come on!" Videl tugs my hand, and we walk until I can physically touch the beams. My fingers become stained with dirty bits of dust or whatever is stuck to the wood. We continue winding our way through its skeleton until we reach the operator's panel, allowing me a closer glimpse at the beast. Parked next to the operator's panel are the carts themselves, attached to each other by screws and bolts. The blue and red paint that once had children clamoring are now so faded I can see the strips of degrading wood underneath. Half the lap bars are pushed down in a locked formation, whereas the other half stick up of their own free will, begging for a rider to enter the cabin one last time.

I turn my attention to the tracks. The lift hill's chains splay broken in half, splattered over the technician walkway like cotton squeezing out the seams of a stuffed animal. There's a two hundred foot climb to the top, and I can faintly discern the drop that dips into a constructed tunnel on the other side.

"You ready?" Videl asks.

"Wait, we're going to ride it?! It looks rickety. The chains are broken."

"Of course not. I don't trust the fragility of the carts, and plus, no electricity. But the support beams are still very sturdy. We're going to climb it."

"Climb? W—wait!" He's already tugging me past the ride's control box, but I pull my hand away from his.

"What's the matter?" He frowns and looks at his hand like I had ripped a part of it off. He's been holding my hand so profusely lately that I wouldn't be surprised if mine had molded into his sometime during.

"I can't." My words slip out defeated and I look down at my boots.

As much fun as it is to ride a roller coaster, climbing one is different. An abandoned roller coaster means no safety net. No protection or any device to ensure survival if an accident—like my affinity toward tripping over my two feet—occurs at a questionable height.

"Can't, or won't?" Videl asks, and I say, "Both." He takes a calculating look at me and then his eyes widen.

"You're scared of heights."

I give a shy nod and blush. "I'm not an adrenaline junkie."

"Don't worry; I've done this several times before myself. I'm still alive, aren't I?"

"For now," I mumble. He takes both my hands in his.

"Listen. Burrow your head in the back of my jacket and watch your feet when we're climbing; we'll get there in a few minutes, tops. I'll hold on to you every step of the way," he promises. "You won't regret it. I promise."

I bite my lip, still unsure but wanting to appease him. "Okay."

He gives me a warm smile and I follow his instructions, burying my face into his cologne-ridden jacket. We begin the trek up the giant. Thank heavens my motor neurons don't betray me, for I don't look down the side of the rails once. And for good measure too, because halfway up my boots slip on a steel panel and I fall backward in what would be my death barring Videl wrapping his other arm behind me and pulling me to a steady halt. He looks at me worriedly, but I just shake my head and give him a cue to go, resisting the urge to scream and bawl like a baby. We continue climbing, and for the rest of the journey, I focus on my feet and count the steps until he suddenly stops.

"Here," he announces after I bump into him. After taking a deep breath, I muster up the courage to poke my head from behind his back.

"Please tell me—"

I never get to finish my sentence, for my words float meaninglessly out of my diminished breath as I take in the sight around me. The textile mills and shopping complexes that usually loom over me are now tiny bricks in the distance. Cars the size of ants slowly chug their way to their destinations. A nearby train blows its horn, and my attention moves to it. Everything looks like a make-your-own-city toy set. And the wind. The breeze is crisper than anything I've ever breathed and spins my hair out of control.

My fear of heights begins to recede into my innermost conscious until only the faintest glimmer can be detected. I laugh at the top of my lungs, and then it turns into a cheer, and then another.

"Having fun?" My head whips around to see Videl focusing intently on me, with an indescribable glint in his eyes.

A wide smile splits across my face and I fervently nod before tackling Videl in a hug.

"This is so beautiful," I claim. "Thank you. This is amazing. You're amazing."

I'm filling with a feeling I can't quite explain. For the last year, I felt like my life was being dragged down by a combination of Roger, depression, and death. Nothing cheered me up the way it used to. But looking out into the cloudless blue sky and standing hundreds of feet above the ground, I feel the shackles chained around my wrists and ankles breaking; crumbling apart, unlocked by the key that Videl holds. I am literally on top of the world, and I am liberated. Free.

"I always go here when I have a lot on my mind. My problems just all seem to vanish by the—"

"Breathtaking view," I finish in a whisper. He turns his attention back to the sky and surroundings.

"I spy our school."

"Oh, you're so on," I snort. With my unparalleled sense of direction, I immediately start scrying south, the direction I know we came from. Not a few minutes later, I let loose a cry of triumph.

"There! That brick building! I can see the soccer field right next to it."

"Well done," Videl approbates. "It took me half an hour to find it the first time."

We spend hours playing random games and talking about each other's lives. Before long, I'm completely mesmerized by the pulchritude of the warm array of red, orange, and yellow streaks in the sky. Videl and I watch the explosive sunset together until the last rays of light recede to the other side of the world, but we don't budge. I bask in the comfortable silence, and the enrapturing view relinquishes my fear of heights.

We remain immobile on the pinnacle of the roller coaster until the sky darkens so much our shadows disappear, and the only surroundings I see are the miniature glow of lights that represent human life many miles away from us. A chilling wind howls and nips my exposed skin, but I don't mind; awe from the breath-taking view of the twinkling lights continue to supersede the frigidness.

The stars have shied away from hiding, and faintly, I spot the Big and Little Dipper sparkling above me. It's hard to imagine that they're dozens of light years away, yet they still penetrate our field of vision on earth. It's metaphoric. The stars search for their place in the universe and ultimately find their fellows and entwine together to create something beautiful. Just like the everlasting friendships humans forge during their lifetime.

I let out a tiny sigh. If only Mom could see this. Love would be an understatement to her emotions.

Wait. Mom! Curfew! What time was it?!

"Videl?" I call for his attention, my voice rasping unattractively from lack of use. I clear my throat and blush. "What time is it?"

"Did you just blush?"

"Videl!" I flush and nudge his shoulder playfully. "I'm serious!" Apparently, the Frenchie has another superpower besides mind-reading—night vision.

"Ouch, woman!" He banters back, and I laugh. There's a shuffling noise as he gets out his phone out to check the time. I return my attention to the cosmos, admiring the eerie, yet majestic celestial bodies glowing brightly in space. Never have I felt so infinitesimal. My story to Mom can wait. She definitely won't die from curiosity.

"My phone's out of battery," Videl admits, and it brings my attention back to earth. "Check yours?" he suggests.

I unclasp my hand from his and pull my phone out of my pocket, trying to unlock it. But the screen remains black.

"Nope, mine's out too." I slip my phone back into my jeans, and we fall into another comfortable silence until a silly thought strikes my mind.

"You know what's funny?" I ask.

"Hmm?" he hums.

"When we first came here, I didn't know of your plans. I was worried about the idea that you were a serial killer and the whole afternoon was just a clever ploy to get me here in your clutches, where you would then dispose of me. Although I don't see the humor behind that, now that I think about it," I voice. "Silly, right?" I await a response, but I don't receive one.

"Videl?"

Still no answer. I begin to panic.

"Videl, you're scaring me here!" I reach my arms out blindly to where I last saw him, trying to make sure he didn't fall off.

"How did you know?" His voice appears out of the darkness and is hardly above a raspy whisper, but I catch every single word. I immediately clam up at how dour he sounds.

"Wh—what?" My breath hitches in my throat.

My hands suddenly become restricted as another pair wraps each of my wrists in a firm grip, but before I can scream, he says, "Just kidding," and begins laughing.

My startled state quickly turns into relief mixed with annoyance and I vociferate, "You asshole!"

He continues to laugh, and I can't stay mad at him for long; I begin giggling with him, and the inexplicable sensation of all the pressure in my life lift off my shoulders and finally make me feel like I belong in this world. A sudden epiphany hits me. Being around Videl vanquishes my depression. He makes me feel again.

"You should have seen your face!" He continues to guffaw, and I muster up the courage to insert hurt in my voice.

"How can you see my face when it's pitch-black?"

"Whatever. I'm sure it was priceless."

"I'm upset. You really had me worried."

"Aw, lighten up. It was all in tasteful humor," he teases.

"Nope," I pop the p and pull away from his slacken grip, crossing my arms in the process. I'm prepared to play hard to get for a few minutes, but then his hands touch me and the idea flies out the window.

I involuntarily jump and squeal, and then start giggling hysterically when he starts tickling my ribs.

"Ahh! S—stop it!" I'm laughing and gasping for air, and in the back of my mind, I vaguely recall saying the same words to Roger. But this is different. Videl envelops me in warmth, and I feel sheltered around him. Protected. Secure.

He continues tickling me, and I can barely pay focus to anything beyond the realm of my enkindled hysterical giggles and ticklish sensitivity. It goes for one or two minutes, maybe five, until my ribs hurt.

"E—enough!" I finally manage to squeeze out between laughs. My arms have long given up their feeble attempts in prying him off.

His hands stop working their magic and leaves me to renew my lungs with air and familiarize my surroundings. Only once my accelerated heartbeat stabilizes to an ordinary rhythm do I realize where I am.

Somehow during the exchange, I had ended up on Videl's lap with my legs wrapped around his back and my hands on his shoulders. The two of us are staring face to face a few inches apart; the only thing separating us is the ghostly air.

The moon peeks from behind the clouds and my breath vanishes as the ethereal glow washes over us and illuminates only half of his face, revealing one of his long-lashed, lustrous eyes while leaving the other half in darkness. The spectacle reminds me of dichotomies: light versus dark, and good versus evil. Secrecy versus candidness.

Because our limbs are entwined, my body vicariously bobs up and down to the rhythm of his breathing. I look into his deep pools and see them bore right back at me, staring at me—staring *through* me, into my soul. And then, his eyes leave mine and dart to my lips. My pulse races again, and my mind whirls at a thousand miles per hour. I involuntarily shift to the side at the thought, biting my lip in the process.

The moonlight encompasses the remaining side to him that was left in the dark and my heart stops beating. Now both his eyes are filled with a smoldering vehemence I've only ever imagined in dreams, and an aura of divinity seems to surround him. Never before have I seen such angelic beauty, and since Altha isn't here to interrupt us, I lean in, abandoning my qualms and closing the gap between our faces, closing the gap between our lips and securing my passion for him.

My mind explodes in a frenzy of live fireworks when I feel the warmth of his mouth wrap around mine, and I gasp. It's my first kiss, and the sensation is foreign and overwhelming. A perfect mixture of citrus and cardamom causes my brain stop functioning in its entirety as his lips send a jolt of electricity straight through mine, striking me at my core. We remain still and unmoving in our connected position, merely savoring the texture and flavor of each other. And then I feel his tongue run across my bottom lip.

I've read my fair share of romance novels to understand the underlying request behind his gesture. In my vulnerable state, I can no longer deny him. My mouth falls open, and his tongue instantly darts inside, exploring every crevice in my mouth and all the nooks and crannies. I let out a whimper into his mouth at his contact.

I'm hesitant and unsure of how to proceed, but my inexperienced thoughts fly out the window when his tongue touches mine. I immediately begin to react, dancing around each other and battling for dominance until my jaw hurts. But it is sensational. It is pure bliss. We kiss until I'm out of breath, but I don't pull away. Only until my lungs are burning for air do I forcefully peel myself off of him. And when we break apart, all I can focus on is him. Videl, Videl, Videl. My brain is wired onto channel Videl. Nothing in the world matters except for Videl.

I let out a shaky breath and try to grasp my surroundings. My heart is filled with an emotion I can't quite discern, but I feel drunk. High on love. Sometime during the exchange, my hand wound its way into his messy hair. One of his hands are on my waist with the other cupping the nape of my neck, and the tingling sensations are so strong I just about faint. The fire that his touch provides suffuses from my ribcage until my whole body is enveloped in a numbing pleasure.

I hardly register any of this before his lips are attacking mine again. I let out a muffled gasp of surprise, which turns to one of hunger as I respond with equal fervor.

Videl pulls away after an innumerable amount of toe-curling kisses, and with a reluctant pout, I do as well. Time seems to have passed so quickly I don't even remember where we are.

It's like the kiss shined an identifying beacon of light on him; every single physical part he holds seems to have been amplified by ten. His hair seems more luminous. His jawline seems more profound. His lips look softer. His eyes reveal more of his soul.

We stay in this position until my thighs are numb.

"What do you say we get back?" Videl's voice is rough and husky, his eyes darkened.

I agree, and we both stand up. Or, I attempt to.

The kiss caused my legs to become wobbly and unsteady, and I begin tumbling to the edge of the railing. My brain is sending me signals to grab Videl's shirt to prevent my death twenty floors below, but my body is reacting seconds too slow, an effect of the soul-piercing kiss experience.

Videl grabs onto me before I can somersault over the edge and draws me back into the safety of his chest.

"Whoa, careful there. I haven't gotten enough of you yet."

The dopamine from my brain is still surging. The high gives me a feeling of immortality; thus, the climb down is much easier and much more doable and enjoyable than the climb up. I appreciatively hold hands with Videl, no longer insecure about my feelings.

The car ride is silent, even with the rain, but comfortable. Our hands remain entwined together over the armrest in the middle of his car. His other hand is on the steering wheel, and I spend a majority of the ride staring at him and admiring his lips, tempted to climb into his lap and continue kissing him.

Maybe it's because my brain isn't thinking straight. Maybe it's because I'm in a state of euphoria. Regardless of the reason, my mouth opens, and the words tumble out before I can stop them.

"Don't you feel the tingles like I do?"

Videl's hand twitches against mine, and he looks at me with wide eyes before withdrawing his. I immediately regret at how unnerved he seems, and I can do nothing but reflexively cover my mouth with my hands.

"That slipped out, I swear! I didn't mean to say that. I don't know why I said that."

"Hope, it's okay."

"No, it's not! I just had my first kiss, and then I admitted this, and now I'm pretty sure I just ruined things between us."

"Hope, listen—"

"No! I blame the high off our kiss! There's something wrong! Maybe my brain has too much dopamine and it's tampering with my thought process and—"

"I feel the same way." His voice is so quiet it throws me off-guard and I shut up.

"You do?" My heart is beating harder than it ever has in my life. He doesn't respond, which makes me want to pull my hair and scream at him.

"Yes. Every time we touch, it's like a wildfire spreading throughout my body. There's this electricity between us, literally. The first day of class, when I collided into you and offered you my hand, remember that?" He gives me an unsure smile. This in itself is a new display of Videl unbeknownst to anyone. The way his index finger taps on the steering wheel implies a vulnerable state of nervousness.

"Of course. The first time we touched, I almost passed out from the sheer intensity of the tingles," I admit, staring at my leggings. I hear Videl breathing a sigh of relief.

"I can't explain this feeling at all because I've never experienced it in my life."

"You must be joking," I snort, finding the confidence to start speaking again after his confession. "I mean, it's appropriate to say that it's *my* first time because I've never been romantically involved with anyone before. But you've, what, been with dozens of girls? And these tingles are just now manifesting?"

"A hundred, give or take a few, is more accurate."

I narrow my eyes at him and growl. "Videl…"

He holds both his hands up in the air as a gesture of surrender. "Just saying."

"I'm trying to be serious here!"

"Well, I *am* serious. You've never had a boyfriend before?"

His question causes my mouth to open. "No," I say. "I haven't." I hastily shut it before anything else embarrassing slips out. Videl runs one of his hands through his hair and sighs prodigiously.

"There's nothing wrong with that. You should be proud of yourself, resisting temptation that offers pleasure at the expense of your personal time. Too many kids who haven't even hit puberty rush into relationships and have no idea what to do in one. Everyone left and right these days is dating, so finding someone who has never been in a relationship is one in a million. The fact that you are one means you're unique. Innocent. This means I can have you all to myself. I'll be your first everything. Dates, company, and even—" he stops speaking and chooses to wag his eyebrows at me instead.

"Okay, okay!" I blush, coming to a sudden understanding of what he's referencing.

"Ah, how I love watching the one in a million girl squirm."

"Squirm, huh?" I dance my fingers slowly between the nooks of his hand, making sure to brush him ever-so-slightly. He is not expecting this, and he fidgets in his seat, much to my delight. "Two can play at this game."

"See," Videl growls. "This is why these damn tingles exist in the first place. You're not afraid to shoot me down with your sassy retorts. Remember all those times I hit on you?"

"How could I forget? You went from full-on ignoring me to giving me your undivided attention."

I might be seeing things, but I swear Videl's face droops for a split second before he erects his smile again.

"Maybe I would've stopped hitting on you had you accepted my advances. Do you have any idea how much your refusals—" he pauses in his speech to crane his neck over so his mouth is in my ear, "—*turned me on*?"

The words from his hot breath fanning over my skin cause my face to heat to an unreasonable temperature of a thousand degrees. "N—No, I don't."

"I guess our bodies knew they were made for each other before our heads did." Videl delivers his trademark smirk along with a fellow wink that drives another wave of a few personal seconds of steeling myself by digging my nails into the armrest.

"I don't like how prurient that sounds."

"I know. You *love* how it sounds."

The double yellow line splitting the road in half on his side of the windshield suddenly makes for good staring material, so I keep my eyes on it for a few seconds while I contemplate on what to say next and pray he can't see how red I am in the dimness of his car.

"So, um, what do we do now?" Great. Excellent job, Hope. Way to relapse back into your glossophobic ways.

"Seeing how we're in a moving vehicle, staying buckled in the seat is the safest course of action. So, nothing."

I give Videl a lighthearted slap on the arm. "So I get to call you my boyfriend?" The word draws up an involuntary smile that splits the side of my cheeks.

Videl takes my hand. "Only if I get to call you my girlfriend. Deal?"

"Deal." Then, my voice grows softer. "I've seen how you act with other girls. I don't want to be your object of affection and then get dumped three days later. I've never been in a relationship," I repeat. "A—and I know this is selfish of me, but I would really like it if we went somewhere with—" I point my finger back and forth, "—what we have right now."

Videl cocks one of his eyebrows. "And what do we have right now?"

"This. A bond, a tie together. A trust."

"A mutual passion. Don't worry, Hope. As I mentioned earlier, you're special. I will never treat you as anything less than perfect, so wave your insecurities goodbye while you still have them."

"Do you pinky promise?"

"Is this an unsanctioned contract you Americans propose?"

"Stop being a goofball and take the finger, Videl."

Videl curls his pinky around mine. "I promise."

What's going to happen down the road? Getting into a relationship leads down two paths—on one end, you break up. On the other hand, you marry. But just because two people get married doesn't necessarily mean they're in love.

In love. These two words in my head keep magnifying in a chaotic storm until a big clap of thunder reveals a distant memory in my past. Like dark clouds parting to reveal sunlight, I remember bits of our conversation on the roof of Veronica's house, about true love. What had he said? *When you brush someone for the first time and get shivers through your spine and tingles racing through your fingertips—that right there is true love.*

My eyes grow to the size of saucers.

"Videl, does this mean that we're—" but before I can finish, he interrupts.

"Looks like someone got into an accident." I peel my eyes off him to see blinding blue and red lights flashing in the near distance.

His interjection both annoys and relieves me. I'm still speaking without thinking, and I realize after the annoyance passes that I would certainly have made things too awkward.

"It's fine." I settle with a content sigh. Live for the moment, Haley always said. "At least this means I get to spend more time with you."

Videl rolls his eyes but chuckles nevertheless. The rainfall is heavier now, and even the near-soundproof capsule has trouble blocking out the clanging thuds on his hood. It makes for difficult conversation, so I direct my attention toward the traffic accident.

The flashes of blue and red begin to overwhelm my eyes as Videl drives through the curve in the road where the officers are. He slows down to a proper speed, in case there is a blockade ahead. I put his reduced speed to good use and peer through the window after wiping it clear from the fog.

His car brushes by what seems to be an overturned vehicle in a ditch; the damage the car sustained makes it look more like a messy blob, but this isn't what catches my attention. A portion of the back bumper of the car is unblemished, and I can easily identify the sticker coated on the paint.

"Stop the car, Videl."

"What? But it's rain—"

"I SAID STOP THE DAMN CAR!" I yell.

He slams his foot on the brake and the car squeals, skidding to a stop next to an ambulance. I fumble with the door lock and slam the door open, banging it against the ambulance's decal and recoiling it back into my face. But I hardly register the pain when I see the unmoving, limp figure splayed out on the hospital stretcher. The face is covered by a heavy blanket that's reduced to a red ruin, but even in the darkness, the glint of an all-too-familiar simple diamond ring catches my eye.

I let out a blood-curdling scream, drawing everyone's attention away from the accident and on me instead. My legs begin carrying me forwards at a calculated pace, and then it turns into a full-blown sprint. But for some reason, no matter how fast I run, it's like I'm in an endless corridor; for every three steps forward, I'm lugged two steps back. And then my minute progress is fully halted when heavily built, uniform-clad man steps out in front of me.

"Miss, you need to stand back," the EMT sternly says, grabbing my shoulders.

"LET ME THROUGH! THAT'S MY MOM! THAT'S MY MOM!" I shout hysterically, wildly waving my arm in front of his face.

The EMT's face contorts into a pained expression, but he remains adamant.

"I'm sorry miss, but as much as I want to let you through, I can't. Standard protocol,"

"Screw your rules!" I bellow at him. "My mom is *dying*!"

"I—" The man tumbles to his back on the ground. I whip my head around, and see Videl.

"Go, Hope!" Videl encourages me. "Go!"

I continue to weave my way through the small crowd of people, darting forward to the stretcher. Some adults shoot me strange looks, but no one else stops me. My feet pound furiously through the slippery pavement, trekking through deep puddles of collected water without care until my balance slips and I fall face-first into the mud. I release a desperate sob before pulling myself up. I hear Videl behind me calling my name, but I don't stop until I reach her. I yank her hand into mine. It's warm, but there is no pulse.

"No...no! No! Mom! Mom!" I hold her unresponsive hand and squeeze it multiple times desperately with my trembling hands. Any sign of life. Please.

"Miss?" Another EMT with a clipboard.

"Please," I plead. "Mom. You have to save her! You have to!"

The EMT's jawline sets into a grim angle.

"We'll do our best, but she's unstable. Your mother is alive but in critical condition. Several of her organs are suffering from internal bleeding, not to mention severe trauma around her head and cervical region. At this rate, we need to transfer her to the hospital as soon as possible. Would you like a ride?"

"What are her chances of sur—survival?"

The EMT sighs despondently and my heart sinks. "I'm going to be upfront with you. It's very low. The odds are against her. She's going to need a miracle. Even if she pulls through, there's most likely going to be permanent damage. We're going to get her to the hospital so the doctor on call can begin operating on her. Would you like a ride?" he repeats consolingly, but my ears seemed to have tuned out everything he says after handing me Mom's chances. I was hoping he would say he didn't know, or maybe fifty-fifty, but he handed me the minuscule fraction like it was nothing.

"I'll take her," Videl interjects from my side, appearing from nowhere. "Come on." He tugs my hand, and my feet begin shuffling with the rate of his footsteps.

"Hope? We need to move faster, come on," Videl encourages, but that just makes me trudge my feet even slower. He stops me a few seconds later and then picks me up in a single flourish; one arm under my shoulders, the other under my knees.

The five-minute drive to the hospital is done in silence and feels like an hour. I'm vaguely aware of the steady dripping of water from my wet clothes onto Videl's interior, ruining it, but I can't bring myself to care. His eyes shine with obvious worry, flickering back and forth between me and the road. The leather seat warmers and the front heater are cranked to the max, but I'm shivering uncontrollably. The foggy windshield distorts the siren lights of the ambulance. Everything passes in a blur.

Videl tails the speeding ambulance closely, and when we arrive, the EMTs unload the stretcher and rush to wheel Mom through the emergency doors. Videl and I follow suit, bursting through the double doors just in time to see the foot of the stretcher disappear inside an operating room. I dart forward with qualms to follow, but I slam headfirst into the unbudging door.

"Let them do their thing," Videl whispers after he catches me from my disequilibrium. "The doctors will save her."

"Don't. Just don't," I breathe out. "Don't give me empty words that hold no promise." I sink into one of three chairs conveniently placed next to the operating room and bury my face in my hands, staring through my fingers at the tile floor with shocked, wide eyes. How can the best day of my life U-turn into this abomination?

Beside me, I hear the sound of Videl shuffling into the next chair. I'm prepared to bunker down into the recess of this grating chair for the whole night if it comes down to it. And that's exactly what we do.

The wait is the longest wait of my life. Only the tick of a clock's second hand and the pitter-pattering of the rain outside offers some resistance from the insanity creeping closer and threatening to consume my psyche. Every now and then I can vaguely discern some muffled voices behind the door followed by some intervallic banging, but it's meaningless. My hands are clammy, and I'm in a state of discomfort from my damp clothing stuck to my skin.

Videl looks no different. His eyes are glassy and focused straight ahead at the blank white concrete wall. Only the steady rising and sinking of his chest lets me know he's still alive. Am I?

I can't even distinguish reality anymore. Although everything is taken in by my visual senses facilely, it's not registering in my brain until a few seconds later. It's like I am riding off another high from the kiss earlier tonight, only there's nothing good about this.

The night drags on, and my distress continues to stampede on. I lose track at how many times I observe the digital clock above the empty nursing station, but the tally's so high that I've now memorized the finer details of the clock. The chipped corner below the six...the pitch of a fifth octave E stemming from the metronomic strum of the second hand…I find myself subconsciously storing these useless bits of information, saving them for later. Perhaps my brain is distracting me from the upending news.

One hour passes and it's midnight. I hear the faint chimes of an unknown church bell through the noisy gale outside.

Two hours and it's one. The hall lights automatically shut off and would be the reason for enveloping darkness, if not for the buzzing 'In Progress' bulb fixed above the operating room door.

Two o'clock passes.

I am misled into thinking the operation is done when the door flies open, but it's the nurses steadying their stomachs. Blood stains are all over their clothes and surgical masks, and both look worse for the wear; pallid skin and queasy countenances are easily distinguishable, even for a poor empath like me. Their discomposed physiques didn't help alleviate my hysteria one bit, and I am too nervous to ask about Mom's condition in trepidation of receiving a negative response. But the answer…the answer is just so *blatant* in their furtive and somber whisperings. So I return back to twiddling my thumbs and superfluous praying. It's the only thing I can do.

Thirty minutes past two in the morning, the door creaks open for the final time, and the doctor steps out. I peel myself off Videl's sticky clothes and make sure to keep my eyes on her bloody, ostentatious leather shoes, sending out one last prayer before slowly scrolling up to her face. But when I see her doleful, downcast, and sanguinary face, my hope instantly disintegrates, disappearing in a puff of smoke.

She shakes her head mournfully and at that exact moment, time freezes, and a part of my soul disappears.

"We couldn't save her," the doctor sniffs before blowing her nose into a ragged tissue. "I'm sorry."

I stand frozen and uncomprehending. It can't be…Mom is…dead?

The doctor suddenly morphs into the last image I had of Mom this morning, and for a split second, I really think it's her standing in front of me. But then the picture shatters, jerking me back to reality, and all I see is the doctor and her blonde hair. And then I snap.

I wring my hand free from Videl's, and I storm over to the doctor before grabbing her collar and pushing her against the wall with fueled strength from my unshackled wrath. She begins wheezing for air when I squeeze my other hand around her throat so tightly that even I can see stars. And the sickest of it all is that in the back of my head, I get pleasure from choking her.

"You call yourself a doctor?! How can you let her die?!" I scream at her, my spit fusing with the remnants of Mom's congealed blood smeared on her face. "How?! I thought you knew what you were doing! I trusted you to save her!" I release the hand choking her throat and claw at her body, trying to inflict physical scars to her as retribution for the emotional ones carved into me. "I—I—"

"Hope!" I hear Videl's alarmed voice at the unexpected outburst, and then my arms are pulled back by his enormous strength. The doctor topples and slinks to the floor with her back against the wall. Her hands shoot to her throat and begin massaging the bruised area. Pathetic whimpering noises escape her lips.

"I'm going to kill you!" I shriek deliriously. "You hear me?! I hate you! You don't deserve Mom's blood on you! Give it back! Give *her* back!"

"That's enough, Hope!" Videl shouts. He apologizes to the surgeon while I have my apoplectic fit. The adrenaline is still coursing through my veins, and because my arms are restrained, I land a successful kick to her shins, laughing as a painful expression works its way on her face.

At this point, Videl is done trying to excuse my irreverent behavior and begins dragging me out of the hospital instead. My legs are dangling loosely on the ground, and I'm still trying to break free from his deadlock like some unstable, deranged patient in a mental institution. I let out a strangled cry of pure fury, a sound inhuman and primal—the kind of emotion reserved only for the deepest pain, and I continue bellowing fatuously until the visibly shaken figure of the doctor escapes from my field of vision.

"Hope, you need to get a grip on yourself. This isn't healthy!" Videl chastises after we're outside of the hospital in the pouring rain.

I laugh emptily. Rain seeps into my mouth. It's blood. My mother's blood.

"Get a grip on myself? Get a grip on myself?! You can't *begin* to imagine how I feel!" I scream, clutching at my heart.

"I know you're upset, but you have to calm down! This isn't you, and at this rate, I'm afraid you'll only end up hurting yourself!"

"Fuck you, Videl! Let—let go of me!" I curse the foul word out loud for the first time in my life, and I'm struck by a momentary sense of gratification at my circumvented release. He withdraws from my hands as if they are a hot iron poker burning into his flesh, but I'm not done venting my frustration.

"Yeah, you hear me, *God*?!" I spit mockingly, whirling around and throwing my hands up in the air. "Fuck you, too!" I scream at the heavens. "First Dad, now Mom? HOW CAN YOU DO THIS TO ME?!" Thunder crepitates dangerously nearby as I pound my fists into the empty air. The rain begins pouring harder, almost as if He himself heard my curse, but my anger is so palpable that it melts the drops away as soon as they touch my burning skin.

Videl's arms snake around my chest, and I try to throw him off by bucking wildly.

"F—Fuck you!" I shout again. But he doesn't release me this time, and after a few failed attempts, my fueled anger seeps out from the pores of my skin and evaporates. The fight goes out of me until I slump in Videl's chest and all that is left is a swarming mass of guilt. Guilt from abusing the doctor in my petulant manner, guilt from cursing the heavens and Videl, and guilt from how disappointed Mom would be if she saw the way I was acting right now.

"When will life stop being so unfair?" I choke out. "When will it get better?"

"I don't know, Hope; I don't know. But let it all out. I've got you," Videl says in a soft, comforting voice.

And then it just explodes out of me. I release an anguishing howl and burst into tears on Videl's shoulder. I sob hopelessly in his shirt. I cry for my messed up life and my bleak future, but most of all, for Mom's absence. I cry my eyes out until the sun's rays peek out from beyond the horizon, until my cheeks are swollen and my vision is blurry.

But it accomplishes nothing. Mom is still dead.

10*

The stars twinkle, millions of miles away, without a care in the world. Why would a celestial being like them care about anything as trivial as earth? They don't care about a measly human. I keep telling myself that to the scope of the universe, Mom's death is nothing—just another lost soul fragment in the abyss. But I can't, because to me, it's everything.

I always thought Dad's death was an accident. And now, every time I close my eyes, I see Mom's bloodied, limp hand. Someone who was so full of life but void of any on the stretcher fills me with an overwhelming fear. I hate fate. I fear fate. I fear how powerless humans are. What are the chances both my parents are gone? What are the chances she died that night? Was it because of me? Because something major in my life changing—going on a date with Videl—drew out a counterforce on my closest loved one?

It's my fault. I'm the source of the vicissitude. If only I had been back in time, before Mom left for the restaurant. I could have gone to the restaurant with her. I could have taken the wheel as it was slipping out of control and pulled the car over on the shoulder until it safely slowed to a crawl.

It's true that my presence could have affected the car's performance and nothing would have actually happened. Even the smallest shift in events can arbitrarily change future phenomena. The butterfly effect. Chance. It's all chance. We would have made it to the restaurant. I could've proceeded to talk with the manager and appeal for a surprise dessert for Mom's birthday.

The uneasiness rumbles in my stomach. It doesn't feel right for Mom's cupcake to spoil away in the depths of the refrigerator. I'm letting Mom's memories wilt away. So I nudge Videl with my arm gently. After ten minutes of copious protests, Videl drives me to my home.

Roger's car is absent from the driveway, and the house lights are off.

Videl sits silently in the driver's seat, watching me as I pull out the key from my pocket and unlock the door before stepping inside. The same unidentifiable book that Mom was absorbing when I came down the stairs that morning is still laying on the table at the head of her seat, its pages begging to be flipped again. My heart clenches so tight the pain is real. I ignore the name of the book—if I didn't know before, then I don't want to know now.

I scurry up to my room and remove the red-wrapped box still tucked behind the vicinity of my dresser and head back downstairs. For the first time in my life, I sit in Mom's seat. Then I unwrap the foil gently until the music box in its entirety is naked to the visible eye, right beside the book.

The fridge's contents are still resting on their respective shelves as I rummage through the groceries—I remember, because I tucked the cupcake in the back. And it's still there. My hands reach past the lightbulb into the reclines of the top shelf until I wheedle out the red velvet cupcake with the inserted candle that I had added in the night after purchasing it. Gingerly cupping the sweet, I walk back to the table and turn off the kitchen light before setting it down on the other side of her book. Part of me is overwhelmed with the desire to take the cupcake and dip it in hot wax to preserve it forever, but that's not how cupcakes, let alone desserts, are meant to be seen as. So with utmost care, I peel the wrapper off and light the candle up with a match. It takes several tries, but soon enough, I can see my hands again.

I wind the key in the side of the music box. The beginning of 'Happy Birthday' begins to play. I turn my eyes to the flickering flame of the candle, steadily watching the fire dance back and forth. And when the music comes to an end, I blow the candle out and make a wish. The smoke lingers in the air, and my nostrils involuntarily flare when I breathe in the odiferous scent.

I watch the wax slide down the candle until it stops moving. The smoke has disappeared. Lifting the cupcake, I slowly lean in before taking a calculated dime-sized bite. My mouth feels like sandpaper, so it takes a lot of effort for me to swallow, but I do so anyway before returning in for another bite. This time, it's bigger.

I eat the whole cupcake in less than a minute. And then I cry.

A/N*

Have you ever lost anyone close to you? You stand in the hallway at school, staring in the desolate corner, but there's no one there. The whole time, you know there's an absence, but it doesn't hit you until you start pondering deeply. Start thinking about all the conversations the two of you had. The hugs you shared. The aroma, the scent of their body covered in the clothes you were so accustomed to seeing. The stupid, snarky change in pitch of voices when the two of you fought and laughed and cried together. Then it's all ripped away. The emptiness strikes. You feel hopeless, nauseous, scared, angry, frustrated, afraid—every negative emotion you could ever think of jumbled into a mess hitting you square in the heart. Never again would you receive a text message. Never again would you hear their voice. Never again would you dedicate your personal time and agenda. You will never see your friend again.

When I was young and naïve, happy in my own little world, I believed nothing bad could ever happen to me. All those shootings and deaths on the news and unfortunate scenarios people found themselves in—I thought I was immune to those things. But then Dad died. You'd never expect to lose a parent so early in your life. But when harsh reality rained down on me, through the whirlwind and torment of emotions, I realized one thing: the just-world hypothesis doesn't define life. Bad things happen to anyone.

After Dad's death, I couldn't have told you how many times the thought of losing Mom perpetually attacked my mind. But I had always shrugged off the nagging entity, placing my hopes and beliefs that no other misfortune could occur after my first loss—bad luck, if you call it that, only strikes once.

But that wasn't the case. Mom had left me too.

You would think in almighty severity that God would give you a break, but no, no one knows how He works. There are innumerable amounts of people in this forsaken world breaking the law and rebelling against morality, and yet they go by unscathed by the hand above our heads to the point where it's laughable. Their deeds continue on the path of self-benefit at the expense of the virtuous—what a convoluted charade. Bad things happen to good people. The innocent get caught in wars. The innocent become victims of petty crime. The innocent lose their lives. There is nothing the innocent does that warrants severe punishment, yet the purity itself isn't enough to keep God satisfied. Iconoclastic, but the only explanation for all the pain and agony is this: there is no god.

The shrilling from the phone's ringtone was the only remote noise that had sounded in the room for the last few hours. A man's voice, void of emotion, had introduced himself and pretended to care by spewing bromides and false reassurances. He had filled me with information from the coroner's office regarding Mom's cause of death and attempted to schedule a time for her funeral. I had told him whenever was fine, but the one thing he had told me right before we parted farewell—that the decedent had no will left behind, and thus, all her possessions would transfer to Roger—made me chuck my phone over to the other end of the room, where it made wall contact with a loud explosion. The sound had alerted Videl, and he rushed into the room and took a single look at the phone helplessly shattered into a million pieces before a look of understanding flitted across his face.

The funeral itself was no new experience—I had already been previously conditioned to the dull, wet weather and the somber environment through Dad's burial. Videl and I had gone together, him in a black suit and pants with a black tie and white undershirt, and me with a black dress accompanied by some accoutrements.

We had walked through the unlocked gates after finding a parking spot outside the cemetery to refrain from disturbing the peace. The priest had garbed himself in a black alb with an even darker chasuble. I had almost wanted to laugh at how attentive people were to funeral attire. Because Mom was Catholic, the priest was in a Eucharistic vestment as opposed to a non-Eucharistic one—but honestly, who the hell cared? Your symbol of respect isn't going to resurrect Mom.

The casket's design had not been a respectable reflection on the attire of the funeral's attendees. Six dirt-caked strips of wood hammered together in an elementary manner were Roger's own creation—he had told the funeral home that Mom would've wanted something handmade and simplistic. He had tarnished her memory.

There had been two dozen chairs, but only four was filled by the time the funeral had started—the low turnout wasn't from how unexpected Mom's departure was, but from how few friends and associates she had ever acquainted herself with.

Videl and I had sat down next to a woman hiding her face behind a black cloth that dangled under her beret. She was sitting next to Roger. After realizing the four of us—excluding the priest and sexton—were the only ones there, the seats were forgotten as we all stood up and bundled in a small semicircle.

The rain had poured harder and harder with each passing minute of the priest's scripture recitation. I had wondered whether there was some entity mourning Mom's departure or if the rain had been a tribute to her accomplishments. Either way, it hadn't mattered. She had already glided over to the other side of the veil.

After the priest had finished his sermon, he asked if anyone had anything to say. Roger took this opportunity and walked to the front of the few. His chest had heaved with fake sobs before he delivered a eulogy about Mom being the love of his life, all while glowering at me during his speech interludes. After a few more minutes of nonsensical sputtering, the priest had asked if anyone else had anything to say after shooting questionable stares at how tawdry Roger's acting was. Ten seconds of silence later, the sexton had lowered the coffin into the grave. Dirt had been spilled on top, and then Mom disappeared. Forever.

I had walked over to the mound of fresh dirt before giving Mom a late introduction as to who Videl was. Tears emerged after a distant memory of Mom and me sitting at the kitchen table discussing piano duets. They casually dripped out and watered the grass that would soon grow on top of her grave.

I was mute. My whole body had been numbed. Denial was my anesthetic.

Mom had seemed so excited that I was doing something new with my life, but I wondered what she thought when the school called the house to announce my disappearance on the day Videl and I went to the amusement park. During junior year, I had skipped many days from the shock of losing Dad, but Mom had made sure to ingrain in my head the importance of education. Through her anger and disappointment, there had been something else: worry.

Unknowingly to me, she had scheduled an appointment and took me to the doctor's office one day. She had paid several hundred dollars to have the man prod me with sticks, only for him to diagnose me with depression through a mnemonic, SIGECAPS. The ride to the pharmacy had been equally unpleasant and silent. After telling me to stay put in the passenger seat, Mom had disappeared through the automatic entryway to the building and was gone for almost an hour before I heard the car door manually unlock. Her face was crestfallen, and I knew it had to be because of the medication, so I took a cheating glimpse at the receipt in Mom's hands as she tried to hastily tuck the medication into the glove compartment of her car. She couldn't though because I had exploded at her, clawing at the bottle of pills in the brown paper bag with my hands in a desperate attempt for her barge back into the dispensary and get her thousand dollars back. I had screamed at her and called her names, ordering her to return them. But then my efforts stopped. Mom had finally moved by turning to her side so that she faced the window, right before she collapsed her head down into her hands and began sobbing.

That was the first time I had ever seen her fall apart into such a vulnerable state—even when Dad died, she would never show any signs of weakness in front of me. Her despair had wrenched my guts together—there is nothing worse than seeing a loved one cry. At that moment, all the fight drained out of me, and I vowed to myself I would give up on the comatose state. If I were to suffer, no one would see it.

My legs had given away on top of Mom's grave, and I collapsed to the ground. My knees splashed into the mud, but I paid them no heed. My face was in my hands, and I began sobbing uncontrollably, the same way Mom had the day of the pharmacy trip. I lost both my parents. Two people that I loved more than anything in the world—violently stripped away from me. If it's one thing I will always remember, it's this: you can't outrun fate.

12

In the last week, the temperature took a sharp plunge from jacket weather to full-blown parkas, but the weather remains dry and freezing with no sign of the usual snowfall. The toboggan hats and balaclavas under the heavy hoodies I spy in the hallways make it impossible to discern whether a student is male or female. At the same time, anonymity provides a sense of security.

The last exams before my finals in music theory, calculus, and astronomy are handed back, scores dropping no lower than an eighty. We discuss entropy and enthalpy in chemistry; Stern continually urges me to practice for the talent show. In psychology, papers are handed back to us with the teacher's spit. I don't understand why they have to lick their fingers clean at our expense.

In fact, school is so mundane that I find myself deliberately causing small bits of trouble to keep my mind off things. Haley and I pass notes in class like prepubescent schoolgirls. I abandon my notes and instead doodle stick figure comics. But the most impressive feat of all is in chemistry lab. An undetected nudge from my elbow and I spill sodium hypochlorite on Altha's cardigan. Bleach. It's only a couple of milliliters but, oh boy, Altha's reaction is priceless.

"Mr. Stern!" Altha screeches. "Mr. Stern!" Around us, every student pauses in what they're doing as their eyes fall on an evident circular patch of white on Altha's red shirt.

These changes help me to stay sane. But the biggest trouble I cause goes far over the edge. One day after class, I spot Veronica and her cronies walking from across the parking lot over to where I am. Even from the distance I'm at, I can spot the snarl smeared on her face as she power walks over. Videl's hand tightens around mine, but before he steps forward, I yank him back. We share a tacit look.

"Hey, *Hope*," Veronica sneers bellicosely once she's standing a few feet in front of me. She has three friends behind her, and by their outfits, they just got out of cheerleading practice. Haley mischievously pokes her head out from Veronica's back and gives me a sly wink.

"You sure are belligerent, aren't you? I see you brought your friends this time," I say with more confidence than I feel.

"You need to be taught a lesson, *bitch*," Veronica sneers again. "Videl belongs to *me*. I don't know what kind of lies you fed him, but you've brainwashed him. Videl would never leave someone like me!"

"Do you realize how desperate you sound, Veronica?" I ask. She takes a menacing step forward, but I put my hand out.

"Listen here, *Veronica*. Videl will never, *ever* get back with you! You're a whore, and a free and ugly one at that. Now piss off and stop bothering us before you get your ass handed to you. *Again*," I taunt. Veronica turns red with anger and embarrassment. The only way to preserve her ego for a close-minded human being like her is to jump into action.

"Get her!" At Veronica's behest, two of her fellow cheerleaders rush forward with menacing looks on their faces, but they instantly go down and smack the pavement with a dull shuffle thanks to Haley's extended foot. It is almost comical in a sense, and I can't help but start laughing hysterically until a fist smacks me in the jaw and shuts me up.

"Oww!" I howl, rubbing the area with the heel of my palm before my senses kick into action. Veronica swings another fist at me—more like a slap—and I easily dodge it before kneeing her in the gut and causing her to start gasping like a ghost timidly trying to scare humans. But this time, she doesn't give up so easily. She recovers fast and then starts running at me until we collide and knock into the ground, with my back against the pavement. Out of the corner of my eye, I see Haley with a pleased smirk on her face, almost as if she's enjoying the show between two enemies trying to kill each other.

"Jesus," I pant, trying to deflect her attacks. "You're so heavy!"

Veronica screams and punches me square in the nose this time, and I immediately feel warm liquid sloshing all over my face. Breathing from my nose is nigh-impossible now. Some of the blood seeps into my mouth, and I hack an uncouth loogie before spitting it on Veronica.

Bullseye. The loogie, mingled with snot and blood, lands right in her left eye. She immediately screams and relinquishes me before tumbling off to the side and rolling about in the grass. I scramble to my feet and kick her three times, giggling at how her butt jiggles in the process.

Veronica's skirt is inverted, pulled up on her stomach, and everyone around us—in the circle they formed—begins laughing at her. When Veronica finishes cleaning her face void of my DNA, she realizes what's going on. Blushing to the shade of almost purple, she yanks her skirt back down and gives up on any plan of counterattack, sitting there like a guilty child.

I feel Videl's hands wrap around my waist. "I'm proud of you. You stood up for yourself without losing your temper this time."

"She had it coming. And she dese—" The words die away in my throat when Videl suddenly leans forward and catches my lips, still stained with blood, in the parking lot for the whole school to see. I find myself responding to his hypnotizing touch, and before long, all background sounds fade away.

We remain immersed in the kiss for minutes or hours. I don't understand how I can't be searing him right now with how red I am. My jaw smarts from Veronica's punch, but Videl's kiss is a remedy, healing all maladies.

Videl gives me one last peck before pulling away, and my eyes immediately dart around to see a variety of emotions stirring on everybody's face. Nearby, Veronica sits with evident defeat on her face.

"Can we leave? Right now, please." I tug his sweater in the direction of the car. Already I hear my name circulated amongst the crowd like some circus act.

"I don't think you'll have to worry. Here comes the principal." Videl's gaze flits over my shoulder, and I follow his eyes to see the principal coming toward us in unconventional jogging attire—a brown checkered suit with matching pants topped with a red tie that, at best, was a fad two decades ago.

"Who is responsible for this insubordination?" he spouts as soon as he reaches us. His face is already a shade of puce—perhaps from his obvious lack of exercise—and his mustache quivers like it has a life of its own.

"Um…you see—" I raise my hand nervously. The student body exercises a wide berth around me, as if I am contagious.

"You. What is the meaning of this?" he directs toward me, exercising his prerogative. Thank god Videl steps in.

"Veronica started picking a fight with Hope. She tried diplomatic matters, but Veronica wouldn't have it, and she resorted to physical violence instead."

"Is this true?" the principal asks, spinning on his feet to look at the remainder of the students who have yet to clear the scene. Most of them are milquetoasts, but a few girls nod their heads fervently. I clear my throat; the last time I checked, me taunting someone isn't interchangeable with diplomacy.

"Well, then." He blinks a few times then points a finger at Veronica and her two friends dumb enough to still be by her side. "You three ladies are suspended for a week." Catching my smirk, he redirects his finger to me as well.

"I'm sorry, but school policy calls for all involved parties to be dealt the same punishment. You and Mr. LaBelle will also carry out a weeks' worth of suspension." My face morphs into one of shock. A week? A whole week?!

"What?! It was all in self-defense! I didn't do anything wrong! This—This *bitch* just came up to me and started harassing me!"

"Language, Miss—"

"Valentine," I answer tersely.

"Valentine," he repeats. "As I just said, all parties involved must deal with the same punishment. I will personally be the one to notify your guardians."

The principal finishes his condemnation and smiles to himself, his mustache quivering like some rodent in the cold. "And young lady, I suggest you wipe yourself off. And as for the rest of you—" he elevates his voice to a yell, "The fight's over! So unless you want to stick around watching nothing, I suggest you all resume your schedules!"

"Are you serious?!" I hiss after we grab our schoolwork from our teachers. "A week of suspension? What am I going to do? This is going to tarnish my college applications!" I know Roger isn't going to do anything when the principal calls him, so all that is left for me to worry is the record that is going to be on my transcript.

"Oh, just *what* are you going to do? It's not like the suspension entitles us to spend our time cooped up alone. Don't know why the bugger gave *me* a week of suspension too."

"News flash, Videl. Just because you take gratification in an uncompleted education does not mean I do!"

He stops in his tracks when we're in the parking lot, spins me around, and fiercely kisses me again, shutting me up.

"Relax," he says after we break apart. "I'd prefer this wouldn't happen either, but there's no use crying over spilled milk. Let's enjoy the time we have together."

I have to admit—although never out loud to Videl—that the five days pass more enjoyably than I ever could have imagined, for several reasons.

I'm so sick of rising at the same time every weekday morning only to attend school, but what choice did I have? School is essential, and if anyone can do it, that means I can put up with a few years of attendance. Waking up whenever I want to gives me a sense of control over my life. Something different. Something liberating.

Altha seems to have given up on her attempts to chide Videl for his pick in a significant other and does not bother me either. In fact, I hardly even see her in the house at all, except for a couple of times when I wake up in the middle of the night craving a glass of water. Bastien's already asleep, but Altha is usually in the living room, busily tampering away on her phone as if she was ready to go somewhere. A quick raise of her head sees me moving behind the sofa, and a quick dip of her head returns her back to her business.

On Wednesday, Videl and I take his car and drive up to Carmines, the Italian restaurant. I was craving gnocchi again. We eat and play games with no interruptions this time. On the way out, we ask an elderly couple passing by to take our photo.

After the meal, he drives us back to the abandoned amusement park, and we climb the roller coaster. The trip up to the sky still gives me an adrenaline rush. I lean into Videl while his back is against the railing. In the distant background where our school lies, students swarm about like ants in a colony, bustling their way to class. I swear I can even hear the bell. We admire the majestic view and the enrapturing display of orange explosions as the sun sets.

"Let's join the talent show. It's after New Year's, a week after school resumes," I tell him.

Videl breaks out into a smirk. The sun casts a beam of light on his head.

"About time. I've been trying to prove just how musically gifted I am without coming off as a complete douche."

The weekend passes in a hurry, and before long, it's Monday morning. No more suspensions. The shrill sound of the alarm pierces through my eardrums and into my skull after a week of absence. Videl and I slowly drag ourselves into the tutoring classroom, where I began quizzing him on ratio tests with several intermittent restroom breaks. We abandoned the library a long time ago. Ever since news of our relationship leaked out, girls have stopped trying to approach him. The stares are still here, but who cares?

The door bangs open and Haley barges in, her eyes growing wide when she spots Videl.

"Hope? Can I speak to you?"

I detect the urgency in Haley's voice, and the dark foreboding tone unsettles me.

I think to myself. I'm sure it's bad news, and I try thinking back a few days. Did we have a disagreement or something? I don't think so…my phone wasn't even on.

"What is it?" I ask her. Beside me, Videl encouragingly squeezes my hand. The pleasant tingles lessen the butterflies swimming in my stomach.

"Alone, please." Haley's voice is pusillanimous and borderline primitive, and I almost do a double-take at how distraught she sounds.

"Um, okay," I agree, turning to Videl. He shrugs, letting me know he isn't sure of the situation either. But he respects Haley's wishes and stands up, planting a soft kiss on my lips before leaving the classroom.

"Where were you? I texted you at least a hundred times!" she hisses.

"Whoa, Haley! I wanted some undisturbed time with Videl. Are you okay?"

Haley's shoulders visibly relax. Then she looks at her feet, shuffling them awkwardly. "Well, I'm not too sure how to start, so I'll just tell you what I heard from Veronica this morning."

"What's wrong? Did Chad do something?" She shakes her head.

"No, that's not it."

"Did you lose your cheerleading scholarship?"

Again, another shake of her head.

"Does it have anything to do with me?" I keep guessing.

"Yeah."

"Is Veronica trying to get me expelled this time?"

"N—No, it's about Videl."

"What did you hear?" I ask her, and my voice holds a strange alacrity to it.

"I—I—" Haley is beginning to stumble over her words so severely she's shaking. She never has an issue stringing words together.

"Haley, Haley! Calm down!" I jump to my feet and hold her hands, rubbing them in encouragement.

"I'm sorry, I'm sorry!" She shakes her head from side to side in distress, panting heavily.

"Look at me, Haley, breathe." I place my hands to each of her cheeks and pull her face to me. She tries avoiding my eyes at first, but at the close range we're in, it only takes a few seconds before her orbs locks onto mine. "Now tell me what's *wrong*."

"I—I heard—outside the hallway this morning—overheard Veronica laughing to one of her friends—she said that Videl was just *using* you for some bet he made with Chad! To d—date you for a month, and that—that he doesn't actually like you!" Her legs buckle below her but I catch her, and she begins to sob into my shoulders. "I'm sorry! I'm so sorry! I should have found out sooner!"

A pit of despair formulates in my stomach, but I try my best to stay optimistic. I've seen the trustworthiness in Videl. Every touch and memory we shared—it couldn't be fake.

"Haley, relax. It's probably just some stupid rumor. Veronica's been trying to get back at me ever since she saw me at his house, and ever since she was humiliated in front of the whole school to see," I tell her. Even though my words hold merit, my reassurance is half-assed; Inner Hope is chanting 'I told you so' at the top of her lungs. The insecurities I've suppressed deep inside are starting to crawl out. What if, by some tiny sliver of a chance, Videl *was* just using me?

"No! You should've heard her, Hope! Veronica wasn't saying it because she knew I was eavesdropping on her! She was bragging about it at the top of her lungs! She said she overheard Chad and Videl talking about it themselves just half an hour ago!"

"Haley, deep breaths, sweetheart. Videl has never given either of us any reason to suspect him of foul play." I pat her on the back awkwardly until her sniffing is reduced to a minimum. "I'm certain it's just a stupid rumor," I repeat.

"I'm worried for you, Hope. I feel like such a monster telling you this because I know how he makes you, but I need to as your best friend. Please talk to him."

"I'll ask him," I promise her.

"I really hope I'm wrong," she lets out a nervous laugh, squeezing me tightly.

Yeah, I really hope so too.

The whole day passes at the pace of a snail, and I find myself staring at the mounted clocks more than my teachers' chalkboard in all of my classes. The sinking feeling in my stomach fails to resolve, and honestly, I'm dreading the confrontation. Maybe I can stall for time. No, no. That won't help.

I've always known many relationships come and go, and I don't want to lose Videl. And if our discussions about true love are true, then we are meant to belong. And if we are meant to belong, that means the bet isn't real.

A couple of times during the day I even catch myself asking whether Haley was trying to sabotage my relationship with Videl, but I quickly dismiss the ludicrous thoughts from my head before they can grow and scold myself. Haley's a genuine friend; there's no incentive for her to ruin me. And her manic state during her confession…something so emotionally jarring in her frenzied caliber can't be feigned, no matter how good of an actress she is.

The bell signals the end of astronomy, and I'm out of my seat and walking toward my usual rendezvous with Videl before anyone else even leaves their seats. I arrive at our lockers, and I wait there impatiently, tapping my foot and breathing irregularly. My guts are coiled up in a tight knot, and I feel like I'm about to hyperventilate, but I'm going to find out the truth.

After what feels like half an hour, I finally see the lumbering figure of Videl turn the corner of the hallway. His face breaks out into the usual smirk when he sees me, and from this distance, I can't tell whether he's nervous or has any idea of the interrogation he's about to be dragged through.

Videl reaches me and offers a simple, "Hey there," before learning into my mouth, and it takes a lot of willpower not to let him cheek me instead. The sparks are still there, but instead of the elation they usually induce, it feels flat and wrong. Off.

"Everything okay with Haley?" is the first thing out of his mouth after we break apart.

The first thing he asks me is that? Is he worried about Haley, or trying to preserve his secret? I look into his eyes—the genuine sincerity is definitely there. Or was it just a cover, a false image? I can't keep questioning his loyalties anymore. In this split second, I make up my mind.

"Can we talk?" I whisper to him. The last thing I want to do is cause a scene, so I keep my voice at a low timbre, attempting to avoid unnecessary drama.

"Nothing positive comes out of that phrase when a partner in a relationship says those three words, you know?" he points out. I cringe at his valid point but compose myself.

"Videl, I'm serious!" My voice comes out in urgency.

"Okay, okay!" he frowns. "What's going on?" He shoves his hands into his pants—one in each pocket. I've never seen him do that before.

"Is—is—" My voice transitions from confident to insecure in a matter of seconds, and my heart is racing.

"Haley told me that...that I'm a bet." There, I said it. I look up to his face, and my eyes immediately begin swimming painfully with tears. Damn my sensitive bundle of emotions. "Is it true? That you're just using me?" The last word cracks in my throat.

"I d—"

"It's a simple yes or no question, Videl!" My composure starts to slip. All the signs are pointing to the worst—he's avoiding my eyes, shuffling his feet, and biting his lip—all at the same time.

"Haley told me Veronica overheard you and Chad talking about it," I whisper. "I wanted to believe it was all a terrible rumor she started but it's been nagging me the whole day and—and now I just want the truth from you!" My voice is an octave higher than normal, and I'm sure I sound deranged. Like I lost my marbles.

"I—"

"Please tell me it isn't true," I beg him. "Please tell me you feel it." I grab his hand desperately and place it over my left breast, nestling it right over my heart. He stares at me for a few seconds with a strange look on his face, and then slowly pulls his hand away from my chest.

"It's true, Hope," he admits. "I'm sorry."

My world collapses, and I freeze in place, my heart shattering into a million pieces. No…it can't be.

I'm so stunned by his revelation that my surroundings recede. School lockers, student chatter, all of it fades away until all that's left is Videl. The small part of my brain that struggles to keep my faith in him is vaporized, crushed to smithereens like a puny bug by the words from Videl himself. I stare at him blankly. It was all a joke?

"I was just telling Chad that—"

"I don't care! How could you?" I hiss. The venom in my voice is so deep-seated I can practically feel it burning my eyes. Or maybe it was my tears.

"Hope?" His voice laces with concern, and I have to remind myself that it's fake. Everything he does is fake. I can't believe I fell for his act. How could I have been so *stupid*? So stupid as to be so blinded by empty words, by his sweet whisperings of nothing. I should've known better. The popular student and the social recluse, dating? Stuff like that only does exist in fictional romance, after all.

And suddenly, I'm flooded with hate. Hate toward Videl, but mostly hate toward me. And I try to quell them, but the demons control me and shake me until all I see is red. I can't even stand to look at his face right now, so I turn around.

Ignoring him, I begin walking out the double-doors to go somewhere, anywhere away from him, before I lose full control over my actions.

But my progress is halted as I feel a brush of air, and then a tug on my hand. I turn back around, a seething glare plastered on my face.

"Hope, wait! Let me explain!" He caresses my hand, but I feel nothing. No sparks, and no love for him. Only a deep, festering abhorrence. I take a look at his vile hand before shaking his firm grip off me with strength only his betrayal could provide me.

"Don't." My voice is calm, and he flinches at how unfeeling I sound. Hell, it scares even me.

"Please, Hope." It's his turn to beg now, but I just shake my head. Besides utter loathing, I am insensate. I feel nothing.

"I trusted you. I gave you my heart, and all you did was toy with it. Did I ever mean anything to you?" He opens his mouth to answer, but I prevent him from doing so by holding my hand up.

"Don't bother with your excuses. I don't want to have anything to do with you or your sick games anymore. We're done," I intone.

I run out of the hallway and through the teeming mass of students, refusing to turn around. Only the inconceivable, bitter sting of Videl's dishonesty and my anger keeps me going until I reach the closest bathroom to me. And when I enter the stall, the contempt turns into sorrow. I sit on the toilet and cry, letting out all my pent-up emotions, allowing them to seep through the façade I had erected until all that remains are dry hiccups and a hollow heart.

13

"Honey, you haven't been eating much lately. Do you not like the food?"

I look up from my untouched plate of pasta and soup and into her concerned frown. "No ma'am, it's not that—"

"Mom," Haley interjects. "I've told you before to back off. Can you leave her alone? Please."

"Are you sure you're doing well, Hope? You used to eat so much when we had you over last year."

"Mom!" Haley interjects. "Seriously! Please, just give her some space."

Haley's mom purses her lips. "I'll clean the dishes if you two are finished."

Haley nods and pulls me out of the large chair. "Thanks, Mom."

The two of us walk up the stairs and into Haley's bedroom. Leaning against one corner of the wall is a large ten-cubby dresser with a mirror; the counter is littered with Haley's makeup accessories and clothes. The wall next to the dresser is where her bed sits, directly opposite to a large plasma television screen. The last wall has a bright window to peer through, and the opening leads right to the backyard, where we sometimes see deer and rabbits. It still mildly surprises me that Haley's room is clean given the amount of stuff she owns.

"What do you want to do?" Haley asks me. I feel the dip of her bed as she joins me from behind, and then the slight tug of my hair as she begins braiding it.

"I don't know."

Haley sighs. "I miss you, Hope. Are you sure you don't want to charge your phone? You can use my charger."

"No, that's okay."

Haley sighs again. "You know I hate seeing you like this. You don't want to talk about anything? Or do anything? We can watch a movie if you'd like, since we finished our homework yesterday."

"I really shouldn't take up so much of your time. You missed church with your family this morning because of me."

"Don't worry about it."

We sit there in silence. The only occasional sound is the small huff of Haley as she finds some imperfection in whatever complicated braid she is trying to weave.

"I can't believe I was a bet. There has to be an explanation."

The fingers stop, and she drops my hair. Haley scoots herself so that she sits cross-legged across from me. "We can go over the details again if you'd like."

I grab the hem of Haley's sweater. "Please. Start from the beginning. Don't leave anything out."

"Okay, on the morning your suspension was lifted, I was home searching for my cheerleading outfit. I found it, but I arrived at school late. And since my first class is English, I had to cut through the P.E. building to get there. During which I happened to catch Veronica's voice coming from the bathroom next to the coach's office. She was talking about you, and that's why I stopped to listen."

"And then…"

"Then I heard her talking about Videl as well, and then Chad. So with my interest piqued, I leaned against the door—you know, the dark gray one that always has the doorstopper underneath it—and heard her laughing to Francine that, and I quote, 'Videl is playing her so well that even I'm starting to believe he actually likes her. Luckily his bet with Chad ends in a couple of days, so he can finally drop his act and start dating me again.' Once I heard that, I came running to you. I didn't find you in the library, so the only other option was the tutoring room."

"What about over the last few days? I haven't seen Videl at all," I say, tilting my head down toward my kneecaps. "Things ended between us six days ago. And I didn't see him in school for the rest of the week."

"And I said I talked to Chad yesterday."

"I bet they had a good laugh," I murmur.

Haley shakes her head. "Chad said he hadn't seen him either."

"Can you repeat what Chad told you?" I ask Haley. "Over the phone?"

Haley nods. "He wouldn't tell me much, but from what I gathered, Chad was partying after our school's first victory against Palm Valley a month ago and Videl was with him. One thing led to another, and you know…"

"And you mentioned before that there was something strange about Chad's hesitancy over the phone."

Haley nods, and I grab her wrists. She jumps, obviously startled.

"Doesn't that sound at least a little suspicious to you? You two confide and tell each other everything, but like you said, he was acting strangely."

Haley scrunches her eyebrows together. "I don't think he was acting suspicious because he had something he wasn't telling me; I think he was just wary because he knows how close we are. Even though you aren't his favorite person, you're mine, and he respects our relationship enough not to directly harm it."

"S—Still, maybe he just—he just—"

I sink back to the bed, on my side. Haley's hands enter under my drab sweatshirt until I feel her warmth resting over my stomach.

"Hope, I think you're looking too deeply into this. The fact of the matter is…" Haley sighs again, her breath fanning over the back of my neck. "I believe Chad. And I believe what Videl told you out in the hallway."

"I do too," I croak. "But that doesn't mean I can't wish for something different."

"I know it will take a long time to get over him, but you *will*, and that's all that matters."

"I just can't imagine him skipping school because he's s—sleeping around with girls. It makes me s—sick to my stomach."

"Then don't imagine it. I'm here for you, Hope. I always will be. I promise."

We fall into silence until the question that has been in the back of my mind since I first met Haley works its way through to the front and forces my mouth open.

"Why, though?"

"Why what?" The warm breath of Haley washes over my skin.

"Why do you do all this for me?" I query.

"Because you're my best friend."

I wriggle out of Haley's arms and scooch myself so that my back leans against the wall.

"But *why*?! Why are you my best friend?! Why did you decide to come up to me in the hallway after biology class last year when I was putting my books away?! Out of everyone in the class, you chose me. Why me?!"

Haley adjusts herself so we're sitting not even a foot away from each other. "It sounds like you're questioning our friendship. Are you, Hope?"

I look into her eyes. "I just—I mean, *look* at you! You're on the cheerleading team, you're popular, you have the attention of everyone, and—and you're *beautiful*! You're everything I'm not! I'm just—no, I don't doubt us! I'm just—you're my only friend."

"Why is that?"

"They usually take one look at my tasteless clothes—" I pinch my sweatpants to demonstrate my point. "Or see how skinny I am, and then just ignore me."

"So you think there was a reason I approached you other than the fact I just wanted to know you for you? That I had some ulterior motive and would use you like some sycophant?" Haley asks. I nod.

"Well, you're not wrong. I'm really the host of a reality television show and you just so happen to be the lucky contestant."

"Very funny, Haley." But my mouth does morph into a small curl.

"Listen. I didn't come up to you that day because of whatever belief you had of me wanting to use you to make an A in biology. I came up to you because I knew you were hurting. When the only open seat was next to you on the first day, I sat there, and I saw you. As sappy as this sounds, I saw how your face always fell when you thought no one was looking. I saw the lost stare in your eyes. So I came up to you. Because it really looked like you needed someone."

"And what about now?"

"I was there for you then when you were recovering from your father's death, wasn't I? What makes you think I'm going to leave now?"

A never-ending supply of tears fills my eyes. Fate. It always come down to fate. There *is* a reason why she is in my life.

"Come here," Haley says, and I oblige, sinking into her arms. She may be smaller, but she's got the strength of an athlete. Haley fiddles around with some voice-activated system that monitors her television, and a random movie pops up. And this is the last thing I can remember. My eyelids droop until I can no longer stay in the real world. I drift off to sleep, but it isn't long before I wake up.

"Hope! Hope!" My eyes burst open to a space of pitch blackness. Someone is screaming and shaking me roughly. And, once again, it takes me half a minute to realize that the screaming is coming from me.

"H—Haley?" I croak. "Is that you?"

Haley's rests her palm on my forehead and wipes off my sweat. My body feels like it's going through hot flashes. "Yes, it's me, Hope. Did you have another nightmare again?"

I try to move around, but my clothes are sticking to my skin. "H— Haley."

"Shh. Don't worry. I'm here. It's me, Haley. You're with me. I'm real." I can vaguely detect her hands brushing my hair. "It was just a nightmare."

"N—N—No," I gasp. "But Mom d—died."

"I'm here, Hope. I'm here. I'll stay with you until you fall asleep, okay?"

I don't want to sleep anymore, but countless nights of restlessness has taken its toll on my body. Combined with the soothing effect of Haley's touch, I fall back asleep in a few minutes. I fall back asleep into an empty void.

~~~~~~

"Today I will read your partners for your psychology project. Since the last few reminders in class, I hope you've given a thought as to what topic you'll pick because your assignment will be due Thursday, one week from today."

I flip open my notebook and pull out the piece of paper, distributed by the teacher two weeks ago. So that's what this is.

The teacher ignores the loud chorus of grumbles at his announcement and begins reading off the list jotted on his fancy, whatever-it-is kind of notebook teachers buy just to get their sense of coolness.

"Poe, Valentine."

I don't feel like moving so I play around with my mechanical pencil, ignoring the rest of the class until I hear the noise of the feet of a chair scraping. The sound is so nearby that it can represent nothing but my partner.

"Hey."

The greeting isn't what makes me turn around. It's the sound of her voice.

The girl is awfully familiar and idiosyncratic, to say the least. You know how one can tell what kind of social group someone else fits in just by one look at them? The girl is a prime paradigm. I immediately get a hipster mien hovering around her. She has an olive-yellowish skin tone and thin, pink lips. These are first things I observe. Fair and well-built, with light, black eyeshadow but no eyeliner or foundation, she possesses a sense of natural beauty. Her left ear has five piercings—I take the time to count, and her right has a dreamcatcher industrial piercing. She has a grey wash tattoo on her neck, partially peeking out. I can't discern it because the majority is being covered by her half-up, half-down black hair that stops just past her shoulders. My eyes wander down below her face to see her wearing a red and black checkered flannel with a white wife beater underneath. The gray pants that wrap snugly around her thighs and calves finally end with a pair of pitch-black sneakers with even blacker laces.

"Name's Jackie," she introduces. My skin burns as her eyes roam up and down my body.

"Is that spelled with a y or i-e?"

"i-e. Real name's Jacqueline, but don't call me that." She offers me her hand, which I take.

"I thought girls hug."

"I don't do hugging."

"You're what, a germophobe?"

"Nah, hugging makes me feel vulnerable. So, you got any ideas for this dumb project or not?" She shifts her chair closer, and my nose catches a whiff of nutmeg and oil essence.

"I don't know, and I don't care."

Jackie snorts and snatches my mechanical pencil and starts writing something on a piece of paper. My eyes catch the black nail polish articulately coated on her nails.

"Well," I adjust. "Maybe we could do something with music. Maybe research on whether personality correlations with musical taste."

"Sounds lame, but it's not a terrible idea. Let's test it out. What kind of music do you think I listen to?"

"I don't know. Probably alternative or rock."

"I listen to everything except country and rap. So while you're not wrong, you're not completely right either."

I don't know what to say to this, so I just stay silent. A few minutes pass where I hear topics flowing around the room from the mouths of other students. Most of their suggestions sound far beyond ethical, but the majority of them are ignoring the assignment and discussing weekend plans instead. I hear party invites and skating rink plans thrown around.

"You know, you're not very talkative."

I shrug, turning my attention back to her. "Maybe I just don't have much to say."

"That may be true," Jackie says. She scoots up next to me so that our chairs are touching, and then cranes her neck out so that her face is a few inches from mine. Her tattoos writhe, seemingly having a life of their own. "But I think you have lots to say. You just force yourself not to."

"I—I do not," I murmur.

Something flits through Jackie's eyes. One moment I think she's going to laugh at me, and the next I think she's going to kiss me, but in the end all she does is smirk. I take notice on how similar her smirk is to Videl's—the only difference is that hers lips curl up to the left.

I clear my throat. "Do you have any ideas on what our experiment can be on?"

"I've always been inquisitive about drugs. The state of your brain with repeated use of them. Although I doubt we'd get a passing grade writing about that since the idea goes against all ethical morals. Can you imagine the teacher's face if we went up to him and said we were going to start distributing cocaine?"

This brings a small chuckle out of my mouth.

"I knew I could get a smile out of you, sunshine. So why are you in this class?"

"I wanted to go to medical school. Neurosurgeon, preferably. It would have been beneficial for me to have some background knowledge on how the brain works. So your cocaine idea isn't all that bad."

"Wanted. What changed?"

"Dreams die," I shrug. "Things change."

"So make new ones," Jackie says. "There's always a dream to replace a dead one. You just have to search hard enough to find it."

"Yeah? And what if it's too hard, and you give up?" I challenge.

"You won't. Not with the right motivation, whether that be a thing…" her eyes roam from my lips to my face again. "Or person. Why do you want to do the assignment on something music related?"

"I play the piano. It's a reliable pastime for de-stressing."

I see. That's what you're in this class for. You have those fast fingers." She curls her fingers back and forth as if to demonstrate, and the philosophical atmosphere disappears. She has a seductive smirk on her face, and I suddenly understand what image she's trying to display with her actions.

The bell suddenly rings, and as if on cue, the classroom goes into an uproar as chairs push back, books dump inside backpacks, and students jostle one another out the door.

"Well, I guess we got a couple of ideas. Are you up to finishing this project after school today?" Jackie asks as we're getting up.

"I don't care. We can do it now if you're free. The sooner, the better."

"Babe, my schedule is always empty." Jackie laughs and packs up her backpack. "My place or yours?"

"Yours." My body shivers.

"Cool. I don't have my driver's license, so you better not mind walking. It's only a few minutes."

I tell her okay, and we make plans for meeting up in front of the psychology building at the end of the school day. The rest of my classes whiz by, and I tell Haley I'll be busy working on a project with someone. Her face lights up at this; I think she is happy that I am making a new friend—if you can call Jackie that. The tattoo certainly looks new, but her face is oddly familiar. I can't pinpoint where I've seen her before.

Once school ends, Jackie and I walk off campus until we are the only two on a secondary road. The street is fairly similar—I think it's only a couple down from my neighborhood. Jackie and I talk about random stuff, like classes we have or personal interests. I notice she strays away from relationships, and for that, I am relieved.

Before long, we wind our way up through the driveway that leads to a beautiful villa-like home. Made of stucco, it gives a Caribbean beach house kind of vibe. To further complete the picture, there are what seem like palm trees planted in the front. The home is large. In fact, it is so large that I'd be able to live out a comfortable life in a small portion of the house alone.

"Come on in." Jackie is already walking inside, and I follow her tentatively. The front entrance makes way to a long hallway, with two winding staircases—one in the middle of the hallway, and the other tucked off to the side at the end of the hall.

"Nice house," I compliment as we take the second staircase.

"Thanks. I don't visit a lot of the rooms. A lot of boring stuff my parents hoard from their expeditions abroad. My area is at the top corner of the house."

"Oh. Are your parents here now?"

"Nah. Parents hardly ever come home. They're always away on business. It's just me." I feel a sudden surge of sympathy for her.

There are three rooms upstairs. One is a kitchen with two fridges—one is chock-full of energy drinks and void of any real food, and the other is full of bags of groceries. The second is a tiny quaint living room complete with a table, sofa, and flat screen, and the third is Jackie's bedroom—a room that at first glance is completely obvious that she put a ton of time into it, because I feel like I'm in a shrine as soon as I walk through the door. The lighting is dim—a low-wattage floor lamp is sitting in one corner, and the other illumination rises from little bulbs with colored shades, the kind that slowly changes the color of the room. There is a lot of memorabilia that Jackie collected over the years. Indie posters cover every inch of her painted forest green wall; dreamcatchers are installed to screws that drill into the ceiling, dangling down and whispering to each other, and there are tall leafy plants on each side of her bed fanning over the mattress. Her bed sheets are black, and in the corner closest to the curtained window is an easel with a half-complete abstract artwork on it.

"This is neat," I speak in a hushed whisper. "I could stay in here forever."

"No kidding. Sometimes the tickle of the cool air from the AC is more than enough to deter me from heading to school. Blinding lights, you know?" Jackie's voice muffles. I turn around just in time to see her pulling her shirt over her head. Her pants are off, and she's in a pair of tiny booty shorts. I pull my eyes away.

"So you think school lighting is too bright."

"There's no peace and quiet either."

I walk over to the corner. "You're into cars?"

Jackie walks over to my side, tiptoeing so that she can reach the poster.

"Foreign imports only. Japanese."

"What's this?" I point at one of the posters.

"*That* is a 1999 Impreza. World Rally Blue paint. I've always wanted to own one. Take the Impreza or an S15 Silvia over to Japan, drive to the mountaintop and spend the whole night there."

"That sounds liberating."

"It is. Come on; I'll give you a tour of the room."

After a description of all of her posters and little gadgets, she takes me out to the living room outside her bedroom, where we sit down at her table. Jackie brings a couple of energy drinks over and scoots her chair so close to me our shoulders bump.

"Alright, so you want to do the music thing you were talking about?" Jackie says after we pull out our material.

"I thought you thought that was a lame idea?"

"You may have heard those words coming out of my mouth, but lame doesn't equate to a bad grade."

"Okay, so do you want to do personality and music like we mentioned?"

"Sure. I'm not a musical genius like you, so I won't be able to come up with any other experiments of the sort." I nod, and we task ourselves to the assignment, exchanging words here and there.

"Participant pool?" I ask, without looking up. Jackie rummages in what sounds like a plastic bag.

"Thirty. Any more and you'd be stuck in the experiment for days." I nod, then scribble the number down. "Control, correlational, or descriptive?"

"This one would be descriptive. You're just collecting data. There's no control group, nor are you finding a correlation between the two variables."

"Okay, so what I think we can do is just go around campus asking students what kind of music they like to listen to before they take a Myers-Briggs personality test. Or maybe even vice-versa." I jot this down in my notes, stop, then cross it out. "Maybe we should use a different personality test. We'd have too many independent variables. What do you think?" There's no response. "Jackie?"

My head finally lifts up and sees Jackie. A small wave of relief washes over me to know she's still here, but then the feeling changes to confusion. Jackie's digging around in a plastic bag filled with a mysterious material.

"Jackie, what is that?"

"This? Just blow," she answers, without looking up.

"What?" My eyes hone onto the white powder inside the bag. Then it clicks. All the discussions we've had about drugs. Her fascination with the various sorts of substances. And when I speak, my voice is quiet.

"Don't tell me that's cocaine."

"It's cocaine." I grab the bag, and she snaps up. "What? You told me to tell you, so I did!" She grabs a straw, and without hesitation, snorts a line. I had a solid three seconds to snatch the straw out of her hands or brush the drug off the table, but I didn't. And I don't know why.

"Don't be a baby," she sighs in satisfaction, throwing the straw over to me. I catch it and hold it between my index finger and thumb, treating it like a bloodied syringe.

"It's illegal." From what I've read and heard, the substance can make you feel euphoric. Confident and happy, the ability to tackle any problems you have.

"Come on, Hope. You're my friend. This is what friends do. And besides, this shit doesn't come cheap."

I shake my head and hand the straw back to her. "We literally just met an hour ago." My notebook remains forgotten, brushed off onto the side of the table. "I—I hardly even know you."

"We have a connection, but suit yourself," Jackie says, before doing another line.

"This is illegal. How do you know I won't report you to the authorities?"

"You won't," she says. "I can see it in your eyes."

"What's that supposed to mean?"

She winks at me. "Maybe I'll tell you if you take a hit."

I shake my head wildly and state, "I need to leave." Before Jackie has a chance to respond, I grab my backpack and almost trip when I dash out of her room, down the stairs, and out the front door. My heart thuds, threatening to break my ribcage. The image of the white powder burns itself into my retinas. I know there are stoners at Starmount, but cocaine?

"Hope."

I whip around and see Jackie at the front door, her feet bare. My limbs seem to be frozen; I don't move a single inch beyond her front porch.

"You forgot this," she says, and then throws my psychology notebook to me.

"Thanks," I mumble. My feet still refuse to move.

I appreciate you, Hope. You see what others don't."

"What's that even supposed to mean?"

She ignores my question. "I've only got a gram on me right now. There's enough for three more lines."

I hear the unsaid offer in her voice, and I weigh the pros and cons. The downside to doing cocaine? Addiction, mental instability, and more. And the upside? No sense of worthlessness. No sense of feeling out of place in this world.

"N—No, I can't. I'm sorry, Jackie. We can finish this project some other time." I pick my notebook off the ground and stash it in my backpack before dashing away. I get a burning desire to turn around and see Jackie still standing at the front door because I know she is, but I fight this urge down.

~~~~~~

Nothing eventful happens the next two days at school. All of my classes are the same, except with heavy tension in psychology. I never paid attention to Jackie during class before, but now that we've been paired together and I know about her existence and secret, my eyes won't stop flickering from the blackboard to the other side of the room. There has to be a reason behind why she started doing cocaine in the first place. Something had to have instigated her drug habits. I want to walk up to her after class and ask her to confide her insecurities in me, because I *know* she as some—who doesn't? But I can't muster up the mental fortitude to do so. The bell rings, and my feet carry me out the door instead of over to her. Cowardice.

"How are you with the nightmares? Do you think they're getting better?" Haley's questions cut me out from my train of thought as she greets me outside the door. She has been walking me to class whenever she has a moment to, as part of her determination to keep me accompanied at all times.

I blush because I can tell my screaming is deriving Haley of sleep—the thick shade of purple bags under her eyes is proof. "They're still there."

"Are they getting better?" she asks, taking my hands in hers.

"N—No."

Haley frowns, but then perks back up.

"So, I was thinking…let's go shopping after school. I don't have cheerleading practice, and it's been forever since we had a girl's day out."

I bite my tongue. "I'd love to, but I'm planning to head over to the cemetery and see my parents." I bite my tongue even harder. It used to be just Dad. "If you don't mind."

"Oh. Well, I can drive you, no problem! Do you want me to wait in the car for you?"

"No, that's okay. I'll be there for hours. I'll catch a bus. Don't worry about me."

The trip to the cemetery is spent in mostly silence. Haley drops me off in front, telling me to be careful before pedaling out. I immerse myself in the walk as I path deeper and deeper into the cemetery until I reach the tombstones I am seeking.

I've always admired how powerful cemeteries are. As soon as I step into the land of the dead, the temperature feels like it drops a few degrees. There's a kind of smell in the air—musty, filled with silent whispers. I feel encompassed, surrounded by the people that are long gone from this world but not from people's hearts. I'm not alone.

For a blink of an eye, I have a momentous urge to dig through my parents' graves and open the casket lids. But then I remind myself to think logically. They're probably decomposed to the point where their faces are unidentifiable. Instead, I touch both the tombstones, hugging them tightly.

When the night begins to grow dark, the rain begins. At first, it's a soft drizzle, and I can ignore it without too much mental effort. But half an hour later, the rain turns into a torrent, so I get out of the open and catch a bus pulling up to the station.

I get off the bus at the eighth stop. Over the past week, I have come to memorize the details of Haley's neighborhood, so finding her house is a cakewalk. The front door is cracked, so I don't need to pull out her spare key to unlock it.

I slip in soundlessly and sigh in relief when my ears pick up some voices, but then I tense. There are protests, like a hushed argument or something. It sounds like Haley and her mom, and because the kitchen is behind a wall, I can eavesdrop on the two without being seen.

"The school has been calling me. You've been falling asleep in class."

"Yeah." I can't see Haley, but I know her well enough to know that she is sheepishly rubbing the back of her head. "Sorry, Mom. I'm just really tired."

"And not only that, but your grades are slipping. How many exams have you had this past week?"

I hear the sharp intake of air. "Three."

"The school's called me again today," Haley's mom repeats. "Not just for your lack of attentiveness, but also for your failing test scores. They gave me a warning, telling me if you didn't pick up your grades, you're going to be kicked off the cheerleading squad! Do you know what that means?!"

"Yes, Mom, but I won't. Don't worry. It won't happen again."

"If you get kicked off the cheerleading team, then that means you won't be eligible for the college cheerleading scholarship!"

"I'm sorry. I'll make sure this won't happen again."

"Won't happen again? Do you even know the reason behind your lapse in concentration? Because I do." There's a heavy thud.

"Don't go there, Mom. Please."

"You are only this way because of Hope! I was trying to be nice at first and take her under our roof, but I've reached the end of my patience."

There's a short pause. "Mom, please. She has nowhere else to go."

"Nowhere else to go? Are you saying she's homeless?"

"N—No."

"Don't think I can't hear her screaming at night! Look at your eyes, Haley! The bags under them are so dark you don't even look like yourself anymore! That girl has been keeping you up every night!"

"It's not that simple! She didn't ask for this! She can't just turn her nightmares on and off like a simple flick of a switch!"

"I don't care! You're my daughter! She's not!"

"I do!" Haley shouts back.

"I am done having this same argument with you over and over again! I can't see my own daughter fall ill, especially if Hope has her home to go to!"

"She can't go home! Mom, please, I'm begging you! Hope needs me! I'm her only friend. I'm her *best* friend."

"Best friend? All she's doing is taking advantage of your hospitality!"

"She's not ready to be by herself! I'm not going to push her. Please respect that. Let her stay."

"I can't anymore, sweetheart. I just can't. She needs to go, and if you don't force her, then I will. I am telling you—as your mother—to get rid of her!"

"Mom, p—please, please don't—"

Another heavy sound. "Haley! Now!"

There's a pregnant pause. The only sound is the strum of the second hand on the clock mounted against the living room. And then Haley speaks.

"I'll tell her."

I want just to disappear right now. To climb the stairs and grab my suitcase and mix all my clean and dirty clothes together, and bolt out the door without a confrontation. But I can't, because the only way upstairs is past the kitchen.

I walk around the corner, revealing myself. Both their heads turn. Haley's mouth falls before she snaps it shut in an effort to recover herself.

"Oh, Hope! I didn't—didn't see you there." Haley's walks to my front. Her mom is at the counter cutting away at some apples, but I know her attention is on us.

"D—did you hear what we were t—talking about?"

"It was hard not to eavesdrop."

Haley's face crumbles and she shuffles her right foot. A habit I've come to realize is her way of expressing her nervousness.

"Listen, Hope. I—I don't know how to say this," she peeks at her mom. "And you're—well—we—I—you can't..." she takes a deep breath. "Can't stay with us. A—Anymore. It's just—not healthy." Haley looks at her feet.

"I heard everything."

"Yeah. I'm—I'm sorry." She finally gets the courage to lift her head up. We stare at each other for a minute in silence before I push myself forward, taking the stairs two at a time.

"Wait, Hope!"

I briskly wheedle out my small suitcase tucked into the corner of Haley's closet, throwing it on the carpet before dumping any stray content of mine I can find in her room.

"Hope! Just listen!"

"What?!" I spin around to face her. Haley looks like she's forcing her entire will to keep her equanimity. "Listen to what?! You fumbling for a ceremonious goodbye speech?!"

"I don't want to do this, Hope!"

"Then *don't*!"

Haley shakes her head wildly. "I'm sorry! I'm sorry! Please—"

"Is that all you have to say?! I thought I was your best friend!"

"You are! You are!" Haley rambunctiously pleads, taking the opportunity to jump toward me. I flinch backward.

"How can you do this to me, Haley? How can you kick me out when I need you the most?" My composure cracks first, and everything that I've kept bottled up—all the negativity, all of the heartbreak—bursts out. "Y—you know I have no one else to t—turn to! You—" My sob breaks off into a strangled gargle. I pull my suitcase up and rush past Haley back into the kitchen.

"Hope! Don't do this! Wait!" Haley yells at me and chases after me. I would have been outside and gone already if it weren't for my shaking hands fumbling with the stupid door lock.

"Hope, no! Don't! Please!" Haley pleads with tears gushing out of the corner of her eyes, her face in the image of a fallen angel. Both her arms are fastened around my wrists, and she's doing her best to pull me back into the depths of their abode through her blurry vision. Her mother is behind her, and even she looks worried at how emotional her daughter sounds. She seems hesitant, as if she didn't wholeheartedly mean the words she yelled a minute ago.

I can't handle this anymore. This emotion clawing out my insides.

Haley's head swivels between me, standing in one corner, and her mom, standing in the other. Her mom purses her lips and gives a curt nod.

"Please, Hope, please," Haley repeats.

I wring my wrists out of her grasp. Or maybe she relinquishes them.

"Hope!"

I shake my head wildly, refusing to look into her eyes. If I do, I won't trust myself stay upright on my two feet. Instead, I yank the door open and disappear outside, leaving Haley's desperate apologies behind me. The rain is pouring harder than ever, and visibility is no more than a few feet. It's cold, but my body is already numb. The physical sting on my face from my freezing tears and the hole punched through my chest are the only two things I can feel right now. Pain and emptiness.

I run aimlessly with no destination in sight or mind. My brain refuses to function as it tries to absorb the destruction of my only friendship, and this causes my legs to snap several times. I fall to the ground, only to get back up with no purpose. I stumble and stumble, the suitcase banging the back of my heels until I can move forward no more. Because through my blurry vision, I somehow managed to stumble to a familiar door. It takes a lot of mustered effort to bang on the door because my fist keeps sliding down from the rain and tears that coat my skin. Even when I do so, I don't expect anyone inside to hear anything. The crackle of thunder and howl of the wind is too loud.

The door opens a minute later to reveal Jackie standing there in nothing but black underwear and a tank top. Her eyes widen.

"Jackie," I rasp, my voice lost in the roar of the storm. "Jackie."

This is all I have to say. Jackie immediately pulls me inside and kicks my suitcase to the side. She scoops me up effortlessly and carries me to her alcove, where she settles my limp body down on her bed. I start panicking when she disappears, but then she returns and wraps me in a heavy quilt, handing me a cup of hot chocolate.

Turning off her air conditioner, she lights up every one of her candles methodically. My eyes follow her every movement like a cheetah does to its prey. The only sounds for the next few minutes are the clashes of thunder outside and the occasional sips I take from the cup.

"More?" Jackie asks, after my mouth presses to the cup again, only to realize it's empty.

"Yes, please." Jackie takes the cup and returns not long after with a fresh brew. She lifts me up and places me so my back is leaning against the cushioned headboard. Then she unravels the quilt and slips inside so that we are in it together, our bodies touching. With the quilt being so large, it fits both of us just fine.

"How do you do it? When your world is crumbling around you...how do you stay calm?" I ask when a few minutes pass.

"Maybe it's not me that is relaxed. Maybe it's you who is too stressed," Jackie replies.

The faint glow of the room illuminated by the candles as well as the roar of the storm offers a strange serenity. I feel…*safe*. I feel secure in Jackie's room, sheltered from the outside. It's almost as if her room is locked away from the real world, and this allows for my mind to steer away from recent events.

My eyes flit over to Jackie's hands as she pulls out a plastic bag.

"You know, whenever I feel like I'm at the end of my rope," she says, her voice rising no higher than a whisper, yet it mutes the thunder and howl of the storm outside. "I realize it could be worse. But who wants to think about the fact that there is someone else in the world that will always be worse off than you? Depression is depression. And what I've found to be the best medicine…is this." Jackie empties the bag directly in front of us, on the sheets, and then organizes the drug into several white lines. My state of sleepiness vanishes and my heart starts pounding. She feels me stiffen, but I stay put this time.

A straw protrudes from somewhere. Maintaining eye contact with me at all times, Jackie gestures to me like a nymph.

"This is more than enough to get you high."

Like a shining revelation, I finally realize: I'm so tired. I'm tired of being a shell with nothing inside. I'm tired of fighting life. I'm tired of trying to get through every single day with a façade plastered to my personality. I'm tired of the rotten core of negative thoughts.

Whatever rational part of me there is left is obliterated by my vulnerable state. With no hesitation, I accept the straw from her. Even in the dim lighting, the small crystals sparkle invitingly.

"If you surrender to your fate, then people will have no reason to play God and intervene," Jackie whispers. "Don't be scared. It's your destiny."

Haley promised she would always here for me. She isn't. And what does that make her? A liar.

I position the straw clumsily under my nose. And then I inhale.

Nutmeg mixed with oriental essence oil wafts through the air. When I look around the room, I see that the candles have expired, and there's something fanning a foot or so over my face—a classroom desk-sized leaf. This is what brings back the memories of the night prior.

Euphoria—giggling with Jackie over nothing, and then laughing at her as she tried to imitate a famous talk show icon. A sense of bubbly happiness, armored and protected so securely that nothing could break it. Filled with aplomb—flirty compliments, roaming hands, rough kisses—

Shit. I need to get out of here. Already I hear Jackie stirring, the weight of the bed shifting.

"I know what you're thinking," she says. I spin around only to find her face in mine. There's no telling what's running through her brain. She's the polar opposite of yesterday. Her eyes are cryptic. Dead.

"What's that?" I ask, ignoring her stare while trying to find my clothes.

"Holy shit, what the hell happened? How am I here in bed with a same-gender, smoking hot girl? Give me a moment while I steady myself and question my true orientation."

"What?"

"You didn't hear a word I said, did you?"

I finally face Jackie after a failed attempt at locating my clothes. A firm, yet gentle tug pulls me to her.

"What are you doing?"

"Calm down, Hope. You're not gay. I could tell the moment I saw you."

My protests slow. "Explain."

"There's nothing to explain. We did what we had to do."

"And that was—" I splutter. "That was—this is—" The word repulsive dies away from escaping my lips.

"See? Finally understand? It's always the ones who are lost in an unfair world. Accept it. It's easier to when you just give no fucks."

"I—I don't know what you mean."

"You have nothing to lose, right? Might as well have fun. And speaking of fun," Jackie says, looking down at my legs. "I think you had a lot of that last night."

A blush wriggles its way onto my face, the first in a long time. "Last night was a mistake."

"Was it a mistake? It seemed mutual to me."

"I—"

"You seemed pretty enthused for a long-needed release. I was supplying it to you."

"Are you always this brazen?" I ask, clicking my tongue.

Jackie disappears over her bed but then reemerges with another bag of cocaine.

"Let's do some more. Yesterday was the most fun I've ever had. And I'm fairly certain I can say the same for you."

"I need to go."

"Go?" Jackie asks, rearranging the powder into lines. "Go where?" And then it hits me. Why I'm here in the first place.

"Come on, Hope. Remember yesterday? Remember when you came running to me?"

The memories I had fought out for so long pour back into me. "Y—Yes. I remember now."

"Remember how you crawled up to my door, face flushed with tears, with no idea on what to do next?"

"Y—y—yes." The lack of warmth as Haley and I broke touch.

"Remember how desperate you were to find somebody who *understands*? Who do you have left to turn to?"

"N—Nobody," I stammer.

"You're wrong. You have me. And we watch out for each other. I'll watch out for you." Jackie hands me the straw.

There are two things that motivate me to snort my lines of cocaine. One, Jackie. And two, and by far a greater factor, the fear of stepping alone out of her home. Because the moment that I do, I lose Jackie. And then, I'll truly be left with no one.

I hand the straw to her after I'm done with my lines, and she quickly finishes the rest. After throwing the straw into the trash can, we both lean back against the headboard in satisfaction. A moderate part of me deep inside knows I'm going to repent it after the high wears off, but the pleasure is worth more than my guilty conscience.

Jackie lights a few new candles then returns to my side. "Now that we've settled in, why don't you tell me what happened? Why you were the way you were."

I shrug, unsure of whether I should tell her or not. But when was the last time I had confided in someone? When was the last time I had openly expressed every grain of hatred and grief and anger choking me to death? When was the last time I had *vented*?

"I just…well, I was staying at who I thought was my best friend's house before she turned her back on me."

"It's Haley, isn't it?" Jackie saying her name only pushed the knife in further into my heart. "It'll make you stronger," she says, kissing my neck.

"How do you know who she is?"

"Just because you don't see me in the hallways doesn't mean I don't see you."

I slump my shoulders. "Yeah, it's Haley."

"Don't worry, I completely understand."

"You do?"

"Of course. I've been backstabbed by someone who I thought was a close friend. Why don't you start from the beginning? The very beginning. There's a reason why you were staying at her house in the first place."

So I tell her. I tell her everything about my life, from when I met Haley at the beginning of junior year up until now, even Dad's death, and it feels amazing to get this burden off my shoulders. I tell her about my first meet with Videl, and how he kept pestering me while I tried to tutor him. I tell her about our first trip alone to the abandoned amusement park, and struggled with Mom's death right afterward. I tell her about Haley and her personality, and how she found out Videl was just using me for a bet he and Chad made. And lastly, I talk about how I was kicked out of Haley's home. I struggle a bit more with the last part—the drugs have started to kick in, and the fact that an attractive girl was nudged up against me was not lost on my body and the amplification of its sensitivity to bare skin.

"You forgot to mention one thing. Why aren't you staying at your own house?" Jackie asks after my lengthy explanation.

"Remember when I told you that Mom was in a car accident? I don't return home because it brings back too many memories."

"Memories you don't want to be reminded of, yet ones that you want to remember forever."

"Yeah." Jackie takes advantage of the short span of silence by running her fingers across my hand.

"And what about your father?"

"He died a while ago. I have a stepfather now. He's not a good person."

"I see. That's why you chose to come over to my home to do that bootless errand of a psychology assignment."

"Yeah."

"You say you're not friends with this Haley girl anymore, but it's obvious to me that she still wants to be. The way you described her pleading—either she's an actress, or she really does see you as her best friend. I'll bet you an 8-ball says she'll talk to you before the week is up."

"Do you think I should?"

"Forgive her? Fuck no! After what she did to you? Throw forgiveness out the window. It doesn't matter if she's your best friend in the whole fucking world or not. Backstabbing is the worst thing someone could ever do."

"Technically speaking, she didn't have much of a choice. Her mom did force her to kick me out."

Jackie's face softens, and she grips my arm.

"Listen, Hope. Her mom didn't do *anything.* Her mom didn't demand you to get out of their home. Who was the one who voiced your dismissal? *Haley.* Not her mom."

"But she's her parent. We were raised to listen to our parents." My argument sounds weak even in my own ears, and Jackie takes this tone of defenselessness into her hands.

"Stop defending her. Best friends don't do that to each other. Best friends *always* have your back, no matter what. And parents? Parents don't understand shit. They were born decades before us and had different lifestyles growing up. What was acceptable then isn't acceptable now. If Haley is willing to listen to her mom over her best friend, especially when she knows about the severity of your situation, then fuck her. Leave her be. Leave her to her own damn life. *You* need to grasp and make do with what you have, not what you had. And you have me," she winks.

"Thank you," I smile.

Jackie runs her hand down my thigh. "Anything for you."

14*

I find it hard to remember things Jackie tells me. My mind is hazy, unable to focus. My surroundings are permanently distorted, and I spend more time high than sober, snorting blow every hour, on the hour. The only time where I try to stay clean is during school so that I can focus on schoolwork, but this proves difficult—all I can constantly think about is another fix, because when the drug is in my system, I feel like an appreciated goddess, able to control time and space. At night, I shift the stars around the sky by a simple snap of my fingers. And the best part of it all? Inner Hope is locked away. I can still hear her screaming, demanding to be released, but the high is simply too miraculous to pass up.

After the incident with Haley, I go out of my way to ignore her. This proves hard because the first few days she would approach me in the hallways or calculus class, eyes full of determination with the full intention of a confrontation. I always slip out of the room before she can call out my name; this results in me skipping class for the most part. But I don't skip alone. Whenever I skip, Jackie skips, and what we do leaves little to the imagination.

A few days later, Haley gives up on trying to approach me. One day— miraculously, I stayed for the whole school day—I see her sitting in her car. The first thought that comes to my head is that she is getting ready to drive away, but it doesn't look like it. She's sitting there with her head down and not even making an attempt to start up her car. I immediately fill with guilt because I know she is thinking about me. I almost give in and walk over to her car with the intention of smacking the windshield until she opens her door and then tackling her in a fierce hug and crying in her arms while telling her how sorry I am, but there's another part of me that wants to spite her. And this part unnerves me because I'm not the type to hold a grudge.

"We've already submitted our stupid experimental project. Let's just walk out of here," Jackie says during the middle of psychology class one day.

"Don't you think we've done enough skipping?" I ask, leaning my head closer to her so that the lecturing teacher won't hear us. "I mean…not that I don't mind hanging with you, but it's only a couple more hours."

"You think that highly of school?"

"I mean, yeah, school is pertinent if we want to survive in the real world. Right now we're all encapsulated in our own little bubble. If we don't receive an education," I recite, mimicking what Mom has told me countless times. "Then we won't be successful in life."

Jackie snorts. "What a load of nonsense."

"Nonsense? Why don't you explain then?" I say. I know she isn't trying to insult Mom, but her disregard can't help but slightly annoy me.

Jackie lifts her desk up and silently scoots over to me behind the teacher's back.

"Listen, Hope. You ever feel like you were born in the wrong world? Destined to have a life in the next? I mean, look around you. Take a glimpse at the rest of society. Everyone follows a strict set of rules. Waking up at the same time Monday through Friday to get through your 9 am to 5 pm labor. Blowing the weekends until you end up groggy and tired the next day, needing your daily dose of caffeine to get you through the morning. For what? Earning money, raising a family, and working every day for the next fifty years before you go into retirement, where you'll age so quickly you won't even be able to wipe your own ass if you make it past seventy. And the saddest thing of all is that that is considered to be a fulfilling life. It's pitiful."

"What are you getting at?"

"Who cares if you don't abide by the status quo? Who cares if you don't finish school or go to college? People squander away half their life away on education while they could out in the world traveling and exploring new places, spontaneously making decisions to their hearts' extent. I'd rather live a life that way than be locked in chains. I'm telling you to live outside that box. Be free, Hope. Just let these trivial matters *go*. As long as we have each other, we can do anything."

The teacher says something, but my full attention is on Jackie.

"If that's the case, then why doesn't everyone delve into this path?" I ask.

"See, that's where the problem lies. Everyone desires this piece of freedom, but not many people can have it. There are too many repercussions to traveling this route. Like I said, everyone's expected to follow the rules and confine to the realities of this world, but just because society enforces an idea doesn't mean that idea is right. Sometimes I feel like life is a game, one big test, and you pass if you realize that social conventions are just restrictions."

"It's like the claw machines at the arcade. Nigh-impossible to win, but once a kid wins a prize by his or herself, it's the best feeling in the world."

The bell rings, and we stuff our notebooks in our backpacks.

"That's right. You have a limitless imagination, so you understand. Humans are so fatally flawed that they follow whatever everyone else does. The few that see beyond the horizon…they're the people we need. That's the kind of person I want to be. And I know you want to be too."

I hesitate and choose my words carefully. "I *had* thought about everything you've said for a while now, even before we met. Something about me has always shifted toward that train of thought. It would be nice to travel the world and learn about every culture firsthand rather than through school. It would be nice to live life the way it was meant to be lived—unrestrained. It *would* be great if we could just drop everything and follow our desires. But we can't," I shake my head. "We can't do all this because this whole—"

"Charade called life centering on going to school, getting a degree, then working forty hour weeks to make a living is sacrosanct. Yeah, I know," Jackie sighs.

"Exactly. People would look down on you otherwise."

"Who cares what other people think when I have you?" Jackie smirks.

I turn around because I'm the first in line out the door and give her a lighthearted shove, to which Jackie returns with more gusto, causing me to lose balance and tumble backward. And since I can't see where I'm going, I fully expect to land butt-first on the floor. But instead, someone very solid catches me.

Spinning around on a dime, I almost crash my head into Haley's. I go cross-eyed trying to keep my focus centered on her face. In a second, I yank my head back and immediately shove her arms off of me while trying to storm past her, but she stands in front of me, unbudging, and this makes me realize a confrontation is finally at hand.

"We need to talk," she says, glaring at me.

"There's nothing to talk about. Are you going to let me through? You're holding up the line."

"Don't play dumb, Hope! You've been ignoring me for the past week! When are you going to drop this act and stop being so vindictive?"

"Act?" I say, cocking my eyebrow in the air. Now that I have a closer glimpse at her, I notice the bags under her eyes are pronounced more than ever—they were bad during my stay at her home, but now the shades are even darker and unhealthier, if possible.

Haley shakes her head side to side. "I didn't mean that. Can we *please* talk somewhere private? I miss you."

I don't know what's wrong with my feet, but they involuntarily begin moving in Haley's direction. I see her face break out into a real smile before it fades away. At the same time, a hand slips into mine and pulls me away from Haley.

"She prefers to stay away from *backstabbers*."

Jackie's face is curled up into something venomous, something ready to strike. The hand that remains by her side is morphed into a fist. Haley sees her for the first time and her mouth drops.

"Who is this?!"

Jackie smirks. "I'm your replacement."

"I'm well aware of who you are, and Hope doesn't deserve someone as vile and fucked up in the head like you!"

My jaw drops.

"Come on, Hope. Don't you want to come back with me? Don't you want us to go back to normal? I can offer you so much more than this—this weird, psychopathic wh—"

"Haley!"

Haley veers back some of her anger, and she uses her palm to hit herself in the forehead.

"Sorry! I've—I've been so cranky lately," she sighs. The fight seems to evaporate out of her small frame. "Look, I don't want to fight, or—or anything!" Her voice grows higher and higher until she looks like she's expending every ounce of her energy to keep back the shining tears threatening to spill from her eyes. "We didn't leave things right between us. All I'm asking for is an opportunity to talk to you, alone! Just talk to me, Hope. Talk to me like we did back then, all the time."

We make eye contact, and it's like she's staring into my soul, staring into where I am most vulnerable. I want to talk to her so badly that it feels like an addiction. My body craves another conversation with my best friend alone on her bed, behind closed doors.

"Whatever you want to say to Hope, you can say in front of me."

"Fine!" Haley snaps. She approaches me and her arms twitch with the intention of touching me, but then she withdraws and sighs. "I've repeatedly played out how this conversation would go in my head, but now I can't think of what I'm supposed to say. I'm sorry, Hope. You have to believe me. I never wanted you to go."

"I've heard this same story over and over again, Haley, and frankly, it's getting exhausting."

"But it's true! You know I didn't want you to go! How many times did I tell you how great it was to have daily sleepovers?! To have your company?! I whispered in your ear every day how much you meant to me!"

"Oh, yeah?" I challenge. "And did you mean what you said?"

"Yes, yes, I did! I wholeheartedly meant them!"

"No," I shake my head. "No, you didn't, because not even ten days!" I shout. "Ten days of sojourn, and you kick me out to the curb!"

"You know it wasn't my choice to! You were eav—listening in on our conversation! You know it was entirely my mom's decision!"

"You didn't even sound like you were *trying*! You put up a half-assed defense that was broken through in a minute! I know you, Haley! If you really want something, then you'll fight for it!"

"It was my *mom's* decision! My *mom's*! Not mine!"

"I don't care if it was your mom's decision! You're the one who told me to leave! You're the one who said all those things! If you were a real friend, you wouldn't let your mom walk all over you! Instead, you just let her manipulate you into doing something she wanted!"

"That is not the case, Hope!" Haley argues. "She's my *mom*, for God's sake! I have to listen to her! If your mom asked, you'd do the same thing!"

"Well that's too bad!" I scream. "I can't do that because my mom is fucking *dead*!"

Haley blanches, and she takes a step back. "Oh god—I for—forgot. It was in the heat of the moment, I'm—Hope, wait! Where are you going?!"

"Leave me alone!" I shout, throwing her grip off. "Fuck off! I don't want to talk to you anymore!"

"Hope!" Haley calls from behind me. "I didn't mean it!"

But I'm too furious to care. Every act of forgiveness I had planned to follow has vanished, shredded apart.

"You okay?"

Jackie catches up to my pace and begins matching it. We ignore all the stares coming our way and walk out the hallway and off the campus.

"I'm fine!" I shout. "I'm just irritated. I need some blow."

Jackie nibbles her lip.

"What?"

"It's probably in my best interest to not tell you during your lapse in judgment, but we're out."

"What?!"

"We're out."

"I heard what you said the first time! Can't you get more?!"

"I can, and that's what I've been doing. My dealer's been on a popularity increase as of late. His quotas are filling too fast. The last bit of cocaine he has as of now is being sold for three times the amount he normally does."

"That's not a problem, right? You have money. I need a fix right now. Look at my hands!" I stick my arms out. Jackie takes a piercing look.

"Funds are being cut. I think my parents are growing suspicious. They know something is up. I only have two hundred on me."

"Shit," I say, running my hand through my hair. "I can probably get some cash from my house. How much do you need?"

"He's selling his last 8-ball for three hundred."

"Alright. I'll check if there's any cash lounging about at home."

"I'll come with you."

The need for more drugs spurs us at a swift pace back to my house. I haven't been there since eating Mom's cupcake, but I have more pressing matters to deal with.

We pass through the empty driveway and slip inside the home. The smell of soot and mold infiltrates my nostrils, and my assumptions are proven when I run a finger across the hallway table, sneezing as a fine layer of dust rises from the unused piece of furniture.

"No one's been here for a while," Jackie's voice rings out from behind me.

I direct Jackie over to the drawers in the kitchen to see if she can find anything.

Even though it hasn't even been a month, being in the house, smelling the house, and seeing the house—it all brings up a powerful sense of nostalgia that wells inside me. I briefly finish reminiscing on the first floor and walk up the stairs, pausing in front of the closed door to my room.

The best place to check is Mom's bedroom, so that's what I do. Her bed is neatly made; only a thin layer of dust settled on the comforter is proof toward the lack of a human body. The curtains—only nice ones in the house, the only memorabilia Mom took with her from our past life with my father—slowly shift back and forth from the air vent underneath.

I immediately head toward the bed, searching under the mattresses for any irregular lumps. Nothing. Next, I check the dresser. To my amazement, after much digging, I scour up a wad of cash tightly bundled by a rubber band inside of a black sock.

Tucking the money in my pants, I walk toward the exit. I'm just about to call Jackie's name, but then something catches my eye. It's the nightstand with Mom's pictures she had collected over the years, all when Dad was still alive. Trips to theme parks, old terracotta ruins, cruises to the Caribbean's; the nightstand could serve well as a collage. I peruse each photo meticulously, touching the woman's smile lightly, as if the slightest graze would erase her face from the picture.

And then my brain takes me down memory lane to the night of the party. To the doorbell ringing, and then Haley coming in with her cute little dress, eyes swimming with mischief. The way she tightly hugged and greeted Mom with nothing but genuine courtesy. Someone like that can't be a liar. They just can't.

The memory disappears in a puff of smoke and leaves me staring at the wad of cash. Suddenly, I just want to throw it back in the drawer and tell Jackie I didn't find anything, but then the awful truth of reality hits. All my memories are just that—visual pictures of the past. The past, not the present. This is the present. No Mom, no Videl, and no Haley. Only Jackie.

I keep the cash in my hands and rendezvous with Jackie downstairs. She's still in the kitchen.

"Nice. How much is that?" she asks after I whip out the money.

"I didn't count, but this is all that I found."

"Are they all twenties?"

"Mostly." What actually happened that evening? Was it me who opened the door or was it Haley?

"This is enough. We're good to go, Hope. Hope?"

"Huh?" I swivel my head to see Jackie staring at me.

"Are you alright?"

"Yeah. Yeah, I'm fine." Am I too stubborn to apologize? Am I obdurate?

"Hope!" Jackie exclaims.

"What?!" I shout. Jackie comes over and squints her eyes in mine.

"You're still thinking about her," she says.

"What?"

"Haley. You're still thinking about her. You still want to forgive her, don't you? Don't think I didn't see you taking steps toward her direction."

There's no use lying to Jackie. "Y—Yeah. J—Just, she's been helping me adjust to life changes for so long that I'm starting to think was a genuine mistake. She isn't capable of hate. Her apologies have verisimilitude. She means them. She—she's really sorry," I conclude.

I lift my head up, forehead bumping into Jackie's.

"Listen to yourself, Hope! Are you *that* desperate? Just because she was there for you in the past doesn't mean she is now. Times change, and when that happens, people do too."

"Yeah, but she's not evil at heart. I believe what she says."

Jackie laughs, but it's not her normal laugh. There's a chill to it. "Do you think I'm a bad person?"

"What? N—No, of course not! You're my saving grace! Without you, I—"

"You saw Haley's face! You saw how disgusted she was when she saw you standing next to me, and your ears sure as hell heard the profanities. So which one is which, Hope? Am I the bad person, or is she?"

I shake my head. "I—I don't know. Neither of you."

"That isn't an answer. There is always a bad side and a good side, and you have the free will to choose which side to walk on, but not both. If you choose her, you best be aware of the consequences. Because once you go back to her..."

I let out a pitiful whimper at her dangling sentence.

"We have a valuable rapport. You don't want to lose that, do you? Don't think I can't see what's happening to you. You're in too deep, and if you leave now, you'll lose yourself."

She leans her head in and bites my earlobe.

"Come on, don't you want to snort more blow? Feel the trickle of powder invade your nostrils and slowly spread through your bloodstream? That feeling of invincibility," she whispers, her breath tickling my neck. "The feeling of accomplishment! Like the world is below your feet, trembling at your power!"

"Y—Yes," I admit, my grasp relinquishing. "Yes!"

Jackie breaks apart and smirks. "Then let's go get high."

She pockets the money.

15*

Mornings are hell. After nights of snorting streams and streams of cocaine, the hangovers progressively get worse. My headaches have a pulse to them, and they're so bad that I regularly pay trips to the bathroom, bent over the toilet until I feel remotely better. Even in my drugged state now, I often ponder on my past. The more I think about it, the more I miss it. Sure, there are benefits of doing cocaine—having a warm shelter with great company, a feeling of acceptance—these aren't liberties to complain about. But I do miss the simplicity of my old life. Working on homework and practicing piano—sure, it was cyclic and sometimes ennui, but it was all for a good reason; because I enjoyed what I did and wanted to make Mom proud.

Simply put: I'm starting to think the high isn't worth the crash anymore. But I can't stop now. I know I'm addicted. If I don't stay on drugs for more than a few hours, tremors start to appear in my hands. I feel exhausted. Body aches, chills, and severe bouts of depression also hits. But more importantly, if I show any sign of weakness, I'll lose her. Jackie.

Ergo, there's only one path to take. I continue on my path to a drug-induced torpor. I can tolerate going to school and controlling myself from any euphoric comments or hysterical outbursts, and I can still consciously understand that my high isn't reality. Maybe that's why I'm still reluctant to skip school.

The relationship between Jackie and me is still kept under wraps. Our sessions in bed are based on drug-fueled lust; it was hardly romantic. I feel guilty toward delivering my body to her and even guiltier when I attribute my actions to a lame excuse for not being in a right state of mind. Her patience with me has been dwindling lately, and this is why I'm currently walking to calculus class. Alone.

I can't even recall the last time I came to class and what we were learning that day. It feels like ages.

Like a honing radar, my eyes land on Haley the second I walk through the door. Her eyes flick up to meet mine at the same time.

Gritting myself, I stroll over to my seat.

"Well, look who decided to show up."

"Don't talk to me." I sit in my seat and refuse to make eye contact.

"Excuse you?"

I glare at her. "Don't. Talk. To. Me."

Haley stares at me. Before I can react, her arm wraps around my wrist tightly and she yanks me so hard I almost topple out of my seat.

"Look. At. Me," she commands, in a fiery voice I've never heard before. I pause before turning my head to stare at her. Her eyes flicker across my face—past my lips, past my cheeks, and past my nose, until they land on my eyes. She continues to watch me, waiting patiently.

"Why the hell are you sitting here? Your seat's on the other end of the room."

"You know, if I answer you, I'd be breaking your request."

"Just answer the fucking question," I grunt.

Haley rolls her eyes. "New assigned seats from the day before." She taps her fingernail on the laminate desk. "Not like you would know, though."

"What do you want, Haley?" I reposition myself in my seat.

"Nothing. Just to ask how your day's going."

"Is this another tactical approach of yours? A dash of passive-aggressiveness as an appetizer and then pretending what happened between us didn't exist as the main course?"

Her face falls. For a split second, the urge to forgive her almost deluges me, but the veil of betrayal and Jackie still shrouds the urge deep inside, locking it in place.

"Hope! Hope, are you okay?"

I elbow her hand back hard, refusing to show any signs of weakness.

"It's just a nosebleed," I explain, pinching my nose together.

Haley digs around in her purse and pulls out some tissues. "Here."

"I'm fine," I protest nasally.

"Just take the damn things," she grunts after sensing my hesitation. I grab them and wipe my nose clean and plug up the nostrils until there's no longer any blood flowing. I feel a little off, so I shake my head to try to dispel the lightheadedness.

Haley scoots her desk closer to mine as if her one benevolent deed earned her the right to do so.

"You know what I think about you, Hope?" she says suddenly.

I try my best to get her to go away by moving my desk toward the other end of the wall. "No, and I don't care to know."

"I'm not going to pretend like I don't know who I saw you with. There are rumors circulating throughout campus, and I've been telling myself that there's no way you'd fall so low, but I can't ignore the facts anymore! You've missed so many days of class, but when you're at school, you just constantly look out of it, like you're absorbed in your own world. You've lost weight. Your hair is falling out, and you're whiter than a ghost. And that nosebl—"

"You know what?!" I yell, kicking my chair back until I'm towering over Haley. She refuses to back down, but a sliver of fear worms its way onto her face. "I'm starting to realize that you and Altha more in common than I thought! I'm tired of your attacks and denigrations! How dare you place yourself in my personal business?!"

"Hope! Listen, Hope!"

"I don't need your invasions, or you! You *betrayed* me, remember?! Or are you too fucking stupid to even realize what you did?!"

"Hope!" Haley's head whips back and forth, her eyes trailing the students' attention. "Calm down! Please, I didn't mean it! I only—"

"Do not tell me to calm down! You—I looked up to you! What did I do to deserve this?! Does my whole life need to be ridiculed?! Do I deserve to be used?!"

"N—no, that's not what I was trying to do, Hope! Please! I'm trying to help you!"

"Fucking *bitch*!" I hiss. "Get away from me!"

"Hope, please!" Haley pushes herself out of her seat and grabs my arm. Her touch causes me to snap, and my hand reflexively rotates back before slapping her in the face harder than anything I've hit in my life.

"Don't touch me again, or I'll fucking kill you."

Haley brings her hand up and presses it against her cheek. A red handprint is already beginning to blossom on her skin. When she speaks, her voice is subdued and tremulous.

"W—what's happened to you?"

"I moved on. That's what happened."

Haley stares into my soul, but can't seem to find what she's looking for. "Where's the real Hope? Where's my b—best friend?" Her bottom lip quivers.

"Best friend?!" Haley jumps at the sound of my morose laughter. "Our friendship!" I keep laughing, spreading my arms out and spinning around, catching nearby students' open stares. "Your best friend is buried six feet under. You and *I*, Haley, never had a friendship. You are *nothing* to me. I fucking hate you, and I sure fucking wish I never met you."

Haley's poise finally crumbles. Her face contorts into an inhuman expression, and she starts crying. A few seconds later, and she's running away. Like a coward. The door slams shut behind her. The class is silent, and the writing chalk is dangling in the teacher's hands like a hypnotist's pendant. Eyes scan me up and down, judging me the way Haley did.

"Fuck you guys," I spit. "Fuck this class. Stupid as fuck." Stumbling to the door, I flip everyone off. That'll show them.

~~~~~~

The next few nights pass by such in a blur that I remember nothing of them. We may have gone mailbox bashing again, but I can't recall. Time is no longer a measurement of hours and days. It's a measurement of how long I can keep my awareness up. It fails, for the next place I find myself is in Jackie's bed. Her alarm clock reads eight in the morning. It might be Thursday. No, Friday.

I try to fall back asleep, but my efforts are to no avail. I give up and groan, pulling myself up to the corner of the bed, my head pounding from a combination of sleep deprivation, drugs, and alcohol.

"Hope?" Jackie is still half-asleep.

"Yeah." This is all so wrong.

"Where are you going?"

"It's getting late. I'll meet you at school." I sound lifeless; nothing in my voice would even suggest any emotional attachment to the warm body sleeping on the other side of the bed.

"Mmm," Jackie grumbles. I don't even think she heard me. I tidy up quickly in the bathroom before getting dressed. I spare another glance at Jackie, and again, I find myself seriously wondering what the hell I'm doing. Skipping school. Drugs. Sex with a girl I've not even known for a long time.

Whatever. I shake these thoughts from my head and walk to school. The parking lot has even less cars parked in it than usual, a result of an overwhelming proportion of the upperclassmen skipping the last day of class before winter break.

I'm the only person inside the tutoring classroom. I mean, who would come in for tutoring on this day?

"Hope!"

Sure enough, Jackie walks through the door. There's a guy that is tagging along behind her, but I don't get a closer look.

"Hey," I thinly smile. "What's up?"

"It's the last day of class, Hope. What're you doing here so early? I missed you this morning." Jackie squats so that we're at eye-level with each other.

"It is?" I feign ignorance.

"Anyhow, it doesn't matter. Come with us. We're going to skip and do some blow." She winks at me. "Courtesy of my friends."

"Yeah, whatever." Maybe it'll get rid of these dumb walls always threatening to crush me from all sides.

"Cool. George, Adam's got his car on campus?"

"Nah. It's parked a couple of streets away. Shouldn't take more than a few minutes to get to." George directs the second sentence toward me, before extending his hand. I shake his greeting, observing his goofy grin and the holes in his toboggan hat.

We make our way through the small crowd of students in a single-file line, slithering through the crowd like a slippery snake chasing after his meal. The hole notorious for the use of escaping by the potheads is still in its usual location, untampered with by school officials. We climb through it until we enter the forest and continue walking in silence until we meet Adam at his car. He's big, burly, and has straggly hair, kind of like the old 80's metal band members—the people that spin their hair wildly back and forth to the swing of the beat on stage.

We make introductions, and before long, I'm sitting in the back with Jackie, while George is in the shotgun. The car is an old Beemer, and the heater doesn't work. Jackie notices my rubbing and holds my hands.

After we're on the highway, George pulls out a bag—no, the biggest bag—I have ever seen, filled entirely with white. There's at least a quarter of a pound.

A few minutes later, all of us are doing lines on rumpled dollar bills balanced in our hands. I find it pretty funny watching George hold out the bill for Adam, feeding him like a mother does for her baby.

Jackie and I mess around in the backseat for an hour or so until the car comes to a halt.

"Throw on your clothes, girls. We're here," one of the guys says.

Jackie and I follow his command. The car doors open and I step outside.

My foot hits pavement overridden with weeds, and my heart instantly freezes.

I hesitantly lift my head up. And right before me is the ancient being. The amusement park.

We wind our way through the same hole-ridden fence until we reach the main plaza. In a cult manner, everyone sits down in a circle. Except me. My eyes constantly flit to the behemoth, back and forth like a trapped spy searching for an escape route. The topic at hand continues to be rebuked by my ears.

"Everything alright, Hope?" Jackie asks "You're distracted."

My first ever kiss, taking me higher than cocaine ever did. The thought that everything in the world was perfect, only to be stripped away by that rainy night. Mom's car. Her death. The bloodied hand.

In the end, I just can't take it anymore.

"I—I'll be back, Jackie. Be back soon," I tell her.

Jackie stares at me intently but then gives a curt nod before disappearing with her friends.

I walk toward the general direction of the rollercoaster. The landmarks along the way remind me that I'm venturing in the right direction. The same mini-game booths, the merry-go-round, and bumper cars brush by my line of sight again until I finally stop in front of the rollercoaster.

Maybe the cocaine gave me the confidence I needed. Or maybe it's because I honestly don't care anymore. Either way, I climb the wooden planks until I reach the top. And when I do, everything hits me at once.

The view is still stunning, even in my narcotic state. The school still sits as a shy speck in the distance, with only the identifiable soccer field guiding me to the cluster of brick buildings. I brush my fingers gently against the wood where Videl and I sat the only time we were here. And then I collapse there.

I always thought Jackie was my savior. The one who helped me out of my endless pit when no one else would. But I was wrong. Her company and cocaine only helped to bury my true feelings deeper inside of me, not replace them. But what are my true feelings? Getting rid of my hated cyclic schedule and separating myself from the rest of society like Jackie mentioned? That would be ideal, but it's something greater. It's with Videl. It's with Haley. I miss them. I miss them both so much it hurts. But most of all, I miss Mom. Dad. The pain—it's insurmountable.

Raising myself up, I sit and look at where I know the school is, rehearsing in my head the conversation I had with Videl on our first date. The moonlight shining in his eyes. The closeness. The heady smell that stripped every one of my senses to nothing. It's hard to believe that that happened in the exact spot I am in now.

A couple of hours later, I can make out two or three voices ringing into the sky, repeating my name over and over again. Jackie. And her nameless friends.

I climb down the rollercoaster, and it doesn't take me long before locating the search party. I catch them right as they are about to pass the bumper cars.

"Hope! We've been looking everywhere for you! You had us worried! Almost," Jackie adds.

I smile. "I was just walking around, thinking to myself." Debating about telling her where I really was seems to taint my memories somehow. As if the top of the rollercoaster is a holy shrine of sorts.

"Existential crisis?"

I don't respond, letting her develop her own interpretation.

"There's a retreat in the mountains. Sky's about to leave for a couple of hours. We can make it to the rendezvous if we rush," one of the guys interjects.

I waylay, unable to stop myself any longer. "Can you take me back to school?"

Jackie shares a look with her comrades, who shrug. "Starmount's along the way," she says. "Sure thing. You do realize today's the last day of school before holidays, right?"

"Yeah. I just left something there," I lie, and then turn my attention back outside the window. Jackie's hazel eyes linger on me longer than her friends do, but she drops the subject.

We drive in silence until the familiar *Starmount High* logo crosses over my eyes. The car stops, and I slide out of it.

"Thanks."

"No problem," Jackie responds. "Are you okay, though?" she asks, caressing the inside of one of my thighs.

"Yeah," I mutter on auto-pilot, replacing her hand somewhere else, but I still accept a kiss from Jackie. She winks, and whispers something unintelligible in my ears. Then she leaves.

I push the door to the first bathroom I locate and stumble to the mirror, not caring if anyone saw the mental state I'm in. I'm not going to sugarcoat it—I look like a zombie reincarnate, and it makes me so disgusted with myself I collapse in a bathroom stall and retch into the toilet. But nothing comes out. It's been—I can't even remember—days since I've eaten, and my stomach is churning at how unhappy it is.

At this moment, absolute hatred fuels my veins. The desire to just feel happy again supersedes all else. Before I know it, I find myself standing in the bathroom stall ripping my jacket off and digging through my backpack, trying any pocket or crevice where I can locate another fix. There's a bag, in my front pocket. I don't even know how it got there, but I yank it out desperately and rip it open.

The contents sit in my hand, and I tackle it with my face, trying to get as much as I can into my system. Most of the drug gets in my nose just fine, but I can feel the mix of my saliva and cocaine smeared on my face, mostly around my upper lip.

Am I so desperate to feel higher than a cloud, to feel like I have a purpose in life, that I resort to being a feral animal? Snorting the drug I hear about all the time on the news that forces an addiction? I always thought I could overcome this, but not anymore. I'm one of those people. The ones who battled. And the ones who lost.

A few minutes later, the effects hit me. I start mumbling some nonsense, but the euphoria is already beginning to fade away faster than I can hold water in the palm of my hand. I don't know if the stuff Jackie gives me is of any quality or if my body is just building up a tolerance, but a gram just isn't enough. It's like my own body is starting to reject me, and my thesis is proven when an involuntary urge causes me to lean over the toilet and begin puking out blood.

I flush the toilet, studying the bright pink mix of water and blood with my watery eyes, and then I sit on the seat, defeated. My head rests on the cool stall wall, and I begin crying.

One minute, everything seemed to be improving, and life was getting better. Mom was making more money at her job, and I had just experienced the first and best kiss of my life. And just in that same day, the walls came crashing down on me. I lost Mom, and then I lost Videl not long afterward when I needed his support the most. And Jackie…it's all her fault. If I weren't partners with her, she never would have gotten me addicted. Maybe I could have repaired my relationship with Haley if it wasn't for Jackie's persuasiveness.

No. It's not her fault. It's mine. I'm the one who accepted her stopgap offer. I fell into the rabbit hole because I am weak.

I bite my lip, drawing blood, but the pain isn't enough to remind me that I'm alive. I don't feel alive. Everything just flies by me without my acknowledgement. I can't concentrate on schoolwork, or even answer a teacher's question. I can't distinguish real life from anything anymore. I could be living in a dream right now, for all I know.

Another half hour passes before I muster up the élan to pull myself together and walk down the hallway. I can't remember the last time I went to class, but I have nothing else to do and nowhere else to turn.

Unfortunately, the last class of the day is physical education. Fortunately, because it's the last day of school before winter break, the coaches let us off easy by allowing us to relax in the bleachers. I use this time to my advantage and curl up in the corner. I just want to sleep. Retire into the realm of dreams.

"Hope?"

"Haley." I forgot she was in this class with me, and at this point, I'm too tired to argue. Too tired to push her away. I'm just *done*. After my unadulterated condemnation, I'm surprised she's even here.

"Don't you want to sit in our usual spot? The coaches are giving us a free period."

"That's good," I smile weakly. "I'm glad."

"Hope, I'm worried about you." Haley rests her cool hand on my face after a brief hesitation. "You're burning up. Are you sure you don't need a doctor? I can take you right now."

"No. It's just a little allergy I have that makes me feel warm. I'll be better soon." Haley eyes narrow.

A warm hand slides into mine and I feel her body shift beside me. She's alive, pulsing, radiating with life; everything I'm not. And suddenly, the urge to speak to her—have a normal conversation with her—supersedes my hatred.

"How's life been? And how's the termagant?" I don't mean to fill my tone with rancor, but I think that's what it comes off as because Haley cringes.

"Let's not talk about her."

"No. I want to."

Haley seemingly takes a liking to the laces on her shoe. "She feels guilty for wanting you out of the house. I've been trying to convince her to let you back in."

"I find Jackie's house more than qualified to provide me shelter."

"Yeah? It sure looks like it. I can tell by the purple bags under your eyes that you still have those nightmares."

I chuckle. "All that matters is that she's good to me." I stare across the court. "How's your life?"

Haley's turns away when she answers me, and her voice is slightly subdued.

"Um, it could be a lot better. The only good thing…well, the restaurant Mickie's I've been working at has a higher customer turnout, so I get more tips, thankfully. I've also been applying to colleges and looking at financial loans if I can't get a cheerleading scholarship."

I laugh raucously. "Fucking fantastic. You have such a great life."

Haley ignores me. "I brought you something," she says suddenly. She begins to rummage through her backpack. "It's past lunchtime, but still. Here." She pushes the brown paper bag over the desk, and I acquiesce, crinkling the paper in the progress.

"It's gnocchi. I saw how much you liked it when we had it at my house. I thought you could use some lunch."

"Thanks."

Haley and I sit next to each other, shoulders touching, for the rest of the class. No more words are said, but then again, I don't think we have anything else to say. The last exchange occurs when the final bell rings, when the coaches wish us a safe and merry Christmas. I tell Haley I'll be heading home in a bit and that she should go on without me and meet her cousins, and she does so, giving me a set smile.

A few students give me strange looks at my unwillingness to move, but leave me alone. I lose track of how long I sit in the dark, empty gym, but it's already black outside by the time I exit the school's front doors. The parking lot is empty, void of any student and teacher cars, even the janitor's. A chilly gust of wind bites me in the face when I begin walking, and it doesn't leave me alone. I walk and walk, my feet guiding me on their own until I reach the cemetery.

Mom and Dad's graves aren't hard to find; after all, their tombstones are right next to each other. The granite surface is slick, unaffected by the cold weather. Every inch of their names my fingers run across leaves me with a hollower heart. It seems forever ago that we were together, we were whole. A family dinner every night, a sitcom afterward, and a bedtime story. Things in my life that will never happen again, because we humans only have one life.

I don't remember what happens next, but I think I stumble into the house with my mind disoriented. The exhaustion that slowly accumulated over the past few days finally reach a carrying capacity, and I collapse on my bed, passing out almost instantly.

The next day, a faint rustling draws me to attention. The window opens, and I see the first signs of snow breaking through the atmosphere and falling to the ground, where it instantly melts into a tear-shaped frame. Before long, the wind is howling and it is snowing harder than ever. In a time that seems too long ago, I would have laughed and immediately went out and rejoiced in the magnificence of whiteness. But no longer. I return back to the bed and pull the covers over my head. My phone, uncharged, is left to die.

Some time passes without my existence, and one day I hear the doorbell ring. Immediately wary, I slip into my pajamas and walk downstairs, slipping my eye into the peephole. Christmas carolers. I almost scoff after checking what time it is on my near-dead phone. It is early morning. I ignore them and drag my feet quietly as not to rouse any suspicions that there is anyone in the house. And then it hits me. It's Christmas.

My eyes flit around the living room. Nothing represents any sign of the holiday. There is no Christmas tree or stockings hanging over the fireplace. There is no food that reflects a large amount of time put into making it—in fact, there's nothing in the fridge at all but some fruit that is so old and ripened the skin is wrinkled. In this home, Christmas spirit is dead.

And because it's Christmas Day, my brain decides to be stupid and offer me what I didn't want to see right now: visions of my past; sitting under the Christmas tree with my parents and drinking eggnog—I hate that stuff—all while hearing Mom's laugh while Dad tells some joke about his coworker's failed attempt at flirting with a new employee. The warm tickle of the fireplace, the stress-free atmosphere—these memories flood into my head and I jerkily jump off my bed and into suitable clothing for the cold weather outside.

The park is empty, but the absence of people is what gives it such a serene glow. There's just something ethereal about seeing a place for social gathering void of anyone shrouded in a beautiful, glistening layer of snow.

I brush three or four inches of snow off the swing seat before sitting down. The moisture dampens my pants and immediately sends a wave of chilliness around my thighs.

The seat of the swing warms up over the next few hours, not just from the sun's torrid rays forming a brilliant sheen over the snow covering the ground, but from my own body heat. The park's location is right next to the main neighborhood road that branches out into several intersections, and many cars drive by. A small part of me hopes that someone will recognize me—even strangers coming to play would offer momentary companionship—but no, the cars don't stop and reveal an adult with their child or pet coming to enjoy the snow or the monkey bars. All the vehicles move with purpose, as if the driver is late getting to their home after a last-minute shopping expedition. I find it ironic. They are moving and gaining velocity, a push forward into the future, while I'm unmoving, stuck in the present. After ten or so cars pass by, I keep my head down.

Over the last few days, solace was a rarity. Every day consisted of me moving around like I normally would when I wasn't in bed, but there was just no purpose. There were moments where I didn't even make it out of bed. There was no point in showering, for I wasn't expecting company.

There is no friendship. There is no social interaction. There is no high. I know for a fact there is no cocaine in the house, and even though I tell myself I would never touch any of it ever again, loneliness shrouds me and somehow manages to coerce my brain into wanting one more fix to feel normal.

The only peace I have is sleep. The only escape I have is sleep. Sleep is so much better—I can just retreat into the blankness and take my mind off everything. There is no feeling of worthlessness. There is no endless pit of angst that makes me want to throw up every few minutes. There are no negative emotions. In sleep, there is only a dark black abyss.

The sky doesn't take long to get dark from the short day. By the time visibility is almost zero, I stand up—my pants make a sticky sound—stretch my muscles, and begin walking home. I debate on visiting Jackie's house along the way and get food, and maybe cocaine, but I decide against it. Nothing is worse than depression. You don't feel like doing anything because you're too down, and you are down because you aren't doing anything. It comes back around in full circle.

Every home in every street I pass have their Christmas lights strung up, blinking and brightly shining, providing warmth for the snowmen and their carrot noses and stone eyes. The inflatable Saint Nicks and reindeer smile at me when I walk past. Families are in the kitchen scrambling to get dinner preparations going and making pleasant conversation with loved ones they haven't seen in ages. One family is in the living room celebrating the holidays—the mother, father, and daughter. The young girl is just now, in the afternoon, opening presents under the tree and her parents are laughing at her joyous responses.

My house isn't very difficult to spot from ways. It's the only one lacking any decorations. The driveway is still empty.

I open the front door and enter my house, not bothering to lock the door behind me. I walk by the kitchen and then up the stairs. The multiple times I've walked by this area of the house does nothing to condition me to the loss. I shut my eyes, but even with them closed I can see Mom walking around, tidying the house up. The pain is so raw it hurts. I've lost everything. Mom and Dad are forever a memory that will haunt my mind.

My footsteps are heavy as I drag myself upstairs, before collapsing on my bed. I lay in bed, surrounded by my thoughts until the stars poke out, and it takes me a while to realize the wet sticky liquid running down my cheeks are my own tears. I wipe them off, but the steady cascade doesn't stop. I check my phone. It's dead.

A sharp pain hits me square in the heart, and I rush to the bathroom and huddle over the toilet, but nothing comes out. I gag until my vision blurs, and with shaky legs, I somehow manage to stand up and rinse my mouth out in the sink. I raise my head to the mirror and gasp at what I see.

My face is sunken, and cheeks are hollow, and the bags under my eyes are almost purple from the lack of quality sleep over the past week. I observe the colors of my eyes, and they're lifeless. Lifeless, like Mom's. Like Dad's.

I walk out of the bathroom, my mind in a haze. My brain hardly seems to be functioning; I don't even realize my legs are moving on their own before they stop in front of my desk like something had called them over.

The teddy bear catches my eye first, and then a picture of Videl and me, and I pick up the frame and stare at the two of us. He looks as handsome as ever, and I ignore the stab through my heart. I shift my gaze to myself. My smile in the picture seems foreign, unbecoming to me.

It seemed like forever ago that we had taken the picture. On the corner where the little Italian restaurant was. The other couple who complimented on how cute we look together before I turned red and, without thinking, furiously said we weren't dating, even though we were. I had everything I wanted. And now—I have nothing. He used me. I should have known better. How could I have been so desperate, so *stupid*? So childish, jumping to any guy that exhibits any attraction to me?

I punch my first through the picture frame, cracking the glass. The teddy bear sits there, mocking me, and something takes ahold of me. My hands flex toward the stupid stuffed animal's head and out of nowhere, I muster the energy to flourish my arm and rip its head off. The wool springs out of the animal like water from a leaky faucet, splaying across the carpet.

I don't know. One moment, I stand there for an uncertain amount of time, and the next moment, I snap. I stumble to the bathroom with determination until I'm standing in front of my medicine cabinet, staring intently at the dusty bottles of depression and sleeping pills held firmly in each of my hands. I've watched my whole life fall apart before my eyes, and I can't do a thing about it. I thought people cared about me the same way I cared about them. I'm not good enough for Haley, Jackie, or Videl. They all exist happily in their own little impenetrable bubbles. I'll never be good enough for them. I'm tired of having nothing to live for. And maybe, just maybe with this, the birthday wish I used in place of Mom's will come true.

I lock the door. The act offers closure, an ultimatum to prevent me from changing my mind if I were somehow to have second doubts. I unscrew both bottle caps and dump all the pills out onto the counter, spilling some onto the floor in the process. The green and white pills mix in the sink ominously, their colors reminding me of wintry M&M's. I pick them up, their grainy surface gently caressing my hand as if they are inviting me over.

I grab my rinsing glass and dump the toothbrush onto the floor before filling the glass up with water from the sink. I glance down at the pills resting in my palm. I shake some pills out of my hand back on the sink counter until only four remain. I look at them intently before dropping them on my tongue, paying no heed to the bitterness they radiated. I quickly drink the water and swallow all four pills before I could change my mind. My legs begin quivering and eyes swim with tears as my brain finally catches up to the situation and I realize that this is really happening. But my resigned state doesn't want to fight anymore. For once Inner Hope is silent, accepting the expedient solution, accompanying me on my final journey.

I pick up four more pills from the sink, not caring about the colors anymore, and swallow them again with only a slight cringe this time. The pills drop down into the depths of my stomach with small thuds.

I reach for four more pills but hear a strange sound downstairs. I'm almost tempted to go out there and check what could have caused the noise. But the picayune idea is instantly squashed and batted away. I return to the pills, but before I can do anything, the bathroom doorknob begins to shake and the absence of tingles I have been subject to over the last month begin to creep back onto my skin.

"Hope? Are you in there?" A voice I never think I'd hear rings out again, and I see the shadow of his feet against the door.

Part of me wonders if I have gone mad, but when the door rattles again against the safety of the lock, I know. I know it isn't a dream. I ignore him. One month of no contact. I can make another half hour.

My focus reverts back to the pills, and I swallow four more. They fall down my throat more easily now. The tears that were threatening to spill are now pouring nonstop down my face and splattering all over the floor.

I realize the glass is empty and I turn on the sink, filling it back up to the brim, ignoring the pain as my hand bangs against the faucet.

"Hope! I know you're in here! I can hear your sink! Open up!"

I can hear the panic pleading entering Videl's voice and I frown, ignoring him again and shoving four more pills into my mouth, guzzling some water to ease them down. Another batch down.

The bathroom door rattles even harder. "Hope! Hope! Open the fucking door now!"

I shake my head, trying my hardest to shrug his voice off. I grab the rest of the pills and place them all in my hand, but before I could take any more, the lock on the door breaks and the door flies open. I whirl around to see a disheveled Videl. His hair is uncombed, and his shirt has a dark stain on it. And then he zones on the pills, eyes bloodshot with tears streaming down his face.

I suddenly panic and pop the remaining pills into my mouth like some hungry animal, spilling some on the floor in the process. I grab the glass of water and try to drink as much as I can, but Videl lunges at me and rips my hand away. The glass breaks free from my grasp and falls to the ground, shattering into a million pieces. I feel the sharp sting as the glass shards cut my bare feet, but the hand on my wrist hurts more.

Before I can offer resistance, Videl has a firm grasp on both of my wrists and pins them with a single hand. My skin burns as his grip tightens.

"Spit them out!" he yells at me, and I furiously shake my head. I try to lubricate my throat with my tongue in order to swallow the pills raw. The tears blur my vision so badly I can no longer see clearly.

I feel a whoosh of air sift by me, and then I feel Videl's body pressed against my back. He grabs both my arms and pins them effectively behind me, and I realize with a stroke of fear that I can't move at all.

Before I know what's going on, he pushes me to my knees with inhuman strength in front of the toilet and forces my head down to the head of the toilet with his vice grip. I flop in his grasp like a fish out of the water and gasp for air, accidentally spitting out the pills that I have yet to swallow.

"Leave me alone! You're ruining everything!" I scream, futilely struggling to escape his clutches.

"No!" His voice cracks into a million different emotions with the single word. "I *saw* you swallow them! I'm not letting you die!" His efforts redouble, and I feel my lips part, and my mouth stretch open as he rams two fingers inside. I instantly began choking as he sticks them in the back of my throat, and I try to stop him by biting down on his fingers as roughly as I can, my teeth screaming in the process. He doesn't withdraw, and after a few more thrusts, I feel myself vomiting, coughing up some pills that I had swallowed. Coughing up my ticket out of this world.

The pills are now in the toilet, and I desperately reach my hand into the toilet and grab them in a last ditch effort, but Videl seems to read my mind and flushes before I can get a firm hold on my freedom. He lets me up, and I instantly start beating him as hard as I can on his chest in an apoplectic fit.

"Get away from me!" I hiss venomously, my hands clawing at every inch of him I can find. "Don't touch me!"

My disgust only fuels his strength, and I feel his arms squeezing, constricting my chest until I can no longer breathe. But I don't need to. Rage, not air, is the catalyst for my existence.

"I fucking hate you!" I scream with as much loathing as I can. "How can you do this to me?!" I continue to pound my fists into his chest, harder than any other time I was angry. This is genuine anger. I want to make him bleed. I want to make him feel pain. I want him to feel what I feel.

"I fucking hate you!" I repeat, my voice elevating beyond a tone of sanity. The tears keep flowing, but the frustration at the opportunity ripped away from me is slowly conquering my ire. "You've ruined everything!"

"I love you," he chokes out. I scream louder.

"I hate you!" My struggling becomes sluggish as my body gets hit with a sudden wave of exhaustion.

"I love you," he repeats over and over again, sobbing and running his hand down my hair.

Before long, the strength slowly seeps out of my pores. I end up collapsing there, in Videl's arms. A deep, soporific languor settles through my body; fatigue begins to drag me under, and my struggles die down as I eventually fall unconscious in his arms.

16

A barricade stacked full of books, clothes, and a couple of chairs block the bedroom door. I sit slumped and quivering, letting out a horrified scream as the door shatters open. Debris flies off to the side and the monstrous shape of Roger steps into my room. His bloodshot eyes sweep the room until they land on me and then he lunges at me. But never reaches me. His hand freezes in place, and at the same time, I hear a beeping sound. Softly at first, but then it consumes my senses. "She's coming back to us," a voice says. And then...blackness.

My eyes flutter as I struggle to emerge from unconsciousness and with a monumental effort, I pull myself out of the dark abyss. Videl and an unfamiliar woman geared in flowery scrubs are the first two things I see after the initial blurriness subsides. The nurse smiles at me charitably. My left hand feels warm, and I peek a glance to see Videl hand clasped around mine. My face breaks out into an involuntary smile that slowly fades away when I capture my surroundings.

I turn my head, grimacing at the stiffness of my neck, and spot the creamy window curtains and a mounted mini-flatscreen. My arms are hooked up with several needles, and I'm in a flimsy hospital gown. And then the most idiosyncratic sensation tickles my chest.

"What's all this?" I baffledly ask. My voice sounds like someone sliced my vocal cords apart.

"Hi, I'm Susanna, the nurse taking care of you," the nurse introduces, making her way over to the foot of the bed. "How do you feel?" She adjusts a couple of pillows and pats me on the shoulder.

I frown. How *do* I feel? Treated like a toddler and a little uncomfortable, perhaps, but now that she mentions it, there's something I can't put my finger on.

I try to swallow, but something bulky in my throat prevents me from doing so.

"W—what's in my mouth?" I croak out. I can feel it winding all the way down my throat and further. It inhibits my speech to a certain degree, forcing me to slur my word.

"You have a nasogastric tube inserted through your throat down to your stomach." I raise an eyebrow at her.

"You've been through a lot Hope, and I apologize for the upcoming question, but the doctor says I should see whether your memory is affected by the incident as soon as you're awake. Do you remember the last thing that happened to you?" Susanna inquires, whipping out a clipboard.

That's the jackpot question right there. I rack my brain in an attempt to recall what happened, and brief visual images flurry through my mind like someone flipping the pages on a pop-up children's book.

Schoolwork, languid tiredness, and sleepovers at Haley's. Why was I spending nights at her house? Oh yeah, Roger. Wait! Does Mom know that I'm here—?

Mom. Waitress. Driving. Car accident. Destruction. Death.

My eyes widen and goosebumps instantly fabricate over my arms as I recall the haunting, crumpled mass of her vehicle. But it is too late now. My memories are roused, angry at my prying, and they don't stop.

Videl. Bet. Heartstrings. Using me. Breaking up. Despair.

My head swivels to Videl, and he notices the alarmed expression on my face. I glance down at our entwined hands.

Catatonia. Weeping. A feeling of absolute tribulation. A lost will to live. Pills. Videl. And—

The conclusion of my thoughts explode into a final bow stroke of an orchestra of strings. The reverberating sound dies in a dull throb inside my head. Almost like I had.

Suicide. *Suicide.*

"You remember," Susanna susurrates. I give her a woozy jerk of my head.

"W—why?" I mutter. My resolution floods back into me, and I'm left with the same angst-ridden, hopeless feeling before my attempted suicide.

"I don't know what prompted you to try, but that's why I'm here to list—"

"No. I mean, why did you save me?" I direct this question at Videl. "Just let me die."

Something almost like raw pain washes over his face, and I have to remind myself it's just a front. He doesn't care.

"I—because I—" Videl is struggling to string a sentence together. He finally settles on an, "I'm sorry," after another futile attempt at explaining himself.

"I'll leave you two alone," the nurse interrupts, sensing the awkward tension between us. "I need to let the doctor know of Hope's progress." She walks out of the room, shutting the door behind her with a soft click.

A few minutes pass without either of us making conversation, and while my attention is on him familiarizing his features that I haven't seen in weeks, his eyes dart anywhere except mine.

"Videl." He looks up at me with an inscrutable expression.

"How are you feeling?" he asks.

"Like death," I mutter.

Videl doesn't respond, but his face drops down a notch.

I shake my head, unable to stop my thoughts any longer. I can already feel the tears welling. "You betrayed me." The accusation causes him to open his mouth, but I continue my rant, leaving him no room for interruptions.

"I—I—I—I can't even explain it. I—I couldn't take the pain anymore, Videl! Every day after M—Mom's death, it was—you can't even begin to imagine! Everywhere I went, the walls just—they just kept closing in on me from all sides. I couldn't breathe. Everything—everything I had once considered important—it just lost meaning! I couldn't keep anything down. I couldn't sleep, yet there you were. *You* were the only thing holding me to this world. *You, Videl!* And when I—when you confessed what the extent of our relationship truly was, it just pushed me over the edge. I had you...and then you were just *gone*." My clenched palm relinquishes, and it feels like whatever is held inside flies away. "I had absolutely nothing left."

He shakes his head, wiping the tears from my cheeks. I can't force his hands off even if I wanted to—the tubes make sure of this.

"You—" I let out a strangled sob, but I am cut off by the sound of the door opening.

"Doctor Lee is here to see you," Susanna announces. My attention diverts from Videl, and I focus on the nurse and the shadow of another person as they make their way into the open space of the room. My breath hitches when my eyes first spot the doctor's ostentatious shoes, and they set off a warning bell inside my head.

"Good afternoon, Hope," the female doctor says, taking a seat in the empty seat. Her blonde hair is a shade lighter than it was back then, but there's no mistaking the straightened composure and clenched jaw muscles. And then the memories I had worked so hard to repress since waking up began surfacing at the sight of her face. The doctor's complexion is void of any blood, but I can still see the specks freckled on her forehead, a clear reminder of what happened that night. The burdened shake of her head. The useless condolences spilling from her lips.

"N—n—no. No, no, please." I whimper raggedly, pushing out my arms before collapsing into the bed. My vision gives out until all I see is Mom's killer standing right in front of me. A black hoodie shadows his face, and I can see his evil smile before he opens his mouth. He points at me with a wrinkly finger as if to say *you're next*.

"Stop it! Go away! Go away!" I scream. He draws closer and begins laughing, his baritone voice planting a dark pit of despair inside me.

"Hope," he slurs. "Hope. Hope." His hand stretches out. I keep screaming, but it only seems to spur him on.

"Hope. Hope. *Hope!*" A hand is shaking me painfully. The menacing stranger vanishes and Videl's face replaces his. "It's okay; nothing's here to hurt you."

"Rest assured, Miss Valentine. You're in no danger here." It's the doctor's voice. My vision clears up within a few seconds and once again, I'm brought face-to-face with her. Luckily, she doesn't trigger any nightmares this time.

"It's you."

No sign of recognition passes over the doctor's face. She probably has so much going on in her career that my mom, a simple-dressed woman, wouldn't leave any memories.

"Yes, it's me," she says blankly. "We're going to have to do some tests. After all this time passed…I'm genuinely surprised you woke up."

"What do you mean?"

"No one told her?" Both Susanna and Videl remain silent. "Take a look at the calendar to your right, Miss Valentine. Above the desk."

I do as she tells me, and my eyes widen at the cursive letter F followed by the rest of the month's letters.

"Impossible," I whisper.

"It's rare, but possible," the doctor responds. "You were in a coma for two months. There was still the power of twenty pills inside your stomach when you were brought to the ER. Chances of you pulling through were slim to none."

Very vaguely I can hear the doctor muttering something to Susanna and Videl, but I can't understand what she's saying from the mess of thoughts in my brain.

Suddenly, I laugh. My ears pick up the startled cries of Videl and Susanna, but they don't do anything in fear of finally cracking my sanity.

I laugh at the heavens, and at whoever is up there making my life a living, mocking joke. *Slim to none*, she said. The EMT had said the same about Mom, but somehow I'm the one who manages to pull through.

After a few more seconds of nonsensical laughter and worried looks shooting my way, and I start wheezing due to lack of air. The nurse puts an oxygen mask on my face, and when she deems me stable enough, takes out a clipboard and begins writing. After five or ten questions about my psyche and a rudimentary checkup, Suzanna and the doctor leave the room.

"How is it *February*?" I ask in disbelief, still having not gotten over the fact that a whole two months have passed without my existence. "How?"

"There's a lot of factors that play into it. That's what the doctor said." He gives my hand a light squeeze.

My eyes must be playing a sick prank. Or Videl must have flipped the calendar to a different month.

"Tell me you're joking. You and Susanna and the doctor must be in some sort of cahoots with one another to mess with me."

"N—no. Today's Valentine's Day." Videl gestures over to a nightstand I had missed in my earlier sweep, and it draws my attention. The desk is occupied by a vase mixed with ivy, hydrangeas, and other flowers I can't identify. Cards, presumably, lay strewn next to them. I wonder who sent them.

"I've seriously been here for two months?" It sounds too absurd to believe. "This room, in this bed?"

"Yeah. The doctor saved your life, and as she said, the chances of you ever waking up again were slim to none. She was worried you might be brain dead. I'm glad you're back," he exhales, squeezing my hand again.

Two months. I've been unconscious for two months? How can someone even live for two months without realizing? Rather, it feels like I just woke up from a long nap, except that my muscles feel like dead weight from lack of use, and my haggardness keeps threatening to drag me under again. And my head feels like an irascible Indian war chief is pounding on it with his personal set of buffalo bone drumsticks.

"Can you—can you fill me in on what's happened?" I ask him.

"What do you want to know?"

"What did I miss at school?" I swallow the lump in my throat. Videl lets loose a soft chuckle.

"Out of all the questions you could ask, you decide to inquire about school? You haven't changed one bit." Videl shakes his head. "The teachers know. The principal sent a staff email so you could retain your privacy, but news of you being hospitalized still managed to reach the students."

"H—how did that happen?"

"Haley's been skipping cheerleading practice every afternoon to come and visit. Because Veronica's her teammate and the asinine gossip queen, she made sure that the news regarding you was spread through campus." Videl rolls his eyes, but then his lips purse. "You need to see Haley, Hope. I know a reunion would do her good. Ever since your…incident, she hasn't been the same. She doesn't reveal much to me, but I know she blames herself."

"It's not her fault." Memories of my abuse toward Haley surface to the front of my mind. "It's mine."

"Well, I won't nose myself into your business. But I won't be surprised if she's angry. The one afternoon she has a mandatory cheerleading practice, and you wake up." He chuckles.

"And is there anyone else that comes to visit?"

He rubs his chin, the only sign of his engrossment. "Now that you mention it, a black-haired girl with a raven-esque appearance has been visiting a couple of times a week. I bump into her quite a bit. Doesn't seem too friendly. She's got the eye-glaring, dagger-wielding expression on her face every time I pass through like she's out to get me."

A rush of relief washes through me.

"And Roger? What's happened to him?" The house we were in before Mom's death was Rogers, and I sure as hell refuse to live with him.

"I don't know. I haven't heard much of what's been going on with his life."

"He's been paying the hospital bills?"

"Yes."

"Do you know why?"

Videl shrugs. "As much as I loathe the guy, I do appreciate this gesture of his. None of your friends were ready to pull the plug on you quite just yet. The bad news is that since your birthday is in August and *he's* the only relative by marriage that's left, you're obligated to live with him until you're eighteen."

"What? No. No way." My free hand grabs Videl's shirt. "You can't—can't let me go back to Roger. You—"

"I won't let that happen, Hope. Have you forgotten that I know what he tries to do to you?" Videl whispers in my ear. "You don't have to worry about him."

We fall quiet again, and I find myself thinking back to that eventful night. I had come home after the park, trudged upstairs, and succumbed. At that point, I had accepted my fate. Then Videl had to ruin it. He just had to break the door down and be the unwanted savior.

"How did you know where I was? And how did you even get in the home?"

Videl fidgets in his seat. "You were sitting on the swing at the park. Altha told me that she saw you with your head down when she drove by. When I went looking for you a couple of hours later in the afternoon, you were already gone. As for your second question, the front door was unlocked."

"You said you loved me when you burst into my room," I try to halter the accusatory tone as I recall the few lines of our dialogue on the bathroom floor. "What's that supposed to mean? Were you just desperately trying to provide me with some glimmer of hope at the time so I could keep living? News flash, Videl. The sentience boat has long sailed. I don't want you in my life anymore, especially after what you did to me." My voice is steady, but it holds an undercurrent bitterness. The heart monitor's beeping rate slightly increases.

"It was a joke," he mutters under his breath, and I don't understand it at first.

"Don't be flippant. What was a joke? That it's February? That you loved me?"

"No! It's so stupid; I don't even know why I took it! How do I even begin explaining this?" He takes a deep breath then looks at me in the eyes. "It was a lousy bet with Chad."

"Come again?"

"It was a bet with Chad."

"When was this, and what did this *bet* entitle?"

Videl mutters, "He bet after our first calculus exam to date you for a month before dumping you and telling you it was all a front. It came up in as discussion right after the first football win against Palm Valley."

It takes heavy digging to get through the cobwebs, but eventually I dig up the memory. "Is that why you were so congenial toward me all of a sudden? Before you came to me for tutoring, you never heeded me."

Videl nods. "Yes. At the time, everything ran smoothly. Haley urged me to go to you for tutoring, so I thought I'd take the opportunity and knock out two birds with one stone: aid my grades, and implement Chad's idea."

"Haley—"

"Was not made aware of this bet. I take full responsibility for my actions." Videl balls his fists and brings them up to rub his eyes. "I just never knew how much the bet would backfire on me."

My curiosity gets the best of me. "So what—what changed?"

"The more we got to know each other—and not just aimless facts—the more I realized you were more than just a toy. After Carmine's, that's when I first understood what we had was more than just a game. You committed a large amount of trust in me. You showed me your vulnerability and entrusted me to take care of you. And that itself opened up a level of attraction I didn't know existed."

"So why didn't you say anything?" I almost shout. If I had just given him a chance to explain himself instead of running away from him, things would be much more different. I wouldn't have lost Haley as a friend. I wouldn't have fallen into the darkness of drug addiction. And most of all, I wouldn't have tried to—

"Don't blame yourself, Hope," Videl whispers. "You're not culpable."

Again with the mind-reading. "That day—the confrontation—if I didn't cut you off, then you would have had a chance to explain."

"You were upset at me for good reason; you had the right to stop me. I should have just told you the truth. Or better yet, not take Chad's stupid bribe."

I snort. "The bribe isn't the only thing that's stupid. Why the hell would you ever befriend Chad? He's a moronic dick."

Videl shrugs. "Same reason Haley used to date him. He was chill. A friendly, frivolous guy—"

"Who is a stud that only thinks about increasing his muscle mass, and the only way he'd *ever* get into college is if he somehow bribed an admissions officer to give him a football scholarship for a sport he's on the team for only because his father and the coach are chummy buddies," I finish.

"You seem to be keeping heavy tabs on someone who you hold heavy disdain for."

"Well, he and Haley are dating. I have to listen to her constantly on Chad this, Chad that." I roll my eyes. "Wait, didn't you use past tense a moment ago? Haley and Chad broke up?"

"I'm not too sure. All I know is that they went to a party on New Year's and then they were over the next day."

"Thank god."

Videl chuckles. "It's the first day of your awakening, and you're already reverting to your old self."

I giggle but fall silent. "How can I trust you ever again?" I suddenly ask him.

A painful expression works its way onto his face. "I'm not playing you anymore, Hope. I love you and always have. But I know the trust we had is severed and needs plenty of repairs."

I agree with him, but I keep my mouth shut.

Videl's eyebrows pinch together, and overwhelming sadness fills his eyes. His face contorts into an expression so painful it would make fate chastise my behavior. And at this moment, I know I will forgive him. Forgive, but never forget.

I click my tongue while I carefully think of what to say next.

"You're right. The trust I had for you is gone, but that doesn't mean I'm not willing to see you anymore. As friends." Just like that, a huge weight is lifted off me. The only burden is the desire to return his confession. Because deep inside, I know I still love him. I always will.

Videl's face completely morphs and breaks out into palpable relief. He offers me half a smirk. "Friends. For now."

I half-heartedly shove him. "Just don't screw it up this time. This is your last chance. Bet or no bet, I'm not going to be used."

"Deal. I can live w—"

The door suddenly clicks open by an unannounced visitor.

"Alright. You've had more than enough time with her. Now get the fuck out."

That voice.

I crane my head over Videl's hair.

"Jackie?!"

"In the flesh," she grins, kicking out the other chair and plopping down in it. "You going to kick this guy out or am I going to have to do it for you?"

My eyes catch with Videl's. "Please," I whisper. Videl reaches a conclusion and blinks before leaving. The door shutting behind him seems to instigate Jackie.

"Hey," she takes my hand and holds it. The feeling of her soft palm puts me at ease. It's soft and so, so *real*. "You almost did yourself in."

"Yeah. You're not going to cry, are you?"

"Hah, me? You can keep wishing. Maybe in a million years." She leans forward, and I recoil so that her kiss lands on my cheek instead. "How are you feeling?"

"Shitty. It's hard to believe two months have passed." I scrutinize Jackie. She wouldn't play a prank like this on me.

"I know, right? You were missed at school. My house wasn't the same without you."

"So I guess you had a lot of fun then," I chuckle.

Jackie snorts. "Yeah, definitely had esoteric conversations with myself while going about daily chores. People probably thought I was crazy, talking to myself all the damn time."

I giggle again. "Come on; it couldn't have been that bad."

Jackie pinches my arm lightly. "It was, because I've never hung out with anyone as much as I did with you."

"What do you mean?"

"Friends come and go, and for me, that timespan is probably only a few days. I never really *click* with anyone. I can't tell you how many times I've had discussions about social conventions and all that unavailing stuff we have to conform to just to have the person on the other end of the conversation give me one of those head nods or mirthless laughs—you know, the ones that don't mean anything outside of an act of politeness as to not offend the other person. That is, until I met you. When I started talking to you, it was like a light went off in your eyes. You and I both want liberation. In the end, we're two peas in a pod."

"I know. I feel it, too. When I take a look at people, they all seem so content. There are people I've talked to who are so down to earth they don't even want to begin to imagine stepping beyond the boundary."

"See? You understand. And since you understand what I want," she says, lowering the pitch of her voice down a few tones, "You up for anything right now?" A naughty glint works her way into her eyes. She whips out a bag and my eyes grow wide. I involuntarily lick my lips and a small glimmer of longing sparks deep down within me.

"You seriously brought that into a *hospital*?" I hiss, my eyes rapidly scanning the room for cameras. "You're crazy!"

"Being crazy constitutes who I am."

I shake my head. My smile slowly vanishes until it disappears altogether at the epiphany that strikes me.

"I can't."

Jackie petulantly sighs and then retreats to her chair. "Makes sense. After an ordeal like that, you must be tired as hell. And this tube up your nostrils and all these cannulas. Wouldn't want those suckers to go any deeper from our roughhousing."

"No, Jackie. Not that." My eyes dart anywhere in the room except her face while I brace myself for the blowing words. I look up to the ceiling and huff. "I can't be around you anymore."

The temperature in the room seems to drop down a few degrees, and I know Jackie's not happy. I take a glance at her and see that her smile is gone.

"Reason? I thought you just said you enjoyed my company." The hurt is obvious, flashing in her eyes like the tears threatening to cover mine.

"I do, Jackie."

"So what's the reason then? Spit it out."

"I enjoyed every moment with you, but the blow—it just—it just fucked me up so much. My mind—my rationality—it wasn't even there anymore. The experience was too out-of-body. I was living under the shadow of some uncontrollable entity possessing the real me. I saw the world in black and white. There was no color."

"You don't have to do blow for us to hang out." Jackie's upper lip trembles and goosebumps grow on her arms. For the first time with my own eyes, I see Jackie's composure crumble to pieces.

"I'm sorry, Jackie, but the pressure to drug myself when I'm around you is too monumental. I can't—" I shake my head back and forth, scared. "I can't. I can't."

"Hope..."

"We both know if it came down to you choosing me or cocaine, it'd be the latter," I resume, pressing down on the urge to ravage the bag.

"That's not—"

"But you can tell me I'm wrong. All you have to do is tell me I'm wrong, Jackie."

She fidgets, her hands tightening around the arms of the chair. At least a minute passes in silent tension.

"I can't," she finally says feebly, much like I did. "As much as you make me, I can't."

I take my free hand and run it across her cheek, already expecting the answer before she gave it. Just one last time. "Come here."

Jackie leans in, and her soft taste I never forgot—nutmeg and essence oil mixed with identifiable traces of cocaine—penetrates my senses and invades my system. My tongue darts into her mouth and begins licking for more. A deep part of me tied in chains moans in desperation and rattles around angrily, like Jackie's kiss is fuel for her determination. I'm in need of her and a need to revert to who I was back a couple of months ago. If it isn't for my willpower, I will have lost. The scary thing, though, is that it is still a close fight.

We break apart and stare into each other's souls, savoring the unmistakable connection between us.

"It's okay. I'm not mad at you."

"You're not?" Jackie breathes, eyes wide.

"I'm not," I say again. "But this is it."

Jackie's face instantly falls and morphs into a more painful expression than Videl's that I almost change my mind. But I know the time I spend with her won't be benefitting for me in the future. She's a bad influence, the rotten apple of the bunch. And it pains me even more in admitting this right after our intimate moment.

"I'm so sorry."

Jackie turns away, and my hand slips off her face. I know she's crying.

"Hey. No tears, remember?" My stomach swoops as a seed of self-loathing spreads inside me. Two months of no contact with Jackie and on the first day I see her in the flesh, I reject her. Disgusting.

"Yeah. You're right." She gives me a clipped response and then turns around. A bright sheen coats her eyes. "But don't think I'm not going to take the opportunity to harass you when you're in the hallways at school."

Just like that, the old Jackie's back—an unbreakable wall obscuring her true feelings.

"You better watch out, because I'm bringing my game."

~~~~~~

My time back to consciousness to being discharged takes another week due to my convalescence. Jackie respects my decision and doesn't visit again, much to my dark disappointment. I also ask the nurse not to let Haley visit—not because I don't want to see her, but because I want to be strong enough to stand face-to-face with her when the time comes. The primary focus during this week is my recuperation.

I leave Monday morning, checking out at the front desk with another hour to spare before the first class of the day at my school starts. The doctor suggested that I spend a minimum of another week in bedrest but fuck that. It'll drive me nuts.

I spend the walk with fluttering butterflies in my stomach. A solid chunk of the second semester has already passed, and I wonder how that will affect me. Has anything changed? How will my classmates react? Not only that, but I don't feel like I belong anymore. There's this blip in the timeline of my life where I was completely irrelevant and nonexistent. The world moved on, while I didn't; I'm living in the past. And that itself is enough for a cloud of apprehensiveness to hover over my body.

Connecting with nature on the way to school is alleviating, but seeing the building, cars, and the bustle of students collectively gathering like ants to their hill is what begins to disconcert me again. Thinking about something is completely different from seeing it with your own eyes. Luckily, no one seems to notice me. Everything seems to be normal.

This atmosphere changes entirely as soon as I step foot inside the Education building. The moment I do, a loud voice rings through the hallway, drawing the attention of many.

"Hope! Hope!" A mellifluous voice rings out. I spin on my feet and see Haley, decorated in a pair of skin-tight light-blue jeans and a burgundy sweater, sprinting toward me. She breaks people apart in the hallway with rapid breaststrokes until she's standing with her face in front of mine.

All nearby sound around me dies away when I see her eyes dart over to my every feature—my combat boots, my leggings that drape loosely around thighs, my shriveled skin, my pale lips, and then my eyes.

"Hi," she says, almost pusillanimously. There is an obvious concern on her face, but something else that I can't pinpoint. But I have it all figured out in a matter of seconds. It's fear.

Even though they're blurry, the memories swarm back. With befriending Jackie came all the drugs, and all the unacceptable behavior toward someone who only wanted to help.

The concern is still manifested on Haley's flawless face when I take another look. Even after what I did, she still cares for me. She still wants the best for me. Just thinking this brings a sudden surge of emotion rushing through my heart. My mouth tumbles open, and everything spills out.

"I'm sorry, Haley," I choke. "I'm so sorry."

"Hope."

I stop her with my hand. "Let me finish! I—I—the way I treated you." I hang my head down in shame. "For how I ignored you and rejected you and turned you away, I'm so sorry. You've done nothing but be the greatest friend I've ever had, and I repaid you by condemning our friendship. There's nothing worse I could have done."

"Hope, look at me."

I lift my head up to see Haley. The next thing I know, my cheek spreads aflame from the hardest slap I've ever felt—even harder than Roger's. Whereas he slapped me for the sole purpose of getting me to behave, Haley's slap held much, much more; hers held the anger of a thousand suns, tempered with her agony and disappointment. But something else is buried—something bittersweet.

"How could you do this? Did you even stop to think about the people who care about you?" She slaps me again. "How do you think *I* felt when I heard you tried to take your life?! When you were in a coma?! How—" Haley's foot slips and she topples forward, but I catch her, even in my weakened state.

"How—H—You—" The stuttering is the only sign I receive before Haley slumps her shoulders and buries her face in my collarbone before bursting out in tears. The sound of her lament is so heart-wrenching that tears begin pouring from my eyes as well.

"I'm sorry, Haley. I'm so sorry," I repeat like a mantra. My brain fumbles to search for assuagements, but there is nothing I can say.

The warmth Haley radiates is like a protective bubble that envelops my whole being, body, and soul, and sets me at more ease than I've felt in ages. My shoulders continue to shake with the occasional hiccup emanating from the girl below me, but I don't care. Even with my eyes closed, my ears still pick up the absence of conversation around us, and I know every students' attention is on us.

By the time Haley's breathing begins to steady, the chatter around us starts back up. A few moments later, we simultaneously draw away from one another. She a few deep breaths before slowly reappearing from the depths of my shoulder. Her nose is rosy, and eyes are moist, but it doesn't detract from her beauty.

"You're wrong, you know," she whispers shakily, brushing my hair back.

My voice catches. "Wrong about what?"

"About the worst thing that can happen," she says. "Because the worst thing that can happen is you never waking up and leaving this world without a chance for us to fix things."

"Haley." Her proclamation almost sends me spiraling into another frenzy of tears.

"I love you, Hope. And I wouldn't have been able to stand you fading from this world knowing I was the one that caused it. Knowing that I could have done something to help you in the darkest part of your life."

I cry again, but not just because of Haley's admittance. I also cry because of fear. I feel no regret for my actions, and this is what scares me beyond disbelief. Because without regret, there is no intrinsic factor that will try to stop me if I were ever to try again. "I don't deserve your friendship. I don't deserve this forgiveness."

"I don't care what you think. You're my best friend. And best friends never give up on each other."

I close my eyes and squeeze her shoulders, fumbling for something to say through my speechlessness. But I don't need to because the bell suddenly blares and I jump in fright. A moment later, I scowl, feeling irritated at how an inanimate object can ruin such an important moment.

Haley also appears to be irritated by the bell because her body stiffens right before she pulls away. I immediately whimper at the loss of contact, but the angst goes away when she slips her hand in mine.

"Want me to catch you up on what's happening around school?"

"Yes, please."

The hallway is at its busiest time of the morning as all the students scramble to get to class before the tardy bell. We begin winding our way through the corridors and walkways, but the hallways seem to stretch infinitely when I catch the stares of many of the students. Knowing that they are only providing me their attention because of whatever fabrications spreading around the school unsettles me.

"Ignore them," Haley breathes, catching on. "They have no room to judge. They know *nothing* about you."

"H—how have you been, Haley? It's been—"

"Three months and eight days since we were on good terms," Haley whispers. "Until today. Until now."

"Yes." I swallow the lump lodged in my throat. "How is everything?"

"Well, I broke up with Chad after New Years. I bet you're relieved. You've been complaining about how he was incompatible with me when I first started dating him."

"Why did the two of you split?"

Haley looks at the ground and clenches both her fists. "He spoke things about you. Cruel, nasty things."

"Oh," I say, understanding. "But the two of you were together for over a year. That's a long time to spend with someone."

"What happened opened my eyes. I thought I loved him, but it was more of the fact that I loved calling someone mine instead."

"And your family? How are they?"

Haley's face darkens before she growls.

"My mom was in hysterics for several weeks after hearing what happened to you. When I told her, she almost fainted. She keeps blaming herself for letting you go. Serves her right," Haley says bitterly, kicking her foot at the empty air.

"Please don't be mad at your mom."

"Too late now. I don't know if we'll ever be the same as we were ever again," Haley reminisces, scowling in the process. "She crossed the ultimate line. For that, I can't forgive her. I won't."

"Please, Haley. It wasn't her fault."

"Wasn't her fault?! Because of her, I almost lost my best friend!" Her eyes begin to swim with tears again, and she quickly rubs her eyes. "Who am I kidding? It was my fault. I'm the one who let you go. I caused all this."

"No." Haley opens her mouth in what I think is another protest, but snaps it shut a moment later. She waits for me to explain, so I continue.

"Don't think I didn't see the dark bags under your eyes and how were always sluggishly milling about during the day. My presence was taking a chunk out of your health—*mine*, not your mom's. *I* was causing you all that distress. If you didn't take initiative, I was going to, sooner or later."

"I just don't understand, though. My mom is usually so calm. Her outburst was so unexpected. I've never seen her act that way."

I cup my hands around Haley's cheeks. "Your mom was just being a parent and putting her child first. Besides, in the end, I walked out of my free volition. Remember?"

Haley looks over my shoulder at what seems like a sheepish manner. When she speaks, her voice is soft.

"I don't know…"

"Haley." At her name, she gives me her undivided attention. "You know I wouldn't have been able to live with the guilt for taking advantage of your hospitality."

"I guess. Although it *was* nice. Your warmth was more than enough to replace the heater. I can't even begin to imagine how much money we saved on the gas bill."

I roll my eyes. "Have you apologized to her? Your mom."

"What? No!" she ghastly declares, looking at me like I've lost my marbles.

"You should. I'm sure she would appreciate repairing the between her and her own daughter."

"I don't know…"

"Would you rather I stand next to you while you're forced to say 'I'm sorry'?"

"No thanks," she blanches. "I'll tell her myself."

The hallway seems to stretch forever, and it isn't long before I turn too self-conscious from indiscreet stares. "All these people staring…"

"You'd better start getting used to it."

"What's that supposed to mean?"

"You know just as well as I do any interesting news in this jejune school spreads like wildfire on campus. You're like a celebrity here."

"Celebrity? Because I tried to—" No matter how hard I was trying to say the word, it just wouldn't come out. Luckily Haley reads my mind.

"N—no, because everyone knows who you are now. The principal made an official announcement to clear up any damaging gossip spread by Veronica."

"I'm not sure how I feel about this."

Throughout half the day alone, I get many stares and hushed whispers. Some familiar faces in my classes come up to me and give me a hug or a small smile, proclaiming that they would've sorely missed me if I had gone. These are people I had never spoken to in my life, and I couldn't help but feel somewhat irritated by the reason why they acknowledge my presence. I think they were just saying all that rubbish to be nice, and probably to give moral support to prevent another 'mishap' to occur in the future. After all, people don't wish for harm on others for no reason.

I let out a frustrated sigh before walking into chemistry a few minutes early so I can grab my usual seat and hide my face. The first thing I see is Stern, and he lifts my spirits. He's writing some foreign equation on the blackboard, but the screeching noise of the chalk halts when he takes heed of my presence.

"Ms. Valentine! It's great to see you." His face splits into a wide grin, and the infectious appearance causes me to break out into a smile of my own.

"Hi, Mr. Stern. You're teaching the second level?"

"Please, how long have we been over this? Call me Greg. And yes, I am. I take it the school's office approved you?"

"Right Mr. Ste—Greg," I nod, catching my error and correcting it. "They cleared me for all my classes, but I have to stay behind after school for remedial chemistry labs and calculus."

"Well, that's great news then!" He gives a hearty laugh. "We're currently in the middle of buffer solutions and titrations, but for someone as smart as you, it should be simple." His compliment causes me to blush. "Your classmates from last semester are all here, so you have the same seat. Next to Altha near the back."

"Okay, thanks." I begin making my way to the familiar black, scratched fire-retardant table.

I put my head down, but not before taking in his proud face before he turns back to the blackboard and resumes jotting down warm-up questions. I kind of drift off into the abyss, yet my ears still perk up a few minutes later when I hear the shoes squeaking on the linoleum floor and the chairs creaking under the weight of their inhabitants.

"Hope?" I lift my head up at the timid voice and see, strangely enough, the concerned face of Altha.

"Yeah?" My voice sounds a little skeptical. I half expect her to snort and then proceed to make an offhand comment about my emaciated figure and how I weigh even less from the improper sustenance the hospital provided. But instead, what she says next takes me by surprise.

"Are you alright?" she asks, and even in my dubious state, I can see the nervous bite of her lip as she thinks of what to say next.

"I'm fine? Are you? You're not one to concern yourself with my wellbeing."

"Yes. I'm fine." She continues nibbling on the corner of her lip, and it drives me nuts.

"Whatever you want to say, spit it out already."

She chews her lip one last time for good measure. "Yes. Look, I not the best when it comes to this, so I'm just going to say it right now…I'm sorry."

"Excuse me?" I'm so surprised at her apology that I lose my inimical tone. Altha fidgets in her chair anxiously. "I mean, why are you sorry?"

"Look, I just am, okay? Can't you accept it and move on?"

"No. You've piqued my interest. Why apologize now? You've been treating me like shit since the first day I met you," I test.

"Look," she says for the third time, and I resist the temptation to roll my eyes. She lets out a tiny sigh. "I know it isn't in my place to tell you this, but Videl told me about what happened. How he found you."

"Oh." I completely forgot the possibility of Videl telling her what happened. "Yeah. The bathroom door is going to cost a fortune to fix."

She squints her eyes. "That's not funny. And that's also not the point."

"Then what is? No offense, Altha, but I've never known to you be one to beat around the bush, and frankly, you're making me exasperated. A little."

"Okay!" She puts up her hands defensively, which throws me for a loop. I don't think I've ever seen her this compliant. "I'm sorry…for treating you so poorly since I've met you."

"Poorly?"

"Okay, terribly."

"Keep going."

"I'm sorry! For treating you like my inferior. For treating you like the dirt at the bottom of my shoes." Altha brings her fists up and rubs her eyes. For once, she doesn't sound dignified. "What am I doing, apologizing to my nemesis?"

"Relax. I'm just teasing you," I say, my lips curling into a smirk. I'm kind of enjoying the omnipotence of the situation here.

"Whatever. Do you want me to answer your question or not? I can sense the seriousness in her voice, so I sew my mouth shut and listen to what she has to say, but not before saying, "We have time before class starts."

Altha's eyes shift past my face to the window I know is behind me.

"It's a long story, so bear with me. I had a friend," she starts, then shakes her head. "Have. Have a friend back in France that I met at the beginning of lycée. French secondary education," she clarifies. "She was my best friend. Much like the relationship between you and Haley, we would see each other every day. We confided our secrets to one another, went shopping together, and had dinner dates together. It was through her that I discovered my identity, and I ended up falling in love with her. She was even my first kiss, and we were inseparable. Up until a year ago."

"What made you two separate?" I ask, curiosity having gotten the best of me.

"She died."

"Oh."

"Out of the year I spent with her, I thought I knew her. I thought I could read her as well as she read me." Altha lets out a strangled chuckle.

"I'll always remember the day it happened. It was our anniversary, and I had planned our day down to the minutest of details. But when I rang the doorbell, it wasn't her who answered. It was a policeman." Altha suddenly turns the other way and hides her face. "Suicide, I was informed. She took her life." My stomach swoops. Altha continues, her voice void of any usual confidence.

"The cop was there, asking her family questions. It wasn't until later that I realized the reticence behind her decision for me to never meet her parents was because of who *they* were. Archaic Neanderthals. Neoconservatives. She had told them about me. She was the subject to their abuse. Because of her sexuality. Because she openly defended her girlfriend after being insulted. Shows how much her parents truly loved her."

"For the longest time, I was lost. I blamed myself, and worst of all, I blamed her. I hated her for not telling me something like that! Why wouldn't she confide in me? I would have done anything for her!" Altha's voice becomes frantic, and her eyes glaze over. "Only a month later did I realize my anger was misplaced. I wasn't mad at her; I just didn't have anyone else to release my frustrations on."

"Look, I'm not saying I'm in love with you. That's not what it is at all. When it finally hit me—that I would never see or touch her ever again for as long as I lived— it was heartbreaking. I realized then that it's the worst feeling ever, to lose someone close to you. You're close to my brother, and when he told me what happened, I couldn't help but be reminded of my past. You and my girlfriend are so different, yet excruciatingly same. And I realized after what you went through, that I was the one who caused you do what you did. *I* became my girlfriend's parents; the source of the pain. Tell me something," Altha whimpers. "Was my bullying what pushed you over the edge?"

"It was mostly the losses in my life. But that's not to say the hurtful words weren't a part of it. I was just tired of it all."

Her face falls. "I knew it," she whispers. "There was always a nagging tug on the back of my head, telling me that I'd gone too far."

"It's okay Altha, really," I tell her sincerely. "I know it wasn't easy confiding me with a piece of your life, and for that, I appreciate it." Altha just confessed to me her deepest secret. To someone she has harbored ill feelings toward since the beginning of school. I have to do something. So I decide to comfort her, taking her hands in mine. She doesn't remove them, but they twitch as she probably wonders what the hell I'm doing.

"I can't live through the experience like you did; that's in your memories, not mine. But I do understand what you went through. And for all it's worth, I forgive you. If she was here, I'm sure she would too." And I did understand. Altha pointing the finger of blame at her girlfriend was no different than me doing the same to Mom when she left me.

"Look at your altruism, comforting me." Altha's body loosens and she smiles at me. Not a mocking smirk or sneer, but a legitimate smile for the first time. One that showed a tender, demure side, normally suppressed under her stoic mask.

"You should smile more often. You're much prettier this way. I like them better than your scowls."

"Don't get used to it," she warns, but I can tell it's playful. Just like that, the atmosphere changes.

I sift through the binder of information she gave me. "So is that why you moved here? So you could start a fresh life?" I ask.

"It's my excuse for running away, yes. But not Videl. His reasoning is different."

"In what way?"

"It's not my position to explain. You'd have to ask him for yourself." I blench. "My fault. I assume you two aren't dating anymore."

"You knew?"

"That you two were together? I knew the two of you liked each other before either of you even knew. The morning after Veronica's party when it looked like you weren't wearing any underwear because my brother's shirt was too large for you," Altha opines matter-of-factly, ticking off her fingers one by one. "The time I ran into you two ready to smear each other's faces off next to the railing. The not-so-secret gossip from Haley declaiming the reason behind the empty seats in calculus was because you were currently on a romantic excursion—bragged about it right in front of Veronica too. Need I go on?" I quickly shake my head, flushing at her apt descriptions. "But you stopped coming around after a while."

"We broke up," I admit.

"He didn't mention that part. May I ask who ended the relationship and why?"

"I did."

"Wow." Besides the one time I beat Veronica up at their home, Altha looks impressed. "A girl breaking up with *him.* Not typical whatsoever. I wonder how he felt being on the other end for once."

"He said I was a bet."

She scowls. "Now that is typical of him." After making sure I'm not about to have an emotional breakdown, she continues, "What did the bet entail?"

"He said Chad dared him to do it. To date me for a month and then dump me; that was the ultimate goal."

"Makes sense. I know for a fact he never would have dated someone like you. Even in France, he always had a thing for blondes who wore too much makeup. No offense."

My lips purse. "None taken."

"So you're just going him go? Like that?" Altha snaps her fingers as to demonstrate her point. "You don't want him anymore?"

"I never said that." She takes a studious look at me.

"You're scared. Scared that he might do something like this again. Along with a loss of trust."

"He said he actually fell in love with me and completely dismissed the idea of the bet even taking place to begin with."

"He's telling the truth," she says straightaway.

"T—that's what he said too."

"If it's one thing I can tell you about my brother, it's this. He *never* asks for forgiveness. Everything he's done in his life he's stuck by with no regrets, even if the people around him disagree with his choices. If he wants to get back into a relationship with you, he wants to get back into a relationship with you. Simple as that."

"I want to believe him, b—but frankly—"

"Frankly what? Besides the fact you're too scared."

"I was going to say he's my first real relationship, and thus, I don't know how to react in a situation like this."

"This is as corny as it gets, but just go with your heart. I live under the same roof as him. I see his gag-worthy mannerisms every day, but even he's been logically thinking about you with his real head instead of lustfully with his other. You're the first girl who's ever made it longer than a week."

"Still. I can't believe you just because you say so."

"Don't worry. I know my brother, and if he wants something, he's going to get his claws on it. I give it less than a week before he has you back in his arms."

"Is that a bet?" I narrow my eyes.

"God no. I can't even begin to believe I'm shipping you and my brother together."

"Don't expect a thank you."

"From you? I'll pass."

"You're still a vainglorious bitch, you know that?"

"And you're still an insufferable know-it-all."

Our insults disappear in the insouciant atmosphere, and we find ourselves suddenly giggling. This catches the attention of Stern, and he breaks into a large beam before signaling us to keep it down while pointing to the rest of the class. The other students are already situated at their tables working on the problems Stern put up on the board. We must have completely lost track of time while talking.

"Alright, class. Today we have a student that—although absent in the flesh, but with us in our hearts—returned to us. Hope," Mr. Stern exalts. Almost all of the students turn their bodies around. Some give me reassuring smiles, while others maintain an indifferent face before quickly turning back to the front.

"Did his speech have to be so ceremonious?"

"I'd say it's worth it if I get to see you blushing."

"Shut up!"

"Back to business," says Stern. "We're going to be reviewing the problems on the board because many of you seem to be having difficulties when it comes to finding the pH using the Henderson-Hasselbalch equation."

"What are you doing?" I whisper when I hear the soft grind of Altha's chair.

"Someone has to catch you up on the material. Would you rather it be one of those unfriendly students who hardly gave you a second look?" she asks, not even a foot away.

"You noticed?"

"I *was* one of those kids."

The rest of the class breezes by in a whim. Although learning buffers are far more challenging than the simple entropy calculations in the prerequisite, I find new joy in the classroom. Not because we are learning something new—no, I've always loved chemistry—but because the person I share the table with is no longer ready to bite my face off at any given time.

For the rest of the class period, the mood between us is completely different. It's as if the old, stale, toxic gas hovering over our heads is replaced by pure, healing-inducing, breathable air. In just fifty minutes, one semester's worth of pain is gone. Gone was the disparaging, please-let-this-class-be-over tone, and in its place is an amiable one; she talks to me as if we've been friends our whole lives—with much resemblance to Haley and me—and I find it bizarre at how quickly she switched teams.

"Homework for tonight are problems two through fifteen located in the back of the buffers and titrations chapter," Stern announces in an outdoor voice. Then a much quieter voice, "Hope, can you stay behind for a quick word yourself?"

Altha and I share a nod before she leaves. I walk to the front.

"Might I just say again it's wonderful to have my favorite student back. Don't tell the principal, though. We teachers technically aren't allowed to have favorites."

"Thanks, Mr. St—Gary, and don't worry. Your secret's safe with me." I know this isn't all that he wanted to say, for he could have just told me in front of Altha.

"I'm sure you were made aware of winter's talent show?"

I nod. "Haley told me about it. Some choreographed yo-yo act won?"

"Right. Such a disappointment you weren't there. Videl dropped out immediately soon after your hospitalization. The two of you would have unanimously won the show."

"What are you getting at?" I fidget.

"Well, as I'm sure you're aware of," he repeats. "The school also holds another talent show, usually a few days before prom. Will you be participating this semester?"

I bite my tongue, wanting to tell him no. But something inside me wants to be different. I want to prove that I'm not the same Hope I was two months ago—weak, meek, and always taking cheek. So I give an earnest nod after making my mind up.

"Sure," I assert.

"Great! I'll keep you updated on when that date will be in Music Club. Oh! Speaking of which, will you be rejoining us? The club meets after school today, in the same room as first semester."

"I'm going to take some time off, but I will be back."

"Okay, take as much time as you need." Stern seems pleased with my answer and then waves me off. "Welcome back."

I almost wish that chemistry class lasted five hours instead of one. Inside, I could take sanctuary. But now that I'm outside, the happiness from Altha and Stern slips away. Peers continue to come up to me and express their concerns for my health. This causes me to stay wary of approaching students, but it also serves as a detector of sorts. I use my newfound 'ability' to spotting some of the more sour, scornful, or disgusted looks on other students' faces. Some of them don't even bother to hide their disdain and look askance at me or begin to talk excessively loud when I am in the near vicinity, spouting pernicious words of hatred—retarded idiot, dumb brunette, suicidal fag—just some of the many examples. I guess they must be living a pretty good life.

The days pass on and on until they stretch to weeks. Haley doesn't leave my side one bit and invites me over to live in her house again. I politely decline. Altha and I get along now, and I even take the chance and visit her house, where she would tease me about resisting Videl past her one week bet—which would end up with us verbally fighting—and then turns into watching television or browsing social networking sites and stuffing our faces with food. I've gained almost all of my lost weight back. And when I spend nights in her room, there are no signs of her doll—Lacey-Macy. Perhaps she replaced her with me. Chemistry labs are also much more fluid with verbal communication between lab partners.

I also discover through our newfound relationship that our classes we have after chemistry are in the same building. Altha takes this opportunity and we walk together to the psychology building. She growls at anyone who stares at me for an extended period of time, as if she is protecting her territory.

The only time I see Jackie is in the psychology building—she's either perching against her locker in deep conversation or in her seat across the room during class. If it's the latter, then it's a guarantee I won't focus, for my body always shivers—a telltale sign of Jackie's glued eyes. Sometimes I have no choice but to pass her, and the nutmeg and essence oil fragrance almost clouds my sense and my saliva suddenly tastes like the white powder I banned myself from using. I tell myself it's just withdrawal symptoms, but yet one time after class I almost find myself groveling in supplication at her feet, begging to take me far away. The unknown tension between us continues to magnetize. She keeps her promise and stays away, and I've come to realize through this that I will always hold a soft spot for her.

The first time Altha sees Jackie is through a sharp glare at her staring at me for too long. Altha threateningly begins to walk forward, only to stop at my brisk tug. It takes a lengthy explanation about the relationship between the two of us in order for Altha to stop treating her like a hostile threat.

News of my return still circulates amongst the student body. The same thing happens—students come up to me and offer me a smile and support, while others ignore me but whisper degrading comments when they think I'm out of earshot. I find myself shying away from the students who offer me words of encouragement. They're the easiest ones to identify. The ones that walk with purpose, I ignore.

So it's with great relief that I finally find a familiar face after the last class of the day dismisses—Videl. I don't care that I'm not on the best of terms with him. At this point, I need to vent my dissatisfaction with the human race. I pull him inside an empty classroom.

"Are you following me or something? You're always everywhere I go."

"Half of my classes are in the same building as yours." Videl frowns and I realize I'm probably gripping him too hard.

"Sorry. I just can't deal with people right now." I sigh and glance behind me just to make sure there is no one here.

"Care to explain?"

"I can't deal with the sympathy! I can't deal with the commiseration! People are talking to me like they understand. They don't understand! People I never, *ever* talk to are saying 'I missed you this, I missed you that,' like they're obligated to make me feel better, but I can hear the undercurrent in their tone. They're blaming me, but they won't even try to understand! They don't know the thoughts that rush through your head at that moment! They won't understand!"

"They're not blaming you. I can't speak for everyone else besides Altha, but she's relieved. And Haley's your best friend; I'm positive she isn't one to point fingers. They're both thankful that you're okay and didn't kill yourself."

"Don't say that," I interrupt, holding my hand out.

"What, kill yourself?" I give him a nod. "Why?"

"I—I just don't want to hear it."

"Why?"

"I just don't want to! Please drop it."

Videl stares at me before saying, "You're scared to admit it because it serves as an unwanted reminder."

I shake my head and remain mute.

"Say what happened," Videl quarrels.

"Stop. I won't say it." I feel myself blanching and retreating into the dark corner of my mind, back to the fateful night. The dim lighting of my bathroom. The resigned state of defeat.

"How do you expect your friends ever to talk to you normally again if you don't confide in them?"

"I don't have any friends," I petulantly argue.

"Hope, you need to accept what happened. The more you keep this bottled up inside you, the longer it'll take for you to start moving on."

"S—stop," I helplessly say, my breathing becoming ragged. My eyes close, and I see everything. The color of the pills. The bitter taste as they dropped on my tongue. The grimy sinking feeling as they dropped into the pits of my stomach, all while I looked into the mirror.

Videl's huge arms wrap around my waist, and he pulls me closer to him.

"No!" I protest. "Stop touching me!" But he doesn't relent, and the next thing I know, his lips are on mine, silencing my protests.

My body continues to tussle against his grip, but I slowly give up when I feel myself floating away. His lips taste of the usual citrus flavor I was so accustomed to, and I find myself hypnotized and entirely under his power until my struggles die away completely. And a few seconds later, my lips begin responding of their own accord, massaging against his with unbridled passion. The smooth texture and perfect fit between us—like a lock and key—sends my brain reeling and toes curling and my mind away from death. This is what I've been wistfully missing—the electric shock that seems to jerk my body to life; the raw passion and fire. This is what my heart has been yearning for—his touch. But then, the contact is gone. He breaks away far too early for my liking, and I let out a loose whimper that turns into a throaty moan as he begins nibbling on my neck instead, planting kisses there before trailing down to my collarbone.

"Beautiful," is what I think comes out of his mouth.

"Videl," I plead, gasping as his mouth reaches a sensitive spot. He finishes up on my shoulder and proceeds to attack my mouth again with carnal hunger. This time, there are no complaints, and we move in sync until he finally pulls away, much to my disappointment.

"W—wow." My legs begin wobbling, and I have to reach for the desk to steady myself.

"I've wanted to do that since the day you woke up."

"Are you used to always getting what you want?" I ask, avoiding his eyes. I can't help but feel a bit ashamed. It's only been a little over three weeks of me trying my best to deny him, and look where that's gotten me. Flushed and horny, having just gone through one of the most heated exchanges of my life. Altha's going to have a field day.

"One of the many tricks I have hidden up my sleeve. Will you say it now?"

I give in, realizing he won't concede defeat. "Fine. I tried to commit suicide, okay?" I pause, waiting for a dramatic emotion to appear suddenly, but none does. The words escape from my mouth easier than I thought they would. Perhaps it's because I'm in a relaxed state of mind. Or maybe it's because of the hormones running rampant through every corner of my body. It doesn't matter, though, because as soon as I say it out loud, some heavy, unknown tension that I was unaware of on my shoulders instantly lift and leaves me feeling healthier and brighter for the first time in a month.

"Better?"

I nod fervently. "You were right."

"Nothing different in the line of work for someone as smart as me," he says cockily.

"Once again, your egotism never ceases to amaze."

He smirks. "So I kissed you and marked you as my territory."

"What are you, a dog?"

"I guess this means we're back together now?"

"Fine." My legs give a steady wobble. "Take me home."

17*

The next few days pass easily; I catch up on all my classes in no time. The next level of math is now easier than ever. Three-dimensional calculus has nothing on me. Luckily for Videl, he no longer is taking any math courses, for his sanity and mine.

The best part is feeling wanted and waking up in his arms. I have a place to stay, and I haven't seen Roger since awakening from my slumber. But there is one disparity on my mind: Videl has been making all of our meals.

"Now that I think about it, where's Bastien? I haven't seen him at all since I woke up from the hospital. I kind of miss the man," I remark, digging ardently into my soufflé after a late morning jog. Videl's attention leaves my lips.

"Who?"

Maybe I have too much dessert in my mouth. I take a swallow. "Bastien?" I ask again.

"I'm not familiar with that name. It sounds like something I'd name my dog."

"Okay, let's not tarnish his name. Bastien, your butler or manservant or whatever you call him?"

"I'm not kidding." At his serious tone, I look up to see a nonplussed expression on his face. "There's no Bastien in this house. Although it would be pretty cool to have someone do my dishes and laundry."

"But he always hovers around in that corner." I jab my finger next to the oven. "You told me he made a great bowl of bouilla-something when I woke up with a hangover." He continues to look at me strangely, so I try to clarify. "I got drunk at Veronica's party? We were sitting on the outside ledge?"

"Bouillabaisse?" Videl revisits. I give him a nod, and the next thing I know his hand is over my forehead.

"You're not burning up…Are you feeling okay Hope? Or does our mind-blowing bedroom sessions fiddle around with your brains?"

"Must you always be so ribald? Surprisingly enough, I can tolerate your megalomaniac personality in bed. But really, you're not messing with me right now?"

"No," he laughs. "I promise."

I must be going insane. I really, *really* could've sworn I know a guy named Bastien. Maybe it was just a dream. I frown and let the matter drop.

"Don't tell me Altha doesn't exist either anymore?"

"No, she's here. Do you want to see her?"

"Why not? I've been so preoccupied with you I haven't had the chance to speak with her lately, so—"

Videl lifts me up into his arms, and I squeal.

"You say it like that's a bad thing. Altha!" he shouts.

A familiar voice echoes from somewhere above. "What do you want?!"

"Hope wants to see you."

The door flies open just as Videl sets me down.

"Hi, Altha." She's dressed in a halter-top with a thin brown belt around her waist and even browner boots. My eyes drift down to her perfectly sculpted, sun-kissed legs. She's beautiful.

"Hope."

"I'm getting out of here," Videl mutters. "Have fun." He gives me a chaste kiss before exiting.

Altha's room is pretty simple. Her bed is directly in the middle of the room; it's larger than Videl's, and the bedsheets are a creamy color. On one end of the room, there is a gargantuan dresser, and a wardrobe at the other end. Other than that, there isn't much else. The room's spotless. Nothing like Jackie's.

My chest flutters as my brain takes a dive into my past. Jackie. Her plants. Her taste. Cocaine. The liberation. The spit in my mouth turns sweet.

I force these thoughts out of my head, locking them away in my heart. I made a promise, and I am going to uphold it.

"I was just getting ready to go grab a bite to eat. Do you want to join? Just the two of us." Altha brings me out of my reverie. "It's been almost a week."

"Um, sure. I am a bit hungry." As if on cue, my stomach grumbles.

"We can go shopping together afterward too," Altha says, as she picks up her leather purse. I double-check to make sure it's really Altha and not Haley.

At *Carmine's*, we get seated in the same spot as my last visit with Videl. Coincidence?

I order gnocchi again, and Altha and I discuss life. There aren't many whimsical remarks shared, but the atmosphere is still convivial.

"I'm running low on gas. You don't mind?" she asks, pointing to the gasoline gauge. The needle is hovering on empty.

"We both know you're going to get gas anyway," I roll my eyes. "Regardless if I give you permission or not."

"You're starting to know me too well. Maybe I should put my guard back up." Altha cracks a grin and pulls into a gas station on the side of the road and opens the door, but not before saluting me.

I'm not going to lie. I enjoy the newfound direction my relationship with Altha is heading. After our conversation in Chemistry, she's become a girl I can look up to and admire. Someone steadfast. Even though she is haughty at times, the trait makes her independent.

A loud clanking sound jerks me out my thoughts and redirects my attention toward a mechanic's shop. *Myer's Tires*, the sign says. A mechanic is in his uniform with his hair matted down under a baseball cap, and his skin is dirty from the oil and grease. But he's munching on his burger and sipping his drink with a grin on his face as he talks to a customer. Jobs…it's pretty obvious he enjoys his career. I wonder what kind of job I'll have after graduating. If I attend college, I know I'm going to major in—music is my life. If I don't attend medical school after, maybe I'll look toward working as a teacher. I shake my head. No, I wouldn't like that job. Too much chaos. Maybe a music therapist—music and medicine combined. I like the sound of that.

The mechanic finishes his conversation and walks back to the garage, tossing away the empty food bag into a nearby trash can. He lets out a belch that I giggle at, before pulling out a creeper and sliding under the car he was working on before his lunch break. Creeper. *Creeper.*

The world freezes. Paralysis strikes me while a tsunami of chills washes over me like a bucket of ice water. The memories rush back to me like a broken dam, and they are so strong I have to grip the seat so I don't pass out. The morning of Mom's death. Driveway. Roger tucked under her car. His refusal for an opportunity to grope me. *Brakes too wiggly.*

Very faintly I'm aware of the outside world collapsing on me until all that is left is the black creeper with the red wheels in my field of vision. The creeper squeakily slides back and forth from under the car like a therapist's pendulum. When it stops, the mechanic whips his head in a demented manner and catches my gaze. His mouth slowly morphs into a sinister grin, and he begins cackling.

I scream. The clang of the gas pump as it gets dropped back into its holster hardly registers in my ears.

The car door opens, and Altha steps inside with a blanched face.

"Hope? Hope! I heard you screaming!"

"Altha, I—I—"

"What's the matter?! Oh my god!" I see her boots disappear around the corner and then the sound of my door opening, and before I know it, I'm outside in the open air, knees on the ground. The next thing I know, I hurl everything from the meal I ate all over the pavement.

"—something wrong—sick—gas—" are the words I can just comprehend coming out of Altha's mouth as she's talking to someone on the other end of my phone.

"V—Videl. Let me—let me talk to him," I rasp. Altha slips my phone to the side of my ear, while her other hand still has my hair pulled back, in case if there was more bile to come.

"Hope?! What's the matter?!"

"It's Roger. It's Roger." Saying his name aloud triggers another bout of nausea through me, and I begin vomiting again.

"Roger?"

"Ye—yeah. He ki—killed Mom. He *killed* her!"

"Get back in the car and come home now."

Altha reclaims the phone and mutters something in French before disconnecting it.

"Come on. Let's get you home." I allow her to pull me up and sit me in the car before she closes the door. A crowd has gathered, a combination of customers getting gas and an employee of the station shop.

Altha walks up to the employee guy tells him to clean up the mess, slapping a fifty dollar bill into his dumbfounded hands before getting in the car. She starts the engine, driving us home like Videl reincarnate.

Videl is already standing outside by the time we pull into the garage. I collapse in his arms and begin crying as soon as I step out of the car.

"Videl! He killed her! He killed her!"

"Shh, Hope. It's okay. It's okay." Videl whispers, brushing my hair. "Tell me what happened," he says after my sobs reduce to nothing more than shaky whimpers. "Tell us what happened so we can make this right."

"I—we were at a gas station, and there was a mechanics shop next door." I take a few deep breathes and steel myself. "I saw a man working on a car with a creeper."

"What the hell is a creeper?" Altha asks.

"The sliding things mechanics get on so they can roll under a car," Videl explains. "Keep going, Hope."

"Our first official date, the one where you took me to the abandoned amusement park?" Videl nods. "That morning I went outside and saw Roger doing something to Mom's car. He said he was fixing the brakes, and he was under the car on one of those creepers. I—I told him I'd take a look instead, but he shrugged me off. I *knew* something was wrong. If—if only I had tried harder—if—that was the last time I ever talked to Mom. If only I kept better track of time. I'd be able to make it home before she left for work. I would've been able to save her! Why didn't I do something? Why didn't I do anything?!"

Videl holds me in the comfort of his body heat while I continue sobbing for the next several minutes until they become nothing more than dry hiccups. Altha disappears from the room for a minute and returns with a glass of water, which I graciously accept.

"We can't cross out the possibility that he has something planned for Hope," Altha astutely says, after accepting the empty glass from me.

"I highly doubt he's going to want to kill her. Her medical expenses were paid for by him. Chances are, he probably wants to take full custody of his stepchild," Videl argues.

"That kind of makes sense, but why would he want to do that?"

Videl turns his head to me, and I deliver him a delicate nod.

"Roger has this…obsession with Hope," he begins to explain.

"Obsession? Like he pines after her?"

"Not in the romantic gesture. One day she left her sweatshirt in my car, so I went to deliver it to her. Upon walking in, I saw Roger trying to force himself onto Hope."

Altha's hands immediately jump to her mouth. Her eyes stretch wide open.

"Is this true?" she asks. I give her a weak smile.

"Hope. I never knew." Before I know it, Altha spans the distance between us and embraces me in a hug.

"Regardless of his motives, we have to do something." The sound of Videl's voice breaks us apart.

"I agree. What you said earlier about custody transferring to Roger makes sense. I never knew he was *that* desperate to get Hope for himself."

"And we can't let him get away from his crimes," Videl adds.

"So do we have a plan?" I ask him. Although the open talk of Mom's death still bothers me, another more consuming desire has manifested in me—the desire to make Roger pay. For him to atone to his wrongdoing. Retribution will come.

"I may have something."

"Let's hear it. What?" Altha asks innocently after we turn to look at her. "Count me in. That's what friends are for, am I right?"

"Thank you."

"Enough with the pleasantries." Videl's eyebrows have been scrunched up in a concentrating manner for the last few minutes, and now he begins speaking. "We're going to need to get a confession out of him."

"You're not going to beat it out of him, are you?" I ask.

"As much as I like to hear those words coming out of your mouth, I'm afraid not," Videl sighs. "If I ask you to confess but you refused, and I resorted to violence, would you actually confess, or would you rather give a false confession to stop the pain?"

"I'd give you a false confession."

"Yeah. My gut says that's what Roger will do if I did start pummeling my fists into him. A slothful man like him doesn't hold many secrets, but for the ones he does, he's bound to protect."

"So what are we going to do?"

"Altha and I. Not you," Videl emphasizes. At my protests, he raises his hand, cutting me off.

"I won't place you in any more danger. Your safety comes first."

"*My* mom is the one who died, not yours. I have a right to see his disgusting face pay," I spit.

"And you will. Just… just hear my plan out, okay?"

I'm almost tempted to continue arguing with him, but I realize we will get nowhere. "Fine. What is it?"

"Well, it just came to the top of my head, but you said he never leaves the house, right?" At my 'yeah,' he continues. "So it's going to have to be in his house. I can install cameras in the living room then pay him a visit."

"That doesn't sound very adroit, if you ask me," I lambast. "If he doesn't clean the house, wouldn't you think he'd notice new shiny cameras installed throughout the house? Wouldn't he know something was up then? Plus, what are you going to say to him? Hi, my name's Videl, I'm Hope's boyfriend, and I need you to tell that camera over there—" I theatrically spin on my feet and point somewhere off in the distance. "—that you killed her mother by tampering with the brakes on her car, with which we'll then send the proper authorities over, and you'll be trialed, convicted, and sentenced to life in prison."

There's a long bout of silence before anyone speaks.

"Hope, you're frustrating me here," Videl finally states. "It just came to my mind; of course the plan's going to need a lot of refining."

"Sorry. Sorry." In an attempt to fix things and reassure him, I plant a kiss on his lips.

"It's okay. And don't worry. These are virtually microscopic surveillance cameras. Unless he has the vision of a hawk, there's no way he'll see these."

"You can buy cameras like that?"

"Probably, but they're the ones in our house. I'll uninstall them and bring them over to your place. When is Roger usually in?"

"Um, his work schedule is subject to change, but he's always out eating around lunchtime. So noon."

"Alright, how about this? You can come tag along when I begin setting up the house with the cameras, but you have to be at my house when I confront him. I'll feed the transmission back to my laptop, and you can watch from there."

"Ahem." Our attention shifts to Altha, who is now sitting with her legs crossed on the white loveseat. "As much as it pleases me to see my brother's lips locked around yours, isn't this plan revolving around your stepfather being an idiot in the first place? No human being with a modicum of intelligence would fall for a plan this stupid."

"Videl is sly when he needs to be," I defend, even though I was just questioning his plan moments prior.

"Yeah, but like Videl said, Roger is an indolent man. Any subtle change in house scenery and he's bound to notice."

"We just have to take the risk."

"Well, if you get caught, you'll be charged and arrested for breaking and entering."

"The worst they can do put me in jail for a day or two."

I shake my head furiously. "That's not the worst! I can't lose you again," I plead, resting my hands on his chest. "If he doesn't confess, they'll ship you back to France, and that'll leave me with—"

"Him. I know. But we need to take this chance, Hope. If we get Roger to confess, not only are you free from his cruelty, but your mother's death will also be avenged. I would do it myself, but this is something you have to be on board with, one hundred percent. I need you to trust me." He takes both of my hands and looks me dead in the eyes. "Trust me. I need you to be brave."

I stare into his jade green eyes. They continue to shine innocently after my analysis, so I give him a meek nod, and then he kisses me hard, letting me taste that everything would be okay.

"We should start planning. The sooner we start, the sooner Roger is behind bars," I hear Altha say.

"Just make sure you're careful."

"Who do you think I am?" Altha gives Videl the stink-eye before hugging me one last time and dragging her laptop upstairs.

~~~~~~

The next couple days tick by slower than the pace of a snail whenever I am alone in class. Videl tries his best to be by my side every hour of the day, leaving his classes early so that he could walk me to mine, his hand and divine lips soothing me. Altha begins to skip school for unknown reasons, and so has Jackie. Maybe she's going through withdrawal symptoms.

I find myself checking the time every ten minutes when I'm by myself in a class that doesn't hold Haley. I continue to gather my bearings, terrified that Roger will pop up out of nowhere and drag me away. If only I knew how soon that moment will come.

Roger calls me and tells me to come home the next afternoon. Videl is currently working on uninstalling the surveillance cameras, but he offers to come over and stand by my side. I refuse. Roger would get too suspicious.

Therefore, I walk alone down the road to the familiar cul-de-sac resting at the bottom of the hill. Roger's car is in the driveway. Bearing myself, I walk in the door with my head held high and find him sitting in his seat at the dinner table.

I warily pull out my chair and sit down, refusing to break eye contact with Roger. He waits patiently as I do so. The clock continues ticking. I find myself subconsciously counting how many seconds are passing.

The first thing he says after I situate myself is, "Where ya been?" His voice is unnervingly soft, but I know better. He is a ticking time bomb.

"School." I pat myself on the back at how my voice doesn't waver.

Roger sneers. "Bein' a smartass will get ya nowhere." He grabs his wallet and pulls out two tickets. Plane tickets.

"You and me are movin'."

The glass of water I had poured myself drops out of my hands and shatters into a million pieces on the wood.

"Wh—what did you just say?" My voice comes out in an undertone. The pieces of the puzzle click together to complete the final project as my brain struggles to keep my emotions in check.

"We movin'. Goin' abroad. Overseas. Maybe somewhere in Europe. Ya like them arts over there, don't ya?" Roger stashes the wallet away.

I try my best to keep my voice steady. "When are we leaving?"

"This Saturday. Take tonight and tomorrow to pack and get whatever belongings ya need. I'll enroll ya in a new school. I know how much you love making straight A's," he sneers. "So I'll give ya the privilege to finish your education over there."

"But why? W—why are we leaving? Why are you doing this?"

"Company's relocatin'. Figured ya'd wanna leave this place behind after Chloe's death and your failed suicide attempt."

"I—I can't leave Mom behind, even if she is deceased. At least let me live here, even if it's by myself. I can visit her and Dad's grave every day this way."

"Sorry." It's the first time I've ever heard him apologize, even if it is fake. "As your legal guardian now, I have an obligation to take care of ya. I know you're beat up about Chloe's death, but believe me, I am too."

This is the final straw that does me in.

"Bullshit!" I spring to my feet, ignoring the sharp jabs of glass as they cut through my flesh. "You're a fucking liar!"

"What did ya just say?!" Roger roars, immediately roused at my opposition. He mirrors my reaction by jumping to his feet, kicking his chair aside where it smashes against the wall. Sudden panic spurs me in a state of fear. I've never seen Roger so angry in a sober state.

"I said you're a liar. You want to take me away and keep me locked up like some animal far away in a place where I can't get in contact with the outside world!" Shit. Shit. *Shit*. What have I DONE?

"Ya little bitch! Who the hell told ya that?!" Roger pounces on me, but this time, my limbs aren't unresponsive. I leap out of the way, just barely escaping his grasp. Roger lands on the table and slides to the other side.

"I'm gonna sew that fucking mouth of yours shut and then drag ya away! Ya hear me?!"

"No! I'm not going anywhere with you!" He straightens himself up and runs around the table. I immediately run the other direction. We continue doing this for almost a minute without him managing to reach me. I might be laughing at how comical the situation looks if it isn't so dire.

"Who told ya that? Who told ya that?!" Roger's yelling becomes more and more overwrought until spit is flying out of his mouth.

I ignore Roger and and pick up Mom's chair—coincidentally—and hurl it with all my strength at him. The chair doesn't manage full-on hit him, but it does slide across the table, accelerated by his spit, and whacks him in the elbow.

Roger immediately begins unleashing a string of curse words, rubbing the injury with his hand. I use his distraction to my advantage and bolt up the staircase to my room, slamming the door behind me and locking it. The power cord splits apart when I yank loose my keyboard and lean it against the door. Afterward, I grab my backpack and fill it up with random clothes from my wardrobe and dresser.

"Phone...Phone..." I continue muttering to myself as I whip out my cell phone and pull up Videl in my contacts.

"Hope?" he answers, not even after the first ring.

"V—Videl."

"Go through your window and to the gas station on the corner of the street. I'll pick you up there," he says without hesitation.

"I'll be there." I hit the red end call button and freeze when I hear the floorboard creaking slowly.

"Hope? Honey? Are ya in here?"

"What is this? You trying to pretend you're nice for a change?!" I yell back.

I flinch as the door starts banging.

"Open this door right now!" he snarls. "I demand ya to, as your father!"

"You're not my father!" I scream, my fingers furrowing on the window latch. "My father is buried under six feet of dirt! You're just a disgusting pig who hides in human skin!"

"Ya little—!" Splinters fly over the carpet as his fist goes through the door. At the same time, I fly off the window and fall to the carpet, eyeing the piece of the object in my palm.

The window latch. It's broken.

A tremendous boom echoes throughout the house as the door finally reaches its maximum limit and flies wide open. Bolts snap off and the hinge is in half so that the door is bent at an angle and swings back and forth.

On the other side of the room stands Roger, armed with a carving knife. He kicks my keyboard off to the side. The instrument makes a dying noise, and my chest constricts when I realize it will forever remain silent.

"Gotcha," he starts cackling, his voice losing the vindictiveness it held downstairs. "I knew I'd win. I knew it all along."

I take one last look at the window, and then my surrounding, eyeing for anything heavy enough to break through the glass. I don't see anything.

Roger's voice snaps me back to reality.

"Now that the two of us are here, why don't we make use of your bed?"

"*No.*"

He brandishes the knife at my chest. "Undress yourself," he orders menacingly, stabbing the knife in the air toward the direction I'm in.

Realizing I don't have any choice, I do as he says.

I do what any desperate, sycophant would in a sticky situation like this. I begin taking off all my clothes. My top, my pants; every last bit of it comes off until I'm standing stark-naked. I cringe as my injured foot brushes against something sharp in the carpet.

Roger eyes me hungrily, licking his lips before throwing the knife to the side and approaching me. "Looks like you've put on some healthy weight now. I like that."

The room is freezing, but that's not where the source of my trembling comes from. Stripping myself naked leaves me with a most dynamic sense of vulnerability with Roger.

Just smelling my fear turns him on even more, and he begins to undress as fast as possible, acting like a dog in heat.

"I like it when you're submissive, girl." His voice turns husky, rough around the edges, and I almost gag. "Get on the bed."

Roger's completely naked now and directly in front of me with his hands on my shoulders and his breath fanning across my face. My disgust, if nothing else, adds fuel to his arousal, and I resist the urge to scream when I feel his manhood brush across my thigh. The contact leaves behind something warm and sticky, and I clench my teeth. I must hold on a little longer. I have to.

The bed is right in front of me, just six or seven feet away. I brush past Roger and dawdle to my bed. My senses scream for me to run—I'm positive Roger is staring at my behind, and even touching himself right now.

I continue to stand upright and still after arriving at the foot of my bed. Then the next thing I know, my head cracks against the headboard when Roger hits me harder than he ever has in my life. Black spots explode out of my eyes, and I begin uncontrollably wheezing in pain as all the air whooshes out of me.

"S—stop," I weakly beg. All Roger does is laugh, and another burst of pain makes me scream when I feel him kick my stomach, and I cough out wet liquid—my blood. I remain in my enervated state, unable to focus, but still conscious enough to sense the dip of the bed as Roger's weight shifts around.

"Tha's the spirit. This is what I like to see, Hope. Ya bein' all submissive."

Finding the strength to open my eyes, I come face-to-face with Roger. He is a mere two inches away from me, on his knees while I am curled up in a fetal position. Swallowing my disgust, I kiss him of my free will.

He tastes like the smell of morning breath, and I let out an involuntary gag into his mouth. The opportunistic pig immediate sticks his tongue in my bloody mouth and begins enjoying himself.

Now! Inner Hope bellows at me. I enact the plan stored in my mind.

I wrap my arms around his large waist to the best of my extent and draw my leg backward, letting the energy course through my body. Then I swing forward with all my might.

Roger's mouth immediately detaches from mine, and he begins shrieking, in pain from his collapsed testicle. He collapses to the ground, writing, and I step back with a small smirk. His privates are deflating at an alarming rate, and he passes out from the pain.

I spit on him four times. Call me unladylike, but to me, Roger doesn't deserve any clemency. I also give him a few heavy—to an extent without rupturing any of my sensitive organs—kicks.

My telescope still sits unscathed. I begin taking the front of the telescope and ramming it into the window. Each consecutive strike sends an aching stab through my heart. The telescope, although bought used at a consignment store, has been with me for as long as I can remember, always inhabiting the spare corner of my room.

The window glass finally breaks eight or nine rams later, and I drop the telescope to the ground, relieved it didn't take twenty or so tries. Luckily my arms aren't crippled—otherwise, I never would have been able to lift the object.

Examining the telescope, I see the aperture and lens are contorted beyond recognition. I allow myself to briefly pine my loss.

Roger is still passed out, albeit there are minute signs of him about to return to the real world. He's stirring, and his eyelids keep fluttering. Hastily, I drop to my knees and search his pants that are discarded to the side of the room. His weathered wallet is tucked in the back pocket, and I search the contents. There's some spare change, which I snag shamelessly. There's also the two plane tickets in there, and I draw them out.

The tickets have our names on them—one reads Roger Sullivan, and the other is my name. The plane leaves two days later, the morning of, at a small international airport half ninety minutes away.

Signs of Roger returning to consciousness are more prominent than ever— his legs are beginning to shift about, and he's muttering nonsense. Hands tremoring, I refold the tickets and stick them under my armpit and grab my clothes, with full intent to put them on. But before I do so, Roger comes to his senses. He props himself up on one arm and shakes his head, flummoxed.

Aside from the cash and plane tickets, I drop my load on my floor and bolt for the window. I look behind me to see him with a disoriented expression on his face, but he's still wary enough to know what I'm planning to do.

"Stop!" he shouts, but it's too late. I jump out my window. I miss the tree, however, and I end up falling to the ground, where I land on my knees. Both my legs and thighs sting as the thick brush—sticks, leaves, and stones—cut into my skin.

Roger tries to follow suit, but because of his distended belly, he has a difficult time doing so. His arms are pressed against the outside wall in an attempt to push him outwards, and I imagine his legs flailing uselessly on the other end of the window, like a fish out of the water. There is nothing attractive about his nakedness.

I hear him bellowing uselessly behind me, shouting gibbering threats, but given the position he's in, he doesn't seem so menacing. I laugh raucously at him, and to highlight the powerless position he's in, I pick up a rock suitable to my strength and chuck it at him. My usually-horrible aim is mysteriously augmented, and the stone hits him dead on the nose. He howls. That's my cue to leave.

I begin running to my rendezvous in the freezing weather. The night is so black that even the streetlamps provide little luminescence. This reassures me. Although I'm more concerned about Roger stalking me, there's a tiny beacon chip in my brain ready to turn my skin color red if any neighbors were to see my unorthodox jogging attire.

Halfway down the road, I palm my forehead in frustration when I realize I could have just left through the front door and saved myself from these scrapes and cuts. Also, my telescope would still be in one mint piece. I'm stupid. Stupid, stupid, stupid! I palm my forehead again several more times in frustration.

I spot Videl's car parked at the street corner, just like he promised. Right when I run under a streetlamp, Videl exits the car and opens my door for me, which I graciously bound into.

"Don't tell me he actually—" Videl starts he covers me with a thick blanket.

"No. I stopped him." Videl sighs in relief but then becomes alert.

"Altha has plenty of clothes for you." Then, taking another look, he curses in French, then switches to English. "Did he fucking do that to you?"

"Just drive," I grit my teeth. "Get me away from him."

"That's easily done, but we have another issue at hand. I hate to add more to your list of burdens, but it's not something we can ignore," he says.

"Is it small or big?" I ask, dreading the worst.

"Think more titanic."

My heart sinks. "That serious? What's wrong?"

"The cameras are bolted in too tight; only a demolition crew could get them out of their bearings. Altha's currently in her room searching for surveillance cameras on the web, but every distributor is too far away from us, and it'll take at least a week, if not two, for the supplies to arrive."

"We don't have that time!"

"I know, Hope. I know!"

"No! I mean, there's something even bigger going on. We need to act *now*. Roger just told me we were moving. Him and me, to Europe!"

"What?!" The car swerves and Videl curses. "No. No. Not good. When?"

"The day after tomorrow." I unfold the tickets and hand them to him. He reads them with his eyes off the road.

Videl's eyes darken. "France."

I nod. "Check the time."

"That gives us…hardly thirty-six hours," he mutters, eyes flickering to the radio clock. "Shit!" he yells. "I'm sorry." His grip on the steering wheel tightens.

"It's not your fault. It's no one's fault. Let's just get home."

Videl clamps his foot down on the accelerator. "We have no other choice. We need to act now, or you can kiss your freedom goodbye. I'm taking this matter into my own hands."

"What are you going to do?"

"First, we get home."

Videl steers his way through the windy two lane road with a blazing fire in his eyes I have never seen before. I chance a glance at his car's speedometer and see that he's driving close to a hundred miles per hour.

"Slow down before you kill us," I scowl, slightly irritated at his secreted attitude. His foot doesn't let up on the accelerator until we approach his neighborhood. Even still, he guns his way past fifty miles an hour until he screeches to a stop.

"Altha! We need you here now!" Videl yells after we pull into the garage. The door opens a few seconds later with Altha on the other end. Videl shoves her roughly against the door and storms inside.

"Jesus, what's gotten in your pants?" Altha stares.

"Hope's stepfather, Roger," Videl sneers. "Is taking Hope away."

Altha's eyes widen, and she drops the laptop, turning to me. "What?!" Her face then blanches when she spots the artwork on my skin. "Oh my god."

"He's taking her to a remote area in France, and no one's going to hear of them ever again!"

"Well, we can't let that happen!"

"Go get our black tracksuits, Altha. Get them now."

If Altha has any questions, she keeps them to herself. The sound of her footsteps slowly recedes as she climbs the flight of stairs to her destination.

"Hope, you're not going to like this, but I need you to liste—"

Altha suddenly manifests and cuts Videl off. In each hand, she holds two coat hangers with black tracksuits on them, as well as two more pairs of clothes. She stretches out an arm, and Videl plucks his tracksuit from her fingertips.

"So, can I ask why you have such a bitchy look on your face? And why are you two are going out on a jog at this time of night?"

"We're not going on a run," Videl says, stripping his body free of his jacket and jeans. "Put yours on, Hope," he points.

"What's this for?" I ask, pulling the shirt over my head.

"It's time I take care of that bastard once and for all. You know what I'm going to do?"

I have my suspicions, but I shake my head at the same time Altha grimaces.

"You were right earlier on about how to deal with this. I'm going to beat the shit out of him. That's how we're getting our confession."

My mouth drops open.

"Videl, you can't do this!" I exhort. "You're going to be arrested!" I run my hands up and down his shoulders to try to calm him down.

"Watch me!" he snarls. "I don't need you to tell *me* what I can or can't do for the sake of my own fucking preservation. I'm *going* to do this, whether you like it or not."

"Let's just think this through, Videl!"

"I *have* thought this through, Hope. There's no other way—time's run out. The two of you will be alone in a little under thirty-six hours. I can't let that happen. I won't."

"T—that's not the point!" I plead. "You're endangering yourself! You're *risking* your safety just to protect me!"

"You don't seem to understand the scope of our situation!"

My eyes widen before I take a threatening step toward him. Altha immediately retreats to a corner, sensing the aura of anger engulfing me.

"How dare you?!" I holler right under his nose. "How dare you say accuse me of being ignorant! I *understand* this situation well enough! You are *so far* removed from the truth! *I'm* the one he puts his hands on! Not you, me!"

"You're construing this the wrong way! You don't think I know that?!" Videl yells. "I was the one who saved you from being raped by the monster half a year ago!"

"If you know what I'm going through, then why are you—" whatever I'm about to say next goes up in a puff of smoke when I stare through his clenched teeth and into his eyes. There's an emotion there—not just indignation or exasperation, but something else.

"You're scared," I whisper. At the reduced volume of my voice, his shoulders slump and all the fight seems to drain out of him.

"I can't lose you again, Hope. I've already fucked up our relationship once, and I'm going to fight with my life so that nothing happens to you."

The fact he is putting me first makes me feel appreciated beyond any words I can formulate, and this feeling overcomes my anger. My voice loses the sharp edge it had not ten seconds prior.

"Fine. Let's do this. Just *please*, if you have any weapons, don't bring them. I'm sure that with your accent, Roger's going to think you're a hitman or something."

"Genius idea, if I have to say so myself. Wait here with Altha; I'll be back." Videl trudges up the stairs.

Altha scooches out of her corner and leads me to the sofa, where we both sit down.

"This is so iniquitous," I laugh throatily. "This feels like a dream. Things are moving too fast for me."

Altha sighs. "Yes, but when my brother is like this, there's no deterring him."

"I know firsthand what you're talking about."

Altha pulls me closer, resting me on her shoulder. "Hope?"

"Yeah?"

"I know this is asking a lot from you, but please—" Altha's voice drops a few pitches. "Take care of him, okay? He's doing a lot for you."

"Are you saying that you don't think I'm worth his time?"

"No! No, that's not it at all. I just don't want you both to throw away your futures by slipping up." Altha gives me a tight hug. "Be careful. I love you both to death."

~~~~~~

"So what's the plan?" I ask once we're in the car. "I mean, you have to have one, right? We can't just wing this."

Videl and I are currently in his car, on the way to Roger's home.

"I'm taking him to the amusement park."

"Why can't we just do what we need to do in the house?"

"He might scream and draw unwanted attention. Also, your house is too recognizable. As soon as we set Roger free, he's going to flee to the police station and file a report. There's going to be detectives swarming around your neighborhood in no time, which is why we're heading over to the park. It's too dark and cold for all the druggies so no one will be there. The more anonymity we have, the harder it'll be for any case detectives to find incriminating evidence."

Videl rummages through the black duffel bag laying at the foot of the back row of seats with one of his hands while driving with the other. A few seconds later, something plops in my lap.

"Recording is your job, and your job only. I'm not going to endanger you for my rash decisions. This is all on my shoulders. Got it?"

I grimace. "How do you work this thing?"

Videl verbally walks me through how to turn the expensive video camera on and how to record.

"The most important thing is that you *only* film and don't speak. Because if you do, he'll know it's you behind the mask."

"Got it."

"Yeah. You need to keep silent, at all costs."

"Do you even think you can deal with him alone? He's a pretty big guy. No offense to you," I hastily say, after Videl shoots me a skeptical look. "And he has a short fuse. Those combined make him scary."

"I know. I saw him at your mom's funeral. I'll be fine; I guarantee he has more fat than muscle, so opposition will be slim. Plus, we have the element of surprise. Kidnapping is the last thing he'll be expecting."

Videl pulls into my neighborhood and slows the car to a steady crawl. Even though it's barely seven in the evening, the sky is already pitch black, a result of the winter season still in office. With the weather barely above freezing, it comes as no surprise to me when the street is void of any visible activity.

We creep our way to where I know my house sits. Not daring to step on the accelerator pedal in fear of the car's engine roaring, Videl lets gravity naturally drag his car to the end of the road.

The light still shining through my window at the corner of the house draws my suspicions that Roger is in my room still, but the driveway sits empty, a different sight than two hours ago.

"No one's home," I whisper, feeling the need to lower my voice to match the stealth of our mission.

"Where could he have gone?"

"I don't know. I haven't been keeping tabs on him. But he doesn't know how to cook, and it's around dinnertime, so maybe—"

"He's out eating." Videl pulls his car to the opposite side of the road, parking it on the grass. The shrubbery next to us provides a viable source of camouflage, and with the darkness and lack of street lamps nearby, there is no way his car will glint.

"So we're just going to wait?" I ask, breaking the silence.

"It seems like it." Videl purses his lips and turns on the radio, and I almost laugh. The two of us are staking Roger while listening to classical music.

"I can always call him on my phone and try to convince him to come home," I offer after fifteen minutes passes.

"No," Videl affirms, shaking his head. He continues to play with the palm of my hand, which he has been busying himself with over the past few minutes. "Police are going to search for any evidence possible. They might label you as a suspect if your phone number pops up on his phone around the time of his abduction."

"Is there *any* way I can help? Besides recording?" I feel slightly disappointed at how I won't be in most of this action. But then the disappointment turns into shame when I realize I should not be taking pride in what Videl is about to do.

Videl ignores me, and I feel the need to poke his side. "Did you hear me?"

He clamps his hand over my mouth, and I inhale the sweet scent of his hand soap. "He's here."

I follow his finger to my house. What was an empty driveway is now occupied by the shadow of a vehicle—Roger's car.

Videl unlocks the door and unbuckles his seatbelt before digging through the contents of his duffel bag again.

"Listen, Hope. When I get back, pop the trunk of the car. It's the latch right beneath the left side of the seat. He points to the black lever for me, and I nod.

"Put this on too," he says, pulling out two ski masks with three tiny holes— one for each eye, and the last one for the mouth. He slips one over his head and hands the other one to me. I comply without complaining and tuck my hair inside. The tightness of the mask makes it difficult to blink.

"And this," he says, pulling out some gloves. "So we won't leave fingerprints."

I do as he tells.

"Make sure you keep your talking under wraps when Roger's in the trunk. I don't want to risk him hearing your voice. Got it?" Videl then opens his door and sticks one foot out.

"Wait!" I exclaim, before pulling him back in for a searing kiss. My fingers dart to his face like muscle memory, trying to feel his skin to no avail due to his mask and my gloves. I give a little squirm in my seat when a dark part of me inside thinks of us as criminals and concludes that this is kind of hot.

"Good luck," I say after we break apart. "And whatever happens, I love you."

All Videl does is nod, but I see the unspoken affection reflecting in his eyes. He shuts the door and quickly disappears from my vision as the black night swallows him up.

Videl left his keys running in the ignition, so I take this opportunity and adjust the radio station purposelessly to try to quell my nerves. I will myself to avoid glancing at the tiny two-story home. I put my trust into Videl when he said he could take on Roger in a one-to-one, and I will follow up on my trust. But that doesn't mean my autonomic nervous system will.

The dashboard clock turns to seven, and again, I almost laugh at the situation. Videl and I are actually doing this. We're committing a crime, if not several. We're doing something illegal.

I used to have this recurring dream back when I was younger, and I quickly labeled them my worst nightmare. In short, the dream consisted of me being arrested and sent off to prison. Most of the time I spent dreaming was in a tiny four by four jail cell, and one of my classmates or friends would always be on the other side of the bars laughing in my face and rubbing in the fact that I took the fall for something they did. Combine the feeling of bitter betrayal with the fact that I'm in jail for life with no means of parole and my freedom completely stripped away from me implanted a seed of hopelessness inside until the despair magnified to such a heavy extent that I woke up drenched in sweat in my bed.

My fingers twitch to my cell phone while I debate internally whether to call Videl and see if he's safe or not. Maybe he's in the middle of a fight right now. Maybe Roger has a gun pointed at him.

But neither is accurate. At first, I think someone is screaming on the radio, but then I realize the muffled sounds are coming from outside the vehicle. With the light from my corner of the room still switched on and providing a modicum of brightness, I see two figures in the distance. Oddly-meshed and lumbering, the shapes can resemble no one but Videl and Roger.

Only by the time they're a few feet away do I remember I need to pop the trunk. I do so, my heartbeat pounding in my eardrums.

I crane my neck to the side and observe Roger only for a split second before he gets tugged out of my field of vision. A bandana covering his entire head and tied around his neck veils his countenance, and a pair of steel handcuffs lock his hands behind his back. Because he's not shouting for help, I can steadfastly assume his mouth is taped shut.

I hear a loud noise and feel the car tires groaning at the extra weight amounted in the back. Videl comes in not long afterward. During the whole ride, we just ignore the intervallic thumping sounds coming from the trunk. Both of us take our masks off, and Videl drives at the speed limit to avoid any chance of being pulled over by the cops.

Before long, the car is shaking back and forth from the dips in the road and potholes stretching as far as my memory can see—a distasteful scenario we have to bear through in order to reach the amusement park.

Videl parks the car in the barren, weedy parking lot. Both of us scurry to get our masks back on our head.

"Do you remember how do work the video camera?" Videl then drops the pitch of his voice a few degrees. "Nod for yes and shake for no."

I nod my head three or four times, and then Videl gives me a thumbs up and flashes a reassuring grin before both of us synergistically exit our respective doors.

The two of us move to the trunk, where Videl lifts the lid. I have to force myself to stifle a gasp that almost rises out of me as I take a closer look at our victim under the trunk light.

What I originally thought was a heavy blindfold is actually a black bag of sorts dumped over his head and tied tightly around his neck. His shirt has   dark liquid stains which I first think is blood until I get a whiff of the fabric. It's alcohol. Roger was probably helping himself to a beer when Videl attacked. The stain continues further down, past the shirt and onto his jeans, until it ends down near his kneecap. In fact, if Roger were walking in public, people would be thinking he wet himself.

Videl manhandles Roger out of the car—I see his muscles ripple in the effect of carrying such a heavy weight. Roger collapses to the ground and tries to stand on his two feet, but because his hands are handcuffed behind his back, finding a center of balance is impossible, and he topples over. But Videl tugs him back up and marches him over to where I know the fence marking the entrance of the park is.

I stand behind the two men, observing silently as Videl pushes Roger over before scrambling over to the duffel bag. He grabs a tool and proceeds to clip the fence away until a gaping hole the size of a fridge looms out before us. Secretly, I'm impressed how Videl has this plan mapped out. I would never have remembered to bring a bolt cutter to make a large enough hole in the fence. Hell, I completely forgot there even was a fence.

The three of us walk through the fence to the other side. My mind seemingly knows where all of the little attractions are. I can tell you what booth is around the corner. I can tell you what color the bumper cars are without looking at them. It's a strange feeling, knowing that my brain can store these bits of visual information in my long-term memory after one glance.

Videl drags us deeper and deeper into the amusement park to the point where even I have no idea where we are anymore. The area is so dark by now that walking without light is impossible. I dig through his duffel bag, pull out a lantern flashlight, and switch it on. The beam powers the next fifty feet in front of us. A few more minutes later, and we finally stop in front of a building—an amphitheater—with dozens of chairs out in front. Videl takes one of the chairs, and we move over to a secluded area infested with weeds with no manmade creations nearby.

Videl goes to work quickly, binding Roger's chest and ankles to the chair with thick rope the size of my wrist. He then takes the handcuffs off and binds Roger's wrists to the chair as well before recuffing him for extra security. Finally, in one flourish, he loosens the black bag and yanks it off Roger's head.

Following his cue, I begin taping, standing back fifteen feet to protect myself from him—the closer I am, the higher the chance Roger will spot the color of my eyes and texture of my lips. I can't afford to take chances, even with the whole camera protecting my face from any scrutiny.

The duct tape is still over Roger's mouth, but Videl makes quick work of this too, ripping it off of him. Roger curses.

"Who are ya?" he immediately asks. "Where am I? You'll regret everything ya did when I get my hands free, ya hear me?! I'm gonna—"

Roger does not get the chance to finish because Videl knees him in the stomach. Roger's head immediately flops down, and he begins wheezing for air. It looks like his body is about to explode from the mass of food he stuffed himself with.

"Shut up," Videl commands. "Now, I can keep doing this to you all night, or you can keep quietly obedient and answer every question I pose to you with absolute honesty. Do you think you can do that?"

Roger lifts his head up and stares at Videl. Through the camera, I see Videl's body stiffen. If Roger recognizes Videl's eye color to belong to the guy that was beside me at Mom's funeral, then it wouldn't take much for him to piece bits of the puzzle together.

However, no sudden wash of grasping comes over his face, and Roger grunts, "Yeah."

"Excellent," Videl says. He disappears off screen for a while but then comes back with another chair and sits it in front of Roger. I shift my angle so the camera can catch both of them, and this small movement causes Roger to notice there are more than just a combined total of two people here tonight.

"Who's that?" he sneers. "Your accomplice?"

"Why, yes, my *accomplice*," Videl mimics. "Don't worry. He's just here for your benefit."

"Benefit bein' what? I'm tied up in a chair with two strangers. I ain't see any benefit from this."

"Why, the benefit of keeping your life, of course. One doesn't realize how much of a liberty life is until they're presented with a dangerous situation."

Roger's eyes widen. "Look, if ya'll are thieves, my wallet's back home. If ya came for the money or whatever, I'll give it to ya! Just let me go!"

"Are you that stupid? Do you really think we'd drag you out all the way to the middle of nowhere just to rob you of your materialistic *money*?"

Roger opens his mouth, but Videl cuts him off.

"Let me answer for you before you hurt yourself. We're *not* here for your money. We're here for your freedom."

"What's that supposed to mean?"

Videl pops a knuckle. He almost seems...exasperated.

"Freedom isn't a gift; it's what you do with it that is."

"So what do ya want?!"

"To start off, I'll ask you a straightforward question. Who do you think I am?"

"How the hell am I supposed to know? With that mask on, I can't see shit."

Videl puts the palm of his right hand threateningly on the side of Roger's neck, and I can see the desired effect it has on him. "I'm afraid I can't take 'I don't know' as an answer. Please do try again."

Roger's body shivers from Videl's touch. "I don't know. Your accent makes it sound like you're a spy or somethin'."

"Excellent," Videl says, pleased that Roger thinks of him that way. I can already see the motors whirring in Videl's head. "Next question. What is your name?"

Roger scrunches his eyebrows for a few seconds before answering, "Roger. Roger Sullivan. But you already knew that, didn't ya? Who are ya?"

"You're pretty smart for a layabout. Since you answered honestly, I'll return the favor." Videl sits back down in his chair and smirks, revealing a pristine set of white teeth. "I'm a contracted killer."

Even from my distance, I can visibly see Roger's eyes bulge out of his sockets as his feeble brain struggles to comprehend the existence of a dark network of people. His obvious but futile attempts of trying to wriggle out of the chair ceases. And then he starts yelling.

"Lemme out! Lemme out of these chains!"

"All in good time, Mr. Sullivan." Videl checks his gloves while Roger writhes around, his forehead coated with a sheen of sweat.

"What do ya want from me?! Why am I here?!"

"Come on, Mr. Sullivan. Think. It's not like I'm doing this by myself. Why would I care about you without any remuneration?" Videl sighs, seemingly bored of his charade already. But patience is a necessary factor—more paramount than fear. The more fear Roger has instilled in him, the more prone he is toward spilling his secrets.

Roger stops fidgeting while he mutters to himself.

"You've got a client. A client, of sorts. Somebody who's out to get me."

"Bravo!" Videl claps. "My client is a dear friend of Mr. Valentine. And lately, well, he's not too happy with the way you've been treating his family."

"Alan? But he's dead. Died a couple of years ago or somethin'."

"True, but that doesn't minimize the fact that my client's not keeping tabs anymore. In fact, he discovered that you have wronged them, and wronged them dearly. On the twelfth of November, as a matter of fact. Do you remember where you were that day?"

"I don't remember. That's an oddly specific date for somethin' that was so far in the past. Why ya want to know?"

"I'll be asking the questions here. Are you going to answer?"

"I already told ya, I don't remember. That's my answer." Roger spits at Videl's feet. His confidence must have increased a sliver when he realized Videl isn't causing more bodily damage.

"Think, Mr. Sullivan," Videl commands. The only sign that he is affected by Roger's germs is through the hardening of his voice. "That day, you woke up and then did something special; something different from your usual slothful path into inebriation. I know you know. Tell me."

"I don't know, I swear!"

Videl sighs. "I'm going to ask you *one* last time before things get ugly. *What. Did. You. Do?*"

"I don't know! I don't know!"

"What did you not understand about me not taking 'I don't know' as an answer?!" Videl rears his fist back and lands a punch right on Roger's right cheek. The echo from the blow weaves through all the attractions near us before dying off somewhere in the distance.

I think Roger finally realizes his life is not susceptible to pain from the stranger in front of him because he starts flailing around in his chair with so much vigor that he and the chair itself actually skids to the side by a couple of feet.

"What are ya doing?! Stop!"

"Answer my fucking question!" Videl barks. "Where were you on the twelfth of November?!"

"I—I already told ya! I t—think I on my way to work! I was—"

Videl winds his fist back before punching him again, this time in the nose. Something cracks in the air, and a horrible stirring rises in my stomach at the sound. The lens provides me with the sight of Roger and his disproportionally bent nose.

Roger lets out an etiolated cough. "I said—said I was drivin' to work."

"Quit lying." Videl knees Roger in the stomach again, with greater force this time. A quivering notion is all the warning we get before he vomits all of his partially-digested food. The smell cuts through the cold breeze, and I instantly gag from the putridness.

Roger seems to be unable to breathe. "I was—driving—work."

Videl balks, and I can sense his desire to turn around and tell me something. But then it seems like his uncertainty vanishes. Videl unzips the duffel bag and slowly draws out a sleek, black combat knife. The blade itself is about six inches and serrated in the shape of waves, and I swear it holds an ominous glint. Videl returns to Roger and tosses the knife up in the air expertly before catching it and twirling it around his fingers. Roger's eyes follow his every movement, and when Videl settles the tip of the blade on the leg of Roger, Roger whimpers.

"Please! You don't want to do this!"

"*I'm* not doing anything. You're doing this to yourself." Videl presses down and draws blood.

Roger eyes the knife. "Okay, okay! I was home. I was at home with Chloe and Hope. I was—"

Videl thrusts the knife into Roger's right thigh.

A hurried gasp comes out of Roger and me and then his mouth tightens. He cries a brood-curdling scream as Videl twists the knife deeper.

"What were you doing that day? What did you do?!" Videl's roaring mixed with Roger's sobbing pleads sounds like two television channels playing at the same time.

My stepfather's hair is in a mangled mess from the amount of his own sweat he's soaking in. Any tough front he had up disappeared as soon as Videl stabbed him, and all that remains of his posture is a babbling baby.

"Please! Please!"

"You're fucking pitiful," Videl snarls, and something about the guttural noise he makes chills my spine. It's a sound I have never heard before. It's a sound that is feral in the rawest sense.

"You're a worthless excuse for a human being," he says again. "Opting to beg your way out instead of confessing." Videl rips the knife out of Roger's thigh, and my stomach threatens to heave when I see the weapon coated with chunks of red flesh and globs of fat drip to the ground.

Videl hovers the knife threateningly over Roger's other thigh.

"I really don't know! Don't do this!"

"Listen here. The first stab wound was a clean point of entry—I avoided any bone and major arteries. But if you refuse to tell me, I'm going to fuck up your leg so badly that you'll never be able to walk properly ever again."

"Okay, okay! I'll tell ya! Just get that knife away from me!"

Videl pauses as if contemplating on whether Roger is going to feed him another lie, but he withdraws the knife and steps back a few paces anyways.

"Speak. Let's hear it then."

Roger doesn't say anything.

"You're testing my patience, Mr. Sullivan."

Roger shudders "I *was* home, but—wait! Wait!" he begs, when Videl moves toward him.

"All I remember is that I was home that day and was workin' on my wife's car. She was tellin' me that there was some smoke comin' from the hood of the car, so I was tryin' to fix it."

"The cooling system?" Videl asks.

Roger nods his head vigorously, trying to take advantage of Videl's calmer tone. "Yeah, so I was just outside workin' on that. In the front yard of the house."

"And?" Videl asks. "Did you fix it? What did you do to fix it?"

"I just removed all the dust inside the fan. That's it, I swear. Let me go. Just let me go and you'll never hear from me ever again, I swear."

Videl rubs his chin with his index finger and thumb.

"Alright," he says after obvious contemplation. "You're free to go."

When Roger speaks, I detect a mingle of considerable relief with a dash of wariness.

"I'm just free to go? Just like that?"

"Of course, Mr. Sullivan!" Roger flinches when Videl approaches with the knife, but all he does is start sawing the ropes in half.

"Oh, thank ya. Thank ya so much," Roger repeats over and over again.

"Not a problem. However…" Videl pauses in his sawing. The rope is just on snapping equilibrium—not too thin so that Roger can break free with his own energy, but not too thick to the extent that a few more strokes will cut the rope in half.

Roger, so bent on escaping, catches the hesitation in a jiffy.

"What's goin' on? Why did ya stop?"

"You know, on second thought, I don't think I believe you anymore."

I see Roger's Adam's apple slide in his throat.

"That was it, I swear!"

Videl tsks. "I think you're just desperate to leave." With that said, Videl stabs him in the other thigh. If I thought Roger's first screaming session was bad, this is nothing compared to it. As soon as the knife tears through his thigh, Roger emits an anguished howl rips through my eardrums and almost damages my body on a cellular level.

The knife embeds so deeply in Roger that Videl has a hard time pulling the blade out. But when he does, Roger's left leg gives a brutal spasm and then languidly flops over on its side.

"This is your last warning, *Roger*. If you don't answer me truthfully, then I'm going to sever your dick. You know what that means, don't you?"

"Please. I have a daughter."

"It's funny that you'd say that." Even with his face facing the other way, I know he's smirking. Videl throws the knife to the side as if he has no need for it anymore because Roger has just awarded him the winning confession.

"When I was debriefed and handed your dossier, young Hope's was also attached. You want to know what I felt when I saw her picture?"

Roger doesn't say anything. Maybe he's in too much pain. From this angle, I can't even tell if he's conscious.

"ANSWER ME!" Videl yells.

"N—no."

"No, what?"

"W—what did you f—feel?"

Videl smirks. "One word." He points his index finger up to the sky to reiterate his point. "*Lust*. I just couldn't help the lust that coursed through my body. She's such an attractive lady, isn't she?" He pauses for a split second. "After you're out of the picture, I think I'm going to pay her a visit in that quaint two story house with the little wind chime next to the purple front door."

"S—stop. Not her. Not her."

"All that will remain of her are the missing child posters around town. I'm going to take her away," Videl says, enunciating every word right next to Roger's ear. "My buddies and I own a whorehouse. I think she'll be an amazing fuck. Think of all the revenue I'll generate from customers lining up outside her room, waiting to use her as a urinal. She'll be the apple of my eye."

Something slips out of Roger's eyes. It takes me a bit to come to an understanding as to what it is. Tears. Roger is crying.

"Don't," Roger weakly mumbles, shaking his head back and forth.

"Don't what?"

"Don't! Don't take her away! I'll do anything you ask!"

"I'll leave her be," Videl says. "All you have to tell me is the truth, and only the truth, of what you did. Make your choice. If you don't confess about your actions on November twelfth, then Hope disappears by the time you return home."

Roger breaks eye contact with Videl, and his head turns toward me—or the camera—for the first time. His eyes are bloodshot and puffy, with tears steadily trickling down his cheek and onto his jeans.

"Promise me," Roger whispers. "Promise me ya won't harm her."

"You have my word," Videl answers. He sits down in his chair. Then, in a much softer tone, he comforts, "Go on."

Roger gives another heave of his chest. I stand still, mesmerized.

"The mornin' of November twelfth—that mornin', I was workin' on the car, but it wasn't to fix the cooling system. I was up under the car, doin' somethin' else."

The camera wobbles dangerously, and I try my best to quell my shaking hands.

"I had planned it for over a week. Chloe told me there was some smoky vapor comin' out of the car whenever she would drive it, and she didn't want to go to the mechanics since it would cost too much money," he pants.

Now that Roger has started his story, he doesn't seem to want to stop—the words tumble out of his mouth like water from a palm. And I think the reason behind this is because he's been keeping this all to himself for so long that confessing leads to a sense of liberation. I don't know whether he wants to confess because the truth is eating him out on the inside, or whether it's because he wants to brag.

"I told her I'd fix it. I was a good mechanic few years back before I switched professions. But instead of her cooling system, I decided to loosen up 'er brakes. Took the studs completely off so the brake would break away while she was drivin'. Worked like a charm."

"What were your motives behind killing Chloe?"

Roger shrugs, and immediately I get the sense that he's hiding something.

"Never really liked 'er. Every single night we'd always get into these petty arguments and I was just tired of it, ya know? Every! Single! Night! I only married 'er in the first place to try to—well, she ain't the woman I thought I loved. No sex, no passion, no nothin'."

Roger spits at Videl's feet.

"There's ya confession. You can let me go now."

"Come on, Mr. Sullivan. Why would my accomplice here be filming you if we didn't have the intention of delivering the evidence to the police?"

Roger blanches. "B—but you said—"

"I said if you don't confess, I'll let you go, at the expense of Hope's future. But since you just confessed to murder, well, that's a whole different story." Videl stands to his feet.

"W—what are ya gonna do to me? Are ya gonna kill me?!"

"No. I could spend days or even months torturing you, but even then, death would be too swift. I'm taking you to the police station."

"But like ya said, i—if ya give the evidence to the cops, then they'll be comin' for me anyways. Let me go."

"You're still trying to bargain?" Videl chuckles. "I'm afraid you have no say in the matter, Mr. Sullivan."

"I swear, I'm sorry for what I did!"

"No, you're not. If I set you free right now, you'd pour all of your resources into leaving the country."

Videl brings out a roll of duct tape and rips a piece off before taping Roger's mouth shut.

"Come on. Get up." Videl yanks Roger to his feet and kicks the chair out from underneath him. Roger fumbles for a stable footing, but he can no longer walk on his own. Even his frame is too large for Videl to lift with ease, so instead, Videl uses both of his hands to drag Roger back toward the direction of the park entrance. I hit the stop reeling button and scurry over to the duffel bag, hauling it over my shoulder.

The walk back is silent, apart from muffling groans coming from Roger. All three of us squeeze back through the fence to the car, where Videl proceeds to dump Roger in the back, slightly cringing at how his blood applies new meaning to his car's interior décor.

The drive to the police station seems to take no time at all, partly because every criminal act we have accomplished—breaking and entering, kidnapping, trespassing, a non-ethical interrogation, and whatever else—sends torrent after torrent of adrenaline shooting through my veins.

By the time we pull up to the curb, the clock reads half an hour from midnight. I can't tell what the building looks like from the outside, but one thing I can discern—even with a lack of windows there for protection—is that there is still a faint glow of light coming from a few areas of the station. There must be police working overtime or detectives delving deep into a case.

Videl clicks the hood of the trunk open and out tumbles a conscious Roger.

"You upheld your end of the bargain, so I am upholding mine. Rest easy upon the fact that your stepdaughter will remain untouched while you can, because once you land in jail, you'll have plenty of other things to worry about."

Twenty feet away lies a bicycle stand firmly planted in the ground. Videl drags him over and protrudes the set of handcuffs he used earlier. Then he locks Roger in place to the rack.

"Video," Videl demands.

After a brief fumbling session, I get the roll of tape to pop out of the little cartridge holder and into his hands.

Videl draws out a tiny manila envelope—about the size of a slice of bread—from his back pocket. The roll of tape makes a clacking sound when it tumbles down into the depths of the envelope. He magically pulls a pen out of nowhere and scribbles something on the outside.

"Goodbye, Mr. Sullivan. It was a pleasure meeting you."

We leave Roger and the mail right there, smack-dab in front of the door entrance. Anyone leaving or entering has no choice but to view the heap of bloodied mass sprawled out in an awkward angle that suggests nothing but a state of helpless agony.

18

Being the young girl that I was, watching crime shows on television always had me hold civil professions in high regards. I admit, I've fantasized about what it would be like if I was arresting a criminal and giving them a slick phrase or two, or being the one who discovers who murdered who based on fingerprint evidence from the crime lab. But all my past fantasies are blown to smithereens by my excursion to the station.

The building is made entirely of brick and is lacking in windows. The front door is metallic and painted royal blue. At the top, the building has the words 'Police' engraved in monolithic letters. All in all, it looked like a normal building—no uniform-clad men or cop cars are in sight, and if it isn't for the building label, I wouldn't have realized the constabulary at all.

However, the inside is entirely different. As soon as Altha and I proceed through the front entrance, a noisy bustle fills my ears. On my left is a bunch of wooden, low-grade desks, each complete with a nameplate and armchair. Police of both gender—though there are far more males—are scrambling to finish reports, drink coffee, or yell at other colleagues for a favor. Some have their coat off, revealing a dress shirt with suspenders as their top, and slacks with polished brown or black dress shoes. These guys are definitely the superintendents or private detectives assigned to cases too intricately dark for a normal police force to tackle. And on the right is a translucent door-window with a name and titles printed in gold font—the chief's office.

"May I help you?" The first man I saw after walking inside is now standing in front of us, a little suspicious frown tugging at his lips.

"Yes. We're here to see Roger…"

"Sullivan," I finish.

"Any idea where he might be? As you can tell, we have probably a dozen visitors here." The officer gestures to a corner of the room that I failed to sweep when I walked in. It's a little waiting room with twenty or so plastic chairs, about half full with people of different backgrounds. I quickly check if Roger is there. He isn't.

"Check your interrogations officer. He should be here," Altha says.

"I sit at the front desk, and I don't seem to recall any 'Roger Sullivan' brought in by our detectives. You sure he's here?" the man asks.

"Positive," I answer.

"Well, let me ask my superintendent. He will know."

Altha and I make our way over to the waiting zone and sit down in the blue plastic chairs. The clock mounted above the door is the same brand as the one that was over the door to the operating room.

"You sound like there's something bothering you," Altha remarks shrewdly, rubbing her thumb across my palms.

I frown because there *is* something nagging me. "It's just—well, out of all the times I've crossed swords with him, apart from yesterday, he's only been sober twice. But out of those two times, he always seemed like—"

"A secret creature that shadows his intelligence behind a mask of stupidity?"

"Right. A disingenuous person full of guile. I just have a bad feeling that he's going to talk his way out of his crime." I rub my shoulders.

"You and Videl have worked hard enough to get solid evidence. There is absolutely no way he will get away."

I chuckle. "Yeah. I almost wish Videl was here so he can see the fruits of his labor."

"You know it'll be too risky for him to make an appearance. There aren't many French inhabitants in Roseden. If he speaks, the authorities will be all over him in an instant."

"He could always just adopt an American accent."

Altha rolls her eyes. "We've discussed this already. One, he's horrendous at accent impersonations. Two, the authorities have eyes of a hawk and are sure to realize that his body physique is all-too-similar to the guy in the mask."

The officer who had just left walks back in with a brand new cup of coffee. His suspicious demeanor is gone.

"Roger Sullivan is currently being detained in the interrogating rooms downstairs. Are the two of you related to him, by any chance?"

"She's his stepdaughter. I'm here to give her moral support."

"Well, I don't see an issue in the two of you going downstairs. A note of advice, though: the best you'll be able to do is watch from the one-way mirror, so if you're here to talk to the detective in charge of your stepfather or your stepfather himself, well, you won't be allowed to."

Altha nods. "Thanks for the tip."

"Not a problem. Hope you get what you're searching for." He takes a final sip of his coffee before throwing the Styrofoam cup into a nearby trashcan.

Altha and I share a silent look before we begin making our way to the blue signpost that says 'Stairs.'

As we work down the steps, the cheerful, noisy atmosphere instantly disappears, giving way to one more ominous and silent. The hallway we walk is much darker than the floor above—the walls are painted a sickly, non-reflective dark taupe color as if its purpose is to scare a suspect into a confession. No light fixtures mount on the ceiling, and the only source of brightness is from the blinding dark-blue colored dome lights gently flickering above each interrogation room. The silence is deafening. I can hear each breath and every step we take.

Altha and I open the door on the left at the end of the hallway. There greets us a woman, brown-haired and steely-eyed with a heart-shaped face, garnered in a dress shirt with a skinny necktie. The shirt tucks into her gray slacks, securely fastened by her standard police-issued brown belt with a bunch of gadgets strapped on.

"May I help the two of you?" She speaks with a British, or maybe Australian, accent.

"Definitely. Is Roger Sullivan here?" She stares at Altha for a moment, perhaps not buying the American accent.

"He's behind this door." She points to another door in front of me.

I speak up. "May I go in?"

"Strictly speaking, the interrogation room is only for officials and people who have been arraigned. If you are his relative, you may stand and watch."

"That's ok," Altha cuts in. "She's his stepdaughter." The woman looks to me for confirmation, and I nod.

"My partner is currently in the middle of questioning, but you are more than welcome to listen in," she instructs before pointing to a window. I take a couple of tentative steps forward and see one of those windows that are one-way mirrors. And on the other side is Roger, sitting with his attorney, while the other detective is in a chair across from them with his back toward me. I can see him scribbling profusely on a piece of paper.

"Can we listen in on this?" I ask. The woman says yes, and then suddenly I can hear the three people's discussion.

"A family man, you say?" the detective rubs his chin before digging out a file. "Says here you live with two other family members, one of which is now deceased."

"Yeah.

"So, would you like to explain to us why you were found bound in front of our station two days ago?"

"Looks like we got here just in the nick of time," I whisper to Altha.

Roger fidgets in his chair. Beside him, his attorney speaks up.

"My client has a right to remain silent. Don't say a word, Rog."

There's a slight pause, and I imagine the detective raising his eyebrows.

"A right to remain silent? What has Mr. Sullivan been telling you?"

Now it's the attorney's turn to look discombobulated. "My client has been assaulted, *victimized* by pranksters insofar he needed to be hospitalized. The attack left him a paraplegic with a broken nose."

My eyes widen. "Oh my god," I whisper.

"It's sad, isn't it?" My attention turns toward the female detective. "Two knife wounds in each leg deep enough to sever his sciatic nerves. With his pre-existing poor health, there was no way for a bypass to occur."

Peering through the glass again, I allow my eyes to roam past Roger's face and the dismal surroundings to a large wheelchair I originally thought was just a normal chair he was sitting in.

"While I sympathize with Mr. Sullivan's paraplegic state, the attack was within reason."

"This is blasphemy! Nothing could warrant crippling my client!"

The detective waves off the attorney with a flick of his hand. "After we're done here, the police are going to get a warrant to search your home."

"You don't have the right to!" the attorney argues. "Claiming my client was brutalized because of something he did is a groundless accusation that does not give you jurisdiction for a search warrant!"

"On the contrary, Mr. Miller, we are within grounds to take action against your client and incarcerate him. This was found in our mailbox two days ago, the same time when Mr. Sullivan was found on our lawn. Let me play this for you." The detective pulls out a manila envelope and digs through its contents until he draws out a camcorder tape.

"What's this?" the attorney queries. "Some foolishly concocted scheme to place my client in jail? You'll have to do better than that."

"Remind me if I'm wrong, but I thought an attorney was supposed to defend his or her client, not kiss their ass and spread apocryphal claims," Altha whispers to me.

"It's about to happen, Altha. I can feel it."

We both turn our attention back to the people inside the room. Maybe it's the lighting, but Roger is paler than usual.

"Any words before I begin playing the video?" the detective asks. Roger doesn't respond. Perhaps he's making one last effort to be tough.

On cue, the female detective enters the room, dragging a cart with an old-school television—one that is bulky—and a media player. Then she leaves the room, situating herself next to Altha again.

The male detective gets out of his chair and slides the tape into the player. The video immediately begins to play, starting at the time of Roger's unconventional interrogation. A foreign sensation engulfs me—knowing that I was the one who was literally behind the camcorder filming makes the experience of watching it on the television screen more way more surreal, perhaps with the exclusion of Altha—I feel the Altha's grip on my arm tightening, and she almost gives me a skin burn during the moments where Videl digs the knife into Roger. And then, after Videl lifts Roger out of the chair, the screen goes black.

The silence between everyone is the static kind that warns you not to breathe first—engulfed with thick tension because no words would ever be appropriate to follow the actions observed.

"I have a few questions for you, Mr. Sullivan." The detective finally cuts through the silence.

Roger cranes his head toward his attorney, only to see that his partner is white around the face.

"Wait!" Roger's mouth starts moving. "I didn't kill Chloe! I promise!"

The detective sighs. "Let's drop the charade, Mr. Sullivan. Evidence here—albeit unconventionally gathered—is more than enough for me to find you guilty."

"I just said that because they were threatenin' to take my stepdaughter away! Chloe died from a horrible car accident that I had no part of!"

"So you deny your admittance that you and your deceased wife ran into marital strife?" the detective asks, flipping over a page on his clipboard.

"N—no," he falters. "That part was true. But that was the only accurate part of that whole video! Even though we argued, I still loved 'er. There was no way I'd kill her because of somethin' so triflin'." He tilts his head down to meet the floor and chokes a little. "I loved 'er so much. When I heard the news, a part of me was ripped away."

Roger's acting is so convincing that I'm even beginning to hold slight pity for him, but the detective shakes his head in what seems to be exasperation, and I realize the only reason he wouldn't be affected by Roger's believable performance is only if he had more incriminating evidence that has yet to been shared. And he proves it.

"Well, Mr. Sullivan, while you were in the hospital recovering from your attack, my partner and I took it upon ourselves to scour up some of your past files." The detective pulls out yet another piece of paper. "To which we found out you sent a request to 'Rufus's Junkyard' to have Chloe Valentine's car crushed."

"I just didn't want to be reminded of my wife's death."

"The company had yet to crush the car, so upon further investigation," the detective continues, ignoring Roger, "The vehicle's brake studs were discovered to be tampered with. Loosened, as a matter of fact. A bit of a coincidence, isn't it?"

"Is this true, Rog?" the attorney asks.

A stretched silence ensues.

"I—I'm being framed! Help me!" Roger turns to his attorney, only to find that even his trusted camaraderie is averting his eyes.

"Mr. Sullivan, you are under arrest for the murder of Chloe Valentine. You have the right to remain silent. Anything you say can and will be—"

"I swear I'm bein' set up! I—I wouldn't kill her!"

"You are behaving like a petulant child, Mr. Sullivan."

"I'm tellin' ya, I didn't do anythin'!"

"The overwhelming evidence says otherwise. You have a lifetime to perfect your poker face in jail, Mr. Sullivan," the detective dryly says, before yanking out a pair of handcuffs. "But right now, you're not fooling anybody."

"Wait!" I yell, before realizing they can't hear me. I tug the door to the room and dash inside, hearing the female detective's surprised protests behind me.

The inhabitants' attention all turn toward me. Roger looks a little dumbfounded, while the other two are giving me bewildering stares. Now that I'm inside, my nerves begin to get the best of me.

"Hi, everybody," I start, giving a meek little wave of my hand. The woman that followed me in seems unsure of what to do, but she doesn't stop me, so I continue.

"My name's Hope. Hope Valentine. I'm Roger's stepdaughter."

"Yes, and what are you here for?" the male detective interjects, recovering from his stupor. "If you're here to petition your stepfather's release, I'm afraid that's not going to happen. The evidence surmounted against him is substantial."

I start to get edgy now that I have everyone's attention.

"I'm not here to absolve him. I've known this man for a year. And I know, with his lack of conscience, he is perfectly capable of breaking the law. But this— this man hasn't committed just one crime, the murder of my mother, Chloe Valentine. No," I shake my head, ignoring the bitter taste of admittance. "I'll just let you all see for yourselves." I take a deep breath before turning to face the mirror. With slow and deliberately movements, I peel my attire off, stripping in a room almost full of strangers. The sweatshirt, tank top, pants, and shoes all are discarded, leaving me almost stark naked. Only my bra and underwear remain attached to my skin, but that's not what captures everyone's attention. For as soon as my clothes come off, everyone in the room except Altha gasps as their eyes come in contact with the pulsating mass of aged yellow bruises and scars splattered across my body like some sick painting, the freshest being those from the night he invaded my bedroom.

"This is what he does to me," I whisper softly, yet my voice echoes powerfully throughout the room. "This is what I deal with." I shift my gaze toward Roger, noticing him clenching his fists and his eyebrows twitch.

"I'm tellin' ya, this is all a setup!" Roger suddenly bursts, pounding his fists on the metal table. His frightened eyes look back and forth between the people in the room, and his mangled hair is flying back and forth. "I wouldn't have done this to my child! I love her. I love ya, Hope," he declares, leaning forward and trying to grab my hand. I immediately spring back.

"Don't touch me."

Roger looks to the detective for help, but his face falls when he sees the disdain etched into his frown.

"I'm positive the scarring isn't just for show."

The room fills with complete silence. I keep my vision on Roger, who's dim; there's a resigned look on his face. He's given up, but I refuse to break eye contact with the man that has tormented me for a year.

My peripherals wander through the room, catching sight of everyone else's eyes still on my body roaming between the bruises on my thighs and stomach, and I'm starting to feel more than self-conscious now. But at least the truth is out of the basket. Roger's chance of acquittal is zero, and I can even see it on his attorney's face—the shake of his head and his lips firmly pressed with a slight queasy look on his face—all before the man gets out of his chair, snaps his briefcase shut, and walks out of the room without a single word to his client.

"Fine, okay! I killed Chloe by doin' exactly what ya said: loosenin' the car brakes!" Roger's tone changes after the departure of his only ally, and I can see the newly-formed scowl on his face.

"We're all ears. How about you start from the beginning."

"Ain't nothin' much to say." Even when Roger know he's done for, his voice still says the same—one with a superiority complex. "Like I said in the vid, I tampered with the car brakes. Chloe was complainin' 'bout how there was some smoke comin' out the hood every now and then. Simple coolin' system malfunction, but a genius idea came to my mind instead. Hope was out there that mornin', weren't ya? You were out there asking me what I was doin' while I was under the car." Roger's nose tilts upwards, and he leers.

"You told me you were fixing her brakes."

He gives a half-hearted shrug. "And? I lied." The simple word causes me to snap.

"Fuck you!" I scream. I wriggle myself out of Altha's grasp and sprint over to Roger.

"Was pretty fun, knowin' her hours were numbered."

"FUCK YOU!" I roar again. Balling my hands into a fist, I immediately draw back as hard as I can and pummel them into Roger's face—clawing at his eyes, slicing at his lips. Every inch of him I can find—anything to make him suffer. Anything to make him feel my pain. Mom's pain.

The room goes into an uproar once I begin scrapping with Roger and many people jump to their feet at once. I feel fingers on the back of my shoulders and arms trying to pry me off, but doing so half-heartedly, as if they didn't care how much harm came to the degenerate whose throat is being strangled in front of their eyes.

Altha is the only one who didn't jump to her feet, let alone flinch when I bolted forward. She remains leaning against the wall, smirking.

"Get 'er off me!"

"No! Fuck you! I'm going to kill you, you hear me?! I'm going to rip you apart!"

"Enough, or both of you go to jail!" the male detective bellows, and I instantly stiffen for a split second before turning around to the detective. And then I start laughing in disbelief.

"You? You're going to arrest me? For—for trying to take action against this insolent swine? I'm sorry," I shake my head. "But I don't think jail is enough to deter me. Forgive me if I do this—" I rear my fist back and punch Roger in the face with the energy of a thousand suns, bleeding his nose in the process. "—but—this—man—deserves—pain—" I grunt, in between hits.

"I'll deal with you later. For now, we need to focus on the topic at hand. Contain your friend," the man warns Altha. The next thing I know, the back of Altha's body presses me against the wall. I pinch her and then feel a sharp pain in my foot when she stomps on it.

"In the video, you said you murdered Chloe Valentine because the two of you didn't get along. Is that the real reason, Mr. Sullivan? Or was there an ulterior motive?"

"There was another reason."

Altha's shoulder moves away from my face, and for the first time since my rampage ended, I see Roger's face in a clear light. His entire face is one bloodied mass; a resemblance of facial reconstructive surgery gone wrong. His eyes hide behind swelling tissue, but what little sclera I can see is bloodshot. The nose is bent at a hooked angle, undoubtedly broken yet again, and his bottom lip is bleeding profusely—the pellets of blood continue to drip on his shirt. He looks like an alien from a horror movie.

"Now we are making progress. What was the other reason? Or reasons," the detective says.

"I had Chloe wrapped around my finger easily enough. She would've done anything to keep 'er daughter happy," he lisps.

"What part of having you as a family member keeps Hope here happy?"

"Financial aid," he grunts. "Supplied 'em with a house. Money. Chloe was workin' shifts at a beat-down restaurant. Didn't make much. Promised her I would pay for Hope's tuition when she went off to med school."

Oh, Mom.

"I see," the detective says, back to scribbling on his pad. "And this is your other reason? To keep Hope here?"

"I couldn't just leave Chloe. That'd mean I'd be leavin' Hope." He juts his head in my direction, looking at me affectionately. I'm going to be sick from his delusional fantasies.

"You murdered Chloe instead of just divorcing her?"

"It ain't that simple. Haven't you ever wanted something so badly ya'd do anything to get it, detective? A bribe? Higher status? Come on, everyone wants somethin'. Society attempts to convince us that there's virtue in resistin' corruption, but in reality, I think you'll find that nothin' in the world is more richly rewarded."

The detective raises one of his eyebrows. "So in short, Miss Valentine would be listed under your guardianship after the passing of her mother. You were trying to get rights to her and her freedom."

"Yeah. Hope," Roger says, focusing his attention on me. "I love you, Hope, I do."

"You're clinically insane."

"Please. I never meant to lay a hand on you that way. I just wanted you to love me back. Love me the same way I love you. We can still start a new life. Together."

"Love?!" I explode. "Beating me and trying to rape me?! Going as far as murdering Mom?! This isn't love! This is a manic fixation, a mad obsession! You need to get this deluded image out of your mind! There is no 'us'! I have never held even a shred of respect for you. I told Mom when she first—"

"Enough!" The detective shouts. I clamp my mouth down, biting my tongue.

"Do you have anything else to say, Mr. Sullivan?"

"That was it," Roger says, and the way he leans back into his wheelchair and sighs demonstrates his acceptance of his fate. "Anythin' else ya got for me, detective?"

"No. That is all."

The lead detective slaps handcuffs on an unresisting Roger.

"A court date which you must attend will later be given to you. But take it from me—you can count your sunny days goodbye," he says. "Because after today, you'll be sitting in prison for the rest of your life." He hauls Roger's wheelchair—with Roger still in it—to the exit. I catch one last whiff of Roger's alcoholic scent before he disappears down the hall. And then, just like that, he's gone forever.

"Here," the other detective says, offering back my clothes littered on the ground. I accept them with quiet thanks before slipping into them.

"Thank you for confiding in us," she says and shakes my hand. "I know it wasn't easy."

I let out a prodigious sigh.

"Please don't arrest her. She wasn't thinking properly."

"I'm thinking just *fine*."

"I'm trying to help," Altha grits out in a hushed whisper. "Look at the man for god's sake!" He's right. The detective—back in the room after presumably transferring Roger to another officer—has his teeth clenched together, and a vein on his temple is throbbing.

"I'll deal with my colleague. You won't have any charges pressed against you," the woman juts in. "Go, go! Before I can't change his mind anymore."

"Thank you," Altha tells her.

"Well, that's that," I say to her after we're outside of the building in the sun's warm rays. I can feel a new sensation evaporate from my shoulders, evaporate from my list of burdens. The dark demon that perpetually pulled me down to the ground is gone. For the first time in a year, I am mentally and physically free from Roger.

I chance a glance at the sky. Perhaps angels do exist.

19*

Altha drives me back to my home, where I cleanse the house of its valuables. Everything that holds a memory to Mom and Dad I store in a knapsack, including the folder of piano music she bought me at the yard sale.

Mom has too many books for me to carry, but I manage to locate the one she was reading on the day of her death. For the first time, I absorb the title that I fought so hard to ignore. And then I keep it.

Upstairs, I take one last look at my broken piano and dented telescope as I pack any spare clothes I might need.

"Ready?" she asks after I meet her back in the kitchen. I give her a nod.

"Let's get out of here." I take one last look of the house and breathe in the musky smell.

No longer do I have to stare at the same drab sofa Roger passes out on. No longer am I ever going to be shrouded by toxic mist whenever Roger makes his appearance. No longer will I ever have to do, see, taste, hear, or smell *anything* Roger.

"How'd it go?! How'd it go?!" is the first sentence out of Videl's mouth as soon as we step out of Altha's car.

"Geez, are you sure you haven't switched personalities with Haley?"

Videl scoffs. "I'm male. She's female."

"I said personality, not gender."

"Everything went well," Altha chips. "Actually, everything went better than expected."

"So, what, he finally got his ass kicked by the cop?"

"The detective managed to coerce him to confess. Murdering Chloe to gain possession of Hope was his primary motive."

Videl slaps his hand to his forehand. "I'm a fucking idiot. That night when you escaped the house naked, we both knew he was going to leave the country with you. Yet when we were at the amusement park, it completely slipped my mind to have him talk about that plan of his."

"Oh," I say. "We also could have used those plane tickets as evidence."

"Like I said, I'm a fucking idiot!"

"Relax," I say, planting a heavy smooch on his lips. "I wouldn't have remembered. I was too excited with what was happening even to realize."

"Roger's incarcerated, so I don't see what you two are complaining about," Altha says. "In the end, it all worked out."

Videl hugs me. "Yeah, you're finally free," he whispers. "Oh, and come. There's a gift. From Altha and I. You can use your newfound time on this fine gem."

I give him a perplexing expression and my eyebrows scrunch together, not just at what present they got me, but from how *choppy* Videl seems to be—he's switching subjects in the blink of an eye, and his demeanor puts me at unease. The Videl I know never bounces up and down excitedly. The Videl I know never had the tone of enthusiasm that this one does. The Videl I know never tucks his hands behind his back like he's doing now.

Maybe it's just me. Maybe my newfound freedom instilled a slight sense of deliriousness, and that is why I am having all of these wary thoughts. So I shrug to myself and decide to play along with his attitude.

Videl leads me to a room at the end of the hallway, one that I've never been inside before.

The door clicks open. For a split second I swear I see a mirror image of myself, but then I just realize it's a room full of junk. Cardboard boxes, wooden pieces of equipment, stuff that you'd find in someone's attic. But my eyes catch onto something in the back. In the back—

"Take the cover off," Videl whispers. I do as he commands.

The cover flies off, and all my early suspicions of Videl's behavior fly out the window. There, right in front of me in all its glory, sits a brand-new digital piano. Burgundy and sleek, it radiates nothing less than infinite power. The power charger is already plugged in, so when I tap on the keys, a thunderous noise booms out, cutting the air clean in half.

"Keys are made of ivory. Not plastic. You don't—"

"—see much of these on digital pianos anymore," I finish in a whisper, before turning to Videl. "I love it. I love you."

I kiss Videl wetly, my eyes crying tears of happiness. It doesn't deter my strength, and he returns the kiss with just as much gusto.

"Uh, hello? I helped."

Videl and I break away to see one Altha with her hands at her hips. I move over to her and give her hug with as much energy as possible.

"I suppose an enthusiastic kiss was too much to ask for," she chuckles.

"Technically speaking, Haley was the one who gave us the idea," Videl tells me.

"How did she know?"

"The mall. She told me about your excursion there and how you were drooling at the display shelf in front of a piano store. This is the one you saw."

My heart swells up exponentially. I send Haley a 'thank you' in my head.

"So," Altha says. "We decided to get you up on your feet and stop you from slacking off on this semester's talent show." She winks.

I whip my head to Videl. "This is why you were so adamant on getting me to join the competition."

Videl lifts his hands up. "Guilty."

~~~~~~

The next day, we dispute which piece to perform. Two hours later, after many shouting matches and heavy kisses, we decide on twelve sheets of a classical, four-handed duet taken from the folder Mom bought at a yard sale many months ago.

Videl and I spend the next week practicing hours a day, every day. We practice before class starts, and before class ends. In fact, we practice anytime we don't have class or need to eat and perform other human behaviors. Videl moves his piano to the practice room, and we huddle up inside the warm, dimly lit room, poking our heads out of the door only when Altha calls us for a meal. Evidently, she's an amazing cook; something I would not have known during her bullying days. The food is so succulent that it melts in my mouth. We've had bouillabaisse three or four times already, but my taste buds still have yet to grow bored of the flavor.

We continue practicing well into the night, the sounds of crickets aligning with our music. After reaching a high enough level of languidness to the point where all we can think about is closing our eyes, the two of us retreat to Videl's room, where we pass out on the bed. My dreams are plagued by a mirror image of myself.

Two days into practice, and we can finally play the piece. However, the synergy is off. Videl is rushing half the time. There is no display of teamwork because both of us struggle with our own tempo and playstyle in an attempt for individual virtuosity. I stick strictly to the tempo and dynamics the composer marked. He pretends to have an endless cadenza.

Four days later, we finally make a breakthrough. Our hands finally stay together throughout the entire song; they wind in and out, in between one another in perfect harmony like a coordinated world-class dance. Like yes and no. Like yin and yang.

The day before the competition, an ominous feeling manifests inside my gut; the sense of something not being right—a malaise. At first, I think it's just my nerves amplified as the hours tick down, but that's not it. I can't identify it. There's a shadow lurking around the corner, with said corner being the night of the competition. It's waiting to pounce, and this feeling in my gut is warning me to back off before an ultimatum occurs.

The night of the talent show arrives. It's a Friday night, and I lock myself in the practice room, practicing my part over and over again while imaging Videl's in my head. Three more times isn't enough. Five isn't either. Ten isn't as well.

"Hope! It's time to eat! Quit brooding about!" Altha shouts. A moment later, and her fist is banging on the door.

I sigh. And then I close the piano lid. It's almost time to go anyways.

I make my way to the kitchen, where the scent of something sweet brews. I can't enjoy the smell; I'm too jittery.

"What's the matter, Hope?" Altha asks after I put my fork down. "You're more subdued than usual tonight."

"Just nervous," I respond. My eyes close and my fingers move across the air, tapping on invisible keys.

I take a few more small bites, but my mouth is drier than usual. So dry, in fact, that swallowing is an impossible chore.

"I can't eat."

"Can't, or won't?" Videl asks.

"Can't. I'm so nervous my teeth won't stop chattering long enough for me to stick food in my mouth."

Videl has a small frown tugging at the corner of his mouth. "We can eat later when we're celebrating. Let's get dressed."

I nod and then slip down from the barstool. Glancing in the corner where Bastien used to stand before heading up the stairs, I wonder again where he went. I'm well sure I did not imagine our first encounter.

Inside the guest bathroom, I strip myself naked down to my underwear before slipping on the rich, forest green gown that Altha bought for me a week ago. The silk fabric exposes my skin and causes me to shiver from the air conditioning.

I open the door right as Altha is opening hers across the hall. She whistles.

"You look hot." We meet eyes.

"Thanks. I have to get going."

"Wait! What about makeup?"

"I haven't thought about it. I can just get Haley to do my makeup. She's done it before."

"Seriously? I'm already here. Just let me do your hair and makeup already."

Finding no other logical reason, I give up to her demands. Altha takes me into her room, where she has me close my eyes. A light touch here and there, and then it's over.

"Wow."

"See? Told you."

I lean in closer to her mirror. For some reason, it's hard to see my reflection, almost as if the mirror is foggy with steam, but I can still make out my eyes. The eyeliner Altha used seems to magnify and darken my lashes by ten. The purple eyeshadow gives me a seductive, coquettish kind of look. I'm reminded of the femme-fatales of the sixties era, the ones with the husky, bedroom voices with dashes of makeup that represented nothing but perfection. Except I don't have the voice. And I also don't have those black gloves they wore.

"Come on. You have half an hour before the show starts." Just like that, my bubble pops, and I remember *why* I am wearing makeup in the first place. A duet performance, in front of hundreds. I take one last look at myself in the mirror. Is this how stage actors and actresses feel? In their dressing rooms, trying to calm their nerves and steady their trembling limbs?

Videl compliments my appearance, and no lie, he looks amazing as well. He's wearing a tuxedo that—at every stitch—is tailored to him. The tux's shoulders fit snugly around his. His pants legs slowly narrow until they reach his polished shoes, giving him a slim fit.

"Ready to go?"

I spend the drive there in brooding in nervousness. Videl's hand clasps around mine and Altha launches into a joke repertoire from the backseat, but my mind is elsewhere. I have always played in my free time, alone in my room. This time, it'll be in the school auditorium. My peers will be there. My enemies will be there.

"Relax. You'll be fine," Videl whispers as we're walking into the school. Just being here at night instead of my regular school schedule is enough to plant rocks in my stomach.

"I'm going to hyperventilate. Oh god, I'm going to hyperventilate."

"Breathe."

"Why did I do this?"

"Because," Videl says. "You're ready to begin again. You're leaving your past behind, and starting a new you."

The two of us take a side door for contestants into the backstage of the auditorium. The curtains are pitch black and drawn over the stage, yet I can still hear all the random chitter-chatter coming through the other side. This only serves to amplify my nerves. Besides Mr. Stern, Haley, and Altha, I don't know whether any other audience members will enjoy the performance. If only Mom was here...she could see how far I've come.

Most of the other contestants are dressed casually in jeans with a simple shirt, but there are a few other contestants dressed sharply. All of a sudden, I feel a connection to them. I feel relieved that I'm not the only one in a breezy dress.

A diversity of students are rehearsing their script under their breath. Maybe stand-up comedians. One person is holding six juggling balls. A couple of other people are musicians as well, their eyes zooming through each line of notes in their sheet music. At least everyone has something in their hands. I glance at my empty ones. If I forget my part—

"You won't forget. We've practiced too much to let this hard work go to waste. You will be perfect. The way you always are." Videl grabs both my hands and looks me in the eyes before kissing me.

The touch of his lips takes me to another world. We move perfectly in sync with each other. Every sensory neuron in my lips cries out with joy at his touch. My lungs are burning from lack of air, but I don't care. If there is a heaven, then is it. With Videl.

Yet at the same time, something feels strange. Off. The taste is salty, like there are tears mingled in our kiss—as if this kiss is a goodbye kiss and the last time I would ever touch him.

The principal makes his way out onto the spotlight, his dress shoes clacking on the oak floor. He begins his spiel, but it gets lost in my ears as none of my senses but my eyes work. The notes from the piece Videl and I practiced for the umpteenth time runs through my vision. A second inversion five chord at measure five. A modulation at measure thirty. A deceptive cadence at the halfway mark.

The line grows smaller and smaller as each contestant finishes. Some students are general favorites; that much is obvious by the audience's uproarious clapping. On the other hand, the less successful students, primarily the ones who tell poorly-received jokes, get sympathy claps.

There are only four people in front of us now. I peek a glance beyond the curtains. A dazzling gleam from the spotlights is so bright that they reveal every strand of hair and every pore on anyone that takes the stage. My gut clenches. I can't take this anymore. The ominous feeling that burrowed itself inside my gut the day before tonight is back, more prevalent than ever.

The next few students step on the stage, and my gut continues to squeeze. Before long, Videl and I are right behind the curtain, waiting for the contestant before us to finish. Even though the crowd is silent during his performance, my ears refuse to focus on the sound of the piece I have engrained into my head.

Then, there's clapping. Clapping means approval, but this clapping only serves to extend my wait for an even more prolonged period. As the clapping slowly dies, I hear the contestant's footsteps growing louder and louder as he walks to the back of the stage where a few other people, including me, have yet to go. Videl gives my hand a hard squeeze, but it doesn't soothe me. I dry heave in my mouth from how nervous I am.

The curtain flips open, and the guy walks through, his forehead all sweaty but his face with visible relief. He nods at us, and then Videl walks through, pulling me with him.

Time seems to freeze when I make my way out onto the stage. All my senses are working in overdrive. The lights are so blindingly bright that it mimics the rays of the sun, and I can immediately feel my sweat pores activate. Whereas Videl walks with his head held high, my eyes are plastered to my feet, taking care as to not trip over them. Every single step I take requires five seconds to do so, and my hands—usually never wet—are clammy and perspiring like crazy.

The program distributed earlier in the evening at the front door gives the audience an idea of who to expect next. My shoes make odd clicking sounds that rumble in my ears. My breathing starts to labor when I see all the blurry faces protected under the dark blanket. But then I hear a cheer, and I immediately recognize who it belongs to—Haley. This brings my confidence level back up a notch, and a few seconds later, Videl and I break apart our hands as we move to our respective pianos.

We take time to adjust our benches, and then we both lay our hands on the ivory. The black and white keys mesh together until I can no longer discern where I am supposed to start. I try playing the piece out in my head, but I can't envision the proceeding notes. I start panicking and rip my eyes off the keys in a desperate attempt to tell Videl I can't do this. But my eyes catch his, and even ten feet away, his orbs trap me inside, soothing me until my heartbeat slows down. He gives me a perfunctory nod, signaling me. And then, ignoring the silent tittering of the audience, my hands press down on the keys.

The sound reverberates through the stage and out toward the audience like a fiery gust of wind on a winter evening. I hold the chord down, allowing my fingers and ears to adjust to the different feel and sound of the piano. And when Videl's familiar tune begins to play, I find myself slowly sinking back into my calm and collected state.

Videl's finishes up his entrance, and in my mind, I can see his left foot pressing down on the damper pedal as he switches from the melody to the accompaniment. My time to shine. Gritting my teeth, I begin playing. I finish the first ten seconds without failing. I finish the second ten seconds without failing. By the time a minute has passed, I finally find my rhythm and my eyes close. My fingers fly over the set of keys like a graceful ballerina, and I almost bark in laughter until I remind myself I am still in front of hundreds.

This feeling doesn't last. After an arduous cadenza, my turn ends, and I recede to the accompanying position. Videl kicks in, the loud dynamics transferring from my end over to his. This is when I open my eyes. And this is when I see Roger.

My hands immediately fumble with the keys and a terrible sound comes out of the piano as I bang my hands down in the formation of a chord that does not fit the key of the piece we are playing. But the dissonant sound is obscured by my voice as I begin screaming. Roger is not in the audience. Roger is right in front of me on the other end of my piano.

"Hello, Hope," he mocks. "Miss me?" In his hand is a glinting, serrated dagger, almost as long as my arm.

"Videl!" I shout. "Videl!" I stumble out of the bench, the competition forgotten, and run over to Videl. "Videl! Help! What are—" my words hitch in the back of my throat when I see Videl with his hands still gliding over the keys. "Stop playing! What are you doing?! Roger's right there!"

Videl doesn't respond, and I yank his arm. He stops playing, but this isn't what freaks me out. He finally turns his attention to me, and I gasp. His eyes are dull and empty, *soulless*, with the usual jade green hue missing. The kind of eyes that that that shows someone there physically, but not mentally.

"Videl, snap out of it! What's wrong with you?! Help!" I scream. "Help!" I scream again, but it gets lost in the chaotic noise. Videl resumes his part and I turn around to my piano only to see the keys moving of their own accord. The pianos are generating sounds so loud my eardrums almost explode.

A tsking noise springs me back around to Roger, who is standing right in front of me. My nails cut so deep into Videl's shoulder that I break one. But Videl doesn't even flinch.

"It's not polite to leave your guest waiting, Hope," Roger smirks.

"How—how did you get out? You were arrested!"

"I broke out," he answers. "It was easy. Almost as easy as you."

"G—get—get away from me you sick freak! Help!" I peer over Roger's hunching figure in a desperate attempt to find out why no one from the audience is helping.

"Is that how you'll repay me?" he sneers. "You little bitch. I've been such a great caretaker. I've put a roof on your head. I've given you your first cell phone. So what if I killed your mom? She was a half-assed human who couldn't even tell the difference between left and right. What a pathetic bitch. Like mother, like daughter."

I'm filled with a strong urge to defend Mom. "Don't talk about Mom that way!" I shout with more confidence than I feel. "You're *nothing* but shit. You think you'll escape the cops? There's a mass manhunt for your alcoholic ass right now as we speak."

Roger snarls threateningly and holds his dagger out in front of my throat, and I instantly shut up.

"Yeah, yeah. Whatever. Let's talk about how you thought you'd get *me* arrested. Do you think I'd let you live to tell the tale? Think twice," he laughs. Out of the corner of my eyes, I see his grip on the knife tighten.

"W—what are you doing?" Alarm bells are ringing inside my head, and my fight or flight response kicks in, forcing my eyes to look for any means of escape. The audience members still refuse to move. It's almost as if they can't even see what's going on, even though it's right in front of their eyes.

"Don't even try it," Roger says. "I'm in sneakers. You're not. I'll gut you like a pig before you even get halfway across the stage. If I can't have you, no one will."

"How are you walking? This can't be real. This can't be real," I chant.

"Oh, this is real. *Very* real."

"N—n—n—no, please. You were—you were arrested! You were sent to jail! There's no physical way you can be here!" My hand jabs Videl again, but he's still a doll. Lifeless.

"Like I said, it wasn't too hard. I just had to pretend like I had given up in that interrogation room. But afterward…turns out the detective was more corrupt than any of us thought. What an experience! The model of justice, falling into the Devil's trap. A bribe later, and I'm walking away as clean as a new whistle. Money can get you far, Hope. Money can get you far."

"No. No," I continue, shaking my head in disbelief. "There's no way. Get—get away from me! Stay away!" I yell as he gradually creeps forward.

"I like it when you resist Hope; I like it a lot. Just make sure you don't resist too much.
These hands—" he pauses, lifting up his palms for me to see. "Have seen a lot of blood. I'd hate to add yours to them."

I stumble backward, falling on the stage floor.

He waves the dagger at Videl. "How could you do this to me Hope? How could you go and fuck that imbecilic little *boy*, when you had a man living in the same house as you?"

"Y—you're insane. Just keep—keep away from me. Leave me alone."

"I don't think so. You're giving me your whole body *now*. Then I might consider your life," he cackles, before launching himself on me.

"No! No!" I flail around in his grasp, but it's no use. In the past, I could always deal with Roger's strength. But now, with nothing to lose, he's fighting with everything he has. I realize with a stroke of fear that the ripping sound I hear is from him tearing my dress down the middle and exposing my breasts and underwear.

"Stop it! Stop it!" My hysterics rise beyond a level of sanity as I do everything to protect my chastity from Roger and the freezing air. I kick, push, grapple, punch, flay, and do every limb movement ever thought possible to man, all while my brain struggles to logically form a reason as to why no one is doing anything.

"Help me! Videl, help me! HELP!"

"Shut the fuck up, you *bitch*!" Roger roars into my mouth and I gasp in surprise and pain. I gasp as I feel him entering me, shredding through every sensor inside me like it is nothing to him. And when my brain finally comes to an understanding of what is happening to me, I start crying.

"S—stop!" I plead, tears now running down my face. "What are you doing?! Stop! St—oww!"

My back arches into the sky as Roger slaps me in the face with a tremendous blow. I wheeze for air and hardly have enough time to get half a breath in before he slaps me again with his other hand.

"This is what you get!" he laughs, continuing to smack me around while ceaselessly thrusting back and forth. "Finally, a good *fuck*."

My muscles involuntarily clench while I'm screaming and I feel Roger growing even more inside of me. Anatomy class from junior year moves to the forefront of my mind as I sluggishly recall what this means.

"NO!" I scream, finally understanding, right as Roger launches a feral snarl of his own before exploding inside of me. He empties everything he has inside of me, and I can *feel* it. I can feel the warm liquid gushing around inside of me. His *semen.*

"NO! I scream again. "No! No, no! NO!" My legs kick him off of me, and I immediately feel the liquid sloshing out and down my thighs.

"What have you done?!" I scream at him. My quaking hands go down to my privates. "No! N—"

A large fist flies and collides with my head, and I get knocked down to the floor again. Cracking open an eyelid, I see someone towering over me, and if I think I can't get any more distraught than I already am, I'm wrong. The person who hit me is not Roger. It's Videl. He disappears from my field of vision for a few seconds before I sense something prodding at me again.

"You're a filthy slut, you know that?" The warm voice of Videl I am so accustomed to is missing. This Videl's voice is dark. This Videl's voice fills with revenge. He laughs, and then with one fluid motion, he enters me as well.

"V—Videl," I choke.

Videl smothers my mouth with one hand and continues to thrust. The only sound in the whole auditorium are my muffling cries and his grunts blending into the music coming out of the pianos.

"Videl, w—why?"

"I fucking hate you, Hope. I always have. You're a fucking slut! How does it feel, to be fucked by someone you gave all your trust to?" Videl laughs raucously, and then I feel another wave of heat as he empties him inside of me with a series of throbs. He finishes and then pulls out, buckling his pants back up in the process.

I scramble to my legs, openly sobbing at the events that just occurred. My brain is yelling at me, telling me to realize that this is *not* my Videl. And then I come to a conclusion: I need to escape. The door is on the other end of the stage, and there's a ray of light shining through the door, beckoning me to come over. I start running, but then my legs give up on me and I fall down into a crumpled heap on the ground. I make some pitiful noise of desperation before I start using my arms to drag myself closer to the exit.

"Oh, no. You're not getting away." Roger walks up to me so his shoes are directly in front of my field of vision, and then he kicks me in my face. My nose erupts in a torrent of blood as it snaps to the side, broken beyond repair.

"Stop," I reply weakly, crawling toward the door inch by inch, trying my best to ignore the pain. "Stop."

"Would you like to do the honors?" he asks someone in the background. A few seconds later and Videl comes to me, dagger in hand.

"Videl! Sto—"

I don't get to say what I want because Videl shoves the dagger down and impales me straight through my stomach and out the other side, where I feel a part of my vertebrae shatter. I immediately let forth an earsplitting scream, yelling in agony for minutes or hours or days until my throat is too abused to scream anymore. My fluids stain the mahogany wood to a dark color, and I gag at the metallic smell of my blood and the acrid odor of my gastric juices.

A swarming mass of people hover over my body, all with darkened, indiscernible faces. Videl stabs me again, this time in my thigh, and I continue sobbing when a new trickle of blood starts to ooze out of the injury. My vision is fading fast, but I can still see Videl pass the knife to someone who breaks through the crowd.

"Ha—Haley. Ha—"

"How could you say such a thing to me, Hope? How could you say we're not friends?!" she sobs, in my face. "Don't worry, Hope. I'll make you my best friend again, just you see. I'll dress you up and do your makeup and tuck you in goodnight." I feel the sharp sting as the knife cuts into my right arm, and then the pain intensifies to an unbearable degree as she saws so deeply that the dagger reaches bone.

"Let me make this right, Hope. We'll be best friends forever. Are you my best friend? Tell me you are."

My eyelids start to droop. I'm losing too much blood.

"I'm s—sorry, Haley. For letting you down."

"Haley?" comes Roger's voice. "Have you finally lost your marbles?" I force my eyes open with whatever reserve of energy I have left.

"P—please."

"Please, what?" Roger laughs. "You want me to fuck you again? I knew you loved being raped."

"Please. K—kill me." I gurgle, managing to tilt my head to meet his eyes. He gives me one last evaluation and deems me too weak to play with.

One voice penetrates through all the chaos like a beam of light in the dark. I can't see who it's coming from, but there's no mistaking the husky voice coming from the exit.

"Join me. Don't be scared. It's your destiny."

The knife tears into my breast and through my heart. The tiredness threatening to envelop my whole entity finally wins over, and my eyes close as I slip into an eternal slumber.

20

"Help! Help!" I try to flail, but cannot.

IV needles. Two in each arm, connected to windy tubes inserted in IV bags hooked on hospital poles.

Somehow I had survived. I frantically peel my hospital gown upwards, only to see an unblemished stomach peering back at me. A monumental wave of relief washes over me when I see a lack of blood and lacerations. Inner Hope kicks in, trying to make sense of exactly what the hell is going on. My initial relief turns into a flummoxed frown, but the closer I get to the answer, the further away it gets.

The door suddenly clicks open and a nurse runs in, her mouth taking the shape of a stretched O as she spots me resting fully conscious in my bed. At the same time, my mouth *also* drops as I realize it's the same nurse. The same one that took care of me when I had tried to commit suicide near Christmas Day.

"You're up."

"Y—yeah," I croak. My voice feels like it hasn't been used in days, but the same familiar feeling encapsulates me. I think it's called a nasogastric tube or something. "It's good to see you again." She knits her eyebrows together and frowns.

"How did I get here? Where are my injuries?" I squint my eyes at my arm.

"I don't quite know what you are talking about, Miss Valentine."

"My injuries! My arm was sawed in half! I was repeatedly stabbed in the stomach! I was—I was…raped."

The nurse shakes her head. Something leaks out of the corner of her eyes. Is she…?

"This might come as a shock, and there's no easy way to say this."

"Say what?"

"This isn't going to be easy, and I have to ask you to try to stay calm—"

"Stay calm? What is it? Please, just tell me."

The nurse takes a long look at me. "You were…in a coma…for eight months," she slurs, drawing out each syllable meticulously.

Very dimly I'm aware of my surroundings receding away until all that's left is Susanna and me in a dark room. And then, my brain stops functioning altogether. All I do is dumbly stare at her, and my saliva turns bitter inside my mouth.

"Eight months?"

"August," she answers, and I gulp. Eight months. *August.*

"It can't be. I woke up on Valentine's Day. You were the same nurse who tended to me then too. Is this some joke you and Videl prepared?" I scan the room. "Videl, you can come out now!"

The nurse shakes her head morosely. "Hope, there is no joke. I don't know who Videl is." She walks to my right side and untacks a calendar from the wall before handing it to me. The calendar slips through my fingers after I see the date circled: August thirteenth.

Suddenly, I laugh. I laugh hysterically until my face is blue and my sides hurt at the ludicrousness of the situation, but she remains standing. Silent. I laugh until I can laugh no more, and my chuckles die down as I take in her indifferent countenance.

"You're not joking?" I inquire. She finally moves, giving a tiny jerk of her head. My eyes widen incredulously.

"You overdosed on Prozac and Ambien and had quantifiable traces of cocaine in your system. You were found unconscious and brought to the ER Christmas Day. Doctor Lee pumped your stomach and tried flushing out the toxins, but you retained your comatose state. Combined with your dehydrated, malnourished, bruised, and anemic condition when brought to us, you fell into a coma and didn't wake up. Until now."

Eight months. Not two. Eight. Christmas. Haley.

"I don't believe you."

"I'm sorry," is all she manages. "But it's true."

I look her dead in the eyes, trying to read through her lie, trying to pierce through this façade, but her face is morphed into pure honesty. She gives a sad little nod, and this unrelenting gesture causes me to snap.

"T—that's impossible," I say. "I was just on stage, and—and—oh god! N—no! I don't believe you! You're lying! YOU'RE LYING!" I roar and begin to thrash about with conniption. I feel the sharp stabs of the needles jerking around in my veins, breaking their thin walls and stabbing into my muscles, but the pain is second to my aporetic state.

"Miss Valentine, please calm down!" The nurse's frozen state dissipates as soon as I start screaming and she jumps into action, trying to dispel my rage. The sound of the heart monitor beeping with faster intensity threatens to consume all my senses.

"Don't touch me!" I snarl, but she refuses to pay heed to my words and continues to grapple with me. I put up a strong fight, but my atrophied muscles slowly give way, allowing Susanna to force my flailing limbs flat. She clamps my arms to the side of my bed, and sits on my legs with her knees.

Her grip is so secure around me that I can't move. And when that happens, my resistance crumbles apart, and I begin sobbing, letting out my frustration and my body's first visible emotion since December.

"It—it c—c—can't be. This isn't real—this—I'm going to wake up any moment. Please—" My hand shoots to her scrubs, and I yank her closer to me, using my free hand to run across her cheek and lips. "Tell me this is a dream. Tell me you aren't real." At our distance, I can see everything in her eyes, and I try to delve as deep as I can into them to uncover the truth.

She shakes her head one more time and mouths an apology. My hand slowly loosens around her shirt and falls lifelessly to my side.

"It can't be," I repeat. "It can't be."

Susanna wanders off but then returns a few seconds later, pressing a tissue to my eyes.

"There, there," she consoles. "You woke up. That's all that matters."

"Is this a dream too? You are fake. You have to be."

Susanna brushes some loose strands of hair out of my eyes.

"I'm real. This is the real world."

Denial's manifestation is still sticking to me like a parasite. "Please take me to the bathroom."

"Sure," she says, seemingly surprised at how stable I am now. "Let me get your wheelchair." I hear her shuffling off to the closet before returning to ease me in.

Susanna helps me to my feet once we're in the cubicle and walks me to the toilet, but I shake my head.

"Mirror."

She lets out a little 'oh' before turning me around to the mirror. And my eyes widen when I see my complexion clearly for the first time—the first time in eight long months. I can see Hope, and what I see makes my grip on the sink tighten. My hair is uneven, like I had gone to a shady barber and received a free bowl cut. They stick out in frizzy chunks, cowlicked from the eternal sleep. My cheeks are sunken in, giving me a bony, old, demented look. The pale, yellow color of my skin on my arms is wizened and saggy. My eyes are the only part of my body unchanged—they remain piercingly clear and perspicacious after my ordeal, but inside swirls emotions so painful I lose control and scream into the mirror, punching it with my hate-fueled fists until the wet trickle of liquid spills to the ground.

Susanna is back on me within a second and drags me away. This time, there's no fight. I let her do what she needs to do. In the back of my mind, there's a feeling coming on. A feeling of regret. Poignancy toward the decision to take my life.

"Promise me you won't do anything rash like that ever again," Susanna reprises after she firmly tucks me into the bed.

I mutter some half-assed response, but it satisfies her because she tells me she'll check on me later. Of course. She has other patients to attend to. And she probably generalizes them the same way as me—with no individuality, copping forced smiles and an attitude of patience.

Susanna has one foot out the exit.

"Who found me?"

She pauses.

"A young boy your age claims he discovered your body and brought you here. He stayed by your side every day for a month before leaving suddenly in the middle of February." She brings herself back in and begins rummaging the contents of my bedside nightstand.

"He wanted me to give you this," she says as she digs through the drawer. I crane my head to the side, watching her upturn objects of disinterest.

"Here we go," she announces, brandishing a white mailing envelope in her hand. "This is for you." I accept the offered letter from her hands.

"Is there anything else you need?" she asks politely, and all it does is infuriate me. I hate those stupid, platitudinous questions.

"Just leave me alone," I bitterly grit.

"I hope you find what you're looking for." And then, she's gone.

I leave the envelope alone and throw it to my side with a heavy huff.

There were so many signs, and yet I missed them all.

I let out a sigh of annoyance as my thoughts reel to an end and are replaced by curiosity mixed with angst. It forces me to pick the envelope back up. I spot some writing on the front of the envelope, and when I focus, I see my name written on the front. The handwriting easily resembles Videl's.

I rip the seal open barbarically, and with trembling hands, I pull the letter out and begin reading.

To Hope—February 14th,

I will be gone already by the time you're reading this. Father has called Altha and me back to France, and no matter how much I want to remain by your side, his word is final. The doctor told me if you wake up, you might experience retrograde amnesia, so it's best that I remind you of what happened.

Your recent catatonic state at school before winter break had me worried, but I respected your wish and stayed away. However, Haley confronted me in person a few days after school ended and asked me to check in on you. I found you in your bathroom, passed out with two empty pill bottles on the countertop.

The doctor and the nurse did what they could to flush out the drugs in your system, but you still didn't come back. You didn't wake up that day, the next day, or any day after.

Every day I prayed for your well-being, but things continued to look grim. The doctor said with each passing day, the likeliness of your conscious return to the real world shrinks. But I believe in you, Hope. I know you're a fighter, and I won't give up on you. You proved it to me by holding your own against Veronica and standing up to Roger. I hope that one day, you will be holding this letter with your own two hands.

Ah, what to say, what to say. I've rehearsed a multitude of speeches, but they all seem to jumble around senselessly in my mind when I attempt to jot them on paper.

First, I'd like to apprise you that Roger has been convicted to two life sentences for the manslaughter of Chloe Valentine. The detectives on the case found plane tickets and forged identities in his office. He confessed in court that his motives were to assume the role of primary guardian and start a new life with you abroad.

Now that he's gone, the focus at hand is finding you a place to stay, whether it be a permanent home or until you turn eighteen. Currently, at this time, you are taken care of by the hospital, with resources funded by my father. If—no, when—you wake up, the idea of foster parents will be a matter of discussion by social services.

Secondly, I want to sincerely apologize for my actions in November. You ran off before I could have a chance to explain, but that does not excuse my behavior. You deserve a right to know. You deserve to know that I made a bet with Chad a month into school. The contents of the bet encompassed me getting closer to you, and the ultimate goal was to end up dating you for a month before I confessed it was all just a game. It was the most stupid, fallacious mistake of my life. At the time, I had taken his challenge because I thought it would be fun to manipulate and mislead you into harboring unrequited feelings for me, but my puerility did nothing but cause us to fall apart. Because somewhere down the line, the game backfired on me. I genuinely fell in love with you. With your innocent smile. With your infectious laugh. But most of all, I fell in love with your tender, rapturous heart. You gave me new life and allowed me to feel emotions I didn't know existed.

I know I don't deserve your forgiveness, and I can't ask you for it. So the only thing I will ask you is this—move on with life. Continue your education and experience all the wild and memorable opportunities in college. Find someone who makes you happy and loves every part of you. And cherish every moment you spend with them.

Happy Valentine's Day,

> *-Videl*

The letter is soaked in tears by the time I finish reading.

I never rekindled my relationship with Haley and Jackie. I never became friends with Altha. I never helped Videl to incarcerate Roger. The talent show didn't exist with me as a participant. But most importantly, I never got back together with Videl. It was all too good to be true.

There were so many signs, and yet I missed them all.

But Roger…it says in Videl's letter he was arrested. And also the bet with Chad. Did these events happen in my dream and real life as well? Coincidence? No. Fate. Maybe my brain subconsciously knew Roger was guilty the moment I saw him outside working on Mom's car and it only decided to piece together parts of the puzzle once I was in my coma. Or maybe, even worse, I'm in another dream. I lift my hands up and ball them into fists. They seem real.

And I scream.

The guttural cries bubble from past the inner depths of my throat until they reverberate around the room. I scream again, and continue screaming. I pause for a few seconds, and then scream again. I scream.

Susanna comes in a few hours later with dinner. She asks me how I'm holding up, and I respond with short remarks. We share a hurried goodbye. The door clicks, and I'm left alone. The sun outside slowly lowers until it's hidden beyond the horizon; all that's left is the emptiness of the room. The only sounds I hear is the heart monitor and the crickets chirping outside.

My heart's beating, but I don't feel alive. The sense of urgency slowly creeps up on me until I can't take it anymore. Knowing that the last eight months had just flown by without my existence pushes me to a feeling that I can't grasp, but it's slowly choking and circling me like black smoke. I wish I had never woken up. Everything in my dream seemed so real—all the gentle caresses and kisses were so *perfect*, that waking up to reality makes me feel so nugatory and cheated.

And then I begin thrashing around in bed. A choked sob flies out of my lips when I come to realize that I can't move my arms or legs. I can't feel them at all. I let out a frustrated noise, one that is supposed to draw the concern of sympathetic humans, but no one hears me. Susanna doesn't come, and I slowly lose my energy. Body exhausted, I fall into the depths of my subconscious. There are no dreams—just blackness.

The next few days roll around. The nasogastric tube is taken out. Susanna walks in every morning with a smile on her face and delivers me a tray of scrambled eggs, French toast, and a glass of milk—the kind of food that companies buy in bulk and stick in their freezer until needed. She proceeds to tell me I am being discharged after I finish my meal. With no will for contentiousness, I finish the muck, grimacing as the low-quality food slides dryly down my throat.

The female doctor walks in not too long after I finish eating. I see her mouth moving, but can't hear the words that come out. She hands me a bag embroidered with the hospital logo, and I look inside to see identification—my passport, since I never took my driving license test, and the same plain gray shirt and sweatpants.

I slip them on and then she leads me through empty, meaningless hallways with her ministrations until I'm at a single counter. The smiling assistant on the other side hands me a clipboard to sign. The automatic doors slide open.

"Hey, honey."

The warm tone makes me look up but it's not Mom I see—it's Haley's mother. She gives me a broken smile.

I mutter an unintelligible response. Or maybe I stay silent.

The car ride is oppressed. She asks me things like how I've been, when I woke up, and what I'm planning to do with my future. I don't know. I answer her desultorily and before long, our short conversation stills.

"Is Haley home?" The question falls from my lips before I know what I am saying. A tiny orb of hope suffuses inside me until it spreads warmth throughout my entire body, reaching my fingertips and toes.

"No, sweetie. She's moved into college already. Her first class was yesterday." She turns around in the seat since we're at a red light and looks at me proudly.

"Oh. Um, congratulations to her."

"We were all worried she wouldn't get into her favorite university, but she managed to get that cheerleading scholarship. She loves it there already." She continues talking about Haley's new life.

Haley has her family and her friends. And me? I have nothing, stuck in this new month and a new season without anyone I know. Stupid coma. I kick the bottom of the seat in frustration. Time took away so much of my life. I was supposed to spend it with Mom. Celebrate Thanksgiving and Christmas with her. Make resolutions for the New Year. Perform for her at the talent show. Graduate high school. Apply for college. Laugh at all the wrong things and scoff at all the right ones. But I can't, because Roger took everything away from me.

At this moment, a rush of intense anger fills me. The rage is so palpable that it courses a roaring fire into my veins, hell-bent on retribution. My vision turns red, and my grip tightens. I imagine it to be Roger's neck in my hands. I squeeze. I can't handle this suffering. I need to vent. I need to—

"Honey. Honey?"

"What?!" I realize the lace of venom in my tone, and I quickly change it. "Sorry, what?" I repeat, this time with a calmer attitude.

"We're…here." Haley's mom stares at me a few seconds longer before pointing to an unfamiliar brick building.

"What is this place?"

"Social services. You have an appointment with them in half an hour. They need to discuss where to house you until you're a legal adult."

"I'm fine. I don't need anyone."

Haley's mom's face softens, and after a brief hesitation, she snaps open the glove compartment before taking out a small manila envelope.

"Take this. It's the extra money Haley earned working her shifts at Mickie's. She wanted you to have it." She presses the envelope in my hand before I can muster up a protest, and then gives me an unexpected hug.

"I'm so sorry. Haley will be back for fall break. Keep in touch," she whispers.

I nod in her embrace and then exit the car, walking toward the building entrance. I hear the car leaving.

The inside of the building has its walls covered in canary yellow paint, and this refreshes my memory of motel that's about to declare bankruptcy. The walls are peeling in several spots, and dark stains spot the carpet.

"Take a seat," the lady at the dirty receptionist counter offers. I give her a small nod before making my way to the antique squashed chairs, taking great care in storing Haley's memento in my pants pocket. I sink so far into the soft chairs that my head is at the chair's arm level.

Someone nudges me a while later, and I see that it's a man garnished in a navy blue suit wearing monocles. His tie is dark blue and striped, the kind my father wore. "Miss Valentine?"

I get up without a word, dreading the following conversation. He leads me through a wooden door to an office area. I sit down in the offered armchair while he makes his way to his. Carl Olsen, his nameplate reads.

"I suppose you know why you're here, Miss Valentine?" he begins.

"You're not my principal. So don't act like one."

He clears his throat. Then he pulls out some papers.

"Hope Valentine, born the twentieth of August?" I give him a surly nod.

"No social security, no credit card, no driver's license, no contact info. Do you have any form of identification to prove your existence?"

"Just my passport." I give a little maniacal chuckle and notice the man gives me a strange, concerned look.

He sets the forms down and looks at me.

"Well, I'll keep this short and simple. Seeing how you turn eighteen in four days, we have two options to work with here." At my silence, he continued.

"Plan A, I set you up with foster care. I know the caretakers personally and can vouch for their good hearts. Or B," he continues. "I'll have a colleague of mine provide you living quarters until you turn eighteen. I daresay you'll choose foster care because going out there in the real world is tough. Your stepfather is in prison, your mother and father are deceased, and you have no relatives in or out of the country. You have no one under listed under emergency conta—"

"Plan B," I blurt out.

"Are you sure? I normally wouldn't offer a choice, but you're only a few days away from legal adulthood."

"I'm sure."

"Well, alright then. Let me introduce you to Amanda." He gets up from his seat, and I follow him back into the main lobby and down another corridor before he knocks on a door.

A woman sticks her head out a few seconds later.

"Amanda," Olsen nods. "This is the girl I was talking to you about. Hope Valentine."

"Pleasure to meet you, Hope." I mutter a quick pleasantry back. She's fairly young, around twenty-five or thirty. She's the kind of woman I always wanted to be, but never could.

The adults talk a little bit more before Carl leaves us alone. She talks to me some more and asks me about my personal interests, like what food I like to eat, my favorite color, whatever. We get in her car and then she drives for ten minutes or so before we reach a small cream, stucco house. The door is a deep shade of purple, yet years of neglect has made it bereft of color. Familiar.

"You can use the guest bedroom," she says after she finishes giving me a tour inside. "You'll have your own bathroom. Hot showers, rejoice!" she chuckles.

I don't smile, and her face slowly loses mirth.

"Say…Hope? I know you made the decision to stay with me until you're eighteen, but do you know what you're going to do after?"

"Yeah. Take the GED. Stay with a friend."

"Okay. I'm worried about you. The real world is intimidating. For someone as young and you are to venture out there yourself…" she trails off. "Anyways, do you have any clothes with you?" she says, trying to change the subject.

"Only what I'm wearing."

"Okay. Why don't you go shower, and I'll laundry your clothes for you. Deal? Go, go," she urges. I have no choice but to do what she says so I go to the bedroom and undress, making sure Haley's envelope and Videl's letter is with me before I leave my shirt and pants in front of the bathroom door.

I make the shower quick and then dry off even quicker, refusing to glance into the mirror.

There are some new clothes that Amanda spread out on the counter, and I gratefully slip into them. They're baggy, but a fresh change.

Amanda's in the bedroom smoothing out the bedsheets when I walk in.

"Feel better?" she asks.

"Yeah," I lie. "Thanks for letting me use the shower."

"I'm your caretaker for four days. What kind of person would I have to be not to let you clean yourself?" She finishes smoothing the wrinkles out and stands back up.

"Are you hungry? I went shopping yesterday, so there's plenty of food in the fridge. Do you like hamburgers? I have beef and pork. Or are you a vegetable person instead?"

I realize she's trying to be an altruistic host, but the bizarre distressed feeling planted in my gut supersedes my scant hunger.

"I'm ok," I answer, half-truthfully. "Just really tired. I think I'll turn in for the night."

She gives me a sad little smile.

"Alright. If you need anything, I'm the last door down at the right end of the hall," she says before leaving. The door clicks shut, and then I'm left alone.

I slowly shake the bedcovers loose and wiggle myself into them. The queen-sized bed is comfortable, and I instantly sink into the soft foam. But no matter what, sleep won't come.

Nostalgia is so raw it rips a hole in my heart, and I moan. And with this nostalgia brings memories of Haley. Her stubbornness. Her refusal to give up, and her unwavering determinism. Her last memory of me was the last day of class before Christmas break—when we were sitting together on the linoleum gym floor. I never made things right.

Videl.

I pull out the worn sheet and skim through the letter, scrutinizing it. I read it again and again, and one more time for good measure. A sharp pang pulses through my chest when I confirm my suspicions. Nowhere in the letter did it say he didn't love me anymore.

Kicking the sheets off me, I leave the room, mind decided. I need a computer, and I find one, a bulky old piece of machinery. I power it on, and luck must be on my side because I don't need an administrator password. I open the browser and search through a list of plane tickets to France. It isn't until I'm asked for a destination that I realize I have no idea where Videl lives. And then, I start having second doubts. He wrote the letter on Valentine's Day. Six months ago. Half a year ago. Plenty can happen within that timeframe.

Tears begin to well up in my eyes. My heart slowly thuds, unmitigating, whispering to me.

And then I realize it doesn't matter if he doesn't love me anymore. It doesn't matter if he's found someone else. It doesn't mater, because in the end, I still love him. I belong to him, and always will.

I snatch computer paper from the nearby printer and scribble a quick letter to Amanda. As short as we've know each other, she has been nothing but the perfect host, and I can't depart without saying goodbye. I leave behind only minor details—that she shouldn't worry, that I'll be safe, and a wholehearted thank you for the short stay.

Within two minutes, I'm out of the house in my own clothes and on the way to my destination. The temperature is cool for a summer night. The sky is clear, and the stars are fully visible. I make out the Big and Little Dipper. They are glowing brighter than usual.

I tuck my head down for the occasional passerby, and half an hour later, the school makes its appearance, looming out before me. Another wave of nostalgia rushes through my body when I see the familiar brick panels and the recently weeded lawn with the glowing school mantle erected in the front. *Starmount— Home of the Titans.*

The hidden back entrance has yet to be patched, and I slip through unscathed into the main building. The office door is locked. Frustrated, I kick the door and ram it with my shoulder. Neither attempt turns out successful, but both leaves me with dull aches. An exasperated sensation begins to consume me.

Seeing no other solution, I run to the front entrance, punch the fire alarm with my fist, and pull the lever down.

The alarms begin screaming in my ears, but my mind is focused on getting that one address. I run back to the office door, and it offers no opposition as I easily push open the now-unlocked door. I scramble in and dash to the filing cabinets. I probably have three minutes tops to leave the school still unseen.

Digging through the horde, I cackle to myself. What am I reduced to? Breaking and trespassing on public property, all for a piece of paper? What would Mom say if she saw me digging around furiously like a homeless beggar in a dumpster? I would have never recognized myself now a year ago. A deranged maniac.

My hands frantically flip paper after paper. The clock's second hand's ticking only grows louder and louder as my deadline draws closer. Sirens are already hovering in the background, maybe only a mile away.

Kwon, Kynton, Labby, Labelle, Lacred, LaCroix—

"Go back!" Inner Hope screams in my ears. My hands are shaking when I draw out Labelle's personal information. My eyes focus in on the dark piece of paper until I find his permanent address. I repeat it to myself four times before sticking the file back in the cabinet. I'm about to leave but then I pause. No one can know that I was here. I move everything back to the way it was right before realizing it doesn't matter if I reorganized the place to the way it was before I broke in. There are security cameras everywhere.

Thinking on my feet, I yank a marker out of a cup. Not finding any paper, I uncap the marker and write out the word 'Sorry!' from one end of the desk to the other. And then I run for my life. The sirens are blaring, and I know for a fact the firetrucks are in the parking lot. But I manage to slip out through the back of school grounds to the forest safely. And then I begin bolting.

I trip a couple of times in the forest but manage to make it out without being caught. Double-checking my pockets, I breathe a sigh of relief when I feel Haley's money and Videl's note still secure.

From what I remember, Roseden has no airport. The nearest one is ninety minutes away. But without any means of transportation besides my own two feet, I have no other option but to drag myself on the desolate two-lane road and hope for a hitchhike.

I only begin walking for a few seconds before it hits me. My footsteps halter into a stop as I let the revelation coat me.

Jackie. *Jackie!*

Due to all the hectic changes in my life, I completely forgot about her. I can ask her for a ride. She didn't have her license around Christmas, but that never stopped her from taking her dad's car out for a spin when her parents weren't around.

With fresh determination fueling my body, I begin jogging, passing down dozens of unfamiliar houses before the fluorescent street lamp tangled in the branches of a gargantuan oak tree that I had become so accustomed to during the wintertime peaks out from around a corner. Knowing this is the right direction, my determination delivers one last powerful punch. I don't stop sprinting until her home looms out in front of me.

The lights illuminating the inside of the house are bright enough to show wilting flowers in their garden and high weeds that haven't been mowed for quite a while, but I don't pay these observations much attention. The only thing I pay attention to are the lights. Lights on means people.

I gently sneak my way up to the front door, careful not to give off the impersonation of a thief. My finger touches the doorbell, and I am just about to press it when logic hits me. Jackie's alcove is at the very top of the house, and that is where she spends all of her time. There is no way the light from there would be able to flash so brightly as it is doing so now, which means it's her parents that are bustling about.

My hypothesis is proven when I spot a pair of shuffling feet through the translucent, frosted glass that is on each side of the door. My eyes shift past the feet to the body, and a blurry, bulky man is who I see.

I'm not about to ring the doorbell and have her father open the door. I've never even met the man. Imagine how awkward it would be trying to explain why I am here at this time of night and why I need Jackie to take me to the airport.

I back away from the door and decide on walking around the back, to where I know the makeshift rope still dangles from the screws of her bedroom window. Jackie always was an affable, aberrant, frivolous girl—even walking out the front door was too conventional for her.

Sure enough, the rope is still there, but the window is sealed. My muscles are still weak from their lack of use, so I search for a small pebble. When I find one, I chuck it at the window. The rock hits its mark, making a sound that is too loud for the inhabitant in the room not to hear but too soft for her dad downstairs to hear.

There is no response. I wait for thirty seconds before throwing another rock. Maybe she thinks a bird flew into her window.

Another three minutes later, and six or seven unsuccessful rouses, I finally give up the notion that rocks will do anything. I take in as much air as my lungs will allow, and then jump onto the rope. My muscles immediately begin to scream in agony, but the determination I felt earlier while running to her home is back.

So I climb. I climb, and I climb, with the intention of banging my fist on the windowpane until Jackie opens up.

When I reach the top and peer inside, this is when the first wave of goosebumps wash over me. The window is dusty, and I can hardly gaze inside. But the dark shapes are obvious.

Cardboard boxes. Cardboard boxes are everywhere, scattered throughout the room. Some of them are closed and securely taped shut, while others still have the flaps dangling. The only thing decorating the room are a few dreamcatchers installed in the ceiling. Jackie's bed is missing, and so are the plants that would hang over her bedsheets. The walls are also bare. There is not even one poster tacked up.

For the first time since I get out of the hospital, I feel genuine fear.

I make sure to let myself down the rope slowly. Even if I burn my hands, I don't think I would have noticed. My thoughts are in a wide array of chaos, fumbling for an answer as to why her room is that way. The only explanation I can think of is this: they are moving.

My feet almost carry me in the opposite direction, but in the end, I end up in front of the door again, for two reasons. One, I still have no idea which direction the airport is. And two, the greater reason by far, is that I need closure. Videl can take a pause. I need to see Jackie.

Even after I finish explaining myself to her dad, and even if he does somehow allow her to take me, what am I supposed to say to Jackie myself? *Hi, Jackie, long time no see. I know it's been eight months, but I'm in a bit of a pickle right now and need to leave the state before I get thrown into prison for breaking and entering our school. Why did I do that? Oh, because I'm still in love with Videl. I had to get inside the school to find his records. Can you drive me to the airport, just so I can leave you again? Maybe we can catch up on the ride there...*

The conversation playing out in my head comes to an end, and I growl in frustration at my behavior. But I am all out of options, so I take another deep breath and jab my index finger on the doorbell.

The shuffling feet I saw earlier stops pacing and by the alignment of his shoes, I know he's looking at the front door. I can feel an eye peering through the peephole. After he deems me harmless, the door opens.

The man is just starting to wrinkle—skin on his forehead that has yet to sag fully but can no longer be deemed as youth crinkle together as he continues to stare at me perplexingly. His hair is black and cut short, and biceps struggle against the tight seams of his polo shirt. The most noticeable feature is the hazel color of his eyes—the same as Jackie's.

"Can I help you?" he asks.

"I—I—ah—" I try to formulate words, but they don't come out. I heave a large sigh before trying again, this time successfully "Is Jackie here? I know it's really late, but I have to speak to her."

The man's face contorts a million times in the span of a few seconds. Surprise, shock, anger, disappointment, relief, love, sadness—every single emotion ever catalogued into words, he matches. But finally, his lips purse, and he disappears back inside the door after shutting it. I hear him hollering for someone.

Not a few seconds later, the door flies open again. My head tilts up and my face breaks out into a smile at what is *supposed* to be Jackie, but isn't. A middle-aged woman, this time, is standing in the entrance.

My smile slips.

"Who are you?" The woman's voice holds wariness and a slight bit of anger. I shrink back at how aggressive the question is.

"I'm Hope. I'm Jackie's friend. Is she in right now? I have to talk to her," I repeat.

"Jackie is no longer with us."

Oh. Maybe she was kicked out of the house for her drug usage. That makes more sense, after all. I don't think she'd want to willingly move out from a part of the house that she spent so much time cultivating. "Is Jackie in college, or?"

She looks me in the eyes and says, "Jackie is dead."

Very vaguely, my surroundings disappear until all that is left is her mother's eyes. I stare into them, disbelieving and trying to unveil some shred of a lie. The temperature drops a few degrees and my goosebumps return. My brain numbs itself as I struggle to decipher how three words can topple everything.

"D—D—Dead?"

"Yes. She overdosed one month ago."

"Oh—oh my god." My hands fly to my mouth.

"Are you playing a joke? My husband and I are trying very hard to move on, young lady."

"I—I'm so sorry." My hands fall from my mouth and clench into fists. "I—I was in a c—coma and didn't know."

The lady stiffens.

"Coma? Did you say your name was Hope?"

I nod.

"Hope Valentine?"

I nod again. The lady takes a calculating stare before her demeanor changes.

The next thing I know, my back is against the wall, and my feet are dangling off the ground. The woman had moved faster than a blink of an eye, and now she's squeezing my neck. Her nails dig into my flesh, and I release a startling cry.

"How could you do this my Jackie?! She died because of you! You're the reason this whole family is ripped apart!" the woman spits. Her hands wrap around my throat so tightly that my vision begins to go black. My lungs cry for air, but her iron grip prevents even a single shred of it from being breathed in.

My hands feebly attempt to pry her off of me, but in the end, it's no use. My current condition is weak. Fighting against any protective mother is unfeasible. The color vanishes from my eyes until all I can see is black and white. My body twitches one last time—

"Margaret, no! This isn't what Jacqueline would have wanted. Stop! Stop!" The sound of the man's voice causes her to hesitate and drop me to the ground. I immediately start making this awful gurgling sound, and my hands reflexively try to ease the bruises that are forming on my neck. Through my blurry vision, I can see the man confronting the woman. A few seconds, he pulls me to my feet. I wobble in place, and my hand shoots out and balances my weight against the same wall I was being strangled on. The woman is nowhere to be seen.

"Listen, I apologize for my wife's behavior. She's still in a state of shock, and it's hard for her to hear about our daughter. She hasn't gotten better over the past month."

It doesn't escape my notice that the man doesn't ask whether I am okay or not.

"T—that's okay," I rasp, still massaging my throat. My feet immediately take a few steps back. This man is at least twice as large as the woman.

A sudden sense of déjà vu creeps on me, and my vision goes back to many nights ago. Pictures of me at the hospital fly into my memory, and suddenly I feel *my* hands wrapped around someone's throat—the doctor's.

"That's okay," I repeat, my voice struggling to return to normal. "I—I understand."

"Do you?" the man asks. "Do you understand?"

I shake my head. I wish I did, but I don't.

"Jacqueline wasn't the same after you fell into a coma. You have to understand that our daughter didn't have many friends. Sure, she had acquaintances, but when it came down to true friends, she could count all of them on one hand. And guess who her best was?"

"Me."

"Yes. I don't know how much you knew about her, but you had a phenomenal impact on her life. Our daughter…she isn't like the rest of her peers. She—"

"I remember," I say. "I know what she was like."

"And she knew you were the same as her. Which is no surprise that when you fell into a coma, she fell into a state of severe depression. My wife and I tried everything we could for her. We tried talking to her, and when that didn't work, we tried therapy. In the end, she was put on anti-depressants, but that only seemed to make her worse."

"So what happened in the end?" I whisper. I have to know. I *need* to know.

"After months without your resuscitation, she gave up on you. I've always had my suspicions about what she did alone in her room, but when I found her body," her dad chokes, "—when I found her body next to her pills and a bag of drugs, I knew Margaret and I failed."

The father rubs his eyes, and under the shadow of the light, he seems to have aged fifty years.

"There was a suicide note," he continues. "Its contents were few, but what it did say was that she did it for you. She thought you would never wake up, so she went off to join you in the afterlife. To provide you with some comfort so that you wouldn't be alone."

He retreats to a tiny lamp table and picks something up.

"Take this," he says with his voice cracking, holding the item to me. "She requested you have this, in the off chance you would ever wake up."

I peer into his hand and see a tiny, silver piece of jewelry. A second later, and I recognize it. It's one of Jackie's five piercings that she wore on her ear; being an industrial piercing, this one is the largest one, a minimized version of a dreamcatcher she had dangling from her room—it has two silver feathers dangling from a circular frame encapsulating a pure, white gem.

I slowly reach out until my hand is resting in his palm, and I scoop the dreamcatcher out with my fingertips. The sharp ends, seemingly with life, stab into me and draw blood.

"Please," her father says. I look up to his face and see tears streaming down his cheeks. "Don't come back."

I tighten my grip.

"I won't," I promise. "You have my word."

He nods and then steps inside, shutting the door. I continue standing and watching the faint glow of the jewelry before realizing my stay is now unwelcome. So tucking it inside my pants, I tread down the stairs and back onto the road.

The industrial piercing jostles around in my pocket, poking me in my thigh every now and then, but I don't readjust it. The pain serves as a reminder of all the memories Jackie and I shared.

I almost wish I never went to her house in an attempt to get a ride to the airport, but then I realize that even if I didn't go, it doesn't change the fact Jackie died. It just changes my own knowledge of things.

I scrunch my posture, pulling the sweatshirt's hoodie over the top of my head as to not garner unwanted attention. A police car zooms by not long after with the sirens on and shrieking, but the driver ignores me. Once they rewind the surveillance tapes and see the perpetrator, they'll post my information on a wanted list. They'll travel door-to-door, asking people I had a class with or knew personally whether they know where I am. Relief washes over me when I realize that I did not tell Jackie's parents where I am going. No doubt the police will question them first.

With no other option but to try to hitch a ride, I beg my feet to start running. In the next half hour, several cars pass me without stopping, but before long, a car slows down, and the person behind the wheel blinks the headlights.

"You okay there?" The passenger door opens and the sight of a hairy hand stretched across the glove compartment greets me. His eyes roam over my body with the exception of my hidden face, taking in the disheveled appearance.

"Yeah. Do you mind if I catch a ride?" Side effects of the determination I experienced an hour ago finally catch up to me. The grueling aftereffects of running for a prolonged period after months of a sedentary existence and a wholehearted strangling marathon has me wheezing for air.

"Come on in," he gestures. The car is relatively luxurious, offering leather interior and a lack of the usual fast food wrappers. I sigh in contentment at the seat warmers.

I flash him a small smile before tucking myself under the seatbelt. "Thanks."

"You can't be out for a jog at this time of night," he states, after shifting gears. "It's dangerous for teenagers. Starmount?"

"Yeah. Or, at least, I used to."

"I teach at Starmount. Used to?"

"Out sick," I respond. "For a semester."

"That's quite a long time."

"Coma," I grunt.

"Huh. You sound like one of my students. She was—"

The man slams his foot on the brake. My eyes widen.

"Hope?"

"Mr. Stern?!"

"Let me compose myself first," Mr. Stern says, pulling his car over on the shoulder.

I yank my hood down and fumble with the overhead light switch.

"It's really you," he breathes, eyes surveying my face.

I flash him a sad smile at the tears swimming in his eyes. "It's me."

Mr. Stern shakes his head like a dog trying to dry off. "I can't—what—how?"

I interrupt him. Something urged me on until I could no longer refuse it, and then I tell him everything while he drives. And I mean everything. In detail. I begin with the first day of school. I discuss Videl. Veronica's party. Mom's death. His betrayal. Haley's mother. Jackie and cocaine. About my inner turmoil near Christmastime. About my suicide attempt and eight months' worth of dreams that I *thought* was reality. I tell him how exuberant he was when I agreed to perform in the winter talent show. I tell him how bright his smile was when Altha and I patched our differences. I traverse the linear pathway between the dream world and reality until I fully exude all the minute details on my break-in and Jackie's death, pricking in the process my index finger again on her piercing—no, *our* piercing—until the wet, trickling sensation of blood slides down my digit while doing so.

"You know what's fucked up?" I ask him, after giving him time to process the information. I don't wait for him to speak before continuing.

"I always used to think we humans had at least a slimmer of control over our lives; just the tiniest amount that still allows us to hold some sort of independence, no matter how minute."

Stern cleared his throat. "And now?"

I chuckle wetly. "Now, I don't know what to think. When Mom passed away, I had no control over anything. I was helpless to do anything but observe."

Mr. Stern sighs.

"We are all victims, Hope. Some more so than others." He pivots his head toward me. "For every good thing in life, there is a bad. But that's how we grow stronger, by living with the weight on our shoulders. It's how we define who we are."

A few minutes later, a bunch of signs with pictures of airplanes on them fills my field of vision. He drives through a sign labeled 'Departures' and then pulls up next to a series of automatic sliding doors. Even at this time of night, people bustle about. The traffic people are blowing on their whistles, and loud calls of farewells and the sound of suitcases dragging on the ground fill my ears.

I open the door.

"Do you have cash or a card on you?" his voice rings out.

I pull out Haley's envelope. "I have enough."

Mr. Stern begins shuffling around in his seat.

"Before you refuse me," he begins, procuring his wallet from his pocket. "I want you to have this. For emergencies."

He pulls me toward him and nestles three hundred dollars into the palm of my hand.

"This is goodbye," he says wistfully.

And then, I throw myself on him and wrap my arms around his back before squeezing as hard as I can.

My chest heaves and wet sobs escape my lips. I'm scared. I'm scared of leaving the only person whom I remotely have a connection with. I'm scared because the solace I have found for the last ninety minutes is going to disappear. I'm scared at taking such a monumental step forward. I am terrified at the black tunnel ahead.

"You can do this, Hope, you can do this. You are strong." Stern breaks apart from me and digs out a pen. He scribbles on the manila envelope.

"Here's my phone number," he points. "I expect to hear from you, do you understand?"

"Y—yeah."

"Consider it one last assignment by your old teacher."

A smile comes to my lips. I grab his outstretched hand and shake it.

"Deal," I promise. "Gary."

He smiles.

Inside the airport, there are only a few baggage attendants due to the hour, but I manage to locate one and tell her where I am planning on going. The one-way ticket takes a sizeable chunk of the money from Haley, and I'm left with a total of four hundred dollars.

I flash my passport under the check-in booth. The official behind the Plexiglass window stares at me intently. My hand squeezes around Jackie's charm, hoping there isn't a wanted status next to my name.

The security guard behind him glances with a heavy frown at me and I begin to panic, but then he waves his arm over, signaling me to go on through.

Before long, I am already on the jet, with only a few other dozen people in the medium-sized machine. My seat is next to an old man, and he slightly stinks of rotten bananas. Craning my head back, I spy most of the empty seats and debate on asking the flight attendant if I can switch seats. I ultimately decide against the idea; the window seat I'm in now offers some consolation, and I don't want to risk being put in an aisle seat, or even worse, a middle seat.

The flight attendant announces some general safety rules on how the flight will last over twelve hours, and that France is seven hours ahead of us. I wake the now-asleep man and ask him the current time. He grumbles five in the morning before going back to sleep. My head whirs into calculation.

We taxi for the next ten minutes before taking off. And during the takeoff, it occurs to me that this is my first time riding an airplane. This feeling of exhilaration suddenly takes ahold of me at the raw speed, the ferocity of acceleration, and the *scream* of the engines deafening all other sound in my ear as we leave the ground. And when we're up in the air, I can see the first rays of sunshine struggling to peek over the horizon.

A new dawn. A new beginning.

I tinker around on the free movies offered on the monitor in the seat in front of me, but most of the time is used for sleep. You'd think I would be immune to sleep for the next millennia, but in what seems like only a few minutes, the plane jerkily touches down on the ground and decelerates to a halt.

Everyone dresses like a fashionista, and I stick out like a sore thumb in the airport. Most passersby gawk at me as I walk by. I let the arrows guide me out of the airport and into the city, and all of a sudden I'm struck with the busy sounds of nightlife. Honking, tinkering sounds, and an array of chatter from outdoor restaurants stupefies my senses, but I manage to hail down a taxi without too much hassle by bunglingly waving my hand in the air.

The taxi driver has a shaggy beard and understands English. I settle myself in the backseat and he takes off.

As the jumble of city life begins to drift away and shrubbery and trees replace the scenery instead, I start thinking about how my life led from one moment to the next. A strange, complacent feeling soon replaces my self-pity. And then, I realize that I wouldn't prefer my life any other way. I always thought there was a fine line between coincidence and fate, but no longer. Fate is inexorable. France. Haley and Stern's money was given to me for a reason. From my birth up until now, my concatenation is meant for this upcoming moment. Dad dying, becoming friends with Haley, falling in love with Videl, Roger murdering

Mom, partnering with Jackie, my attempted suicide—it is all for this. The last stop, and the last chapter of my old life.

I have no idea how it will end. Because this is how destiny works. Fate is the governess of my existence, and all I can do as a human is ride the path she has created for me.

I start to see the silhouette of a building. It grows by the second, and I realize it's a large castle. The taxi grinds to a stop.

The dim lights surrounding the property casts ominous shadows over the environment, and I can't help but wonder if it's a dark omen. But it is too late now. I pay the taxi driver, forking more money I had exchanged to Euros in the airport. He mutters something before taking off. Before long, the bustling sound of the car's engine fades away, and all that's left is the noise of the cicadas.

My footsteps click on the stone pavement when I move from the sidewalk up to the front entrance. When I arrive, the wooden door peers over me. My hand hovers only briefly over the ornate door knocker before the last of my doubts vanquish from my mind.

In a foreign nation with only a bit of money, a letter, my passport, the clothes on my back, and Jackie's piercing, I grip the knocker firmly and bang it three times. Somewhere, a clock tower strikes midnight. *One chime, two chimes, three chimes.*

I wait with bated breath. *Eleven chimes.*

On the twelfth, the door opens, greeting me with the person I sought out for so long. The person behind my existence.

"Videl."

Epilogue

The door slams shut as I dash inside, my backpack flying off to the side and the contents—a notebook and a bunch of pens and pencils—spilling out due to my distractedness at not shutting the zipper after Eva's writing class. I hang my car keys on the mounted hooks next to the garage. No one is home yet, but that won't stop me from getting a head start. Heading over to the kitchen, I grab a clean bowl from the cabinet before digging up the leftover gnocchi that the grocery boy brings every weekend. I scour down half the contents with one hand while reviewing my notes with the other, occasionally absentmindedly bringing up my hand to finger the piercing fixed in my ear. The fine china cup—adorned with red and blue flowers—is half-full of Mariage Frères. The cup itself makes a clinking noise as I set it down on its accompanying saucer. Wiping my mouth, I lift the lid of my laptop, entering my password before opening a new page under my finished prologue. The new teddy bear receives a quick smile from me. With fingers poised over the keys, and my thoughts taking a trip down memory lane, I rhapsodize.

"Honey! It's time to get up!"